Nora Kay's novels:

'If you enjoy Cookson you will love this.'
Bradford Telegraph & Argus (Legacy of Shame)

'Strong characters and a persuasive storyline make this a memorable tale.'
(Tina)

'An enjoyable, warm-hearted tale.'
Publishing News (Beth)

'A stirring tale rich in heartache and warmth with an unquenchable zest for life.'
Northern Echo (Gift of Love)

'This is a strong, warm story.'
Middlesbrough Evening News (Lost Dreams)

'An unforgettable story of love and heartache.'
Dundee Courier (Lost Dreams)

'A rich and rewarding tale.'
Bolton Evening News (A Woman of Spirit)

'Absorbing tale of the twenties.'
Chester and District Standard (Best Friends)

'Packed with atmosphere and strong characters.'
Newcastle Evening Chronicle (A Woman of Spirit)

Also by Nora Kay in Coronet

A Woman of Spirit
Best Friends
Beth
Lost Dreams
Gift of Love
Tina
Legacy of Shame

About the author

Nora Kay was born in Northumberland but she and her husband lived for many years in Dundee. They now live in Aberdeen.

For Better,
For Worse

Nora Kay

CORONET BOOKS

Hodder & Stoughton

First published in Great Britain in 2001 by
Hodder and Stoughton
First published in Great Britain in paperback in 2001 by
Hodder and Stoughton
A division of Hodder Headline

A Coronet Paperback

10 9 8 7 6 5 4 3 2

A CIP catalogue record for this title
is available from the British Library.

ISBN 0 340 76831 2

Typeset by Hewer Text Ltd, Edinburgh
Printed and bound in Great Britain by
Clays Ltd, St Ives plc

Hodder and Stoughton
A division of Hodder Headline
338 Euston Road
London NW1 3BH

For Bill and Raymond

Chapter One

Jenny Richardson turned her head when she heard the back door open. It was usually left unlocked until the girls got back from school.

'Hello, dear,' she said sounding surprised. 'What are you doing home at this time? I thought you said—'

'I know what I said,' he interrupted, 'I said I wouldn't be home for the evening meal and that still stands.' He had taken up a position in the middle of the kitchen, a tall, good-looking man with broad shoulders who held himself well. His dark business suit was regularly pressed and with it he wore a white shirt and a dark blue tie with thin gold stripes. 'When do they get in?' he added.

Jenny frowned. She knew he was referring to the children but why ask such a question? He knew, or he certainly ought to know, when the school got out and the time of the bus.

'The girls get dropped off at the end of the road and they should be home some time between half past four and a quarter to five. Why?'

He ignored that and glanced at his watch. 'We can count on being alone for the next – say – three quarters of an hour?'

'I should think so,' Jenny said quietly. She put down the vegetable knife and dried her hands on the towel. The family had their main meal of the day at six o'clock and Jenny had just started on the preparations. The girls took sandwiches preferring them to school dinners and Paul got himself a snack lunch in a restaurant close to Easton & Hutcheson, the well-established engineering firm where he worked as an accountant.

Something was wrong, Jenny could feel it. Why else would Paul be home at this time?

Jenny Richardson was a pleasant-looking woman of medium height with a tendency to put on weight if she wasn't careful. Her thick, dark chestnut-coloured hair had a natural wave and she wore it short. It was easy to look after, requiring only a trim every four or five weeks. For special occasions she would have a shampoo and set but those times were few and far between. Jenny didn't mind, she was a home lover devoted to her husband and their two daughters. She didn't bother about fashion and wore what she thought suited her.

Thoughts kept clicking round in her head. Had she imagined it or had Paul been tensed up of late? If he was it could only be due to overwork. It angered Jenny that the firm was for ever piling on extra work. She did all the complaining, not Paul. He said that was the wrong thing to do if you wanted to get on and her husband did. He wanted it quite desperately. As for Jenny she would much prefer that he relaxed. If promotion came, well and good, but she was perfectly content. Indeed Jenny considered herself very fortunate. They managed to pay the mortgage on their three bedroom, semi-detached villa with enough left over to give them a reasonable standard of living. Paul had the use of a company car which meant they didn't have the expense of buying one. All they had to do was provide the petrol.

Jenny frequently counted her blessings. She had a handsome husband who worked hard to provide for his wife and two daughters: Wilma, fifteen, had blonde hair and long thin legs; Katy, just turned ten, was a happy-go-lucky girl with brown curly hair and laughing blue eyes. They had been blessed with two lovely daughters. The pity was that she hadn't given Paul a son but it wasn't too late, it could still happen.

'We'll talk better in the sitting-room,' he said abruptly.

Jenny took off her apron, put it over the back of a chair and followed him. Had Paul lost his job? Surely not. It didn't seem very likely. According to reports the firm had a full order book and even if they hadn't the white collar workers wouldn't be affected. It would have to be something very serious before that happened. Paul was a much valued member of staff. He was popular, that was evident at the office Christmas parties. He moved around with confidence, joked easily with his seniors and spoke courteously with their wives. No, his job was safe, she was sure of that. Then suddenly Jenny was smiling with relief, remembering her husband's little idiosyncrasies. He liked to pretend he had bad news when, in fact, it was the opposite. Jenny considered it juvenile and irritating but Paul appeared to find it amusing. He liked, he said, to see the changing expressions. Alarm giving way to joy. They sat down. Jenny waited with her hands in her lap and a smile hovering at her mouth.

The room they were sitting in had a tiled fireplace with a large gilt mirror above it. Jenny's mother hadn't been too happy about it hanging there, not with two young girls in the house. She said it was a dangerous place to hang a mirror but Paul disagreed and the mirror remained where it was. There was a shabby moquette suite that had twice been recovered and a large square of carpet which had been turned round to hide the signs of wear. When she and Paul had started out in married life most of their savings had gone on a deposit for the house. They had decided to make do with second-hand furniture and replace it when they could afford to, only that had to be shelved when Jenny found herself pregnant. Then refurnishing got pushed further and further down the list as more pressing needs took away their savings. This was to be the year when the house got a facelift. Downstairs first and then the bedrooms unless it was going to be too much of an upheaval and the upstairs could be left until the following year.

'What's so funny?' he said, sounding annoyed.

'You, Paul. This is your little joke, getting me worked up and worried. I think I know what this is about. You've got your promotion, that is it, isn't it?' She almost beamed.

He looked blank.

'You did say you stood a good chance,' Jenny faltered.

'Oh, that!' he said dismissively. 'I got it weeks ago, didn't I tell you?'

Jenny shook her head. He knew he hadn't. Had he done so there would have been some kind of celebration. Her mother would have looked after the girls and they would have gone out for a meal. A very special meal, possibly with champagne. Not that she liked champagne but Paul did. And what he liked she tried to like too. Jenny was suddenly very afraid and her mouth had gone dry.

'What is this all about, Paul?' She waited for his answer, every sense strung taut.

There was a film of perspiration on his brow and Paul's finger had gone to the inside of his collar as though it had suddenly become too tight.

'There is no easy way of saying this—'

'Saying what?' She felt cold, so very cold yet the room was warm with the May sunshine streaming in.

'I'm leaving you, Jenny.' There it was out, he had said it. She stared at him. 'You can't do that,' she said stupidly.

'I'm afraid I can and I am,' he said gently. He hated hurting her but it had to be done now, not put off any longer. This was a turning-point in his life, he kept telling himself. He was gloriously and hopelessly in love. That he had fallen out of love with Jenny was no fault of hers, yet she was the one to suffer most. The children would suffer too but not so much and he would see them from time to time. That was something they would have to arrange.

'Why do you want to leave me?' she whispered.

'Jenny, I'm in love with someone else,' he said softly, 'these things do happen you know.'

'I'm aware of that.' To other couples, she added silently, but not to us. It wasn't possible that Paul was telling her their marriage was over. Or was it?

'It's not true, you can't mean it.' She was shaking her head. Paul was going through some sort of crisis, a temporary madness. It was well known, wasn't it, that men of a

5

certain age, forty or thereabout, had a need to prove that they were still attractive to women? A sort of last fling. She hadn't expected it of Paul but she would be good about it, be prepared to forgive and forget. No, that was asking too much. To forgive was one thing, to forget quite another. One had no control over one's memory. The bad memories would surface from time to time and sadly it would be like discovering a weakness and never again being able to trust the one who had behaved so badly.

'I do mean it, Jenny, and please try to keep calm.'

'I am calm.' And I am, she thought, I'm shattered but remarkably calm. It shocked her a little that she could be so calm when her whole world was falling apart. But, of course, none of this was happening, this was some sort of nightmare and she would waken up with her world secure.

'Jenny, are you listening?'

'Of course I am.'

'Believe me, I hate having to hurt you.'

She did believe him. 'Then don't, you don't have to,' Jenny said quietly.

'You just won't accept it, will you?' Paul was sounding exasperated. 'Our marriage is over, Jenny, get that into your head. If we are both honest we know it has been over for some time.'

'That isn't true,' she said hotly.

'All right, tell me this, when did we last make love?'

Her soft brown eyes were full of pain but there was anger there as well.

'That's rich coming from you. You were the one who turned away. You were always too tired or just not interested. Innocent fool that I was, I put it down to overwork and exhaustion. Now I know the reason. You had her, you didn't need me.' She shook her head wonderingly. 'All that time you were unfaithful to me and I never suspected, not for a single moment. I trusted you, Paul, and I honestly thought we had a good marriage, that we were a happy family.'

He shrugged. She wished he wouldn't, he seemed to do a lot of it. 'We did,' he said, 'but we all change.'

'I haven't.'

'Perhaps you should have.'

'What do you mean by that?'

Another shrug. 'Maybe you've got too settled.'

'Boring, uninteresting?'

'I didn't say that.'

'It's what you meant.' She waited for him to deny it but he didn't.

'Who is she?'

Paul took his time about answering as though he was reluctant to part with the information.

'Her name is Vera Cuthbertson,' he said at last.

That rang a bell. 'Isn't that the name of Andy's secretary? Wasn't it she who got Miss Dewar's job?'

'Yes.'

It was all coming back. Miss Dewar had been plain and efficient, a good reliable secretary who had taken a great pride in her work and encouraged others to do the same. Her replacement had come as a shock and Paul had told Jenny about the new member of staff being a stunning-looking girl with excellent qualifications. She remembered

7

being secretly relieved that she wasn't Paul's secretary and telling him laughingly to keep his distance, that he had three girls at home, two young and one not-so-young, who adored him. He had laughed and said there was absolutely no danger. Why would he look elsewhere when he had a lovely wife and two smashing daughters? Yet here he was talking about leaving them and presumably going to live with this Vera Cuthbertson. Was it possible to hate someone you hadn't met? Yes, it was, when that person was going to ruin your life and cause heartache to two innocent little girls.

'The girls, think about them.'

'I have, believe me I have. Children are remarkable, they very quickly learn to adapt.'

'Do they?'

'Yes, they do and ours will. Jenny, for heaven's sake, this is 1952, the world is changing. Couples no longer stay together just for the sake of appearances. In our parents' day they did and it caused a lot of misery. Our generation has more sense. They look at it sensibly and get out.'

'They get out, as you term it, when the marriage has failed but ours hasn't, Paul. We don't yell at each other, we don't have rows. Perhaps the occasional disagreement but nothing serious. No marriage remains on a high all the time.'

'I'm not getting into an argument. I arranged time off to tell you that I'm leaving you, Jenny, and that is it. Of course, you and the girls will continue to live here and I'll pay the mortgage. Obviously you'll have to make do with less but you can always get a job. What a good thing you

kept up your typing – good typists are always in demand.'
He was talking much too quickly.

'You've got it all worked out,' Jenny said bitterly. She remembered being pleased when Paul got her a good second-hand typewriter. Some firm he knew had gone into liquidation, everything had to be sold and the type-writer had been a genuine bargain.

'Yes, I have got it worked out. You need to know the financial position.'

Jenny hadn't been thinking about the financial position, that worry would come later. What she was thinking about was getting her more worked up by the minute. She could feel her colour rising.

'All that talk about extra work, all those late nights at the office. I felt so sorry for you and so angry at the firm and they were only excuses. You were with her, weren't you?' she said accusingly.

He shrugged and sat more comfortably in the chair. 'Some of the time but there was extra work as well.'

How could I live with someone for sixteen years, she wondered and yet not know them? She closed her eyes for a moment to lessen the pain.

'How long has this been going on?'

He shrugged.

'Don't do that,' she shouted. 'I asked you, how long?'

'A few months, I can't say exactly and keep your voice down.'

'Why? In case the neighbours hear? Possibly they know already. Isn't it always the wife who is the last to know?'

'I'm sorry, I really am.'

'So you keep saying. How old is she?'

'What difference does that make?'

'None, but I'd like to know.'

'Twenty-five.'

'Single?'

'Yes.'

'No problems for her then?'

'No,' he said looking increasingly uncomfortable.

'She gets her clutches into a married man and breaks up a family. That doesn't say much for her.'

He remained silent.

'You are forty, quite an age gap.'

That angered him as she knew it would. Paul had hated that step from thirty-nine to forty. He could very easily pass for early thirties with his youthful appearance, his fresh complexion and his plentiful dark blond hair. Nevertheless there was no denying what was on the birth certificate.

'It doesn't bother us, the difference in ages.'

Liar, she thought. It bothered him that the years were slipping by or he wouldn't flinch the way he did when he was reminded of his age. Jenny was thirty-eight and didn't mind anyone knowing.

'I give it a year at the most then she'll tire of you, dump you, Paul, and look for a younger man.'

He smiled, so sure of himself. 'I don't think so and I'm more than willing to take the risk.'

'What are they saying about it in the office? They can't fail to notice what is going on.'

'I don't know and I don't care. It has nothing to do with them. It's our business, Vera's and mine and no one else's.'

'I beg to differ. This is very much the business of your wife and children.'

'I'm trying to sort that out.'

'What are you going to tell Wilma and Katy?'

'I'll leave that to you, you'll make a better job of it.'

She gave a strangled laugh. 'Oh, no, Paul, I'm not having that, you can do your own dirty work. None of this is my doing.'

'Why are you so determined to make this as difficult as possible? I thought better of you, Jenny.'

'I thought better of you too.' She was shaking but surprisingly her voice was quite steady.

'I'm going.' He got up and just then came the sound of voices and the back door opening.

'Too late, Paul, here they are.' She walked ahead of him back to the kitchen and lit the gas under the kettle. Six o'clock was a long time for them to wait for their meal and a scone or a piece of plain cake helped to keep away the hunger pangs. It struck her then that from now on there would be no need to wait until six o'clock.

Two pairs of eyes registered surprise.

'What is Daddy doing home at this time?' Katy demanded of her mother as though her father was incapable of answering for himself.

Wilma threw her bulging schoolbag on to one of the kitchen chairs. It stayed for a moment then fell to the floor. She waited for Jenny to tell her to pick it up and not to be so careless. She didn't. Wilma looked surprised to be let off, waited another moment or two, then lifted the bag and put it on the chair. Her mother was smiling and managing to

11

look stricken at the same time. Her father was smiling too in a funny sort of way. She wondered if they had had a row and she and Katy had arrived home before they could sort out whatever it was. They didn't row much, come to think about it they didn't row at all. Not a real barney just the occasional disagreement. Not like her friend Evelyn's parents who, according to their daughter, were either shouting insults at each other or barely speaking. Wilma didn't believe it was as bad as Evelyn made out, she always had to exaggerate as though that made it more interesting.

'Don't your parents ever fight?' she'd asked.

'Not really. If they don't agree they just agree to differ.'

Evelyn couldn't quite understand that. 'Must be awfully boring in your house,' she'd said.

'Daddy has something to tell you both, that's why he is home at this time,' Jenny said with false brightness.

'Something nice,' Katy said hopefully.

Paul shot his wife a look that was close to hatred and she found herself trembling. Jenny realised in that moment how unpredictable were human relationships and how quickly they could turn to hostility or worse. She wished now she hadn't antagonised him. Had she not she would have been spared that look. It seemed to speed up the end.

On the other hand why should she protect Paul? He wasn't the one to suffer. That young woman, that Vera Cuthbertson, would be waiting for him with open arms. Jenny tried to imagine Vera Cuthbertson's home. Probably it would be a modern flat, maybe she called it an apartment, and it would have every latest convenience.

Jenny was feeling the bitter pain of rejection. She had

lost out to a younger and more beautiful woman. She wasn't the first to go through this and she wouldn't be the last. People would pity her, she would be pointed out as the abandoned wife and she didn't want to be pitied. Some would put part of the blame at her door saying men didn't stray unless there was something lacking in the marriage. She couldn't think where she had failed. Her whole life had been devoted to her husband and family. She had been a good wife. What more could she have done? Nothing.

The children, what of them? She would learn to contend with the pain and humiliation but the girls, how would they deal with the situation? They were so different. Wilma would try to hide her suffering and that could leave its mark in later life. Fifteen was a difficult age, her own mother described it as half woman, half child. Katy would be inconsolable for a short time then she would recover as happier events took over. Lucky Katy who could never be sad for long. Wilma was the worry. Their first-born enjoyed a close bond with Paul. She had always adored him and Jenny had accepted second place. Their other daughter had evened things up, it was always her mother she ran to with her troubles. Damn you, Paul Richardson, Jenny said silently, damn you for what you are putting us through.

'Nothing for you two to worry about.' He was smiling that crooked smile she had always loved. 'It's just that your mother and I have agreed to separate for a while. I won't be living here.'

There was a stunned silence. Jenny bit back the words. She had been about to say that she had agreed to nothing of the kind but what was the use. This wasn't quite so final for the girls. It was wise to be civilised about these things and who knows, perhaps in a month or two Paul would realise his mistake. He had been a good husband and father, perhaps he could be those again. She would leave the door open. Pride was something she couldn't afford. It seemed impossible to Jenny that only a little time ago, hours just hours, she had been so sure of Paul. Had that been her mistake? Had she taken him for granted? She still loved him, you didn't just stop loving someone. What did stop was respect. How could you respect someone who put his own selfish pleasure before the happiness and well-being of his family? In her book that was despicable.

'Where are you going to live, Daddy?' Katy asked as she reached for the biscuit tin and had it removed from her hands.

'No, Katy, no biscuits, you'll get a scone and butter when I'm ready.' Katy made a face. 'Daddy, where—'

'Not very far away.'

'Can we come and see you?'

'Not right away but later on.'

'You can't leave Mum and us.' Wilma sounded horri-fied.

'Wilma, don't upset yourself. I'll see you both from time to time and now I must get back to the office.' He sounded flustered and desperate to be on his way. 'First though I need a few things from upstairs.'

Jenny, needing something to do with her hands had made the tea and was splitting scones and buttering them. She looked up. 'Your clothes, you mean?'

'Yes, I'll take some and pick up the rest in the next day or two. I'll phone you first.'

'What for? You have a key.'

'It was to give you time to get them packed.'

She drew in her breath at the nerve of him. After an inward battle she said quietly, 'Very well, I'll fold your suits, I'll do that for you. There are a number of shirts and some underwear and socks in the dirty-clothes basket. I'll sort them out and put them in a separate bag. You can see to the laundering of them yourself.'

He was very obviously taken aback. 'Surely—'

'Absolutely not,' she said firmly.

He gave her a long look which she returned. It had been a small victory, but still a victory of sorts. No wonder Paul was shocked, it was so unlike her to be disobliging but already she was changing, she could feel herself doing so. Surely it was diabolical cheek to announce that their marriage was over and expect her to do his washing or at least what was in the tub. His mistress could jolly well do it.

Without another word Paul went upstairs. They heard drawers opening and shutting then a little later heavy feet on the stairs. Rather than face them he was going to use the front door. They heard it shut and looked at one another.

'Daddy's gone,' Kate said unnecessarily.

'He'll be back,' Wilma said sitting down at the table. Katy was already there and Jenny poured the tea. Her hand wasn't quite steady and some of it spilled into the saucer. 'Did you have a quarrel or something?'

'No, Wilma, there was no quarrel.'

'All right, no quarrel. Dad didn't walk out without a reason. You can tell us. We aren't babies, I'm not anyway.'

Why not just tell them? It would be common knowledge before long that Paul Richardson had left his wife and was living with another woman. She began crumbling the scone on her plate.

'Why are you doing that?' Katy demanded. Something would have been said if she'd done it.

'Doing what?'

'Making that mess with your scone?'

'I didn't realise I was doing it.' She paused and moistened her lips. 'You had better both listen. I was going to try and spare you, but I think that would be a mistake. Your father didn't tell you the truth. This isn't a short separation and I most certainly didn't agree to it. The truth is your father is leaving me—'

'For good?' Wilma gasped. 'I don't believe it.'

'It was just as big a shock for me.'

'Why would he leave us?' Wilma said miserably.

'He told me he had fallen in love with someone else.'

'Do you know her?'

'No, but she is someone who works beside him. Apparently she is very lovely and he wants to be with her.'

'What will we do?' Wilma whispered.

'We'll manage, darling, we have each other and there is always a way as your gran would say.'

'But nothing will ever be the same?'

'No, Wilma, nothing will ever be the same.'

Katy began to cry.

Chapter Two

———◆———

After a night of tossing and turning in a bed that was too big for one person, Jenny waited until it was her usual time for getting up. Her head ached and she took a couple of aspirins washing them down with a glass of water from the bathroom. She had never been one for wandering about in a dressing-gown, preferring to dress straight away in one of her older skirts and a jumper. Once the housework was completed it would be time to put on something better. That was the way she had been brought up. What was important, what she must do, was keep to routine as much as possible. There wouldn't be the same rush since it was one less for the bathroom. Paul had gone first and taken a long time. He wouldn't be rushed and cries of 'Hurry up Daddy' were ignored. Occasionally Katy had to wash herself at the kitchen sink.

If they could get over the first few mornings it would become easier, or was that wishful thinking? Jenny felt the weight of responsibility and wondered if she was strong enough to cope. She had to, there was no one else. Paul had opted out and she alone was left to care for her daughters.

They came into the kitchen together, both in school uniform and looking smart. The usual banter was missing and they sat down at the table like two schoolgirls in a restaurant who had been told to behave properly. There was a muttered good morning in answer to their mother's greeting. Jenny filled the toast rack, took it to the table, and joined them. The unoccupied chair drew all eyes and Jenny wished she had removed it to somewhere else. She should have thought about that.

'Mum, will Daddy stay away for ever?' Katy was dragging her spoon through the cereal without making any effort to eat.

'Yes, you were told that last night, don't you ever listen?' Wilma said angrily.

'Mum!' she wailed.

'I know, dear, that wasn't very nice.' Then turning to Wilma. 'There was no cause for that. Katy is a lot younger than you.'

'She doesn't listen though, does she?'

'I do so. Doesn't Daddy love us any more?' Katy said on the verge of tears.

'Of course he loves you both, that won't change. It would hurt him terribly if he thought you believed otherwise.'

'Why has he stopped loving you?' she sniffed.

Jenny gave a sad smile. 'Maybe he's just grown tired of me. Please, could we leave it there? When you come home from school we'll talk again if you want that and remember that bus isn't going to wait for you,' she warned.

'I need the bathroom,' Katy said scraping back her chair.

'At the double then.'

They heard her racing up the stairs.

'Mum, I'm sorry, I'm not blaming you, it's just I can't understand.'

'I know, dear, it's a difficult time for us all and that includes your father. I'm sure he misses you and Katy.'

'If he did he wouldn't be leaving us,' she said in a hard voice.

Jenny shook her head wearily. 'I'm not sure about anything any more.'

'I'll skip school and stay with you.'

Jenny looked at the young anxious face and felt like weeping only she must not. She had to put on a brave face. Wilma wasn't making this an excuse for a day off, she liked school.

'No, darling, that was thoughtful of you but I'll be all right. We just have to get on with life without Daddy.'

'Will you phone Gran and tell her?'

'Yes.'

'Maybe she'll come over and keep you company.'

'Yes, maybe.'

Katy had come downstairs and Jenny almost chased them out of the door. She waited. It was possible to see the bus approaching and there it was on the brow of the hill. They would catch it but only just. She closed the door and was about to start clearing the table when grief caught up with her and the tears came. She couldn't stop them and putting her head down on the table Jenny gave in to a paroxysm of weeping. After the outburst she felt drained but it had helped. She could face the housework, get that over and done with quickly then phone her mother. Grace Turnbull, her next door neighbour and a good friend, would have to be told. Perhaps she already knew and couldn't bring herself to say anything. She would find out. There was still some tea in the pot and Jenny poured it into her cup. It was lukewarm but she drank it.

Jenny's mother had only recently had the phone installed. She and Paul had suggested when her father was alive that they should think about a phone, but her father had refused saying it was an unnecessary expense, that they had managed all these years without one and for an emergency wasn't there a phone box at the end of the road? No more had been said. Tom Scrimgeour was a dour man, honest and outspoken, qualities not always appreciated. His wife seldom complained, she knew the futility of it. Tom Scrimgeour was the man of the house and his word was law.

After his death and a decent interval, Janet had the phone installed and began to have a social life. Jenny and Paul had encouraged her to take up bridge where, they said, she would meet new friends. And no it wasn't too difficult, it was just a case of concentrating. At first she had been reluctant, it was a big step for someone like her, but she had taken that step and never looked back.

Jenny went through to the hall, sat down on the chair beside the phone and dialled the number.

'Hello?' Her mother sounded out of breath.

'Mum, it's me.'

'Jenny, is this just for a chat?'

'Sort of, I mean—'

'Darling, this really isn't a good time. I have my bridge ladies coming for coffee and you know how I like to have everything just so. Everybody fine?'

'Yes.'

'Good. I'll ring you in the afternoon, early on. You don't mind, do you? I really am in a rush.'

'No, that's all right, my news will keep.'

'Goodbye, dear.' The phone went dead.

'So much for a sympathetic ear,' Jenny muttered to herself as she put the receiver down. Then she smiled. It was nice to know her mother was enjoying life, she deserved it.

The need to confide was strong and the afternoon seemed a long time away. She could always talk to Grace. Grace and Arthur Turnbull and their son, Jonathan, had come to live next door to them about three years ago and a friendship had quickly developed. Grace was a slim-built, attractive woman in her early forties with a sympathetic manner, the kind of person who listened and only gave advice when it was wanted. Her husband, Arthur, was a tall, pleasant-faced man who had gone prematurely bald and was seldom seen without a cap. He had a hardware store in Blackford High Street, a good-going business and the only one of its kind for miles around. The nearest was in Perth. His hope was that their only son would join him in the business but Jonathan had other ideas. When he left school in a year's time he wanted to join the navy and see the world.

Jenny was on the point of getting up when there was a tap at the door. She went to answer it but already knew who was there. She recognised Grace's own particular knock.

'Grace, come in, I was just coming round.'

'Two minds with but a single thought. You know it's cold away from that sun.' She gave a small shiver.

'Coffee?'

'Actually I'd prefer tea if you don't mind.'

'Tea will do me nicely. You could put out some biscuits.'

'Absolutely not, I'm taking myself in hand. No more eating between meals. I'm putting on weight.'

'If you are I fail to see it. All right I'll go without too. I don't need one, it's just a habit.'

'A bad one.' Grace grinned then began to look concerned. 'Jenny, are you well enough or have you a cold coming on? Quite a bit of it around and no wonder with the changeable weather.'

'No, I haven't got a cold.' She sat down opposite Grace at the kitchen table. The tea was made but required a few minutes to draw. The treacherous tears were close but she fought them. Grace would understand but even so she didn't want to break down.

'What is the matter, Jenny?' she said gently.

'Paul has left me.'

Grace looked thunderstruck. 'That I just do not believe.'

'It's true, Grace.'

'You mean,' she said incredulously, 'he's moved out?'

'Yes. Paul has moved in with the new love in his life.'

Grace was very still.

'You knew, didn't you? Damn it, did everybody know about this but me?' Her voice broke.

Grace got up, poured the tea and sat down. 'Drink that then we'll talk and no, I didn't know or at least I didn't believe it,' her voice trailed off. She took a drink of tea. 'This is it and it is all I know. Mary Marshall and her husband were celebrating an anniversary or something. At any rate they were dining at that new place between here and Glenagnes. Apparently it's all subdued lighting – Arthur says that's so they won't see what they are eating—'

Jenny smiled. That was like Arthur.

'—and alcoves. Mary told Edna and it eventually reached me. She said she was nearly sure that she saw Paul Richardson sitting in one of the alcoves with a young glamorous blonde. I told Edna that Mary needed her eyesight tested, that whoever she saw it certainly wasn't Paul Richardson.'

'It would have been Paul.'

'Do I ask questions or wait until you tell me what you want me to know?'

'Ask what you want. I need to talk about it and I phoned Mother but she's too busy with her bridge ladies. No, that's not fair of me, she thought it was just for a chat.'

'Had your mother known she would have put off her bridge ladies and come over.' Grace had met Jenny's mother on several occasions.

'Yes, she would but what would be the point? There is nothing she can do, nothing anyone can do.'

'Friends are for times like these. Who is she or don't you know?'

'I asked Paul. Her name is Vera Cuthbertson, she's twenty-five, works beside him or at least they are with the same firm. She is a tall, stunning blonde, his own description when she came to the office. With that kind of opposition not much hope for me, is there?' She tried to laugh about it.

'Paul needs his head examined. You've done far too much for him, always putting his needs and everybody else's before your own.'

'You do that with Arthur and Jonathan.'

'I know I'm as bad as you.'

'Maybe in some way I was to blame, but I can't honestly think where I went wrong.'

'You did nothing wrong. The girls, what about them?'

'Upset but OK I think. Paul came home early yesterday to drop his bombshell and he wanted me to break it to Wilma and Katy. Unfortunately for him he was about to leave when they arrived and I told them their father had something to tell them.'

'He would love you for that.'

'If looks could have killed I wouldn't be here now. He played it down a bit saying we had agreed to a separation for a while and that he wouldn't be living at home.'

'Did you correct him?'

'Very nearly then I thought what was the use. I let it pass and told them later.' She shook her head. 'Wilma is taking it badly.'

'She was always Daddy's girl and Katy clings to you.'

'Was it that noticeable?' Jenny said sounding surprised.

'I'm next door, remember.'

★   ★   ★

24

Wilma's mind kept straying, earning her a reprimand from the teacher. She was glad when the bell rang at three o'clock. Today they went to the sports field. Neither Wilma nor her friend Evelyn were sports enthusiasts. They sloped off, fairly sure they wouldn't be missed.

'You look down in the dumps.'

'So would you be if you were me. My dad's left us.'

'Why would he do that?'

'What do you think?'

'Not—'

'Yes.'

'That's awful. You're not kidding me?'

'I wouldn't kid about a thing like that. He's gone to live with another woman.'

Evelyn's face showed a mixture of concern and curiosity. 'You said they never had fights.'

'Neither they do. Maybe they had one yesterday when he told Mum.'

'Funny that when you think about it. My parents fight but they would never, ever walk out. Yours don't and your dad ups and goes.' She was a kind-hearted girl. 'He'll get tired of whoever it is and come back.'

'My mum doesn't seem to think so.'

'What'll you do for money?'

'What do you mean?'

'If he has her to keep there won't be so much for your mum.'

Wilma hadn't thought about that. 'Dad won't keep us short.'

'I've got money, we'll go into Brownlow's and get a bar of Highland Cream toffee, it lasts for ages.'

Wilma had money but she didn't feel like spending it.

Evelyn broke off two squares and gave them to Wilma. They would wander around looking at the shop windows until it was time for the bus.

Jenny's mother phoned before one o'clock.

'Sorry about this morning, but everything went off well and my Victoria sponge rose a treat. It was as light as a feather and everybody praised it.'

'Your sponges always rise.'

'Thank you, dear.'

'Mum, Paul has left me.'

'This line's gone funny.'

'No, it hasn't. You were hearing correctly. Paul has taken up with another woman and left us.'

'Why would he do a thing like that? I mean you two get on well. I wouldn't have said that Paul had a roving eye.'

'Neither would I.'

'If I had him here I'd give him a piece of my mind. Men are just like children you know. That woman has buttered him up, made him feel six feet tall.'

'Mother, Paul is six feet tall.'

'Ten feet tall then, you know what I mean. They like to feel they are wonderful and appreciated. Maybe you've been neglecting your man.'

Jenny felt a surge of anger. 'Thank you very much, it's my fault now.'

'Stop it, you're being childish. I'm going to ring off and get the next bus over.'

'You don't need to.'

'Yes, I do. The girls—'

'Shocked but OK I think.'

'Expect me when you see me. The bus service is like everything else here, the powers-that-be need a good shaking up.'

'Yes, Mother.'

Jenny was half laughing and half crying when she put down the phone.

Mrs Janet Scrimgeour arrived at a quarter past two. She had been hurrying from the bus stop and was slightly out of breath. She wore her good navy costume that was mostly kept for Sundays. Her felt hat had a small brim and was also navy but was relieved by a feather of various hues. She looked what she was, a kindly woman in her early sixties.

'Mum, it was good of you to come.' They didn't kiss, they weren't a demonstrative family but that didn't mean they cared less.

'I wanted to, you haven't been a moment out of my thoughts since you gave me your news.' She unbuttoned her jacket, remembered her handkerchief was in the pocket, got it and tucked it up the sleeve of her blouse.

'Aren't you going to take off your hat?'

'It would be as well.' She took it off carefully so as not to disarrange her hair.

Jenny went upstairs to put them on the bed.

'Mum, I'll put the kettle on.'

'No, I think we should talk. I'll last out until the girls get home.'

Jenny nodded. 'We'll go through to the sitting-room and get a comfortable seat.'

'Didn't you see it coming?' she asked once they were seated.

'No, Mum, I noticed nothing different but then I wasn't looking for anything. With hindsight I should have questioned so many late nights at the office.'

'You were too trusting.'

'I thought marriage was all about trust.'

'Now you know better.' She paused. 'How are you going to be placed financially?'

'Paul is to continue to pay the mortgage and make me an allowance. He didn't say how much, only that it would be a lot less and I'd have to start looking for a job.'

'Your father wouldn't have allowed me to go out to work. He was the bread-winner and it was my duty to manage on what he gave me.'

'Dad didn't leave you, that's the difference,' Jenny said bitterly. 'I don't mind going out to work, I might even enjoy it but who is going to employ me? There are young girls without a job.'

'You worked in an office before you were married.'

'That was sixteen years ago for heaven's sake, Mum. There have been lots of changes in that time. I can type but that is about all.'

'Something will turn up, something always does, dear, it's a case of having faith.'

'Faith won't pay the bills.'

'Paul won't see you want. I've always liked Paul and I remember how good he was to me when your father died.'

'Yes, I know, it's only—'

'Only what?'

'Paul has changed, it showed in his manner when he told me our marriage was over. He hated hurting me, I'm sure of that but I think he is so besotted with that young woman that he'll do whatever she wants.'

'Then, Jenny, you'll have to look out for yourself and make sure Paul meets his obligations. Legally I don't know how you stand.'

'Neither do I but I'm inclined to think I'm at Paul's mercy.'

'Take steps and find out,' Janet Scrimgeour said grimly.

'Yes, I must but I'm still in shock. A part of me doesn't believe it has happened.'

'I know, dear, it is very hard for you. Who is this besom?'

'Her name is Vera Cuthbertson, she's twenty-five, single and intelligent. Paul said she had excellent qualifications.'

'You mean she works beside him?'

'In the same office, yes. And, Mother, she is tall, blonde and beautiful.'

'If she's all those things why is she bothering with a married man?'

'I asked myself that too. Maybe she sees it as more of a challenge and remember Paul is a very attractive man.' The lump in her throat got larger and she paused. 'Let's talk about something else.'

'All right, dear, we'll give it a rest for now.'

She swallowed and managed a smile. 'What's the latest gossip from the bridge ladies?'

'We shouldn't call them that. Maggie was there and she isn't a bridge player and, my girl, we talk we do not gossip.'

'What do you talk about?'

'This and that, sometimes politics.'

'Dangerous. Politics and religion should be kept out of the conversation.'

'Nothing heated. Mostly we were talking about Moira Ramsay buying that place just beyond Glebe Farm.'

'That white elephant.'

'She thinks she can make a go of it and Moira won't sink money into something until she is reasonably sure it has good possibilities.'

'It is still a big gamble.'

'We would think so. Moira looks on it as a challenge. She is very comfortably off so even if it isn't a success she won't be down to her last penny.'

'Lucky Moira.'

'She's a worker, she can't abide to be idle.'

'What plans has she? It's a bit far out for passing trade.'

'Yes and no to that. More people than ever have cars and there is a bus service that passes close by.' She paused and a faraway look came into her eyes. 'Remember, Jenny, when you were little we used to have picnics there?'

Jenny did remember and nodded. 'It is a lovely spot. A few have tried a shop there but there wasn't the trade to make it pay.'

'Moira has a lot more than a wee shop in mind. She is to extend the premises and do a lot to it. What she plans is a gift shop, not the small rubbishy things found in these places although she'll have to stock some. She wants more upmarket goods, the kind of display that would encourage folk to browse around and then visit the gallery next door.'

'The what?'

'A gallery, Jenny, and not so daft as you might think. There are a lot of artists just waiting to be discovered and they won't have much chance if their work isn't displayed. Moira has an interest in art in any case. She knows that most hardly have a penny to their name and they will be very glad and deeply grateful to be given wall space.'

'What is Moira getting out of it?'

'She'll take a percentage of those that are sold. Nobody loses.'

'Some might never be sold.'

'That's a strong possibility. She'll have to have a time limit, three months or six, whatever she decides.'

'If that were me I'd have teas and refreshments. People want that before all else.'

'She is doing teas, I forgot to mention it.'

'How about staff?'

'That's a problem for later.'

'Tell her to keep me in mind,' Jenny said jokingly.

'You could do worse. Moira, I imagine, would be a good employer provided the work is done to her satisfaction.'

Jenny looked at the clock and got up. 'The girls won't be long, I'll get the kettle on and toast yesterday's scones.'

Janet Scrimgeour tut-tutted. 'In my rush to get that bus I forgot to bring you the leftovers. Not all that much left, but we could have finished them off.'

'Never mind, we'll make do with a lightly toasted scone.'

'That'll suit me. Don't bring the tea here, I'll come to the kitchen.' She got up and followed Jenny.

The girls came in not quietly but certainly quieter than usual. They both showed pleasure to see their grandmother there.

'You came over to keep Mum company?' Wilma said sounding very grown-up.

'Yes, Wilma, I did.'

'You know?'

'Yes, dear, I know and I know, too, that you and Katy will help your mum.'

'You mean with the housework?'

'No, although that as well, I meant in general.'

Jenny shook her head at her mother. 'I'll manage the housework, I'm going to have less work not more.'

'Mum, I told Evelyn.'

'I didn't tell anybody,' Katy said, 'because I didn't want anyone to know. You shouldn't have told Evelyn Bannerman, she'll tell everybody and it will be all round the school.'

'Evelyn isn't like that, she knows how to keep a secret.' Wilma wondered if that was true. Sometimes Evelyn told her things she had heard that were supposed to be secrets.

'It doesn't matter,' Jenny said, 'everybody will know soon enough. Katy wash your hands at the sink then sit down. Your gran is dying for a cup of tea and so am I. Wilma,' she turned to her elder daughter. 'Evelyn is your friend and it is only natural that you should tell her.'

'She was very surprised. I told her you and Dad never quarrelled. Her parents do all the time but – but they stay together.'

'There are those who think a good row clears the air,

Wilma,' her grandmother said, then looked in horror at the blackened scone before her. 'I was expecting a lightly toasted scone not a cinder.'

'Scrape it, it isn't as bad as all that. Katy, bring the biscuit tin.'

Katy didn't have to be asked twice. She didn't mind a burnt scone if there was a cream biscuit to follow.

Janet finished her tea. 'You'll have to excuse me, I'll have to get on my way,' she said getting up.

'Stay for a meal – there's plenty.'

'No, thanks, Jenny, I won't. Wilma, lass, pop upstairs and get my coat and hat.'

'I'll get them,' Katy said almost knocking down the chair in her haste.

'No, you won't. Gran asked me not you.'

'My, it's nice to be popular or could it be to hasten my departure?'

They all laughed. At the door the four of them stood in a group.

'I'll ring you tomorrow?'

'Yes, and thanks, Mum, thanks for everything.'

'I just wish there was something I could do.' She hurried away not wanting them to see how upset she was.

Chapter Three

———◆———

Paul had pressed the doorbell as though he were a visitor. Jenny went to answer it wondering who could be calling at this time of day. It was just before one o'clock and five minutes earlier Jenny had finished eating her snack lunch. A slice of toast topped with two rashers of bacon, crispy bacon the way she liked it.

He stood there at his own front door and she moved aside to let him enter. Neither of them said a word. Paul closed the door behind him and followed Jenny into the sitting-room.

'What brings you?' she said at last. It had been three weeks since he departed with his clothes and other personal belongings.

'To see if you were all right. May I sit down?'

She shrugged then smiled to herself. She must have caught the habit from Paul. Jenny watched him take his usual chair. She didn't take hers but sat down on a straight-backed chair they always avoided since they found it uncomfortable. It had been a bad buy from an auction sale. Paul named it the invalid chair, perfect for those who suffered from a bad back. He had his briefcase with him and placed it at his feet. Jenny noticed that Paul was as smart as ever. Either his shirts went to the laundry or Vera Cuthbertson was handy with an iron. She found herself hoping it was the former.

'I'm perfectly all right, thank you,' Jenny said stiffly.

'Wilma and Katy fine too?'

'They keep wondering when they are going to be invited to your new home.' That wasn't completely true. They or rather Wilma had mentioned it the once but just now Jenny wasn't too troubled about accuracy.

'I'll arrange that.'

'When?'

'Soon,' he said frowning at her. 'And as regards the house, as I said before, the mortgage will continue to be paid and I have made arrangements for a monthly allowance to be sent to you.' He paused. 'With time on your hands you can take a job.'

'If I can get one.'

'Bound to be something you can do. You are intelligent, you have office experience but, of course, you'll have to make the effort.'

'A job won't come to me,' she smiled.

He took that as a good sign and she saw him relaxing. 'No, Jenny, it won't.'

'Let's get back to the girls. I take it you don't want to lose touch with them?'

'There is absolutely no fear of that and I hope you aren't suggesting—'

'I'm not. Are you going to have them stay overnight?'

He looked at her as if she had made an improper suggestion, either that or taken leave of her senses.

'For God's sake, Jenny, we are only a few miles apart. I'll drive them home.'

'They might quite like the idea of staying overnight,' she persisted.

'That's completely out of the question. You can't expect Vera to go that far.'

'Why not?'

'They aren't her children for heaven's sake.'

'No, but they are yours.'

'The cottage is quite small. Vera will meet them and we'll take it from there,' he said irritably.

'Meaning you'll take orders from her, you'll do what she wants. Why should she be the one to dictate?' Jenny said furiously. She didn't want Wilma and Katy staying with the woman, she didn't want that at all but neither did she want her to get off scot free. 'They already feel abandoned by you so see to it that they are not made to feel unwelcome in your or, should I say, her house.'

'You have no right to judge Vera,' he said angrily.

'Haven't I? I haven't met the new woman in your life and I think I am glad about that but it doesn't stop me having a picture of her in my mind. I see her as a selfish, hard-hearted young woman who takes what she wants and doesn't give a damn who gets hurt.' She laughed and the sound startled Paul. It was pitched too high as though she was about to become hysterical.

'Calm it, Jenny, you appear to be on the verge of hysteria.'

She shook her head. 'I am far from that. Unfortunately I can't afford the luxury.' She paused and it really was to help calm her. The conversation was upsetting Jenny more than she had expected but it was obviously upsetting Paul too and she was pleased about that. His previously good-natured and ever-obliging wife was showing another side, a side that was dismaying him. 'Do you know this, Paul, it is three weeks since you walked out and I don't even have an address or a telephone number to contact you.'

'You have the office number and if I am not available you can leave a message with Betty and I'll get back to you.'

Office jargon – I'll get back to you – that hurt. Jenny looked with cold dislike at the man she had once loved so dearly, perhaps still did though she wasn't as sure about that as she had been. Betty Morgan was middle-aged, a pleasant woman whom Jenny liked and she couldn't help wondering what Betty was making of this. To phone her would only be embarrassing for both of them.

'If you think I am going to phone your secretary you can think again.'

'You are going out of your way to be difficult.' He opened his briefcase, took out a notepad and scribbled on it. 'There you are, that's what you want, isn't it?'

'For the girls, not for me. Surely they should know where their father is living.'

'They'll know now.' He paused and looked directly at her. 'There is something else I want to say. I want a divorce, Jenny.'

'You aren't putting off much time. She wants marriage then?'

'We both do.'

'What about me?'

'You will be free to make a new life for yourself.'

'Not really. Have you forgotten Wilma and Katy?'

'Of course I haven't.'

'If my new life should be with someone else why should he be expected to take responsibility for your daughters when your mistress isn't prepared to give them house room even for one night?'

'That's different.'

'I bet it is.'

'I'm going now.' He got up.

Jenny got to her feet as well. 'If I agree to a divorce I'll let you know but don't bank on it.'

Without another word he went ahead, out of the room and out of the door almost but not quite banging it behind him.

Jenny found she was shaking and had to sit down. She felt so ashamed. That had been a show of bitchiness and completely out of character. It had done no good, angry exchanges seldom did. All it had done was alienate them further.

She was finding the nights worst, the sense of loss greatest then. Was it the darkness that heightened fears? Certainly there were sleepless hours when she all but panicked. She felt so ill-equipped to deal with life on her own. Paul was the one who made the decisions and she had happily gone along with whatever he suggested. From now on the decision-making would be hers.

Money wasn't an immediate problem though it very soon would be. She had a little of her own saved from the housekeeping. It had been her mother who had encouraged her to open a post office savings account and put by a little each month and not to touch it unless for an absolute emergency. You never know she had said, when it might come in useful. How very true that was proving.

The real position when she got down to thinking about it was that she and the girls had no security. Paul might say and believe what he was saying, that they had nothing to fear, the roof over their head was safe. That was no guarantee. The day might come when he or more likely Miss Cuthbertson, might decide to put the house up for sale and force Jenny to find cheap, rented accommodation. Jenny didn't really think it would come to that but it didn't take away the nagging fear.

A divorce would give her greater security or she imagined it would. At least she would know where she stood. The trouble was she didn't want a divorce. It was a step too far. A divorce was so final and wasn't there a small hope in her heart that after this affair had run its course Paul would come home?

It was evening and the three of them were playing snakes and ladders. Katy was yawning, it was past her bedtime but with no school next day it didn't matter. She could have a long lie-in in the morning. Wilma was pretending boredom at playing such a childish game but she didn't mind. The game didn't demand concentration and it gave her a chance to think about tomorrow. She still loved her father but he was no longer perfect. No one was but in her eyes he had been pretty near that. Maybe there were faults on both sides although her mother strenuously denied that. She would, of course, people didn't notice their faults until they had them pointed out. That aside surely it was pretty terrible to walk out on the three of them. Evelyn, who had promised on pain of death, not to mention a word to anyone, was kept up-to-date with developments.

'If whoever she is is really and truly beautiful, beautiful like a film star I mean then maybe your dad couldn't help himself,' she had said.

'My mum is nice-looking,' Wilma said loyally.

'Nice-looking and beautiful are not the same.'

Wilma conceded the point.

'Once in a while my mum treats me like a grown-up,' Evelyn said proudly, 'and she said it was a well-known fact that women are much stronger than men, not physically but in every other way. Not many women up and go even when they want to. They just can't do it if there are children to consider.'

Wilma was suspicious. Why would they be having that kind of conversation unless – 'You told your mum about me,' Wilma said accusingly. It certainly sounded like it.

Evelyn had bright auburn hair caught back in a ribbon. She had very pale skin and had been spared a freckled complexion. Only a few across the bridge of her nose that looked attractive. There was a slight flush on the pale cheeks.

'I did not, I didn't say anything.'

Wilma wasn't sure if she believed her friend but she didn't want it to lead to a quarrel. She needed someone to talk to about her worries.

Wilma and Katy had returned with the shopping and Jenny was putting the groceries in the cupboard.

41

'Mum, what will I wear?'

'Whatever you like, you don't have to dress up.'

'No.' Wilma giggled but it was a nervous giggle. The arrangement was that her dad would collect them at two o'clock or shortly after. They would go to the cottage to see *her* and then the four of them would go somewhere for a meal. Wilma was looking forward to seeing her dad, she missed him more than she said. And she couldn't help being curious about the woman who was causing all the trouble. Wilma thought her mum was being very good about it but she couldn't be happy. She was the only one left out and that must feel awful. To show pleasure at going at all seemed like disloyalty to her mother.

'I don't want to go,' Katy announced suddenly. 'You can go, Wilma, and I'll stay with Mum.'

Wilma looked at her sharply. 'You have to go. Hasn't she, Mum?'

'No, I don't, do I?' She looked at Jenny.

'You don't have to do what you don't want, Katy, but I think Daddy would be very hurt if you didn't accept his invitation.'

'I suppose that means I *have* to go,' she said with a very pronounced sigh.

Wilma would have died rather than admit to needing the support of her little sister and she was relieved that her mum had more or less made sure that Katy would be there. On her own it could be an ordeal, the two of them together would make it easier. She wondered if her parents would get divorced. She wouldn't be the only one in the class with divorced parents. Thelma Paterson said it wasn't all bad that her parents tried to outdo each other by giving her gifts and special treats. Wilma wasn't interested in gifts and special treats. She just wished her parents could get together again and as long as they weren't divorced she thought there might be a chance.

Jenny wished that she hadn't said they could wear what they wanted, it had been foolish but she couldn't go back on that now. They had taken her at her word.

'Katy, your kilt is far too short, Gran hasn't had time to lengthen it.'

Mrs Scrimgeour was good with a needle. She would take the kilt home with her and insert a piece of material in the bodice, a good two inches and Katy would get another year out of it. Kilts were expensive.

'You said I could put on what I wanted and I want to wear my kilt and my green jumper.' She didn't say 'so there' though she might as well have.

'You won't be too hot?' A last hope.

'No.'

That was probably true. The weather continued to be disappointing with what sunshine there was spoiled by a chill wind. So much for flaming June.

When Wilma came downstairs wearing an old favourite which had twice had the hem lowered, the second time with a false hem, Jenny closed her eyes. Paul would think it deliberate. The pinafore dress in shades of yellow and orange was worn thin. The very fact that it had been a favourite meant it had been worn done and was only fit for wearing about the house or around the doors. The choice of a bright pink blouse to wear with it sealed its fate.

'No, you needn't look like that, Mum, I'm not changing it. Gran gave me this blouse for my birthday,' Wilma said defensively.

'It is a very pretty blouse but not to wear with that. The colours clash.'

'No, Mum, you are wrong. Miss Hunter, our English teacher, told us that nature knows best. You always say that red and green should never be seen but they should. The grass is green and green goes with every colour of flower.'

Jenny nodded. She couldn't argue with that.

As the time went on Wilma was beginning to look unsure. It had been a fit of bravado to choose her oldest dress. What had she been wanting to prove? She couldn't remember. 'Maybe I could run up and change into my—'

'No time,' Katy said triumphantly. 'That's Daddy's car stopping at the gate. He's got out but he's not coming in.'

'Don't worry, Wilma,' Jenny said giving her daughter a hug, 'a pretty girl can get away with anything.' And that was true, she thought with amusement. The colours clashed badly no matter what Miss Hunter said, yet after that initial shock the dreadful combination became striking. It was all to do with youth and that lovely shoulder-length blonde hair.

'On you go then, don't keep Daddy waiting.'

'Cheerio, Mum. You won't be lonely without us?'

'No, Katy, I've lots to do and on my own I'll get through it. Be good both of you.'

She stood at the door and waved. There was a fixed smile on her face and the lump in her throat was nearly choking her. Maybe they would be won over, that young woman's charm had worked for Paul, it could work for his daughters.

'Jenny?'

She had been about to close the door when Grace Turnbull came hurrying from next door.

'Hello, Grace, come in.' Jenny would have preferred to be on her own. She could have howled her head off and no one would have been the wiser.

Grace closed the door and they both went through to the sitting-room.

'That was Paul, you might have noticed?'

'Recognised the car, I didn't actually see him.'

'Wilma and Katy are off to meet his lady love,' Jenny said bitterly.

'Try not to let it upset you.'

'What if they decide they like her?'

'Would that be so terrible?' Grace said gently. 'Better really that they should.'

'I'm being unreasonable and selfish.'

'No, you are not, I would be exactly the same in your shoes.'

'I was going to have a good howl, you've cheated me of that,' Jenny said trying to smile.

'You're going to get through this, believe me you are. Is your mother coming over?'

'Not until tomorrow.'

'Fine. Arthur has a bowling match so I can keep you company, if you want me that is?'

'I do but I warn you I'll be rotten company.'

'A pot of strong tea then we'll talk. No use skirting round it, far better to bring your worries out. Even hearing yourself talking about them will help.'

The tea was made and the cups filled.

'I'll have to do something about finding a job, Grace, but I can't see me getting one. Apart from lack of qualifications the little confidence I had has gone. Paul made all the decisions.'

'We are good friends so I take it that anything I say you won't take amiss.'

'You mean I won't take offence? I'll try not to. No, honestly, go ahead, it will be for my own good, I know that.'

'Jenny, you don't make the best of yourself.'

'Meaning I'm dowdy?'

'Meaning nothing of the kind.' She paused. 'What I mean is you are a nice-looking woman who, if she took the trouble, could be quite lovely. No, let me finish. You have thick hair with a natural wave and that glorious chestnut colour, your complexion is good, nothing wrong with your features or your teeth, in fact you have such a lot going for you that I'm positively envious.'

'That last bit is a load of rubbish and the rest is just to make me feel better.'

'Partly that but I did tell the truth.'

'I've lost a few pounds over the last few weeks.'

'You could afford to,' she said brutally.

'Thanks.'

'Try to keep it that way. I know worry has done this for you and provided you stop worrying you'll be fine.'

'I was putting on weight and now that I have lost a bit I'll take your advice and cut down on sweet things.'

'That's right don't nibble during the day. With your figure taken care of we'll talk about your hair. When did you last have it styled? Don't answer that, you've worn it that way since I met you.'

Jenny frowned. 'I'll have you know, Grace, that I get a trim, shampoo and set every four or five weeks.'

'Same old style.'

'Next time I go I'll ask Helen to suggest something new.'

'Helen Dempster doesn't know how to cut hair.'

'That's a bit unkind, I always get a good trim and I've no complaint with the way she sets it.'

'You get a trim when your hair is shouting out for a professional cut. Honestly what I'd give to have your hair with its natural wave. I never wanted curly hair just a natural wave. There are endless possibilities with yours.'

'Nothing wrong with your own.'

'No, but it needs a lot of looking after to keep it like this.'

'What do you advise?'

'A visit to Pierre's in Glenagnes.'

Jenny almost screeched. 'That fashionable stylist, the Frenchman who got the huge write-up?'

'That's the one. I've seen what he can do and I'm going to book up for my birthday treat. Arthur never knows what to give me so I'll suggest a very special hairdo.'

'I've never had my hair done by a man.'

'Then make it a first. Male hair stylists take a great pride in their work. Pierre is special. I've heard he takes ages but the result is worth it.'

'Expensive? He has to be. Grace, I'm trying to economise not throw money away.'

'Yes, Jenny, he is expensive but look on it as an

investment. A new-look you and you'll have the confidence to go after a job and get it.'

'You are very persuasive.'

'I hope so. Remember you will have to book up well in advance, his fame has spread. There are two female assistants who are probably very good but you make sure when you book an appointment that it is with the great man himself.'

Jenny laughed.

'I mean it, don't let anyone else touch your hair apart from shampooing it.'

'Grace,' Jenny smiled, 'I'll give the matter my serious consideration.'

'As regards a job—'

'You've heard of something?' Jenny said eagerly.

'No, I'm afraid not, this is just a one off. If you can stand the sheer monotony of addressing envelopes, typing them I mean—'

'I'll gladly do them and it will help me get back my typing speed. Who wants them done?'

'Arthur was asked if he knew anyone who would be interested. When he mentioned it to me I immediately thought of you.'

'I'm very glad you did.'

'Won't pay much, I'm afraid.'

'Never mind, the little I do get will help pay for this hairdo.'

There had been a mad rush to get into the front seat beside Paul and he was laughing. 'Just for that you can both go in the back.'

They settled in and the car moved off. Both of them twisted round to wave to Jenny, a lonely figure at the door then she was lost to sight.

'Dad, we don't know—'

'Don't know what, Wilma?'

'How will we address – what will we call—' she stopped.

'We were discussing that before I left. Vera wants you to call her by her Christian name.'

'We can't, Daddy.'

'Why not, Katy?'

'We are not allowed to call old people by their first name.'

He smiled. 'Vera isn't old.'

'How old is she?'

'You don't ask a lady her age, Katy.'

'Why not?'

'It's impolite.'

'Mum said she was twenty-five,' Wilma said quietly.

'Bet you don't know Mum's age?'

'Yes, I do, she makes no secret of it. Mum's thirty-eight and Dad is two years older.'

'Two on to thirty-eight, that makes you forty Daddy. That's old.'

'It is not.' Paul was feeling unreasonably annoyed and blamed Jenny. This was her doing, making what she could about the difference in ages. 'No more about ages if you please. Miss Cuthbertson is too formal. You will call her Vera and that is an order.'

This wasn't starting out very well he thought. Jenny was to blame for a lot. She was doing her best to spoil the day for them all. Look at Wilma wearing that ancient pinafore dress. What Vera would say when she saw it he shuddered to think. On the other hand she might be amused, but he wasn't.

They were unusually quiet and Paul stole a glance in the mirror. Poor kids, this wasn't easy for them and he shouldn't have shown his annoyance. The truth was he was a bit on edge himself. Maybe he should have taken the two of them for a meal and they could have met Vera another time. Vera hadn't exactly suggested that but had he done so he had no doubt she would have agreed. Too late now.

They were leaving Blackford behind and approaching Glenagnes. Both places had started out as villages. Blackford had grown but not as much as Glenagnes. People commuted from Glenagnes to Perth. It was a pleasant place to live and the houses were less expensive than in and around the city. As well as a mixture of villas and bungalows, all privately owned, there was a sprawling housing scheme. The latest to be built was the Courtyard. The flats had been described by the builder as very desirable residences for the young executive. As they drove by Paul glanced at the building which was near to completion. He had been shown around the apartments and been very impressed with what he saw. As a young man, he thought this was the life he would have wanted for himself and he gave the construction company full marks for being so forward-looking. Describing the apartments as desirable residences for the young executive was a touch of genius. A year or two of freedom in a place of one's own with every modern convenience, was the stuff of dreams. It was space between leaving home and taking on the responsibilities of marriage. Admittedly not many young men could afford to live in the Courtyard but for those who could it was an ideal life.

Katy was getting impatient. 'Dad, are we nearly there?'

'Yes, Katy, won't be long now.'

The executive apartments were left behind and about ten minutes later they were approaching a row of pretty little cottages. The end house, known as Bramble Cottage, was home to Vera Cuthbertson. On his first visit, Paul had been surprised that someone as sophisticated as Vera would have chosen a cottage.

'Darling, I didn't choose it,' she had said with a laugh. 'It was left to me by a great-aunt of mine, a maiden lady.'

'You could have sold it and bought something more to your liking.'

'Not so easy,' she said raising well-shaped eyebrows, 'the cottage wouldn't have fetched enough to let me buy what I would have wanted and you must remember, dear, that lawyers are not exactly falling over themselves to give mortgages to single women. It doesn't matter a fig if one can afford to pay the instalments or not, in the eyes of a lawyer we are too big a risk.'

Paul wasn't going to be brought into an argument. 'So you settled for the cottage?' he said.

'That was pure chance, fate taking a hand you might say. I noticed in the Situations Vacant that Easton & Hutcheson were advertising for a secretary and I decided to apply since it would be convenient to work there and live in the cottage.'

'You got the job.'

'Of course I did, I never doubted my ability to get it.'

Paul slowed down, signalled left then drove a few yards and stopped. A wooden sign showed that this was Bramble Cottage. There was a tiny strip of garden.

'Out you get, we've arrived.'

They got out of the car and stood looking at the cottage.

'Why is it called Bramble Cottage?' Katy wanted to know.

'Presumably at one time there must have been bramble bushes.'

The girls were waiting for the door to be opened any second and for a smiling Vera to welcome them into her home. Surely she must have heard the car stopping or maybe not, Wilma thought, if she was at the back of the house. There had to be a reason.

Paul opened the gate, waited until they were inside and then closed it. That had made quite a noise, a creaking sound but still no one appeared. Wilma was about to ask if maybe they'd got the wrong day but she didn't when she saw her father take out a bunch of keys, select one and open the door. There was a long carpeted passage and a mat just inside the door, the kind you used to clean your feet. Wilma used it. Katy had gone ahead but returned to clean her shoes though she wondered how she could have dirtied hers. It wasn't raining and all the walking they had done was from their house to the car, then the car to Vera's house.

'Vera, here we are,' Paul called.

Chapter Four

Paul went along the narrow passageway with his two daughters close at his heels. Only one door was slightly ajar and Paul gave a light tap. If it was to announce their arrival and Wilma thought it looked that way, no one flew to the door to greet them. The first glimpse of Vera Cuthbertson came when Paul pushed open the sitting-room door. She was lying stretched out on a cream leather sofa and when they entered she let the magazine she had been reading fall to the floor. Slowly and gracefully she got to her feet and Wilma shivered, it was like something from the movies. Her dad, too, was playing his part. She hadn't paid much attention to what he was wearing but she had a good look at him now. She thought he looked very smart in well-pressed or maybe they were new flannels and a navy blue blazer with brass buttons. It gave him a nautical air and Wilma liked that. He seemed different somehow from the way he looked at home. For one thing she hadn't seen him in a blazer before, that must be Vera's influence. Her mother might not like to know that her husband had taken to wearing a blazer with brass buttons down the front and on the cuffs so she wouldn't tell her. It was important that she didn't add to her mother's hurt. Everything was black enough already.

'Vera,' Paul said smiling engagingly, 'I'd like you to meet my two daughters. This is Wilma and Katy.'

They went forward a little self-consciously to shake hands.

'Do sit down.' Vera gestured in the direction of the chairs but Katy had opted for the sofa. She sat well forward in it with her feet in their brown brogues planted firmly on the russet carpet. After a small hesitation, Wilma joined her sister. Paul waited until Vera had claimed one of the easy chairs before taking the other. For a moment or two no one spoke.

'First meetings are quite dreadful I always think. No one knows what to say.' Vera had a pleasant voice and spoke almost lazily.

Wilma was smiling with relief. It wasn't going to be so bad after all. That had been clever of Vera acknowledging the awkwardness and since she had the awkwardness would cease to exist.

'Believe me, darling, neither of my daughters suffers from shyness, chatterboxes the pair of them.'

Wilma thought she should say something. 'This is very nice,' she said looking about her, 'I thought being a cottage the rooms would be smaller.'

'They were small and I happen to like space. There was only one way to make that possible.'

Both girls were giving her all their attention.

'I had the workmen knock down a wall and make two rooms into one.'

'That must have made a big mess,' Katy said.

Vera laughed. 'The cottage was emptied first. The furniture was old and shabby and it all went to the sale-room. I made myself scarce until the job was completed and everything cleaned up. Then it was time for the redecoration and choosing new furniture.'

'What a lot of money you must have—'

'Katy!' Paul said warningly.

'Don't scold, why shouldn't the child say what she wants, I always do?' Vera turned to Katy who was worrying her lower lip knowing she had said the wrong thing. 'I spent practically every penny I had, Katy, and didn't grudge a penny. This way I can enjoy what money can buy. Others, like your father,' she made a face at him, 'get enjoyment or at the very least satisfaction from having money in the bank. I am not one of those. The money, let me whisper, came from the same great-aunt who left me the cottage.'

'Wish we had a great-aunt like that, Dad,' Wilma said enviously. 'We don't, do we?'

'No, I'm afraid not.'

Katy had slipped down from the sofa to pick up the magazine.

'You dropped that when we came in,' she said handing it to Vera.

'Is that a fashion magazine?' Wilma asked. She had been squinting at it when it was on the floor.

'Yes, it is. Are you interested in fashion?'

Knowing she looked a mess, Wilma blushed to the roots of her hair.

'How old are you, Wilma?' Vera asked kindly.

'Fifteen.'

'I would have been about fifteen when I became interested.'

Wilma brightened. 'Evelyn, my friend, brings a magazine like that to school. Her mother gets it.'

'Which must mean her mother likes to be the first of fashion.'

'No. Evelyn says she wouldn't have the nerve to wear them. She just likes to look at the styles.'

'That is a pity, they aren't all extreme,' Vera said getting up to adjust the curtains. She was a tall, very slim woman with smooth pale skin and golden fair hair piled high on her head. The pale green sleeveless linen dress she wore had a square neckline and showed her long neck to advantage. She had no jewellery. Wilma knew her mother would have worn beads or a string of pearls with a low neckline. Wilma thought her mother was wrong. Vera looked wonderful.

Glancing down at the now hated pinafore dress, Wilma could have wept. Vera would think she had no fashion sense whatsoever.

'I'm sorry about what I'm wearing,' she said in a rush, 'I used to like this pinafore dress an awful lot but it's old now. My mother didn't want me to wear it.' Wilma wanted to make that very clear and not have Jenny blamed. 'I could see that dad was mad when he saw it, though he didn't say anything.'

'That was nice of your father but then he is a very nice man,' she said turning to him. They exchanged smiles, loving smiles that made Wilma feel left out.

Katy thought she had been ignored long enough. 'Mum didn't want me to wear my kilt because it's too short. Gran hasn't had time to let it down.'

'About time it was let down or you got a new one. You are hardly decent.'

Katy was offended. 'I've grown, that's all and it isn't as short as you're trying to make out,' she pouted.

Vera stepped in. 'Is that the Stewart tartan?'

'Yes. Our name doesn't have a tartan.'

'That's lucky.'

'Why?'

'That way you aren't tied to one tartan, you can choose the one you like most.' She paused. 'Incidentally, we are going to Maitland's for high tea. I hope that is all right with you both?'

They nodded happily. It was more than all right, it would be a treat. Eating out in a restaurant was usually reserved for birthdays.

'Paul, did you say you had booked a table for five thirty?'

'I did.'

'In which case I don't think we should have anything to eat. The servings are more than generous and you must keep a space for what follows. We could, however, have a drink.' She looked at Paul.

'Fine,' Paul said getting to his feet. 'The usual for you, Vera?'

'Yes, please.'

Wilma wondered what that would be. She thought about asking what Vera was having and saying she would have the same. She didn't get the chance.

'Straight choice you two. Lemonade or orange?'

'Is the lemonade very gassy?'

'Same as you get at home, Katy.'

She nodded. 'I'll have lemonade.'

'Make mine an orange,' Wilma said with the faintest of sighs. It would have been nice to have been able to tell Evelyn that she'd had a grown-up drink. Evelyn said her mother liked gin and orange, that she'd had a sip and hadn't liked it, in fact she had thought it quite disgusting. Maybe it was an acquired taste.

Paul disappeared to see to the drinks and Vera followed him. Maybe she went to help him since it was her house or maybe they wanted to be together. People in love couldn't get enough of each other and Wilma thought that her dad and Vera must be very much in love. He would have to be, to have it really bad, to leave her mum.

Katy had wandered over to look out of the window and Wilma took the chance to study her surroundings. At the far end of the room was the dining area with a sideboard, table and four chairs. Wilma loved the cream sofa and matching easy chairs. They were so big and comfortable. Against one wall was a china cabinet not unlike the one they had at home. Only this one had hardly anything on the glass shelves. What was there was attractively displayed and got Wilma thinking about her mother's display. There was so much of it that very little of the glass shelves could be seen. Most of the china and crystal had come from elderly relatives as keepsakes. Paul, ever hopeful, had taken a few pieces to be valued only to be told they had no value other than sentimental. One day there might be a market for them but that day was far off.

Katy had moved away from the window. She didn't seem terribly impressed judging by the way she was looking about her but then she was just a kid.

'She's hardly got any furniture,' Katy said in a stage whisper. 'Maybe dad will take her some of ours if mum lets him.'

'Don't be so daft,' Wilma said witheringly, 'this is modern, what we have is ancient.'

'Here we are girls.' Paul had the drinks on a tray and Vera went ahead to bring over a small table.

'That do?' she said putting it between them.

'Yes, thank you.'

'Katy, lemonade for you,' Paul said turning the tray so that she could get at it easily.

'And Wilma.'

'Thanks, Dad,' she said taking hers and putting it on the table.

Dad's drink looked like whisky. Vera's might be gin or it might be something else.

Vera took a sip and began twirling the glass in her fingers.

'At fifteen, Wilma, you must have some idea of what you want to do when you leave school.'

'Wilma is hoping to be a teacher and working hard towards that goal. Isn't that right?' Paul looked across at his daughter and raised his eyebrows.

'Yes,' she said shortly.

'I'm going to be a nurse,' Katy said importantly.

'First I've heard of it. I was under the impression you were bound for Hollywood. A film star no less or failing that an actress.'

'I've changed my mind.'

Vera laughed. 'I didn't set my sights as high as a film star but there was a time, like you Katy, when I wanted to be an actress. Maybe I did have some talent because I was nearly always chosen to take one of the leading roles in school plays.'

'I didn't know you could act, Vera. Now I'll never be a hundred per cent sure of you and what your true feelings are,' he joked.

'Are any of us ever totally sure of another?'

'Darling, that's bit cynical.'

'Yes, it did sound a bit that way.' She turned to Katy. 'Plenty of time for you to change your mind.'

'You are a secretary aren't you, Vera?'

'Yes, Wilma, I'm a secretary.'

'And a very good one,' Paul added.

'Is that what you wanted to be? Did you never want to be anything else, I mean other than an actress?'

Vera laughed delightedly. 'Oh, yes, my dear, I had my hopes and dreams but sadly they didn't come to anything.'

'Why not?'

'I had my head in the clouds was what my father used to say.'

'What about your mother, was she more sympathetic?' Wilma didn't look at her dad. He would be frowning at her asking so many questions.

'My mother,' she said with a trace of contempt in her

voice, 'never had an opinion of her own. In fairness maybe she didn't think it was worth the effort. My father's word was law.'

'Mum said that about her father.'

'Paul, my dearest, be warned. If you want to continue to be loved by your offspring then go easy, don't be domineering.'

'I'm going to refrain from answering that,' he laughed.

Wilma didn't want this conversation to end. 'Vera, what did you want to be?'

'A model.'

'You mean modelling clothes,' Katy said.

'Yes.'

'Why didn't you just go ahead?' Wilma said greatly daring.

'Wilma, dear, there was the vexed question of money. How could I have survived? My father was generous provided I did as I was told. Had I chosen to disobey he would have washed his hands of me and that would not have been an idle threat.' She smiled. 'He probably did me a favour. Very few make it to the top in modelling and it was unlikely I would have been one of them.'

'I bet you would. You look just like a model, doesn't she Dad?'

'I can only agree with that and let me say I am truly glad that Vera's modelling didn't get off the ground. Had she been floating down the catwalk it is highly unlikely our paths would have crossed.'

'What's a catwalk, Dad?'

'Models walk up and down it to show the fashions, but

don't ask me how it got that name. I can't imagine it had anything to do with cats.'

Wilma decided she couldn't let this chance pass. It might be the only one she would get. Her dad wouldn't ridicule it in front of Vera, not when she had been honest enough to tell them her early ambitions.

'Teaching isn't what I want to do,' she said boldly.

'I thought it was. I understood you wanted to teach primary school children.'

She shook her head. 'I never said that, Dad. It got spoken about and you and Mum and Gran decided I should teach, it wasn't me.'

Paul was frowning and looking distinctly annoyed. Vera, seeing it, shook her head warningly and whatever he was about to say remained unsaid.

'Tell me what you want to be, I'd like to know.'

Wilma took a deep breath. 'We've been talking about careers at school and I want to be a reporter on a newspaper or work on a magazine,' she said sounding breathless. 'I wouldn't have to go to college so that would be less expense. I could go straight from school.'

'How many others will be after one or at the most two vacancies?' Paul said sarcastically.

'I don't know and I could be the successful one though you obviously don't think so,' she flashed back sounding angry and hurt.

'Your dad means it won't be easy but you knew that anyway.'

Wilma nodded. 'You think the same as Dad, you don't think I stand a chance.'

'On the contrary I think your chances are excellent. Do remember though that your school record is very important.'

'I work hard.'

'I'm sure you do. To succeed one must work hard and I speak from experience. This is not to put you off, just to have you prepared. It might sound glamorous to be a reporter but an experienced one will tell you that most of it is just hard work and unsocial hours.'

She smiled. 'I know, I heard that.'

'You will be expected to have other qualifications as well as academic ones. If I were doing the interviewing, Wilma, I would be looking for someone with good appearance, a pleasant personality, a clear speaking voice and a genuine enthusiasm for the job. I would pass you on all counts.'

'If I could get a word in—'

'Yes, Paul, did you think we were ignoring you?'

'It crossed my mind,' he smiled. 'Haven't you forgotten shorthand and typing? Aren't they essential?'

'Very much so. Not a problem though. If the school doesn't teach commercial subjects there is always night school. That, I imagine, would be encouraged.'

'Mum has a typewriter.'

'Good! Listen to me going on and none of this is my business. Maybe I've said too much already.'

'No, Vera, no, you haven't,' Wilma said earnestly, 'I'm just so glad I spoke about it.'

'Don't get carried away, Wilma,' Paul warned. 'Don't dismiss teaching. Become a teacher and you'll have a short working week and long holidays. Worth bearing that in mind.'

'I'm not bothered about that. It is more important to enjoy what you do.'

'Time enough to discuss this at a later date.' It was said firmly and the matter was closed.

Maitland's restaurant was busy, the waitresses rushed off their feet. Since they were booked, the four of them went ahead of those waiting in a queue for a table, and were shown to one with a reserved ticket on it. Vera had put on a matching jacket before leaving the house and Wilma was filled with admiration. It was awful to have to feel guilty about liking somebody but what could you do if you couldn't help it.

It wasn't like going out for dinner, people were casual about dress when it was high tea. Wilma was thankful it wasn't an hotel or she would have been very embarrassed. Though thinking about it she could have swanked a bit to Evelyn.

They each got a menu to study and there was quite a choice. Katy was concentrating on the sweets and once she had decided on that she would go back to the main course.

'Well, girls, have you made up your mind?'

'Cold meat and salad for me, dear,' Vera said putting down her menu.

Wilma thought about having that too though it certainly wasn't her favourite. Haddock and chips was very ordinary but seeing it being served at the next table made it irrisistible.

'Wilma?'

'Haddock and chips, please.'

'Ready to order?' The waitress was there with her notepad and pencil.

'Yes, I think so,' Paul said. 'One cold meat and salad, one steak and kidney pie and one—'

'No, Dad, make it two – I'm having the same as Wilma.'

'Two haddock and chips.'

'Tea, bread and butter?'

'Yes.'

She went away.

'Why didn't she ask about the sweet?' Katy said anxiously.

'Not to worry,' Vera said. 'We'll order that later. I have to confess a weakness for the sweet course.' Katy smiled, well satisfied.

Jenny watched the clock, impatient for their return. She wouldn't ask anything, just wait and let them do the talking. Had it been very awkward for them? How could it not be? Their father was living with a woman who wasn't his wife. The girls knew right from wrong, she had done her best to give them proper values though she had never been guilty of preaching to them. They would see this Vera Cuthbertson for what she was.

The girls were almost home. Vera had been dropped off at her home and she had said before getting out of the car that they would be welcome to visit her again.

Paul slowed down as they neared 16 Abbotsford Crescent.

'Are you coming in, Daddy?' Katy said.

'No, pet, I'll just get back. Did you enjoy yourselves?'

'Yes, the tea was great.'

'Vera is nice, Dad, I didn't think I would like her but I do.'

'Thank you, Wilma, that makes it a lot easier for me.'

'If we are all friends you mean?'

'Something like that.'

'You can't expect Mum,' Wilma said showing anger.

'No, I can't. I accept that it is out of the question. Out you go then, I've petrol to get before the garage closes.'

Jenny looked up and gave them a welcoming smile when they entered.

'Did you lock the door, Wilma?'

'Yes, I turned the key.'

'Mum, I'm not a bit hungry, we got lots to eat.'

'We had high tea in Maitland's,' Wilma said as she sat down.

'That would please you both.'

'Yes.' Her mother wasn't going to ask questions about Vera and Wilma thought that was probably going to make it more difficult. It was easier answering questions than making up what to say.

'Mum, Vera is—'

'Katy, I don't think you should be using the woman's Christian name.'

'She wants us to.'

'I see,' Jenny said pressing her lips together.

'She's all right, Mum, and she's got white furniture but hardly any of it.'

'It is not white, the sofa and chairs are cream leather.'

'White and cream are nearly the same and we've got far more furniture than she does.'

'That's because our sitting-room is—' Wilma stopped.

'Just say it, Wilma, cluttered is the word you are searching for. Families tend to have over-furnished rooms.'

'I didn't mean that, Mum,' Wilma said wretchedly.

'I know you didn't, but it happens to be the truth.'

'What I meant was, it is a cottage Vera has modernised and what looks well in it wouldn't be right for here.'

'That's true.'

'You know this, Wilma doesn't want to be a teacher, she told Vera she wants to be – what is it again Wilma?'

'Reporter,' Wilma said through clenched teeth. She could have throttled her young sister. She had wanted to broach that subject gradually and when Katy wasn't around.

Jenny felt pain like the thrust of a knife. Vera Cuthbertson must have made a very favourable impression on Wilma when she got that out of her. Why hadn't she told her own mother?

She swallowed. 'Nothing to hinder you going into journalism if that is what you want. Did you think I was forcing you into teaching?'

Wilma shook her head. 'I thought that was what you wanted for me and I wanted to please you,' she gulped.

'I want to be a nurse.'

'That's good, Katy. When I'm old and frail you'll look after me.'

'I don't want to be that kind of nurse.'

Jenny didn't know whether to laugh or cry. She didn't seem to be able to get anything right.

'Vera wanted to be a fashion model but she wasn't allowed,' Katy said ignoring her sister's dark look.

'Her father was against it,' Wilma said by way of explanation.

'Mum, she's skinny, like a beanpole.'

'She is not,' Wilma said hotly, 'she's got a super figure. Mum, just ignore what she says, Katy doesn't know anything. Vera is tall and slim and wears her hair swept up. Actually she would pass for a model. Fancy being a secretary when you could be a model.'

'Do you want to hear what we had to eat?'

'No, thank you, Katy, I think we'll talk about something else. Your visit is over and I'm glad you both enjoyed it.'

Wilma heard the finality in her voice. There would be no objections raised to further visits but the hope would be that those would be few and far between. She felt a sadness. Vera was young and she was interesting. It would be nice to have someone like that on her side. Then back came the guilt. Her mother wasn't insisting she went in for teaching. She could be a reporter or at least try to be one. Her mother was so good and so reasonable. She didn't deserve to be left out, yet that was what was happening. Dad had Vera and Vera had made it clear they would be welcome if they wanted to come and if they didn't she would understand. She couldn't have said fairer than that.

The only one to miss out on everything was Mum.

Chapter Five

—◆—

Jenny thought she needed her head examined, not her hair done by an expensive stylist. That was all very well if one had money to burn, but she wasn't in that fortunate position nor likely to be. Jenny sat in the bus thinking these thoughts. A visit to the hairdresser didn't mean dressing up but Jenny thought she should look smart. She chose a lightweight beige costume and an olive green blouse bought the previous year for a cousin's wedding on Paul's side of the family. The outfit had been kept for best though she thought she ought to start wearing it before it became old-fashioned. Skirt lengths kept changing. She got off the bus in the High Street and from there it was a short step to Bernard Street. Walking towards the premises Jenny saw nothing special about the outside and felt slightly cheated. She had expected the frontage to be more, well – à la mode or at least different. Admittedly the paintwork, cream and pale green, looked fresh, otherwise it was just a very ordinary shop that had been taken over and fitted out as a hairdresser's.

There was no mistake that this was Pierre's salon. The name was in gold lettering above the door. Feeling foolish and blaming Grace for putting her in this position, Jenny opened the door and went over to the desk. There was a faint whiff of perfume. A smart, pretty young lady with beautifully manicured nails looked up and smiled.

'I have an appointment for two thirty with Pierre.' She felt self-conscious saying the name Pierre. It was as though they were on friendly terms.

'Your name?'

'Mrs Richardson.'

The eyes were lowered to the book open in front of her. 'Here we are.' She ticked a name. 'Please take a seat Mrs Richardson, Pierre is a little behind time with his appointments but he shouldn't be too long.'

Jenny knew she was five minutes early, she had checked with her watch before coming in.

'Thank you.' She went to sit down on the couch and reached for a magazine from the pile on the glass table. She opened it as though preparing to read or glance through it but instead kept the magazine in her hand and looked about her. The premises were bigger and more spacious than one would have expected from the outside. Two attractive girls wearing pink overalls with brown piping were expertly winding hair on to rollers and talking non-stop. An anxious looking junior was beside one of the wash-basins and was being given a demonstration on the correct way to shampoo hair. After the shampoo itself came a very thorough rinsing until the hair squeaked, Jenny heard the assistant say. Finally, and with the fingertips, the scalp was given a massage. Jenny compared the procedure with her local hairdresser. There it was just a quick shampoo, an equally quick rinse and over to the mirror for the next stage. It all went like clockwork.

Common to them all was the babble of voices. There must be something about a hairdresser's that invited confidences. How many rumours began there? How many secrets were whispered as busy hands coaxed difficult hair into curls? Jenny thought she must be one of a small minority who preferred to be quiet and use the time to think her own thoughts.

There was a slight disturbance and Jenny turned her head. Someone had come out of one of the cubicles and was gesticulating wildly. It could only be Pierre and an assistant was quick to give him whatever it was he required. Her reward was a huge smile that lit up his face and Jenny couldn't keep from smiling. There was something endearing about the little man with the goatee beard and the excitable manner.

Twenty minutes later Jenny was minus her costume jacket and sitting in the cubicle. She had expected to be shampooed first but, no, Pierre had to study her face and hair. Her chin was lifted in surprisingly strong fingers while he examined first her profile and then full face. Satisfied, his attention turned to Jenny's hair and he smiled as though well pleased. Darting away he called for someone to shampoo Madame and Jenny was whisked away to go through the procedure she had just witnessed. After the massage her scalp tingled and she felt wonderfully relaxed.

The Frenchman muttered to himself while he worked but there was no attempt at conversation. Freed from the effort of talking to a stranger and a foreigner at that, Jenny closed her eyes and listened to the snip, snip, snip of the scissors. She didn't want to watch. Jenny had told him she wanted nothing elaborate and Pierre had thrown up his hands in horror. Pierre did not do elaborate hairstyles. Pierre was an artist, the hair was his canvas. She had felt like giggling but managed to keep her face straight. The Frenchman was very serious.

The result was so much more than she had dared hope. It was a transformation and Jenny all but gasped. This couldn't be her?

Pierre was beaming. An artist satisfied with his work.

'Madame is pleased?'

'Madame is more than pleased. I didn't know I could look like this,' she said foolishly. It was true. The short layered hair curled becomingly, like a large chrysanthemum, and suited the shape of her face. It made her look younger she thought and dare she say it, sophisticated. No, not sophisticated, she corrected herself, she could never be that. Attractive, she would settle for that. 'How long will it stay like this?' Jenny asked coming down to earth.

'Until you come to see me. All you need, Madame, is a cut from Pierre, only Pierre. You have the lovely hair and it is not appreciated,' he said mournfully. He walked with her to the desk and left her to pay the bill. She didn't blanch. Grace had warned her what to expect.

'He is good, isn't he?' the receptionist said as she admired Jenny's hair.

'Yes, very good.'

'Mind you, he can't do that for everyone. Some ladies

72

with thin wispy hair expect Pierre to do wonders. Shall I make another appointment for you?'

'I'm afraid I can't, not at this moment. I'm not sure of my plans.' Jenny was making excuses.

'Here is our card. Phone for an appointment but if you want Pierre,' she smiled, 'you will have to book well in advance.'

'I'll do that.'

Jenny closed the door behind her and stepped into the street. She was an abandoned wife with all the worries that brought, but just for now she felt carefree. If this is what a visit to Pierre could do maybe it wasn't such an extravagance after all.

'Told you, didn't I?' Grace said looking smug. 'Seems a shame not to be going somewhere special to show it off.'

'No hope of that. This, you might recall, was to give me a better chance with the job situation.'

'It can't do any harm.'

'Is that all you can say when it was you who bullied me into it.'

'I did, didn't I? Makes you feel different, you have to admit it.'

Jenny smiled. 'I do feel different, I feel a new woman. The feeling won't last, of course, but nice while it does.' She stopped and looked thoughtful. 'Maybe I'm partly to blame for Paul looking elsewhere. I ought to have taken more interest in my appearance.'

'You are not to blame, most certainly you are not. That said, Jenny, an interest in your appearance can only be good for you. Good for us forty-somethings to take a pride in ourselves.'

'Speak for yourself, I'm only thirty-eight.'

'Slip of the tongue,' Grace grinned.

'I'll put the kettle on.'

'No, thanks, Jenny, I just came in to see how you got on.'

Jenny gave a rueful smile. 'As regards the job situation, there isn't a single one I could apply for with any hope of success. Nobody wants a thirty-eight-year-old woman with no qualifications other than typing and even there I doubt if my speed is enough for them.'

'Don't worry – something will turn up. And now I really must dash, I'll see myself out.'

Jenny had another look through the job vacancies in case she had missed something but there was nothing. She wandered over to the window and looked out at the garden. The grass could do with a cut. That was the gardening job Paul had done, cutting the grass and trimming the edges. It would be her task now. The phone rang and she went to answer it.

'It's me, Jenny.'

'Hello, Mum.'

'Where were you, I phoned earlier?'

'Having my hair done.'

'I must phone Helen, mine is needing a tidy.'

'I gave Helen a miss. Grace recommended someone.'

'Any good?'

'Very, very good.'

'In that case I must try her.'

'It's a he not a she.'

'I wouldn't mind that.'

'You would mind the cost though.'

'As expensive as all that?'

'Yes.'

'A bit extravagant for you. I thought money was tight.'

'It is. I thought a new hairstyle might cheer me up and help me to get a job.'

'You're being very silly, Jenny.'

'I know.'

'Any luck?'

'With a job? None at all. I'm twenty years too old. Mum, I honestly don't see me getting an office job.'

'Would you consider something else?'

'I might. It depends. I'm not reduced to taking just anything.'

'Of course you are not.' She paused. 'Wilma and Katy all right?'

'Yes, Mum, they are fine. You don't want to come right out with it and ask but I'll tell you. Paul and that woman—'

'That woman has a name and bad though she is, she is entitled to it,' Janet Scrimgeour said severely.

'Yes, Mother, I stand corrected. Paul and Miss Cuthbertson entertained the girls on Saturday. They had high tea at Maitland's restaurant.'

'That would be to save her the trouble of making something.'

'Possibly. Whatever, they enjoyed the meal and—' Jenny's voice broke.

'Now! Now! That won't do, you mustn't let it upset you.'

'Of course it has upset me. I have feelings you know.

75

They like her, not only like her,' she gulped, 'that young woman has apparently made a great impression on Wilma. Poor girl, she is doing her best to hide it from me so as not to hurt my feelings—'

'Just your imagination,' Janet said briskly, 'you always had plenty of that.'

'No, not my imagination.' She stopped until she had gained control. 'Wilma doesn't want to be a teacher, she wants to be a reporter on a newspaper.'

'What's wrong with that? It's a job and I imagine it will be reasonably well paid.'

'That's not the point. I'm not against Wilma becoming a reporter, she can be whatever she wants to be. What is so hurtful is that she discussed it with Miss Cuthbertson and not with me.'

'Yes, I can see why you're hurt. That wasn't very nice of Wilma but maybe it just came up in conversation the way these things sometimes do. Not worth getting upset about, dear, that isn't going to help.'

'I know,' she said miserably and sounding very sorry for herself.

Janet wanted her to snap out of it. She would change the subject.

'Moira Ramsay,' her mother began.

'How is she getting on? I meant to ask. Didn't the press do her proud, it was quite a write-up?'

'That's what we all thought. Comes, of course, from having the right connections.'

Jenny wasn't all that interested in Miss Ramsay's venture, she had more to think about.

'And she has those?'

'Oh, yes, Moira knows the right people. From what I gather she is quite happy the way things are going. Now will you be quiet while I say my piece.'

'Sorry.'

'This is not what you are looking for, I know, but would you be prepared to help Moira out? She would consider a part-time assistant or as she said, hours to suit if she was sufficiently impressed with the applicant.'

'What is the job?' she said carefully.

'Serving in the shop and I imagine just being generally helpful,' Janet said vaguely.

Jenny was wary, generally helpful could mean anything and she wasn't reduced to going down on her knees and scrubbing floors.

'She shouldn't have any difficulty getting staff.'

'She hasn't. Getting staff is easy, getting suitable staff is more difficult. Moira has just sacked her assistant, not for breaking an expensive vase, but for her attitude. She made no apology, just said it wasn't her fault that it slipped through her fingers and broke.'

Jenny smiled. Katy let things slip through her fingers. Helping with the dishes often meant a cracked dish or the handle parting company with the cup.

'You are smiling, aren't you?'

Jenny laughed. 'Could be our Katy.'

'No, Katy apologises and shows genuine regret. I remember how upset she was when she broke a saucer of my good set of china.'

'So were you.'

'I was because I knew I wouldn't get it matched.'

'You told Katy you could.'

'I had to, the poor lass was in tears.'

'This Miss Ramsay, tell me more.'

'Tell you what?'

'You've met her?'

'I have. Maggie introduced us but I only met her the once.'

'What is she like?'

'I remember a small attractive woman, very neat and quick on her feet. Let me think. Early fifties at a guess but I'm not all that good with ages. Anything else you want to know?'

'Is she pleasant?'

'I thought so, I liked her.'

'Does she want to see me?'

'If you are interested in the job. I had told Maggie you see that you were looking for something and she must have mentioned it to Moira. Don't delay or someone else will get in before you. If you take my advice you'll get the ten o'clock bus tomorrow morning.'

'I'll do that. Won't do any harm to go and see what is expected.'

'I would come with you but I'm to be assisting at a coffee morning. It's in the church hall with the proceeds going to help the aged and infirm.'

'You are elderly yourself, Mother.'

'I don't see myself as elderly,' Janet said tartly. 'I'm getting older like everyone else but I'm still able and thankful to be so. Mind you, when I think about it I could give my excuses and come with you. It would be nice to see the place for myself. She's calling it the Log Cabin.'

'I know.' Jenny smiled. Her mother would come like a shot but if this was to be an interview for a job she would prefer her mother not to be there. 'Mum, you keep your promise and lend a hand with the coffee morning. There will be another time for the Log Cabin.'

Jenny wore her pale blue summer skirt and a dark blue blouse and over them an oatmeal linen jacket. She loved the way she could pull a comb through her hair and see it fall into place. If she got this job maybe a visit to Pierre every four or five weeks would be possible. She hoped so. Wilma and Katy had thought their mum looked marvellous. They hadn't used the word drab but Jenny thought it must have been how they had seen her. She didn't know whether to be flattered or dismayed.

Jenny got off the bus and walked the short distance to the cut off leading to the Log Cabin. The sun was shining and the overnight rain had freshened the countryside. The sky was high, and there was a pleasant breeze blowing. The depression that gripped her from time to time had lifted. Life went on no matter what.

The design for the Log Cabin had been drawn up by someone sympathetic to the countryside and with plenty of imagination. It could have been an eye-catching monstrosity but it wasn't. The Log Cabin blended in with the country scene. It was a solid structure – it had to be to withstand the harsh winters – with a timber frontage, green shutters and an awning that stretched the whole length of the one-storey building. There was a large gravelled area to the front and tubs of flowers at the entrance gave an attractive splash of colour. Jenny thought the wooden benches would be for those who wished to sit outside and admire the lovely Perthshire scenery before going in to browse around, be tempted, and perhaps enjoy a refreshment.

A few years ago the Log Cabin would have been an impossible dream. The area was too remote. Now that was one of its attractions. With more and more cars on the road and a much improved bus service, folk were going further afield. They were looking for the unusual and Moira Ramsay was doing her best to provide it. Jenny went up the two wide steps, opened the door and went inside. She could hear voices then hurrying footsteps. A smallish woman with a neat figure and hair just turning grey, appeared. She gave a welcoming smile and Jenny liked her on sight.

'Good morning.'

'Good morning. I'm Jenny Richardson. My mother told me you are looking for an assistant. That is if you are Miss Ramsay?' It suddenly occurred to her that it might not be.

'Yes, I am Miss Ramsay and you must be Mrs Scrimgeour's daughter?'

'Yes.'

'We, your mother and I, met through a mutual friend. You probably know that?'

Jenny nodded.

'We'll talk better over a cup of coffee and then if we are to suit each other I'll show you around the premises.'

'Thank you. I'm very impressed with the outside.'

'Not an eyesore?'

'Anything but. It seems to blend in.'

'That was the idea. Some people, and friends of mine among them, thought I was making a big mistake, an expensive mistake. They pleaded with me to think again.'

'You didn't, your mind was made up.'

'I did have some misgivings,' she laughed, 'but, no, not serious misgivings. I felt there was a need for something like this. Folk had to get rid of the after-war blues and breathe in the fresh country air.' They walked across the parquet floor to the far end and up a few steps to an area set out with tables covered in red and white checked tablecloths. One table was occupied by a business representative who was just finishing his coffee and reading a newspaper. There was a counter and behind it a woman was arranging cakes in a glass case.

'Is it coffee, Miss Ramsay?'

'Yes, please, Lily. Two coffees. How do you take yours, Mrs Richardson? Black or white?'

'Brown, please, I only take a little milk.'

'Just as I do.'

The woman brought the coffee to the table and a plate of assorted biscuits. Jenny helped herself to sugar and accepted a plain biscuit.

'You may already know that my husband has left me.' Jenny thought she ought to get that out of the way.

'I did hear that and I am sorry. When there are children it makes it more difficult.'

'Yes.' Jenny drank some coffee and put the cup carefully

back on the saucer. 'Let me say right away, Miss Ramsay, that I have no experience of shop work, no experience of anything apart from running a home. Before I was married I worked in an office. That was sixteen years ago and a lot of changes have taken place since then.'

'That's what I like, no dithering, cards on the table. I'll be equally honest. I want someone who would be genuinely interested in the job, someone with a love of beautiful things. Maybe in this day and age I am asking too much. A job to most is a pay packet at the end of the week.'

'In my house there aren't many treasures,' Jenny smiled, 'but that doesn't mean to say I wouldn't like them. Be assured I would handle with care.'

'I have a feeling you would.'

'I want to say I would be reliable but if one of my daughters – Wilma is fifteen and Katy is ten – were unwell—'

'They would come first and so they should. We'll finish our coffee and then I'll show you the gift shop and the gallery. I'm glad you came at this time. In the afternoon there are ladies coming from some organisation or other, and I'll be kept busy as will Lily. The weekends are the busiest as you would expect but Edna, a friend of mine with time on her hands, helps out. Extra staff will be employed as and when required. A venture like this, Mrs Richardson, takes time to be established. Start small and grow as the saying goes.'

'It would be part-time?'

'Hours to suit, let me put it that way.'

'Provided I am home for the girls coming out of school and that is usually four thirty, I could work Monday to Friday. If you were to be rushed or your friend wasn't available at the weekend I could help out. My mother would come over to be with Wilma and Katy.'

'Mrs Richardson, I have a feeling we could work well together. It would be a case of giving and taking.'

Jenny smiled. This was looking very promising.

'You are interested?'

'Yes, I am, Miss Ramsay.'

'Good. Are you finished?'

'Yes, thank you, that was very nice.'

They got up and Miss Ramsay smiled to Lily.

'The gift shop is where you would be spending a lot of your time. The gallery is my own special love. So many artists, very good artists, Mrs Richardson, live a hand-to-mouth existence and a few become disheartened and give up, feeling it is too much of a struggle. This is my way of helping. Once people come in they like to see everything. There are those who give the gallery no more than a quick look but others take their time and study the paintings and once in a while we make a sale.'

'Much to the joy of the artist,' Jenny smiled.

'My dear, I have had tears of joy and one young man almost crushed me to death in a bearlike hug.' She laughed. 'Never a dull moment or not too many of them.'

Looking about her, Jenny was impressed with the gift shop. It was well stocked and beautifully arranged. No wonder it was attracting visitors. For so long they had been deprived of beautiful things. The country was just beginning to recover from a long war. No one had expected it to take this length of time. For years everything was scarce. Furniture shops stocked utility goods. Not all of it was inferior but the label utility immediately branded it as such.

Fine china was only now beginning to be seen. There was a mad rush when word got round that such and such a shop had a small quantity for sale. Brides were overjoyed. A half tea service comprising six cups and saucers, six tea plates, one bread plate, sugar bowl and milk jug, was the traditional gift from bridesmaid to bride. Money wasn't plentiful but more of it was in circulation with women holding on to their part-time jobs.

Miss Moira Ramsay had waited until she thought the time was right. A great deal of care had gone into the stocking of the shop. She wanted something for everyone. A small part of the shop was given over to the more affordable items. Holidaymakers and day trippers liked to take home a souvenir. There was a wide choice of trinkets. Butter dishes and small plates showing local beauty spots were on display. Children were well catered for and the toys included tiny cars for little boys and dolls of all sizes for little girls. The ever popular tartan dolls in their boxes were displayed on a shelf along with other tartan novelties. A special attraction was the mohair jackets which immediately took Jenny's eye.

'I love those, they look so cosy.' Jenny went over to touch one.

'I couldn't resist them. In time I hope to sell tartan skirts.'

'And tweed?'

'Possibly.'

The show cases held Dresden china figures and Wedgwood dishes, whisky glasses, sherry glasses and much much more. A section was given over to linen, some boxed some loose.

'This is quite perfect, Miss Ramsay. No wonder folk come back and back again. Working here is going to be an absolute pleasure. What I especially like—' She stopped.

'Go on.'

'There is so much space to walk about.'

'Yes, I wanted that and the more fragile articles out of the reach of children. Mothers can't enjoy looking if they have to be for ever checking on their little ones.'

Jenny nodded in approval.

'This isn't like a busy store in town, Mrs Richardson, where possibly you would need some training. All that is needed here is a pleasant manner, a show of patience and common sense. You, I would say, have these. I don't think I am a difficult employer though the young woman whose services I dispensed with would no doubt disagree. She was bored and made no attempt to hide it. The fact that she broke a vase had nothing to do with her removal but it did give me the excuse I needed to be rid of her. Breakages happen, accidents cannot be avoided, they happen to all of us. All that was needed was a show of regret.' She smiled. 'Any questions?'

'I don't think so, Miss Ramsay, other than when would you want me to start?'

'As soon as possible. Shall we say Monday first and the hours . . .' She stopped to consider. 'How about 10 a.m. to 3.45 p.m.? There is a bus at four o'clock and you must leave in plenty of time to catch it.'

'Thank you, that would suit me very well.'

'Splendid, I'm so glad to have that settled. We'll talk about remuneration and holiday entitlement but I don't see us disagreeing there.'

Chapter Six

Jenny's first week had gone well and she was enjoying working in the Log Cabin. A few business reps had become regulars since they found it to be a convenient stopping place where they could get a coffee, a rest and a read of the newspaper. No one rushed them out and that was much appreciated. Unlike some restaurants where the bill was put on the table without being asked. It was a hint that they had already overstayed their welcome.

Families and friends of the artists who had been given wall space for their paintings came to see the display and word began to spread that the Log Cabin was well worth a visit. The same happened with a party of women on a day trip who had made the Log Cabin a stop and been very favourably impressed. Word of mouth was the best advertisement. Business was slowly but surely building up.

Jenny was willing to turn her hand to anything and when Lily was harassed in the tea room she was quick to offer assistance. Her employer noticed. Mrs Richardson was proving to be a find and she just hoped the woman would stay and not take an office job if one was offered. Occasionally she saw a fleeting sadness in her face and Moira wondered how deeply wounded she was. Once they were better acquainted perhaps she could broach the subject and offer help. What kind of help she didn't know but there might be something. Once, long ago, Moira Ramsay had loved and lost and it had been a painful experience. She had recovered but it had taken a long time. A betrayal was more difficult to get over than a bereavement. It was heartbreaking and humiliating. It made one feel a lesser person. She understood only too well what Jenny was going through.

Jenny was understandably nervous one morning when she was alone in the gift shop and a well-dressed woman came in. She walked about then took a good look at the display before pointing to one of the show cases.

'Would you let me see that crystal vase, the large one, please?'

'Certainly.' Jenny knew it would be very heavy and she was apprehensive about bringing it down and putting it on the counter. Miss Ramsay made her appearance at the right moment.

'Netta, how lovely to see you.' They touched cheeks.

'I was seeing friends off at the station, had time on my hands, and decided to drive this way and find out how you are getting on.'

'I'm so glad you did. This is Mrs Richardson, my new assistant.'

The women smiled to each other.

'I was asking your assistant about that crystal vase, Moira, the large one.'

'Lovely isn't it? No, Mrs Richardson, don't attempt to take it out, not unless you are seriously interested, Netta.'

'Really! What a way to treat a prospective customer,' Netta said pretending to be insulted, 'you'll chase folk away.'

'Are you a prospective customer?' Moira laughed.

'I could be. It just happens that Michael and I have been invited to a wedding down south. My poor dear husband isn't keen on the long drive so I don't expect we'll attend but we will have to send something decent.'

'Didn't you suggest sharing the wheel?'

'Of course I did and you know what he said to that?'

'I can guess. It wasn't well received,' Moira laughed.

'It was not. Isn't it awful that men always consider themselves to be better drivers than women. Absolute nonsense, of course, I have much better road sense than Michael. I had to be good. After all I did drive an ambulance during the war.'

'So you did.'

'About this gift, I might as well buy it here as anywhere else.' She had another look at the vase. 'Crystal is always acceptable.'

'It is, crystal makes a lovely gift but if you are contemplating sending this through the post, Netta, there is the risk of breakage. It can happen even though it is well packed. Indeed I don't know the maximum weight the post office allows or if there is a limit. Someone, I can't remember who, said there was no limit for letter post but that there was for parcels and that legally—'

'I've heard that too,' Netta interrupted, 'legally one can send an elephant by letter post.'

Jenny was laughing. It was plain to see they were good friends.

'While we are on the subject of parcels have you seen the way they are thrown about at the railway station? I've seen a parcel clearly showing a "handle with care" label, being thrown from one basket into another, occasionally not even reaching the basket. That said, I have no quarrel with the post office.'

'I wouldn't be posting it. Transport is no problem. Some of the family will be going down by car and they would take it.'

'In that case—'

'No,' she shook her head, 'on second thoughts they might not be too keen to be responsible for the vase if it is as heavy as you are making out. Maybe I could settle for linen which, I imagine, would be equally acceptable.'

'I would think so. Come and see what we have and don't feel obliged to buy.'

'I'll see something. You do have a lot of lovely things but then you've always had good taste.' She frowned. 'After that compliment don't I get the offer of a cup of coffee?'

'Of course, Netta. Shall we have it now or later?'

'Now. I feel the need of one.'

An hour and a half later Moira helped her friend carry her purchases to the car. She had bought a lace tablecloth for a full-sized dining table, an embroidered linen teacloth and matching napkins and four silver napkin rings. The two pottery plates decorated with tulips were bought because Netta couldn't resist them.

Moira came back smiling. 'One of my more eccentric friends, Mrs Richardson, but a dear for all that. Netta loves to shop and fortunately has the means to do so. She has a beautiful home and Michael is a darling. She can be very difficult and he puts up with a lot but then he adores her.' Moira laughed as though remembering. 'Shoes are Netta's passion, she must have a wardrobe full of them. I think she tries on every size 4 in the shop before making up her mind. That said, Jenny – do you mind me calling you Jenny?'

'No, not at all – I prefer it.'

'Netta isn't one of those awful women who put the assistant to endless trouble then leave without making a purchase. My friend is likely to end up undecided between two pairs and buy both.'

'A worthwhile sale in the end,' Jenny smiled.

'As you say. Now off you go and have your coffee and don't rush. This is your break and you are entitled to it.'

Summer was giving way to autumn with the countryside looking particularly lovely. Jenny could never make up her mind whether her favourite season of the year was spring or autumn. Spring was the fresh green shoots showing everywhere. Spring was lovers strolling hand-in-hand. She and Paul had fallen in love in springtime. Autumn was very different, there was a hint of sadness. Summer was left behind. It was like saying goodbye to a friend and knowing it would be another year before they met up again. In autumn the trees were beautiful with the leaves showing russet and yellow among the green.

The girls knew no difference. Their mother was there to give them breakfast and to prepare their lunch boxes and she was back home from the Log Cabin before they returned from school. Paul as yet did not know that she had got herself a job. She saw no reason to phone and tell him and he hadn't called. Why should he? They had nothing to say to each other. Jenny surprised herself by asking Wilma and Katy to say nothing to their father about her working. Her excuse was that she wanted to do it herself. Once they would have questioned anything that didn't make sense to them but not now. It would appear Paul was right when he said that children quickly adapt to changed conditions.

Paul, though he didn't know it, was out of favour with his elder daughter. She was hurt and angry and very surprised when she heard that they would only see Paul and Vera once a month. Paul and Vera were of the opinion that too many visits would only unsettle the girls. How could they possibly think that? Katy didn't care, she wasn't bothered one way or another. Unlike Wilma she hadn't much to say to Vera and her dad wasn't as easy to talk to as he used to be when they were all at home together. As long as she had her mum Katy was fine.

Wilma couldn't get over it. She was too upset to tell her friend Evelyn. She couldn't talk to anyone about it. Certainly not her mother or her gran or Katy. She was the odd one out. She liked and admired Vera and thought of her as a friend. Surely it wasn't pretence on Vera's part? Of course it wasn't. Hadn't Vera said that Wilma reminded her of herself at that age? Saying with a laugh that they were both blonde, long-legged and that she, too, had been painfully thin. Being slim she had said was different to being thin. Thin was to be shapeless, whereas being slim was having a good figure with curves in the right places.

Her dad had laughed at that and Vera had thrown a cushion at him. All good fun and she had been part of it. Yet they only wanted to see her once a month.

Janet Scrimgeour hadn't as yet visited the Log Cabin. Each time she made plans to do so something got in the way. She didn't particularly want to go on her own and when Maggie Halliday, the friend who had introduced her to Moira Ramsay, offered to take her she jumped at the chance. To be upsides with her friends Maggie had learned to drive. It had taken a long time and tempers had been frayed but eventually she was declared fit to be in charge of a vehicle. Two cars were out of the question but Maggie, after a hard fought fight, would have the use of her husband's car for one day a week. It had been below her husband's dignity to travel by bus to his place of employment but a sympathetic and obliging colleague had come to the rescue and offered to give him a lift there and back. Maggie got the car. She drove very slowly and very carefully.

Just after two o'clock Maggie breezed in with Jenny's mother just behind her. Mrs Halliday was a buxom lady of medium height with a round happy face and a huge laugh.

'This is absolutely wonderful, Moira,' she enthused. 'I'd heard the others rave about it but you know how they do exaggerate. Not this time though, full marks I give it.'

'Don't make such sweeping statements, Maggie, you're hardly in the door,' Moira smiled extending her hand to Janet Scrimgeour. 'I'm so glad you could come, Mrs Scrimgeour. We did meet before and I have you to thank for my very able assistant.'

Janet was slightly flushed. She still wasn't quite at ease with the bridge ladies though no blame could be attached to them. She had joined them as a lonely widow and been given a warm welcome. Bridge wasn't an obsession with any of them though they enjoyed a game. The social side was more important.

'Jenny is very happy working here and no wonder, everything looks so fresh and attractive.'

'And spacious, Moira,' Maggie added. 'Very important for those of us carrying a bit of bulk. Getting around some shops is no joke. This, I have to say is a pleasure. Do we look around ourselves or do we get a guided tour?'

'Which would you prefer?'

'To wander around on our own. How about you, Janet, I shouldn't be speaking for you?'

'Fine by me,' Janet said as she waved a hand to Jenny who was busy clearing up after a customer. This particular customer had no intention of buying but insisted on picking up each article, examining it carefully then putting it down in the wrong place. She moved away saying she would go and have a cup of tea and something to eat provided it wasn't too expensive. These out of the way places usually are was her parting shot. Free for the moment Jenny joined the ladies.

'Another satisfied customer?' Maggie smiled.

'No, just one of those women who like to look with no intention of buying. We don't mind that at all, we encourage people to browse, but it can be very annoying when they pick everything up.'

Moira Ramsay was nodding. 'If only they would keep

their hands off. That doesn't apply to friends of course,' she said hastily.

'Not to worry, whatever we pick up will be returned to its rightful place. Come on Janet, we'll browse to our heart's content then go and look at this gallery. I do love to see paintings especially by unknown artists. Moira, there might be a masterpiece hanging on your wall.'

'I wouldn't be at all surprised. Some of the paintings are extremely good and you would be surprised how many folk have come back for another look. In some cases it has meant a sale.' She turned to Jenny. 'You must take time off and have afternoon tea with your mother and Maggie.'

'That is kind of you.' The ladies had moved away. 'My mother will want to bombard you with questions. She has a great admiration for women who make a success of their life.'

'And I have?'

'I would say so.'

'Circumstances, a twist of fate can so often dictate the course of our life.'

Jenny looked at her quickly but Moira said no more.

Lily had set a table for four. There were no customers and Lily had volunteered to keep an eye on the door and report if anyone should come in.

'A very obliging lady,' Maggie said as she settled into her chair and opened out the paper napkin.

'We work as a team, isn't that so, Jenny?'

'Yes, it is by far the best way.'

The tea was poured and they began eating.

'These are baker's scones,' Maggie said in a voice of censure.

'Yes, Maggie, Maxwell the baker delivers fresh every day. Why, don't you like them?'

'Not bad, but you can't compare these with home baking.'

'I'm aware of that,' Moira Ramsay said and looking just a little bit annoyed.

If Maggie noticed she decided to ignore it. 'Janet, your scones and sponges would go down a treat.'

Jenny's mother flushed with pleasure. 'I'll take credit for my sponges but when it comes to scones Jenny's are better than mine.'

Jenny smiled and shook her head. Paul had always said that her scones were extra special. Did he miss them and her home cooking or did he think being deprived of them was a small price to pay for what he had now?

'I'll get up early, do a baking of scones and bring them in.'

'Seriously, Moira,' Maggie said as she finished the scone, 'there are women who are very good bakers and would be more than happy to bake in their own homes and earn some money. Trouble would be to get the stuff to the Log Cabin.'

'That needn't be a problem provided it isn't too far. Tommy, the man who does odd jobs for me, has his own car and he's always keen to earn a little extra.'

'May I make a suggestion?'

'Of course, Mrs Scrimgeour, all suggestions will be given careful consideration.' Moira smiled encouragingly.

'I was thinking of the counter in your tea room.' All eyes went to it. 'There is plenty of room to have jars of home-made marmalade, jams in season and maybe honey. You could even have tablet, look how well it sells at sales of work. Folk don't always want to buy from the gift shop, they can't afford to, but they will always buy something to eat. Not everyone makes their own marmalade.'

'Mrs Scrimgeour, you have given me a lot to think about. Your daughter and I will put our heads together and see what can be done.'

The ladies had thoroughly enjoyed their afternoon and were not going home empty-handed. Maggie had bought half a dozen dish towels. She said she would keep two and the others would be handy to give as a small gift. Janet selected two small autograph books for her granddaughters and then wondered what use they would be. What would Wilma and Katy do with them? Say a polite 'Thank you, Gran' and pop them in a drawer where they would lie forgotten.

'What a stupid thing to buy,' Janet said wretchedly, 'I need my head examined. Why didn't I just buy note-books?'

'They can be exchanged.'

'No, Jenny, don't do that, it would look bad.'

'It would not. Give them here, I won't be a minute.' Jenny made the exchange and saw the look of relief on her mother's face. It got Jenny thinking how silly we are to worry about such trifles. But then, what was a trifling thing to one person could be important to another. Worrying to some people came as natural as breathing. She wondered about herself. Was she a born worrier? She didn't think so, not in a general way. She did worry about the girls but most mothers worried about their families. That was as it should be. We had brought them into the world and they needed our protection and our love. A husband was different, he could change. Paul had and it still hurt. She wondered if she would ever be free of the hurt. It wasn't as bad as it had been at the beginning and that could be because she had a new interest. The days didn't drag the way they would have done had she been home all day.

'I do like your mother, Jenny. She has a pawky sense of humour.'

'She enjoyed today, Mother likes getting out and about. When my father was alive she led a very quiet life because he never wanted to go anywhere. Paul . . .' she faltered.

'Your husband?'

Jenny nodded. 'Paul was good to her and good for her, they really got on very well. After dad died I tried to encourage mother to take up an interest, something to occupy her but she paid more attention to what Paul said. Learning to play bridge was his idea. I didn't imagine she would even consider it. She plays whist but bridge needs a lot more thought and I didn't see her mastering it.'

'You were proved wrong.'

Jenny smiled. 'She admits to not being very good but at least she made the effort.'

'None of them are particularly good. An exclusive club caters for the keen ones, I don't like to use the expression card sharpers but it could be a fair description.' She paused. 'Jenny, I wonder if you could help me out?'

'I would like to if it is possible,' she said carefully.

'The next two Saturdays if you could manage that. My friend isn't available. I have a feeling she wants to give up and is gradually getting round to it. This will spur me on to making a greater effort to engage more part-time staff.'

'Yes, I'm reasonably sure that can be arranged. Mum will come over unless she has other plans but that is unlikely.'

'I would be grateful.'

'Wilma thinks she is old enough and capable enough to be left in charge of the house but I wouldn't be happy.'

'Neither would I. And you, Jenny, would be unable to relax.'

'I'll let you know for certain tomorrow but it will be all right I'm sure or nearly sure.'

'Thank you.'

'What did you really think of my mother's suggestions?'

'Worthy of consideration.'

'May I add my pennyworth?'

'Please do,' she smiled.

Jenny took a deep breath. She was a fairly new employee and didn't want to appear forward.

'The weather is getting colder,' she began.

'Alas that is true and winter will soon be upon us. There will be a falling off of trade as one would expect. I took that into consideration when I decided to open this business. The Log Cabin is not in the wilds. It is quite near to a bus route and the authorities will make a great effort to keep the road clear.'

'That's what I thought. Some people will still come but

more willingly, Miss Ramsay, if hot food is served in the tea room.'

She shook her head. 'No, Jenny, I'm afraid that is not possible. We don't have the facilities. Tea and coffee are all we can manage.'

'I wasn't thinking of proper lunches but rather of hot snacks. Folk would enjoy a plate of home-made soup and you could have a variety of sandwiches.'

'Jenny, you leave me breathless. We all have to crawl before we walk. While I am not dismissing your suggestions, as I said before the facilities are not there. There is plenty of kitchen space. I was advised to allow for expansion but I feel I haven't reached that stage.'

'I'm sorry.'

'Don't be. You may have hit on a splendid idea for the future. In fact come to think about it, a good-sized stove and an oven wouldn't be hugely expensive. If I sound wary, at the back of my mind I am thinking about shortages. Even seven years after the war we are not completely free of rationing. One can only hope that the end is in sight.'

Chapter Seven

———◆———

Janet was agreeable to come over on both Saturdays and be with the girls. Remembering she had promised to bake scones for the Log Cabin, Jenny got up early. She left a few on the cooling tray and put the rest in a clean tea towel. Tommy was to call and collect her and save her waiting for the bus which on occasions was full and didn't stop. It was a long wait for the next.

Moira had an early cup of tea and a scone and said it was delicious. The rest were to be kept for the afternoon teas.

Saturdays were hectic and Jenny was kept busy between the gift shop and the tea room. Lily was very quick and efficient but she did need assistance from time to time. Moira remained in the gift shop. Between noon and two o'clock there was a lull and then the occasional car would stop and the occupants wander over to the Log Cabin.

What made Jenny glance out of the window and then stay to take another look, she couldn't have said. Was it the car she recognised first or the broad back of the person getting out of it. Whichever it was she remained rooted to the spot. Her heart began to pound then give a sickening lurch as two people walked towards the entrance. Her first thought was that Paul must not see her. She would hide herself until they were gone. Like a scared rabbit she mumbled something to Lily who stared after her. Jenny made for the cloakroom unaware that Moira had seen her. Was Jenny unwell? She went along to see.

'Jenny, are you sick?'

She shook her head.

'Sit down and let me get you something.'

'No, I'm all right.'

'That you are not. Your face is white.'

'I'm sorry, it was the shock. Give me a minute and I'll be fine.'

'What kind of shock? Jenny, you are not making sense.'

Jenny looked up and swallowed painfully. 'Paul and the woman he is living with have just come in. I think they must be in the tea room. I – I just happened to glance out of the window and saw them. Lily must think I've gone mad, I'm supposed to be helping her.' She gave a nervous laugh.

'You stay here and let me deal with this.'

Moira came back. 'A tall, broad-shouldered man with fairish hair and a tall woman with swept up blonde hair?'

'Yes, that fits their description.'

'If Lily is busy I'll serve them.'

'I feel all kinds of a fool acting this way. I wish I could help myself but I can't.'

'Perfectly understandable. Tell me, does your husband know you are working here?'

'No, he doesn't.'

'I thought not.'

The colour had come back into her face and Jenny was

beginning to feel better. She was also becoming increasingly angry with herself. Why was she getting into this state? If anyone should be embarrassed, that someone should be Paul.

Moira was imagining what was going through Jenny's mind and with some accuracy. She would wait. The best thing to happen was for Jenny to face her husband. Did she have the courage?

'If this was someone else I would say to that person to face up to it and not be a coward.' Jenny smiled and bit her lip to stop it trembling. 'I'll serve them, that is if Lily hasn't already done so.'

'Good for you, that is what I was hoping you would do.'

Jenny shivered. She didn't want to go through with it but with Miss Ramsay's eyes on her she couldn't back out now.

'Jenny,' Moira said softly, 'remember this, you have the advantage. Your surprise is over, his is still to come.'

'I hadn't thought of that.'

Leaving the cloakroom with her head held high and the faintest of smiles on her face, Jenny returned to the tea room. She stopped to apologise to Lily for leaving her so suddenly then went across to the corner table. The woman was leaning over to say something to Paul and he was smiling.

'Excuse me, Paul, is it the set afternoon tea you wish?'

The way he turned and the shocked incredulity on his face was comical to see.

'Jenny, I didn't, I never,' he was stuttering, 'you didn't tell me you were working.'

'How could I when I never see you.'

His face darkened. 'You could have phoned.'

Jenny's eyes widened. 'I seem to recall you saying that I was only to phone in an emergency and finding myself a job could hardly be termed that.' Jenny was amazed at her seeming composure when inside she was churning with nerves.

The woman moved as though to draw attention to herself. And it did appear that she had been forgotten. Jenny saw Paul make an effort to pull himself together.

'Sorry, dearest.' He put his hand over hers. 'Vera this is Jenny.'

She was quite lovely, Jenny thought with a pang. Wilma hadn't exaggerated. Vera Cuthbertson was stunning and that air of sophistication would impress a young girl. Impress most people.

Wife and mistress looked at each other and each gave an uncertain smile. Jenny would have been very surprised if she could have known what Vera was thinking. She had expected Paul's wife by his description to be a plain, homely woman, a shy retiring person. That was far from the truth. She wasn't overwhelmed by the situation and Paul clearly was. Mrs Richardson was no raving beauty but she was attractive. Probably her hair did it and whoever gave her that style knew what suited her. She couldn't fault her own hair but it required a lot of attention to keep it looking the way she liked it. Jenny's hair would bounce back. She felt almost envious.

'You look different, Jenny.'

'Do I?' Was that admiration in his eyes or wishful thinking on her part?

'Your hair, you never used to wear it that way.'

'That's true. I wanted a change, a whole new me. I'm so glad you like it. Wilma and Katy do. Forgive me, I must get on. You did say afternoon tea for two?'

'Yes, please.'

Jenny turned away, relieved that was over. She would get Lily to serve them afternoon tea and she would assist behind the scenes. When Jenny left them Paul made a pretence of mopping his brow.

'Not such a good idea coming here after all.'

'I have to say your wife was the more composed. Could be, of course, that she saw us coming in and had time to prepare herself.'

'That would be it. She wouldn't have handled it so well otherwise.'

'She isn't what I expected, Paul.'

'What did you expect?'

'Someone mousy.'

'I never described Jenny as mousy. All the same she has changed.' He didn't know why he was finding that disturbing. Always he had a picture of Jenny moping at home and missing him. She didn't give that impression, rather she appeared confident and contented. Jenny had no right to be either. That was irrational. He should be pleased not annoyed. Paul stretched out for a scone, buttered it and added a spoonful of jam.

'Have one, darling, best I've tasted for ages.' It reminded him of the scones Jenny made. That was what he missed, not Jenny. He missed the meals she used to prepare. Vera was the love of his life but he did wish she had more interest in food. Going out for a meal once in a while was fine but too often and it became monotonous. Expensive too. Vera was expensive, worryingly so at times.

Shortly after lunch Paul collected the girls for their visit and had them back home for seven o'clock. That was long enough for Katy who secretly would rather they didn't have to go at all. Why couldn't her dad come and see them? It might be awkward for Mum, Katy accepted that, but she was nearly sure she wouldn't object. Vera wouldn't be there and for a little while it would be like before. Her dad might even change his mind and find back home was better than being with Vera.

The worst part of going to Vera's house was Wilma acting so silly and hanging on to every word Vera said as though she was someone very special. She wasn't half as special as Mum. And as for Dad he hadn't been as cheerful as usual. Had he been like that when they were a proper family, Mum would have said he was sickening for something and given him hot drinks and things like that. Vera didn't seem to notice or care.

There was a warm smile for them when they came in. Jenny had the workbox out and was sewing a button on Katy's school blouse. The scissors weren't handy and she snapped the thread with her strong teeth. Paul hadn't liked to see her doing that but Paul wasn't here and she could do as she liked.

'Did you have a nice time?' They would have eaten out and that was always a treat.

'Super,' Wilma said throwing herself on the sofa and grinning broadly.

'It was all right,' her sister said and went upstairs. She didn't want to hear Wilma going on about it. Her mum wouldn't want to listen to all that stuff. Wilma thought herself very clever but Katy thought she had more sense.

'Mum, what do you know! Dad and Vera have been in Paris.'

'Good for them.'

'Vera bought some smashing clothes when they were there and she showed them to me.'

'That would please you.'

'Not the sort of clothes you could wear.'

'Thank you very much,' Jenny said drily.

Wilma frowned. 'I didn't mean that the way you are taking it. What I meant was that it would have to be someone like Vera to show them off to advantage. And,' she laughed, 'more to the point, have the nerve to wear them.'

'As daring as that?'

'Not terribly daring, just fashionable. Slinky and tight-fitting is this year's look. That is what the Paris fashion houses say and, of course, our fashion houses follow,' she said as though she knew all about it.

'You seem well informed.'

Wilma was on the defensive. 'Vera tells me things like that because she knows I am interested. You saw Vera,' she said almost accusingly, 'so you must know she looks like a model.'

'Yes, Wilma, I did see Miss Cuthbertson and I agree she is a very attractive young woman.'

'Why do you keep calling her Miss Cuthbertson? She doesn't like being called that.'

'I am not concerned with what she likes or doesn't like.'

'Dad thinks you are being difficult.'

'Your father has no business discussing me.'

'You were not being discussed, you were merely mentioned, that's all,' Wilma said rudely. It was always the same when they got back from Vera's, she thought furiously, her mother only pretended an interest.

It was no use getting angry with Wilma, far better to ignore it. Jenny checked on the other buttons in case one was slack but they all seemed firm enough. She put the blouse on the back of the chair.

'One job done.'

'Why can't you call her Vera, she calls you Jenny?'

'Does she indeed! Tell her your mother prefers Mrs Richardson, Jenny is for my friends.'

Wilma went out slamming the door behind her.

Chapter Eight

Jenny was down on her knees in front of one of the show cases and looked up with a smile when Miss Ramsay came over.

'You know that's rather nice with the silver to the front. Yes, leave it like that.'

This was the part of her work Jenny especially liked. Where before she had just dusted and polished and returned the articles to their same place, now she was doing some rearranging.

'I enjoy this.'

'You do have the knack which must mean you have a lovely home.'

'Sadly that is not the case, Miss Ramsay. Our home is comfortable, I could call it that, but it is no showpiece. One day I had hoped to furnish it just as I would like but that day is further away than ever.' Jenny got up off her knees. 'When we got married and to keep the mortgage as low as possible, Paul and I put practically every penny we had towards a deposit. I must say we had a lot of fun going to sales and searching second-hand shops for bargains. The result as you can imagine, was that nothing ever matched.

Then we were going to wait for two years before starting a family and I was to keep on my job.'

'You got careless,' Miss Ramsay smiled.

'Must have. Wilma arrived and then a few years later Katy put in her appearance. Paul thought the children needed their freedom and I went along with that. The refurnishing would wait until they were a bit older.' Jenny laughed. 'If you saw our china cabinet you wouldn't say I was good at displaying. All the little treasures the girls collected over the years went into it along with china and glass and I don't know what else.' She laughed again. 'I keep promising myself that I'll empty it, put the junk in the bin, and display only the best.'

'If you do, be sure you don't throw out something that might be valuable.'

'Not a chance. Much of what we have are bits and pieces given to us by elderly relatives now long gone. Paul kept hoping there might be something worth a bit of money and he even went to the trouble of finding out. Alas there was nothing to get excited about.'

'That would only be one person's opinion so take my advice and hang on to what you have, you never know. Incidentally why haven't I met your two daughters? Aren't they curious to see where their mother is working?'

'Very curious. The pair of them have been pestering me to bring them.'

'Why haven't you?'

'It would have to be a Saturday, our busiest day and I didn't want them getting in the way and making a nuisance of themselves.'

'They wouldn't. Good heavens, Jenny, they aren't toddlers. Isn't one fifteen and the other ten?'

'Nearer sixteen and eleven. They both have birthdays next month.'

'Old enough to want to earn a little extra pocket money.'

'They wouldn't say no to that, but it would have to be real work.'

'Of course it would be real work and you know, Jenny, with the girls here on a Saturday you wouldn't have to depend on your mother to look after them.'

Jenny nodded. 'Mum doesn't mind, but I do feel guilty saddling her with Wilma and Katy every Saturday. 'Wilma could, perhaps, help Lily in the tea room. She has a little experience of serving teas and coffees in the church hall. As for Katy,' Jenny shook her head, 'it would have to be something behind the scenes for her.'

Katy's face was pink with excitement. She felt very grown-up and important standing in the kitchen of the Log Cabin with Lily. Lily was nice. Mum said that she and Wilma must remember to call the lady Miss Anderson though she was Lily to everyone else. Katy wore a large apron, one of Miss Anderson's, over her new grey skirt. She had, without being told, washed her hands thoroughly and her nails were clean.

When Katy was out of earshot, Jenny slipped along to the kitchen to have a quiet word with Lily.

'I have to warn you, Lily, that Katy is like a bull in a china shop.'

111

'Not as bad as that?' Lily was smiling.

'Maybe not but I'm afraid my daughter is one of those children who are naturally clumsy.'

'She'll grow out of it.'

'It's to be hoped so.'

'Don't worry, Jenny, Katy will be fine with me. I'll keep her occupied.'

Katy was back. 'Miss Anderson, what do you want me to do?'

'You can help me fill the cakestands.'

The cakestands were three-tiered and each plate was covered by a white paper doily. The special afternoon teas were served between quarter to three and half past four. People could eat at other times, Lily told Katy. They could eat all day if they wanted but on those occasions they ordered whatever they wished and paid the full price. The set afternoon tea was much better value.

'What are you going to put on them?'

'We'll start with the scones. Take four from the tray, Katy, and put them on the top plate.'

Katy did that and had them evenly spaced.

'Good. I'll cut the sponges and the Dundee cake. Watch how careful I am. The cake and the sponge, Katy, have both to be cut as near the same size as it is possible to make them. Some folk feel very upset and cheated if they see they have been left with the tiny piece.'

'Not fair when they are paying the same.' Katy was on the side of the person getting poor value.

'Exactly and that is why I am being so careful. Put these on the middle plate.'

Katy did so but not to Lily's satisfaction and she quickly rearranged them.

'Now for the macaroons and you have to be extra careful how you pick them up.'

'Oh, dear, you didn't tell me in time and my finger has gone through the top of this one.' Katy bit her bottom lip and raised her eyes. 'Nobody will notice, will they?' she said anxiously.

'I would notice, wouldn't you?'

Katy nodded miserably.

'It's all right, accidents will happen.'

'What'll I do with it?'

'Put it aside.'

'And take another?'

'No, better leave the macaroons to me.'

'What will happen to it?' Katy said a little wistfully.

'No one is going to want a broken macaroon.' Lily's lips twitched. 'Would you like to eat it?'

'Oh, yes, please.' Katy cheered up at once.

Lily was smiling to herself. She was a delightful child, Jenny's younger daughter, but she wasn't going to be much help in the kitchen. Or, wait, maybe she could sort out the cutlery. She couldn't do much damage there.

The tea room which now advertised home baking, was becoming ever more popular. Edna, Moira Ramsay's friend, who had been helping out on a Saturday, had withdrawn her services and in her place had come Mrs Doris Roberts, a childless widow, who was willing to work all day on Saturdays in the tea room and assist at other times wherever it was needed. Doris was a pleasant, quietly spoken woman who after the untimely death of her husband had returned to live with her parents in their tied farm cottage. Her mother, she told Miss Ramsay, was an excellent baker and would be happy to supply the tea room. Moira had sampled a selection of her baking before committing herself. The woman had a light hand with pastry, her sponges were all that could be desired as were her scones. From now on there would be no more shop cakes and scones served in the Log Cabin.

Mrs Wallace, Doris's mother, was an early riser and always had been. She said it would be no bother for her to get up at the crack of dawn, heat the oven and get started to a big baking while other folk slept. The trays of home baking could be collected early in the day.

They were country folk the Wallaces, Sandy was a farm labourer and all farm workers were considered to be poorly paid. The farmers disagreed. Hadn't they a rent-free house? They wouldn't starve, they could exist off the land. Most of them grew their own vegetables and they were permitted to help themselves to whatever was growing in the fields. Eggs and milk were cheap enough and there was no scarcity of rabbits. If Mrs Wallace complained it was only because everyone else did. She didn't think they did too badly. Even so this was a grand opportunity to earn money of her own and put it by for a rainy day. It wouldn't be frittered away. They would manage as they always had. There was something very reassuring about having a few pounds in the bank since none of us knew what the future might hold. Look at their daughter, their only child and widowed at thirty-nine. A bairn would have helped but

114

there had been no living child from that union. One still-birth and whatever had gone wrong at that time had taken away any chance of Doris having more. It had been so sad. No grandchildren. That had been a big disappointment but she'd got over it. What was the point of grieving over something you couldn't change. It had been the will of God. Sandy had disagreed. He was a good man and he could be that, she knew, without him being a churchgoer. The only times Sandy had seen the inside of a church had been at his own wedding and then at his daughter's. Sandy Wallace said and believed, that what happened in life was all in the luck of the draw.

None of the locals believed that the Log Cabin would last long. No one else had made a go of it so why should Miss Ramsay? It would close down just as soon as the novelty wore off. Another month they would give it, then they had to give it another and then another. Far from closing down, the Log Cabin was going from strength to strength. It was gaining a reputation as an interesting place to visit. There was something for everyone and in the bonny days families could picnic nearby. The burn running close by was a magnet for the children. With a jam jar and a net purchased from the Log Cabin they could fish for minnows and fill their jam jars to take home. With their children happily occupied and their husband behind a newspaper or stretched out on the grass, mothers could browse at leisure and be tempted by something on display. Winter was another story. They would have to wait and see what would happen then but folk wouldn't be in such a hurry to write it off.

Mrs Wallace was quietly happy. The Log Cabin was a godsend to them. Doris had perked up, there was less time to be depressed. She was in employment and it had given her a purpose in life. As for Mrs Wallace she was congratulating herself. She felt proud to be playing her part in bringing in the customers. Admittedly the shop and that gallery were the main attractions. The gallery brought in some weird-looking customers, arty types but nice for all that. Not many departed without having visited the tea room and sampled her home-baking. Jenny had been the first to make the suggestion about hot snackes and Mrs Wallace was all in favour. Nothing elaborate, she said, folk weren't looking for that. What would go down well, especially on a cold day with a bitter east wind blowing, was a plate of piping hot soup. Ring the changes, have a different kind each day. Sandwiches, freshly made to requirements, was another suggestion but Mrs Wallace wasn't so keen on sandwiches. Pies and sausage rolls, her own of course, would have more appeal or so she thought. Jenny, that nice woman, seemed to have the ear of her employer and she was in favour of lunches. It could all happen. Amazing the way her mind kept jumping ahead. Her Doris had been well taught. She knew how to prepare a good pot of soup – and who knows, the day might come when her daughter could be in charge of the tea room.

Wilma wore a small white apron with a frilly edge over her navy blue skirt. Her mother hadn't been anywhere near when she described the Log Cabin. It was much, much better than she had made out and Wilma was greatly impressed. No wonder people wanted to make a return visit. She would tell Evelyn every little detail and have her green with envy. All poor Evelyn did on a Saturday was to go shopping with her mother for boring groceries and then tea and a bun in some café. After that it was window shopping. Her mother was supposed to be very fashion-conscious but they hardly ever went into a clothes shop. Evelyn said it was because her mother might see something she wanted and couldn't afford and that would make her a bit miserable for the rest of the day. Wilma didn't believe it, that was Evelyn making it up as usual. It didn't tie up with all the fashion journals her mother bought or there again maybe it did. Looking at a fashion journal was a bit like window shopping.

Wilma was glad Miss Ramsay was so friendly. She wasn't putting it on, she really was pleased to see them. She said that Mum should have brought them weeks ago. Wilma had wanted to say it wasn't her fault, that she had wanted to come but the look on her mother's face had kept her quiet. There was something else she noticed. Miss Ramsay and her mum got on really well. They were more like friends than boss and employee. That could be good news for her. If she made a good job of being a waitress and Katy didn't break anything maybe they could come every Saturday. Her mother had hinted it might be possible.

'What do I have to do?'

'To be a good waitress? Be pleasant but not forward. Be obliging and smile but do not giggle.'

'Not like at the Guide and Brownie coffee morning?' She giggled at the memory.

'Not like that,' Jenny smiled.

117

'It didn't matter there though, did it? We were only serving mothers and aunts and grannies.'

'You'll be serving strangers here, that's the difference.'

It had been a busy day. The good weather had brought the people out and for a while folk had to wait for a table to become vacant. By the end of the day Wilma was tired though if asked she would have denied it. Mrs Roberts told her she had done very well and Wilma hoped that word would get to Miss Ramsay. She need not have worried, Moira Ramsay had seen for herself how well Wilma was coping and said as much to Jenny.

'You have two delightful daughters, Jenny, they are a credit to you.'

'Thank you. I hope nobody found them a nuisance.'

'Nobody did. Both Lily and Doris said how smart and efficient Wilma was. There was no awkwardness whatso-ever.'

'Thanks to her helping at the church coffee mornings.'

'Whatever it was she did well,' Moira smiled. 'Now if you would send the pair of them along to my office.' Jenny guessed that Miss Ramsay was going to give them money. She hoped it wouldn't be too much.

'Wilma, Katy,' Jenny said going over to where Wilma was looking longingly at a mohair jacket in sky blue, 'Miss Ramsay wants to see you in her office. Remember to knock and don't enter until you are told to do so.'

'Why does she want to see us?' Katy said a little fearfully.

'I don't know, dear, you'll find out when you go.'

They went together and Wilma knocked.

'Come in.'

Katy pushed Wilma ahead so that she had to go in first. Miss Ramsay was seated at her desk. She had been wearing spectacles but took them off and laid them on the desk.

'Wilma, close the door if you please.'

Wilma did so then returned to stand beside her sister. She looked unconcerned and her sister a little apprehensive.

Moira Ramsay was smiling as she picked up two small brown envelopes and handed one to Wilma and the other to Katy. 'That is a little something for your assistance.'

'Thank you, Miss Ramsay,' they said almost together. Wilma's fingers closed round the shape of coins. She had worked for it and deserved to be paid not like Katy who wouldn't have done very much. It wouldn't be fair if they were paid the same.

'You have both been a great help and thank you.'

'I enjoyed serving the tables,' Wilma said.

'I'm so glad and from what I heard you have been a splendid waitress. You didn't get flustered, not even when you were rushed off your feet.'

Wilma flushed at the praise and dropping her eyes began to study her shoes.

Katy shifted on her feet. Her mother always said to own up and not to wait until you were found out. She swallowed and licked her lips.

'I'm very sorry about my finger going through one of the macaroons, Miss Ramsay,' she said in a rush. 'It was an accident. Did Miss Anderson tell you?'

'No, she didn't.'

She hadn't needed to confess after all. Katy could see

from the corner of her eye that Wilma was trying to keep a straight face.

'Are you angry with me?'

'My dear Katy, why should I be angry? I'm far from that. What an honest child you are.'

Katy brightened. She wasn't in disgrace. 'Miss Anderson said no one would want the macaroon so I got to eat it.'

'Was it good?'

'The macaroon? It was lovely.'

'Katy gets called butter-fingers, she's always dropping things.'

'No, I don't. Well not very often.'

'Katy, I can sympathise. I, too, used to get called butter-fingers.' It was completely untrue but Moira felt sorry for this charming, clumsy child. She liked both girls but there was something very endearing about Katy. She was the kind of child you wanted to hug.

Katy's smile stretched. 'You couldn't help it either.'

'No, it just seemed to happen.'

They shared a smile of complete understanding.

Outside the office, Wilma was desperate to see what was inside the envelope but knew she would have to wait. Mum would say it was bad manners to rush and open it. She would make them wait until they were home. Wilma thought two of the coins were half crowns.

'Mum,' Katy waved her envelope. 'From Miss Ramsay and there is money in it.'

'You shouldn't have accepted money.'

'We had to,' Wilma said.

Jenny knew that but she didn't want them to expect

payment. She wanted her children to be helpful without looking for a reward.

'Mum, we had to,' Wilma repeated. 'How could we hand something back when we don't know what is in the envelope?'

'Yes, yes, I know. The point I want to make is that you must not look for payment. Miss Ramsay has been more than kind to us.'

Miss Ramsay came out of the office to see them go.

'Goodbye girls, I hope to see you next Saturday unless, of course, something more exciting turns up,' she smiled.

'Nothing will,' Wilma said and Katy nodded in agreement, then changed that to a shake of the head in case it was misunderstood.

They were home and Wilma was very pleased with the contents of her envelope until she discovered that her young sister had got the same. That rankled and she complained to Jenny.

'Aren't you satisfied with what you got?' Jenny said showing her annoyance.

'Yes, I am satisfied, I'm very satisfied,' she added for good measure. 'I just don't think it is fair that Katy got the same for doing hardly anything.'

'Katy did her bit. She did her best and she is a lot younger.'

'That is always the excuse. When I was her age you didn't make those excuses for me.'

'How could I?' Jenny smiled.

★   ★   ★

Their grandmother came over on Sunday and she was hardly in the door before being told about the lovely time they'd had in the Log Cabin and that they would be going back next Saturday and maybe the one after that.

'You've been there, Gran and you liked it.'

'Yes, Wilma, I had a very enjoyable visit.'

'We got paid for helping,' Katy told her.

'Helping is an act of kindness and does not require payment,' Janet said severely.

Wilma made a face. 'Don't you start, Gran, that's what Mum keeps saying. We didn't ask to be paid but anyone hearing you two would think so.'

'Very well, we'll say no more about it.' Janet paused. 'Did either of you give a thought to your poor grandmother being left all alone? No, I'm sure you didn't.'

Wilma looked up from reading her magazine. 'Would you have come?'

'Chance would have been a good thing.'

Jenny had just come downstairs and heard the last part of the exchange. The voice had been decidedly peevish.

'Mum, I didn't think to ask you.'

'No, you didn't, did you? I'm fine when I'm needed and ignored when I'm not.' She sniffed and kept her hat on. A sign that this might be a short visit.

Jenny sighed. 'Mum, you are never ignored and I honestly thought you would be glad to have some time to yourself. You've been so good coming over to be with Wilma and Katy.'

'And pleased I was to do so. Have you ever heard me complaining?'

'No.'

Jenny thought how easy it was to cause offence. It had never occurred to her that her mother would have wanted to accompany them. A bit much to expect Miss Ramsay to welcome her mother as well as her two daughters. To keep the peace Jenny thought she must invite her for the coming Saturday. She would explain the situation to Miss Ramsay.

'Gran, you never want to go into Perth and look at the shops and you won't let me go on my own. I could meet some of my friends there. They have a lot more freedom than I have.'

'That may or may not be the case and I am not concerned with other girls.' She looked at Jenny. 'When your mother isn't here I am responsible.'

Jenny nodded and Wilma grimaced as though in pain.

'You always say you get tired trailing round the shops.'

'So I do, Wilma. One day you'll be old yourself and then you'll know something about it.'

'If Gran came with us to the Log Cabin that wouldn't be like trailing round the shops. She could sit down whenever she wanted,' Katy said as she played with next door's cat.

'Very true, Katy, I'm glad there is someone on my side.'

'We are all on your side, Mother. You are just in a difficult mood. Take off your hat for goodness sake. When you have it on I'm never sure whether you are coming or going. I'll go and make a pot of tea,' she said sounding exasperated.

Janet eased off her hat and then patted her hair into place. 'Do keep that cat away, Katy, you know I always get a sneezing fit when it comes near.'

'Put it out, Katy,' her mother called.

Katy picked up the animal and opened the outside door.

'Shoo, go home.' She closed the door smartly before the cat could slip past her and back in.

'Mum, I'll put the cups out.'

'No, Wilma can do that.'

'I'm reading.'

'Do as you are told,' Jenny said sharply then turned to her mother. 'Now that you have got that off your chest and I've said I'm sorry can we forget it?'

'Of course. I'm not one for holding grievances as you well know.'

Jenny smiled. She loved her mother dearly but she could be very awkward when she chose.

'Then I take it you would like to come with us on Saturday?'

'Yes, I would and don't worry, Jenny, Moira Ramsay won't find me a hindrance. I'll make myself useful. There is always work for those that seek it.'

'And knowing you, Mother, you'll seek it.'

Miss Ramsay had a good laugh when she had it explained.

'Poor Mrs Scrimgeour, she felt left out and none of us like to feel that.'

'She *was* very hurt and I do hope you won't mind if we all come this Saturday.' Jenny bit her lip and waited.

'Why should I mind?'

'It is a bit much the four of us being here.'

'Nonsense. There is plenty of room for everyone.'

'You are being very kind.'

'Jenny, I am not being kind. Your mother is very, very welcome.'

'Mother will want to work she doesn't believe in being idle.'

'Don't worry I'll give Mrs Scrimgeour enough to occupy her but she is not to be run off her feet. I don't want her going home exhausted.'

Jenny smiled. 'She would rather that than be left on her own. Funny really, I did think she would enjoy a bit of peace and quiet but I was wrong. During the week she is happy enough but come the weekend—'

'She likes to be with family and quite right too.'

Chapter Nine

'Mum, don't you think it is about time we were getting down the decorations from the attic and sorting them out?'

'Yes, dear, I suppose it is.' Jenny was having a few minutes with the evening paper and only half listening to Wilma.

'Not long now before Christmas,' she added.

'Mmm.'

'You are getting two days off, aren't you?' she continued with a hint of exasperation creeping into her voice.

Hearing it Jenny looked up. 'I've already told you that. The Log Cabin will be closed on Christmas day and Boxing day.' She went back to her paper.

'Wouldn't be anything doing so why keep open?'

'Exactly.' Jenny sighed. She wasn't going to get peace to read so she folded the newspaper and put it down. The mention of Christmas made her thoughts run back silently to happier times. A time of joy and laughter, was that what it had been or had she just thought that? Had Paul been acting the part even then, pretending to be the happy, caring, family man and all the time wishing himself elsewhere and with someone else? There could have been other women before Vera Cuthbertson came on the scene.

'I've got some of my gifts bought. Mum, you are paying absolutely no attention to what I'm saying.' Wilma had raised her voice.

'Sorry, dear, my mind was wandering.'

'I said I've got some of my gifts bought.'

'That's good, it's wise not to wait until the last minute.'

'I've got gran's and yours and I think I know what to get Katy. That leaves Dad and Vera. I don't know what to get them. Any ideas?'

Jenny didn't answer, she couldn't. How could Wilma be so insensitive? Bad enough that she had to hear about the wonderful Vera Cuthbertson when Wilma got back from a visit, but this – this was too much.

'Well?' Wilma said impatiently.

'Have I any ideas? No, I have not,' she said in a dangerously quiet voice that should have warned Wilma.

'What have you bought?'

'For whom?'

'Them. We are talking about them, aren't we?'

'You might be.'

Wilma fixed her mother with a cold stare. 'What about the Christmas spirit?'

'You could say it is lacking.'

'That is just *awful*. You can't mean you are not going to buy them anything?' she squeaked.

'That is exactly what I mean.'

'A gift they could share would probably be best. What if they give you something, that would make you feel terrible. Then you would have to dash out and buy them a gift.'

'No danger of that.'

'No danger of what?'

'Dashing out for a last-minute gift.'

'You've got this all wrong, Mum.'

'What have I got wrong?' Jenny looked at the clock. 'Katy should be in by now.'

'Never mind Katy. You've got it all wrong about Dad and Vera. You only have to see them together to know they are in love. It might happen to you one day and then you would understand.'

Jenny raised her eyebrows. 'This is a very interesting conversation. How about if we use a hypothetical situation.'

'Why?'

'Because, Wilma, I think you might learn something. Just suppose I have met someone with whom I want to spend the rest of my life.'

'But you haven't,' Wilma said in a tone of voice that suggested there was little chance of that happening.

Jenny ignored her and spoke as though there had been no interruption. 'Let us imagine that I have met someone and that someone wants to take me away.'

'This is daft,' Wilma said but beginning to look uncomfortable.

'Is it? What, I wonder, would happen to you and Katy?'

'You can't just leave us.'

'Why not? Your father did.'

'That's different.'

'How is it different?'

'Mothers can't leave their children.'

'And why is that?'

'I don't know, they can't that's all.'

'They can't, that's all, how very true and that sums it up perfectly. Mothers put their children first and give up their own chance of happiness. That is the way of the world but that doesn't make it fair.'

Katy burst in.

'About time, young lady. I don't like you being out this late.'

'Brenda's brother was going to bring me home but Jonathan was there and he said he would.'

'That was nice of Jonathan.' And surprising too, she thought. Grace's son didn't have a lot to say for himself and a mumbled hello was about all Jenny got.

'He, Jonathan I mean, doesn't want to go to sea, he never really wanted to be a sailor.'

'Then why pretend to his parents that he did?' Jenny wondered if she were alone in not understanding the young people of today.

'Because he doesn't want to work in the shop.'

'Jonathan told you that?'

'That and a lot more,' she said smugly. 'Jonathan and me are good friends.'

'Jonathan and I that should be.'

Katy looked at her sister's scowling face. 'What's wrong with her?'

'There is nothing wrong with me. We, Mum and I, were having a serious conversation when you barged in with all that about Jonathan Turnbull. I could have told you ages ago he didn't want to work in his dad's shop.'

Katy put out her tongue.

'If you want to know we were talking about Dad and Vera.'

'I wasn't,' Jenny said mildly.

'What about them?' Katy asked.

'I think Mum should buy them a Christmas gift and she doesn't. What have you bought?'

'That's none of your business.'

'For Dad and Vera I mean.'

'I'm going to send them a Christmas card, that's all. They have more money than we have.'

'That is not the Christmas spirit,' her sister said loftily. 'What have you bought for them?'

'Nothing as yet. Mum is not in favour.'

Jenny took a deep breath. She could have slapped Wilma. The girl was becoming more difficult by the day. If her father had been here she wouldn't have spoken like that. Then Jenny thought they wouldn't be having this conversation if he was.

'No, Wilma, don't get up just stay right there. You'll hear what I have to say first. What you do with your own money is for you to decide. If it means so much to you then buy your father and his mistress a gift.'

Wilma was shocked. 'You've never used that word before.'

'No, I haven't and that was to spare you.'

'That was hateful of you. It's awful having to live in this house. All you do is find fault with everything.'

131

Something snapped. 'If you are so unhappy living here then I suggest you pack your bag and go and live with your father and Miss Cuthbertson.'

'They wouldn't have her.'

'No, Katy, you are absolutely right they wouldn't. Once a month is enough for them. However, Wilma can try her luck and find out for herself.'

Wilma was looking frightened. She had never seen her mother so angry and she didn't want to leave home. She wasn't stupid enough to believe that she would be made welcome in Vera's house and apart from that they only had one bed. She wished now she hadn't said all that and upset mum. If she wanted to make it all right she would have to apologise. That wouldn't be easy, in fact it was going to be very hard, but she would have to do it. Gran always said it was better to apologise as soon as you knew you were in the wrong and that waiting only made it harder.

She mumbled an apology.

'Did you say something, Wilma?' Jenny said coldly.

'I said I'm sorry.'

'Sorry for what?' Jenny wasn't going to let her off so easily.

'Sorry for what I said. I didn't mean any of it.'

'Very well, I accept your apology.'

'I'll buy Dad a box of handkerchiefs with the initial P on them, but I won't buy Vera anything. She'll think I'm mean.' Her voice wobbled.

Jenny relented. 'Buy the woman a gift if it means so much to you but spare me the details.'

Wilma was subdued for the next day and then the

unpleasantness was forgotten. The decorations were brought down from the attic and those that had seen better days were thrown out. Grace handed in some holly and the three of them set about giving the sitting-room a festive look.

Jenny had been dreading Christmas day itself but in the event they all enjoyed it. Jenny's mother had prepared the Christmas pudding and baked the mince pies. There was no turkey but Jenny had cooked a chicken, roasted potatoes and had a variety of vegetables. The four of them tucked in and Gran said she was so full she could hardly move. There had been no gifts from Paul and Vera. Jenny felt angry that Paul hadn't remembered the girls. It turned out he had. An envelope had been put rather belatedly through the letter-box. It contained a cheque and a scribbled note to the effect that the money should be used to buy a gift for Wilma and Katy and with what remained Jenny could buy something for herself. Jenny divided the money, it was a fairly modest sum, between the girls. They could spend it or save it.

'Did you have a nice Christmas, Jenny?' Miss Ramsay asked as they began removing the Christmas goods from the display. Some would be kept for another year and others reduced in price for those people who took advantage of a bargain.

'Very nice, thank you. What about yourself?'

'I spent the day with friends. Actually it doesn't bother me being on my own, but it appears to worry others and to avoid hurt feelings I accept their kind invitation. Christmas is really a family time, all laughter and goodwill.'

'Not all of the time,' Jenny said forcing a laugh.

'Oh, dear, problems?'

'Nothing serious. Wilma is – difficult just now.'

'Do you want to talk about it?'

'Nothing much to tell. We just seem to rub each other the wrong way,' Jenny said ruefully.

Moira smiled sympathetically. 'I don't see us being inundated with customers today so we can safely leave Lily and Doris to keep shop. Come along to my office and we can have a chat. Often an outsider can see things clearer.'

'I'm making too much of this I know and I shouldn't be troubling you.' Jenny was feeling embarrassed.

'I offered, do sit down, Jenny. You must remember I know and like your daughters. They are completely different from one another which is not unusual in sisters. Katy has a lovely nature. She is a happy child and it shows.'

'Meaning Wilma isn't?' Jenny said worriedly.

'Wilma is older. Maybe the separation has been more traumatic for her. I seem to recall you saying she has always been a daddy's girl.'

'Yes, that's true, she and Paul were very close. Miss Ramsay, Wilma can see her father at any time as far as I am concerned, I have never objected and she knows that. It was Paul who said a monthly visit was enough.'

'Enough for whom? Enough for him and his mistress or enough for the girls?'

'Enough for him and Miss Cuthbertson. They appear to have an active social life but the excuse was that frequent visits would only unsettle Wilma and Katy. Katy, I have to add, doesn't get the same pleasure from the visits as her sister.' She paused. 'We are not a quarrelsome family and that's what made it worse. Wilma and I had a real fall-out. I'd better explain. Wilma asked me if I had any ideas about what she could buy for Paul and Miss Cuthbertson and I'm afraid I nearly hit the roof. Another annoyance for Wilma is that I keep calling the woman Miss Cuthbertson. I can't bring myself to call her Vera, the name just sticks in my throat.'

'There are those in your position who would call her a lot worse.'

Jenny smiled. 'I do but not out loud. You see how petty it all is? Wilma thought I should be full of the spirit of Christmas and buy my husband and his mistress a gift, presumably accompanied by my best wishes.'

Moira Ramsay frowned. 'How insensitive. Wilma is old enough to have more sense.'

'I think she is all mixed up.'

'Possibly.'

'Thinking back I do feel ashamed of myself. Wilma is little more than a child, but I was so angry and hurt too I suppose that I told her to pack her bag and go and live with her father and his mistress if staying at home was so awful.'

'Good for you. A sharp shock was what was needed and I bet that did the trick. Wilma wouldn't have expected it of you.'

'No, she didn't. I've never seen her looking so frightened. Anyway,' Jenny smiled, 'Wilma apologised and things are back to normal.'

'That's fine but don't you dare feel guilty. She will have more respect for you after that.'

'I didn't tell Mother. She might have said too much and made it worse.'

Moira nodded. 'I always meant to ask Wilma what she intends doing when she leaves school.'

'There hasn't been much said recently but there was talk about her becoming a reporter.'

'A cub reporter on a newspaper?'

'Or working on a magazine. A journalist. I have to admit being hurt about that. I had thought she wanted to go in for teaching but apparently she had only gone along with that because she thought Paul and I wanted it. Miss Wonderful discovered that my daughter had dreams of becoming a reporter.'

'What advice did she give Wilma?'

'Wilma had told her she was leaving school at the summer holidays and the woman, very sensibly I suppose, said she should try to be taken on by the local paper and get experience.'

Moira pursed her lips. 'She could be lucky I suppose.'

'What would your advice be?'

'Is Wilma good at English?'

'Yes, English is her best subject.'

'Must she leave school at sixteen?'

'No, but she appears determined to do so.'

'Pity. If she stayed on to get her certificate, her chances would be very much better. Forget the local paper. Dundee is the home of journalism and if she was fortunate enough to be taken on she would get a first-class training.'

'Maybe you would have a word with Wilma, Miss Ramsay, she would pay attention to what you said.'

'I'll do my best.'

'Wilma, there you are. Come along and get your envelope.'

Wilma followed Miss Ramsay into the office and closed the door at her request.

'Have a seat for a few minutes.' Moira handed over the envelope and Wilma took it and put it in her pocket.

'Thank you very much, Miss Ramsay.'

'Not getting tired of serving in the tea room, are you?'

'Oh, no, I like it.' Wilma wanted to make that very clear. She had come to depend on her waitressing money as she called it.

'Your mother said you had hopes of becoming a journalist.'

'Did Mum tell you that?' Wilma sounded surprised.

'Was she not supposed to?' Moira smiled.

'No, I don't mind at all. Wanting to be a journalist and getting to be one isn't the same.'

'No, it will mean a lot of hard work but once you pass your exams and have your leaving certificate—'

'I'm leaving school at the summer holidays,' Wilma interrupted.

'You don't like school, you can't wait to get away?'

'No I'm not, I happen to like school.'

'Then why leave before you have the all-important certificate?'

'It's sort of complicated.'

'Surely not. You either want to leave school at sixteen or you don't. The extra two years' education would be enormously helpful.'

'I know all that,' Wilma said dismissively. It sounded cheeky but Moira knew it wasn't intended to be. 'Mum must have told you how it is. You know Dad left us and it doesn't look as though he'll come back.'

'Yes, Wilma, I do know,' she said gently.

'Well you see the thing is that Mum doesn't have as much money as she used to have. She never used to economise the way she does now and if I was working that would help.'

'That is very considerate of you but you could be making a mistake. You could end up with a dead-end job and I know your mother wouldn't want that.'

'Maybe not but I have to do what I think best.'

'What about your father, he must want the best for you.'

'Of course he does. Dad still thinks I should go in for teaching.'

'Won't he assist with the financial side?' Moira was stepping carefully. Other people's financial affairs were private.

'My dad has a well-paid job,' Wilma said proudly, 'but he's like Mum and not finding it easy. He laughs and says it in fun but I think he means it all the same.' She stopped.

'Means what, Wilma?'

'Dad says Vera has very expensive tastes.'

'I take it she works.'

'Yes, she is a secretary in the same office as my dad. She is super looking. I forgot you saw her didn't you when she and Dad were in the tea room?'

'Yes, I did.'

'Don't you think she looks like a model?'

Moira had thought she looked what she was, a good-looking woman out for what she could get. Jenny's husband would be dropped if someone else with more to offer came on the scene. Maybe Jenny was waiting for that to happen. She was the forgiving kind.

'She has good appearance but then so has your mother. Beauty is in the eye of the beholder.'

'Vera likes expensive clothes and she's got this liking for Paris. They were there not long ago for a few days and she wants to go back for their next holiday. Have you ever been to Paris, Miss Ramsay?'

'Yes, many years ago. Paris is a beautiful city.'

'Then you can hardly blame Vera for wanting to go back.'

Miss Ramsay didn't answer and Wilma got up feeling awkward. 'I'll better go.'

'All right, dear, off you go.'

Wilma closed the door behind her and wondered if she had said too much, only she didn't think Miss Ramsay would repeat any of it.

Snow had fallen in the night, big soft flakes dropping slowly. The first real snowfall usually came after the new year and a white Christmas was unusual. It was now a few days after the beginning of the year and on the fields the light covering made the undergrowth appear a blue green. Then it snowed in earnest and from the Log Cabin and as far as the eye could see it was a smooth, silent, untouched white almost eerie in its beauty. Dangerous too. With hardly any warning a blizzard could whip up in the country and sheep could be buried in deep drifts with the shepherd or the farmer unable to get to them.

In the towns and in the villages there was an on-going struggle to keep the main routes clear and folk were warned to travel only if their journey was absolutely necessary.

The phone rang and Jenny went to answer it.

'Jenny, Moira Ramsay here, this is quite dreadful, isn't it?'

'My neighbour says it is the worst for ten years and he remembers it didn't completely clear until the month of March.'

'A ray of sunshine, your neighbour,' Moira laughed. 'I'm speaking from home to tell you to stay put and not even to think about trying to get through.'

'I thought the main roads—'

'No, at the moment the snow ploughs are fighting a losing battle. The Log Cabin will remain closed until this clears. In any case, who in their right mind would want to come out?'

'There's always the foolhardy.'

'Then they will get a locked door.'

'I wonder how Doris and her parents are but they are probably fine. Country folk have the good sense to be prepared for this.'

'I was about to tell you how fortunate I am to have that family working for me. Doris, being a wise country lass, had the foresight to ask me for a spare set of keys.'

'Did she?'

'She did and said that even if the roads were blocked solid her father would manage to get through to the Log Cabin and check that all was well.'

'That must be a great relief?'

'Jenny, I couldn't even begin to express my gratitude. What a good soul he is and it has taken away an enormous worry. I would have been dreadfully concerned for my stock with the possibility of a burst pipe or some other disaster.'

'How did the Wallaces get in touch with you? They aren't on the telephone.'

'Mr Wallace must have trudged through the snow to the farmhouse and phoned from there. Thank goodness their phone was still working.'

'Yes.'

'What about you and the girls?'

'We're fine. The girls are quite excited, they've never seen so much snow. They are dressed for the weather and at the moment are trying to clear a path to the gate.' Jenny knew that Miss Ramsay's house was on the outskirts of Perth. 'Are you very bad where you are?'

'Probably much the same as yourself. I went out armed with a shovel to do my bit but before long one of my neighbours relieved me of the task. Whether that was because I was making a poor job of it or just gentlemanly chivalry, I couldn't say.'

'Definitely gentlemanly chivalry,' Jenny laughed.

'This will give us a chance to get those jobs done that one keeps putting off. I'll get down to replying to some long overdue letters so at least the time will be well spent.'

In a week the snow had turned to slush and for many that was worse. People felt the cold more and there were sore throats and coughs and other winter ailments for an overworked doctor to attend to.

Chapter Ten

'Dad is very pleased you've got a job and earning money,' Wilma said mischievously.

Jenny stopped what she was doing. 'Why should he be so pleased about that?' she said carefully. 'I have never at any time suggested that he should increase what he gives me.'

'Sounds more like he wants to reduce it,' she was grinning.

Jenny looked at her sharply. Wilma was sitting on the chair with her stockinged feet tucked under her. 'Did your father suggest that?'

'Of course he didn't,' Wilma said scathingly, 'you do jump to conclusions.'

'No, I don't think I do.'

'Dad didn't suggest anything.'

'Fine, he didn't suggest anything. Just tell me exactly what he did say.' Jenny wanted to get to the bottom of this.

'In fun, Mum, you know funny ha-ha.' Wilma was wishing she hadn't said anything. Trust her mother to take it the wrong way. Honestly these days you weren't safe to open your mouth.

'All in fun but I would still like to hear what was said.'

Wilma gave a deep sigh. 'All Dad said was that Vera had very expensive tastes and they couldn't go on spending money at the rate they were doing. It means absolutely nothing. They do have two salaries coming in so how could they be hard up?'

Jenny didn't answer. She felt the cold hand of fear grip her. If money was becoming a problem, and that is what it sounded like, she knew who would be the first to feel the pinch. She would get less and less. The roof over their head might be threatened and there was nothing she could do about it.

Moira Ramsay was becoming increasingly concerned at the change in her assistant. Jenny did her work as conscientiously as before but she smiled a lot less. It wasn't just a fleeting sadness which was natural enough when she was separated from her husband. This was so much more, this was a deep worry and it showed. They knew each other quite well by now and Moira liked to think they were friends as well as employer and employee. She would wait for an opportunity when they could talk without being interrupted. That time had come.

Jenny admired Miss Ramsay in every way and today she thought the woman looked particularly attractive in her fine-knit aquamarine suit and navy blue court shoes with a narrow medium heel. She glanced up when her employer approached.

'Jenny, when you finish that come along to my office, will you?'

'Yes, I'll only be a few minutes.' She went on folding the

scarves and putting them away in the drawer then went quickly along to the office. The room she entered was not large but had been carefully designed to make the best use of the space available. Fitted shelves took care of the files, ledgers and boxes of stationery. The desk was handsome and had been bought from an antique dealer in Perth. There was a leather chair behind it and two chairs, both padded, were against one wall. At the window which looked out to green fields and softly rolling hills, hung pretty gingham curtains. Jenny admired the bowl of snow-drops on the wide sill.

'I discovered them in my garden at home, tucked away in a corner. The very first sign of spring and so welcome.' Moira Ramsay brought over one of the chairs to be nearer the desk. 'Do sit down, Jenny.'

'Thank you.' Charming though the woman was, Jenny was still a little in awe of Miss Ramsay.

'I'm going to come straight out with it, Jenny, and ask you what is the matter?'

Jenny looked alarmed and had paled. Was her work suffering? Had she allowed her personal worries to show? She prayed it wasn't that. The very last thing she needed right now was to be told her work had deteriorated and that her services would no longer be required.

'Nothing is the matter, Miss Ramsay.' Her hands were clenched in her lap.

'That I cannot accept, Jenny. I have eyes that miss very little.'

'Truly, Miss Ramsay, nothing is the matter,' she said rather desperately. 'Is my work not to your satisfaction?'

'I have no fault to find with your work. Please believe me when I say that I am talking to you as a friend first and as an employer second. I do want to help. Has it anything to do with the girls?'

Jenny shook her head. 'No, Wilma and Katy are fine and doing well at school.'

'Then it can't be too dreadful,' she smiled. Moira was a moment or two before she continued and Jenny thought she was weighing up her next words. 'Forgive me asking this but would you have financial worries?'

The truth was always best. 'I do have those like so many others but I manage or – or—' She bit her lip.

'Go on, please, I cannot help until I know what is worrying you. Money or rather the lack of it, is that the trouble?'

Jenny looked horrified. Miss Ramsay might think she was after a rise in her wages. 'I didn't say that.'

'No, you didn't. Believe me that might be one of the easier problems to solve but I have to know the true position. Let me guess since you are so reluctant to tell me. Your husband is being difficult?'

'Oh, no, Paul meets his obligations. It is only that it may not be so easy for him in the future. It was just something Wilma said that made me think that Paul has his worries too. It would appear that Miss Cuthbertson has expensive tastes and I suppose that is giving him cause for concern. Paul is by nature careful.'

Moira Ramsay recalled Wilma mentioning something of the sort. 'Yes, it would be of concern to him and a man as obsessed as your husband apparently is would be more likely to reduce your maintenance payments than tell his mistress to cut down. Am I anywhere near?'

'Spot on.' Jenny gave a nervous laugh.

'This is interference I know but you are not going to resent it, are you?'

'No.'

'You will answer my questions truthfully?' A raised eyebrow.

'To the best of my ability.'

Moira leaned forward. 'The housing situation, your home, how are you placed with that?'

'Paul is continuing to meet the mortgage payments.'

Moira nodded, picked up a pencil and began to doodle absentmindedly on the back of an envelope.

'If he was to fall behind with the payments you would be in trouble?'

'I would be in very deep trouble and even bigger trouble if Paul decided to put the house on the market. I can't see him doing that but should it happen we would have to go and stay with my mother who doesn't have room for us or I would have to try and get a cheap rented house.'

'You say unlikely but the possibility is there?'

'I suppose so,' Jenny said reluctantly. She wasn't enjoying discussing her private affairs.

Miss Ramsay was silent for a few moments then nodded as though she had made up her mind. 'Jenny, I think I may be able to help. You have been very open with me and I could see it wasn't easy. I think I should return the compliment and tell you something about myself. This is strictly confidential and nothing said will go beyond this room?'

'Of course not.'

'And rest assured the same applies in your case.'

'I know that,' Jenny said quietly. She thought there were some people one trusted without question and Miss Ramsay was one.

'This is going to be a glimpse into my early life. However, before that I think we should have a cup of tea. Would you mind popping along to the tea room and asking Doris to bring tea for two?'

'No, not at all,' Jenny said getting up. She was glad of the short break to sort out her thoughts. She hoped she hadn't said too much and it worried her that she might appear the complaining sort, a real moaning Minny. Compared to many abandoned wives she was lucky. Jenny thought she should try and remember that. In the tea room she stopped at the counter where Doris was wiping one of the glass shelves. She was always busy, her hands never idle. That was the way she liked it, she said. If she wasn't occupied time would drag.

'Doris, when you have a minute Miss Ramsay would like tea taken to her office. Tea for two.'

'A visitor?'

'No, not a visitor, the other cup is for me.'

She smiled showing slightly buck teeth. 'In that case I'll cut a piece of mother's iced sponge, a bit more interesting than a biscuit.'

'You spoil me.'

'A bit of spoiling won't do you any harm. You've been looking a sight peaky this last wee while,' Doris said as she brought out two cups and saucers. She was very fond of

FOR BETTER, FOR WORSE

Jenny and couldn't imagine what kind of a man would leave her and those two nice girls. She'd heard it said that Jenny's husband was living with some glamour piece and anyone with an ounce of sense knew that kind of relationship didn't last. Once he got his walking ticket he would appreciate what he had given up. Jenny might take him back more's the pity or there again maybe not if there was to be a divorce. Jenny was no weakling, she had strength of character and maybe she wouldn't want him back. Then again for the sake of the two girls she might.

'On you go and I'll follow with the tray.'

'Thanks, Doris.' She hurried back to Miss Ramsay. 'Doris is just coming.' Jenny left the door open and sat down in her chair.

Doris arrived, put the tray on the desk, gave a quick smile and departed closing the door quietly behind her.

Miss Ramsay smiled and shook her head. 'Just looking at Doris has me exhausted, I've never known anyone with so much energy.'

'My mother would call that nervous energy.'

'She would be right and possibly Doris just needs to be on the go. I do find myself wishing she would ease up and stop making me feel like a slave-driver.'

'No one could call you that.'

'Thank you. I am extremely lucky with my staff, we are like a family working together.' Moira lifted the jug. 'How much milk, Jenny?'

'Just a spot to colour it and no sugar.'

'Sugar in coffee but not in tea?'

'Yes.'

'My mother used to have a little notebook she kept in a kitchen drawer and in it she jotted down the likes and dislikes of her visitors. People were pleasantly surprised when she didn't have to ask. They took that as a compliment.'

'Which it was to have taken that much trouble.'

'Sadly it hasn't been passed down from mother to daughter.' She filled the cups and handed one to Jenny. 'That sponge looks delicious,' she said taking a piece and pushing the plate nearer to Jenny.

'Thank you.' Jenny took a piece and put it on her own smaller plate.

'We'll enjoy this and then get back to what we were talking about.'

Once they were finished, Jenny stacked the dishes on the tray. She would take it back to the tea room when Miss Ramsay had said her say. Jenny wasn't curious, indeed she would rather not hear what was obviously very personal. Folk did this and then regretted disclosing what should have been kept secret.

'I was going to tell you a little about myself and let me begin by saying this was not the kind of life I had planned. No, Jenny, I had expected to be married with a family but here I am an unmarried woman.'

Jenny thought it must have been from choice and was about to say so when she decided it might be wiser to be quiet and listen unless an answer was called for. It would appear one was called for.

'Did you lose someone?'

Jenny thought there was a sadness in the smile. 'You

could say that,' she said and raised her eyes to Jenny. 'I was engaged to be married and I was as happy as any girl has a right to be. Blindly in love one could say. Roger was perfect or so I thought. He was charming, good-looking and clever. What more could I ask? The firm he worked for was sending him to America for two years and I was so excited that we were to begin our married life out there. Only one thing marred my happiness. My mother never said a word against Roger but I knew she didn't like him.'

'That worried you?'

'No, it didn't worry me but it made me sad. The two people I most loved should like each other and they didn't. Roger was never at ease with her. That said, Jenny, I didn't let it alter my feelings for Roger or let it make any difference to our plans.' She stopped and her eyes met Jenny's. 'How trusting we are when we are young. I should have seen the signs but I wasn't looking.'

'Love is blind,' Jenny said softly, 'I think I know something about that.'

Moira smiled sympathetically. 'Friends of ours had a hotel up north and my sister Gertrude was supposed to be learning the business but she very soon decided the work didn't suit her and gave in her notice. Our friends were annoyed but probably relieved too. Gertrude was a particularly attractive girl and used to getting her own way. She came home, was introduced to Roger and I was happy to see how well they got on. It would have been awkward if both mother and Gertie had disliked Roger. Perhaps you are ahead of me now?'

Jenny looked at her quickly. 'You can't mean your sister and your fiancé?'

Moira nodded. 'They came to tell me, to break the news. I suppose they needed each other's support and would you believe it when it was staring me in the face, I didn't guess, not even then. Only when they became increasingly embarrassed did I begin to suspect. Then I had to listen to them, one helping the other out and each saying how they hadn't wanted this to happen. They were in love and so terribly sorry to hurt me but these things happened and surely it was better to find out now rather than when it was too late.'

'How awful for you.' Jenny was trying to imagine the scene.

'Yes, it was. I thanked God that the invitations hadn't gone out though some wedding gifts had already arrived. Mother took charge, she was quite wonderful. The presents were returned with a small note to say that the wedding would not now take place. I remember wondering if I should have handed them over to Gertie since she was taking my place.' She laughed and Jenny joined in the laughter.

'It was anything but funny.'

'A tragedy for me, Jenny. I wept oceans of tears, most of them into my pillow. My heart might have been broken but it did mend. My pride took a lot longer. The humiliation was the worst, I had received a huge blow and I felt like something cast aside. Friends tried to be kind and find the right words but there were no right words and I hated their sympathy. Mother admitted then that she had never liked Roger. He was too smooth and not to be trusted. She said it and said it so often that I wanted to scream, that I was better off without him, that there would be someone else for me and that Gertrude and Roger deserved each other. She never forgave Gertie and neither did I. To my dying day I will always regret it.'

'Why should you? Your sister behaved very badly.'

'She did, no question about that but I ought to have been big enough and generous enough to forgive. Sadly I wasn't, the hurt went too deep. Before they left for America Gertie pleaded for my forgiveness but I refused even to speak to her or Roger.'

'No one could blame you. They didn't deserve to be happy.'

'If they were it was cut short. Gertie became ill not long after they arrived in America and she died a few months later. That upset me terribly as it did mother. I felt so wretched and ashamed. It was easier for mother, she was able to put all the blame on to Roger.'

'You must have had other proposals of marriage.'

She smiled.

'Did you let what happened put you off?'

'I imagine it did. Learning to trust again takes time. As it happens I had two what I like to call serious offers of marriage and one I did consider very carefully. In the end though I turned him down.'

'Do you have any regrets?'

'No, I can't honestly say I have any regrets. You see, Jenny, I was beginning to value my independence. I found it very satisfying being able to do what I wanted, when I wanted, without having to consider anyone else. What, I began to wonder, was to hinder me having the best of both worlds. I had men friends and enjoyed their company and, Jenny, I had become ambitious. I wanted to succeed on my own. Money was no problem so I had a head start. My family had always been very comfortably off and with Gertrude gone and no other family everything came to me including the house where, incidentally, I still live.'

Jenny nodded. Miss Ramsay was a very remarkable woman she thought.

'You are puzzled and wondering why I am telling you all this which is, after all, history. It all happened so long ago and I seldom think about it. My reason for subjecting you to all this was to let you know that I understand a little of what you are going through. Being jilted is difficult to talk about even now and you can't find it easy to talk about your husband's infidelity.'

'No, I don't.'

'Sadly you have to come to terms with that yourself. You are strong, Jenny, and you'll come through it. Without my help you would manage but with it will make it easier for you.'

'You have done enough for me already. I have a job I enjoy and you have been so good to Wilma and Katy.'

'Don't forget I benefit too. I don't want to lose you.'

'No danger of that, I know when I am well off,' Jenny smiled.

'Will you forgive me if I take the liberty of calling your husband by his Christian name, it will be easier than always referring to him as your husband?'

'By all means call him Paul.'

'Paul would find it a relief if he didn't have to pay the mortgage on the house?'

'A huge relief I imagine.'

'Don't give me your answer immediately, take time to consider it. Do you think Paul would be prepared to put the house on the market and should it sell would he give you half the proceeds once the mortgage is paid to the building society and the solicitor has taken his dues?'

Jenny took her time before answering. 'I honestly have no idea but I wouldn't want that. Where would we live?'

'You would have to trust me on this but I can assure you, Jenny, that you and the girls would be all right. That is all I can say at present.'

Jenny bit her lip. 'Miss Ramsay, I do appreciate that you are trying to help me but I have to tell you that I am not the kind of person to take risks. With only myself to consider perhaps I would be willing to take a chance but I couldn't do that with Wilma and Katy.'

'Of course you couldn't but in this there would be no risk. What I need to know before I take this further is are you happy with the kind of work you do here?'

'I love it,' Jenny said simply.

'That is what I wanted to hear. In you, Jenny, I know I have found the right person. I can trust you and you have a genuine interest in the Log Cabin. Running a business like this on one's own can be lonely. Sharing the responsibility, talking over changes, discussing what merchandise is likely to be popular, is so much easier if one doesn't have to make the decisions on one's own. You are still with me?' She smiled.

'Yes.'

'Then here is what I propose. Jenny, I want to give you a share, an interest, in the Log Cabin.'

Jenny stared. 'I – I—' she stammered.

'Let me finish,' Moira Ramsay said gently. 'A share of the profits won't amount to a great deal for some time to come though I am optimistic for the long-term future. Any new venture is a risk and a shop and tea room in the country, at the back of beyond someone said, has to be a high risk. I knew all that but I did feel I was coming in at the right time. The tourist trade is improving each year, rationing is all but over or so we hope and many more families have their own transport. They want to get away from the town but not too far.'

'This is ideal?'

'I like to think so. We are rather straying, Jenny. What I would like you to do is suggest to Paul that he sells the house.'

'He won't.'

'He may find a good offer difficult to refuse particularly if this Cuthbertson woman is in favour and why should she not be?'

'I'll put it to him,' Jenny said feeling she couldn't refuse to do that.

'Are you so sure he will refuse?'

'Paul is an accountant, Miss Ramsay, he'll be suspicious and look at this very carefully.'

'I would hope he would. Don't worry everything is open and above board. Whichever way he looks at it he can't lose. The house market is fairly buoyant at present.'

Jenny's head was beginning to ache. Miss Ramsay was going too fast for her.

'Poor Jenny I've got you completely bewildered.'

'You have.'

'You must not worry about being homeless because that would not happen.'

'I can't help worrying.'

'Don't you trust me?' Was there a hint of disappointment in the voice?

'I do, of course I do, only—'

'You can't help being concerned but really you have no cause to be.'

Jenny was vaguely remembering her mother saying that Moira Ramsay owned property. Maybe there was a house about to become vacant. That was all very well but she didn't want to leave 16 Abbotsford Crescent. She liked having Grace next door. She liked the neighbourhood, it was friendly and she didn't want to start over again with strangers. She wouldn't say that because Miss Ramsay would never understand.

'We'll go into all the details later but you should know how you will be placed. Starting immediately, Jenny, you will receive a monthly salary. That is the way we work in business. I take my salary and expenses as though I were an employee. Your salary will be more than adequate for your needs, in other words a good deal more than you earn at present. This should mean peace of mind for you whatever happens.'

'I can't believe you are doing all this for me.'

'You had better believe it and I can be a hard task master you know.'

'And you should know that I am completely ignorant about business.'

'You can learn.' She smiled. 'You are prepared to do that?'

'I'll do my very, very best and just hope that will be good enough.'

'Your best will do me. Back to work then,' she said getting up. 'The others needn't know just yet, that will give you a chance to get used to your new status.'

Chapter Eleven

———◆———

Going home in the bus, Jenny found herself smiling foolishly. The money worries that had plagued her and become worse of late could be put aside, perhaps for good. That, of course, would depend on the continuing success of the Log Cabin. From the day she started work its success had been important to Jenny but never so much as now. Her future was tied up with the Log Cabin and she would give it her all. Miss Ramsay deserved no less.

Jenny was glad her new status would not be recognised immediately. She needed time to grow into it and Miss Ramsay was wise enough to see that. Not so the salary, it was to take effect from now. No longer would she be earning the wages of a shop assistant, she was salaried and what a lovely ring that had to it. For the first time in her life Jenny felt important. Important in the sense that she had achieved something by her own efforts.

She waited another day before phoning Paul by which time she felt more composed. She didn't want her voice shaking with nerves when she was talking. Lifting the phone she dialled his office number and was told her husband was available and just to hold on.

'It's Jenny, Paul,' she said to his 'hello'.

'What's wrong?'

'Nothing.' Why did he immediately jump to the conclusion that something was wrong? 'We need to talk, that's all.'

'What about?'

'I would rather not say over the phone but it is important.'

'A bit inconvenient. I'm pretty well tied up this week.'

That infuriated her. 'My time is important too.'

'Waitressing!' She could imagine the smile on his face and how it would be wiped off if he knew how she had gone up in the world.

'This is worth putting yourself out for,' Jenny said sharply.

'All right, don't get yourself worked up. Shall we say one o'clock tomorrow and I'll take an extended lunch break?'

'No, that doesn't suit me. I won't be at home at that time. Make it tomorrow morning as soon after nine o'clock as you can manage.'

'Very well, I'll be there. If this is some trivial thing I am going to be very annoyed.'

Jenny put down the phone. It was the first time she had ever done that to Paul. He had always been the first to ring off. How had it come to this? Their life together had not been an empty shell, once they had been happy, it hadn't been all pretence. She sighed and went through to the kitchen to prepare the meal.

There was a drizzle of rain when the girls left for school. Jenny hadn't told them their father was coming. By the time Paul's car had stopped at the gate the heavens had opened. He got out and sprinted along the drive. Jenny had the door open.

'You choose your times.'

She smiled. 'I'm not responsible for the weather. Would you like a coffee?'

'No, thank you. Let us get on with whatever it is.' He had gone ahead to the sitting-room and was seated when Jenny went in. She sat down.

'This concerns the house.'

His face darkened. 'What about the house? I pay the mortgage, what more do you want?'

'Not having to pay it would be a relief?'

'What kind of stupid question is that? Of course it would be a relief. It is a huge drain on my income.'

'Come! Come! A drain but certainly not a huge drain.'

'Get to the point, Jenny, I haven't all day.'

'Neither have I. This is it, Paul. How would you feel about putting the house on the market? In the present climate it might sell quickly.'

'Where did you pick up that expression?' He was amused.

She ignored it. 'Once you pay off the building society what is left can be shared equally between us.'

'Who put you up to this?'

'No one put me up to anything.'

'You didn't think up that yourself.'

'You underestimate me.'

'I would have to give this some serious thought.'

'Take all the time you need. No, on second thoughts, I

want this settled one way or the other. You used to pride yourself on being able to come to a decision quickly.'

He smiled and got to his feet. 'You will have your answer very soon. As a matter of interest if the house was to be sold where would you and the girls live?'

'I have no idea but that needn't concern you.'

'You are becoming very independent all of a sudden.'

'Yes, Paul, thanks to you. By the way, if you do agree to the house being sold you can have your divorce.'

He nodded and walked to the door.

Paul was thoughtful and a bit uneasy as he drove to the office. The rain had stopped and a weak sun was shining but he barely noticed. Jenny had changed and he wondered why. Was there a man behind all this? It seemed like it when all of a sudden she was offering him a divorce. Funny that. He and Vera had wanted the divorce so that they could marry and belong to each other but marriage was seldom mentioned these days. He supposed it was better the way they were. Was it his imagination or was there a restlessness about Vera? She needed so much to keep her happy and though he kept warning her that they couldn't go on spending the way they were doing she paid little attention. Paul didn't know how long he could keep her happy. The day would surely come when she would leave him but he wanted to put that day off as long as possible. Maybe he should do what Jenny suggested and sell the house. He would discuss it with Vera in the evening.

'Darling, set the table will you while I prepare the salad?'

Paul groaned inwardly. He hated salads, hated the kind

of food Vera produced and expected him to like. He certainly wasn't putting on weight, he would give her that. Occasionally he found himself longing for Jenny's home cooking. That was real food and after a long, busy day was what he needed. And the baking if he could bear to think about it. Apple tarts, scones, pancakes, sponges and more besides. Very little was bought from the baker's.

'Heavens! You are a slow coach. You're going about in a dream.'

'Sorry, love, I have a lot on my mind.' He arranged the cutlery and got out two paper napkins from the drawer. There were linen ones but washing and ironing them meant more work and Vera liked to keep work down to a minimum.

Neither of them was any good at cooking. Vera had little interest in food. She ate sparingly. Paul joked that she could exist on a lettuce leaf. Maybe he should invest in a cookery book. Tasty meals for the beginner. The only decent meals he got was when they dined out but one couldn't do that too often. Not the restaurants Vera chose.

They sat down to eat.

'Paul, where did you disappear to this morning?'

'Jenny phoned. She wanted to see me, said it was urgent.'

'When did she phone?'

'Yesterday.'

'You didn't say.'

'Slipped my memory.'

'And was it important?'

'It could be. I thought we could talk about it over coffee.'

'Why wait? I'm curious.'

'Jenny suggested that I sell our house, pay off the mortgage and the money remaining to be shared between us.'

She raised her eyes and smiled. 'No mortgage to pay?'

'That's right.'

'Sounds fine, where's the catch?'

'I can't find one.'

'Maybe you aren't looking hard enough.'

'I've looked at it from every angle, there is no catch.'

'Why is she doing this?'

'She wouldn't say. In fact she didn't seem too bothered whether I took up the offer or not.'

'Someone is behind this.' She gave a hard little smile. 'Our Jenny is playing tricks.'

'No, Vera, Jenny isn't underhand. She wouldn't do anything dishonest.'

'You said she had changed.'

'So she has, but I meant in herself. She is much more confident.'

'A lover?'

'Jenny?'

'Why not? She's quite attractive if you like the homely type and some do.'

'No, Vera, I can't see it and how would Wilma and Katy be able to keep something like that from me?'

'You don't see them all that often and Jenny could have sworn them to silence.'

'Not her style,' he said shaking his head.

'In that case, darling, take Jenny at her word and put the

house on the market. Should it sell that will save you having to pay the mortgage.'

He smiled and nodded and pushed the lettuce aside. 'Jenny also said that should I go along with selling the house she will agree to a divorce. Thinking back I'm almost sure she doesn't expect me to sell.'

'Then why all this?'

'Wish I knew.'

'Regarding the divorce it isn't all that important is it? We are perfectly happy as we are. You would agree with that?'

'Never been happier,' he smiled.

'Then we'll forget the divorce. Even so,' she said thoughtfully, 'I would love to know what brought on this sudden change. Your wife was so dead against a divorce. Paul, it could be that Jenny has got over you. Maybe she doesn't want you back.'

He didn't think that, not for a moment, he didn't want to think it either. Jenny was the sort of woman who, when she gave her heart, it was for always. Till death us do part. He wouldn't say any of that to Vera, she would find it quaint and rather pathetic.

'Maybe she has got over me and to tell you the truth I'm not bothered one way or the other. Just so long as you haven't. Got over me, I mean.'

'Not yet, dearest,' she said with a smile to soften the words. 'Have you finished?'

'Yes, thank you,' Paul said handing over his plate.

'Tut tut, darling, lettuce is very good for you.'

'I took some.'

'Not very much but you did enjoy your meal?'

'Yes, it was very nice,' he lied. Paul watched Vera take the plates to the kitchen. All her movements were so graceful, she was lovely and he couldn't imagine life without her. Yet he knew that time was running out. One day she would tell him to go, he couldn't hide that from himself. Paul had already seen enough to alarm him. When they dined out he was always aware of the admiring glances she got from other men and at one time that had pleased him enormously. He had the prize and others envied him. Now he saw it as a threat. Vera didn't exactly encourage them, nothing so vulgar, but neither did she totally ignore them. They got that secretive smile that once had been for him alone.

When his time came and he got the push he could always return to 16 Abbotsford Crescent, he told himself, provided, of course, there was no divorce. And there wouldn't be one he would see to that. No divorce and no selling of the house. In the position he was in, it was a huge relief to know he could return to 16 Abbotsford Crescent and more or less resume the life he had once known. Jenny, naturally enough, would be cold and unwelcoming for a start but the old charm would work, he hadn't lost it. Even if she decided to be difficult she couldn't refuse him entry to his own house. Which meant that the house would not go on the market. Paul found he was interested to know what the house would be worth and he could do that without selling.

Jenny stood outside the front door and fumbled in her bag for the house keys. Before she had the door open the phone began to ring and thinking it might be Paul she got herself in quickly, shut the door and hurried to answer it.

'Hello.'

'Paul here,' he almost snapped.

Jenny found herself smiling. It wasn't 'Hello, Jenny, it's me' but cut short to 'Paul here' as though she was no more than a business associate and not his wife and the mother of his two daughters. That was what estrangement did. It wiped away all the happy, carefree, family days as though they had never been.

'Lucky you caught me. The phone was ringing when I opened the door.'

He didn't answer. Maybe the remark was too trifling to elicit a reply.

'About the house.'

'Yes, Paul, about the house.' She held the phone in one hand and used the other to unbutton her coat. 'You've come to a decision?'

'Yes and no to that.'

She didn't ask him what that was supposed to mean and after a few moments he went on.

'I may not consider selling the house to be to my advantage.'

'In which case I take it you are not interested?' She could breathe easily, it wasn't going to happen and she could say to Miss Ramsay in all honesty that she had asked Paul and the answer was no. He wanted to hold on to the house.

'I didn't say that. It might be interesting to find out what the house would fetch.'

'A pointless exercise when at the end of the day you are

not selling. And there would be some cost involved I imagine.'

'Not all that much.'

Jenny was silent for a moment. She didn't want this uncertainty, this maybe yes, maybe no, but she had better play along with it. 'I wouldn't expect you to sell our house unless you got a very good offer.'

'One I couldn't refuse.' She heard his laugh. 'That would surprise me.'

'Nothing surprises me,' she found herself saying. It had been said softly. Maybe he hadn't heard or chose not to answer.

'Don't expect a steady stream of people arriving on the doorstep to view the property. It won't generate that kind of interest.'

What kind of a fool did he take her for?

'I'm quite sure it won't,' she said her voice icily cold, 'we have a very ordinary house in a good neighbourhood. No more than that.'

'Quite.' Did she imagine the suppressed anger?

'You may or may not know, Paul, that there are a great many people who simply love viewing houses. It is a sort of hobby with them while curiosity brings others. The genuinely interested are usually thin on the ground.'

'You appear to have become remarkably knowledgeable about the sale of houses,' he said sarcastically.

'That and a lot more I'll have you know.'

'Nevertheless it is impossible to distinguish between those who are looking for a house and those who are just looking.' He laughed as though he had said something smart. 'Which means, Jenny, that you will have to be on hand to show them around and answer their questions.'

She let that go for the moment. 'When will you put the house on the market if that is your intention?'

'Better to do it right away. I'll get things moving at my end.'

'Viewing by appointment only.'

She heard the shock in his voice. 'That won't do, Jenny, that won't do at all, folk won't go to that bother.'

'Folk will go to any amount of bother if they are genuinely interested. That way you discourage the time-wasters.'

'I'm not in favour.'

'Perhaps I should remind you that you are not the one who is to do the showing around.'

'That is your job.'

'Not necessarily. I am no longer simply a housewife – I, too, go out to work.'

'I must say you don't appear to be greatly concerned as to whether or not the house gets sold.'

'I'm not. All I did, Paul, was make a suggestion. You either sell or you don't, it is up to you.'

'What about the girls?'

'What about them?'

'Do they know about this?'

'Not yet. Why bother to tell them if you are not interested in selling.'

'I agree.'

Thank goodness they could agree about something.

'Let me suggest, however, that you tell Wilma and Katy

and anyone else who asks that we are only testing the market,' said Paul.

'Do people do that?'

'Regularly. Some go on to sell if the price is right. Others withdraw the property from the market and try again at a later date.'

'I see.'

'Jenny, I'm somewhat perplexed.'

'Are you?'

'You must admit you are not exactly forthcoming about your own plans and you must have some.'

'Perhaps I have but I'm not ready to disclose them.'

'Let me hazard a guess. Your mother hasn't the room to take the three of you but maybe she is to give up her house and—'

'Get a bigger one,' Jenny finished for him. She was shaking her head. 'Completely wrong. In fact that possibility never occurred to me. Mother is perfectly happy where she is and the last thing I would want to do would be to upset her life.' She didn't add that she knew it wouldn't work. Katy, with her sunny nature, wouldn't be a problem but Wilma was older and perhaps at the most awkward stage. She was stubborn, a bit selfish and with a mind of her own. Their grandmother was set in her ways and she thought young people got far too much freedom. Perhaps they did, but times changed and it was wise to go with the change at least part of the way. No, it wouldn't work out. They were better living apart.

'My mistake, I thought she would enjoy having you and that it would be company for her.'

'You thought wrong. Mum likes a bit of peace and quiet and at her age she is entitled to them. When you walked out Mum was very supportive and I honestly don't know what I would have done without her. She saw me through the worst days and now I'm fine. Better than fine, Paul, I'm enjoying being a person in my own right.'

'When were you anything else?'

'Paul, you made all the decisions and I just went along with everything. Not necessarily your fault,' she said hastily, 'but it made the separation that bit more traumatic.'

'Do I have to hear all this?'

'It won't do you any harm and I think I must want to get it off my chest.'

'And now you have?'

'Yes, now I have. As I said, I'm fine and you need have no worries about Wilma and Katy. The three of us will not be homeless and that is all I intend saying.' She could have added that she was as much in the dark as he was.

'There should be no misunderstandings–'

'There won't be,' Jenny interrupted. 'Should you get an offer for the house that satisfies you and you decide to go along with the sale I demand to see everything in writing.'

'In black and white,' he said sarcastically.

'Yes, in black and white.'

'Jenny, for your information that is a solicitor's job.'

'I am well aware of that. I am also aware that he, the solicitor, will take his instructions from his client. Those instructions,' Jenny spoke slowly, 'will state clearly that half of the proceeds from the sale of the house will come to me.

171

That is, of course, after the mortgage is paid off in full and the solicitor has taken his whack.'

'God, Jenny, you amaze me.'

She laughed. 'I amaze myself.'

'You are certainly looking after number one.'

'Not at all, equal shares.'

He was silent for a few moments. 'Very well, Jenny, I accept your conditions and that is extremely generous of me. Remember I don't have to go along with it.'

'Neither you do. To sell or not to sell that is the decision you have to make,' she said sounding flippant.

'And in return you must accept my condition.'

'Which is?' She took the weight off one leg on to the other. She could have done with a seat but the chair had been removed because it took up too much space. Maybe she should bring it back.

'Which is, Jenny, that my responsibility for you ends with the sale of the house.'

'Agreed,' she said without hesitation. 'You will, however, be responsible for Wilma and Katy and that to continue until they are of an age to provide for themselves.'

'Certainly, I take my responsibilities as a father very seriously.'

She couldn't stop herself. 'Was walking out on them an act of responsibility? Don't bother to answer that. You can't know this, Paul, but leaving me as you did may have done me a good turn, a very good turn.'

Paul didn't like what he was hearing. 'In what way?' he said sharply. Jenny was a changed woman, he wouldn't have believed that anyone could have changed so much.

Paul had the uncomfortable feeling that she was holding out on him but for the life of him couldn't see how that could be. It had nothing to do with the house since she wasn't bothered about whether or not he sold it. Was Vera right and there was a man in her life? He had been so sure there was no one, only now he wasn't so sure.

'In what way?' She repeated his question. 'Now that would be telling and I find I am not ready yet. Was there anything else we needed to discuss?'

'No.'

'In that case I'll ring off. I'm a busy woman these days.' She was smiling as she put the phone down. Paul would think she had gone crazy. Maybe she was a little crazy. So much was happening in her own little world that she was having difficulty keeping up.

Before she left for work in the morning, Jenny backed up the fire and it only needed a poker through it to bring it to life. The house was never cold because she made a point of keeping the house well heated during the cold winter months. She didn't want to risk the pipes freezing and having to call in the plumber if, indeed, she could get one. There was no saying how long one would have to wait or how much would be charged. Trying to save on fuel was false economy.

Taking off her coat Jenny hung it on the coatstand. There was an assortment of old coats, two black umbrellas and a walking stick that had once belonged to her father and Paul had decided to make his own. His mother-in-law had put it aside together with other things for a jumble sale in the church hall. She was delighted when Paul expressed an interest.

'Take it by all means,' she had said.

Jenny was pleased with her performance but the conversation with Paul had exhausted her and her throat felt dry. She would make herself a cup of tea and sit down at the table to have it. Once it was made and had been standing a few minutes, Jenny poured herself a cup and drank a little. She was thinking back and trying to remember all that had been said. She had felt it was important and the need was there to let Paul know that she wasn't just managing her life but managing it very well. One day, and her heart quickened with excitement, he would learn that she was a successful business woman. She could imagine his astonishment and somehow she didn't see him congratulating her.

She wasn't too worried about the house, she was reasonably sure that he would hang on to it. Hadn't he always said that property was a good investment and probably the safest. An offer he couldn't refuse was so unlikely it could be dismissed. Only someone very desperate would make a ridiculous offer and 16 Abbotsford Crescent was very ordinary and badly in need of redecoration.

All the same Jenny wished she hadn't been put to all this bother. Miss Ramsay had done it out of kindness but there had been no need. Not now that she had a generous salary. Jenny saw herself free from financial worries. They could have carried on with Paul paying the mortgage and even if he did fall behind with the instalments she would be able to meet them without hardship. It was a heady feeling to know she had earning power and there were times when Jenny had to pinch herself in case she wakened up to find it had all been a dream. A short time ago she had been an employee, a shop assistant, earning a wage and needing every penny of it. And now she had a lot more responsibility and was being rewarded handsomely. She loved being part of a business that was steadily gaining recognition as a place to visit and discover something different. Miss Ramsay never bought in bulk no matter the incentive. She chose carefully, going for the unusual and people appreciated that. They wouldn't be likely to find such goods in the town stores.

Wilma and Katy liked their home, it was the only one they had known and to leave it and their friends would be very upsetting.

'Why would dad do a thing like that?' Wilma asked in a shocked voice. They were sitting round the table having their main meal of the day. 'Why, Mum, why is he doing it?'

'It really is nothing to worry about, Wilma. Your father wants to know what the property is worth, that is all.'

'Which must mean he is considering selling.'

'No, it doesn't mean that at all.' Jenny gave a laugh that came out rather forced. 'If someone was to offer a huge amount for the house then he might be tempted but no one is going to do that.'

'How can you be so sure?'

'Believe me I am. Wilma, I didn't know this either but apparently it is normal practice to put a house on the market without any intention of selling. The owner wants to know the present-day value and how much interest is shown.'

'Sounds daft to me and he would have to pay for it. Dad doesn't throw away money as a rule, especially now when he's living it up.'

'Wilma!'

'He is. When he was at home we hardly went anywhere but now he forks out for whatever Vera wants.'

Was Wilma becoming disillusioned with her father and Vera Cuthbertson?

'The Vera Cuthbertsons of this world don't come cheap as your father is finding out.'

'Mum, that isn't a nice thing to say.'

'Mum can say what she likes.' Katy had been eating and listening. 'Vera is extravagant, Dad says that to her face. He didn't use to but he does now.' She forked a piece of meat and spoke with her mouth full. 'Know what I think?'

Jenny smiled and Wilma raised her eyes to the ceiling. 'Do we have to hear this?'

'Yes. I think Vera would leave Dad if he didn't give her all she wanted.'

'You do talk a lot of rubbish,' her sister said scornfully. 'They are in love for heaven's sake. Dad likes to give her things which is only to be expected.'

Katy's fork clattered on to her plate. 'Mum, supposing, just supposing, our house did sell for a lot of money.'

'Which it won't.'

'I said supposing. Would we all be rich or would Dad and Vera keep most of it for themselves?'

'Of course Dad wouldn't do a thing like that, you nitwit.'

'I wasn't asking you, clever clogs, I was asking mum.'

'We would not be rich, Katy. The house was bought with building society money and that has to be repaid. We would get half of what is left after all the deductions and that wouldn't come to a great deal.' Jenny thought she should make this very clear to them. 'Listen carefully, both of you, I don't see us leaving 16 Abbotsford Crescent and I have a feeling that next year at this time we will still be in the same house.'

'That is what I think as well,' Katy said happily.

Wilma nodded but didn't say anything. She looked thoughtful.

Jenny got off the bus and seeing Grace ahead hurried to catch up. Grace turned round at the sound of hurrying feet.

'Hello, Jenny, I hardly ever see you these days.'

'I know, life has been pretty hectic. I'm not complaining but a few extra hours in the day would be helpful.'

'Job getting a bit much?'

'Far from it, I love the work.'

'Good boss?'

'The best. Slow down will you, I've something to tell you.'

Grace all but stopped. 'Good news I hope.'

'The house is going on the market.'

'What?' Grace screeched. 'No, I didn't hear that, I didn't.'

'Grace, it won't come to anything. I'm only telling you before you see it being advertised. Paul isn't selling but he does want to know what the property is worth in today's market.'

'Easy enough to find that out without going to that length and it wouldn't cost him a penny. Heavens! all he has to do is to look at a similar house or just phone up to ask the solicitor what it is likely to go for. They always give a figure.'

'I wouldn't know about that. Paul likes to do things his way.'

Grace looked worried. 'Could he sell over your head if he wanted?'

'I suppose he could.'

'You're sure he won't?'

'Nearly sure. If Paul was to be offered well above the asking price then, yes, he might sell. That won't happen, Grace.'

'It had better not. You'll have to show prospective buyers around?'

'Yes, but I insisted it should be by appointment only.'

'Let me know when they are coming and I'll make sure they lose all interest in your house.'

Jenny was laughing. 'How would you go about that?'

'Oh, problem drains, difficult neighbours – heavens! that's me. Never mind all in a good cause. Seriously, Jenny, I do feel upset. You could be right, no doubt you are and there is nothing to this, but I can't help wondering what Paul is up to.'

Jenny did feel some guilt. She had set the ball rolling not Paul.

'Paul isn't up to anything, Grace. People do this regularly. It seems silly to us but they must get some satisfaction from it. I just wanted you to know before anyone else and don't worry, as I told Wilma and Katy, we'll be here in 16 Abbotsford Crescent next year and well after that.' She sighed. 'I have to make Mother understand and that won't be easy.'

'No, I don't expect it will.' She paused. 'Change of subject. Jonathan has suddenly declared his intention of studying to become an architect. Right out of the blue.'

'You have to be pleased, Grace.'

'We both are. Admittedly Arthur would have liked to see Jonathan take over the shop one day but he has accepted that it won't happen. All that nonsense about joining the navy was just that, nonsense.'

'I know.'

'You do?'

'Jonathan brought Katy home from Brenda's house and Katy being Katy would have pestered him until she had all her answers. Let me hasten to add that there was no mention of architect, just that he wasn't going to be a jolly tar.'

'Thank goodness we were the first to know about him wanting to be an architect.'

'Katy said he didn't want to work in his dad's shop and the navy was just an excuse.'

Grace looked exasperated. 'Jenny, why don't our children trust us? We just want the best for him. They can be very hurtful.'

'Don't I know it. That Vera Cuthbertson knew before I did that Wilma had no interest in teaching.'

'What does she want to do?'

'Journalism, you know work on magazines or something like that.'

'You wouldn't mind?'

'Of course not, she can be what she wants to be, I told her.'

'Which means, Jenny, that they will both be staying on at school.'

'That's all to the good. My boss, Miss Ramsay, is very good with both girls and she was advising Wilma to stay on at school for her certificate and not risk finding herself in a dead-end job. To give Wilma her due and I didn't know this until Miss Ramsay told me, she was only leaving school at the holidays to get a job and help me financially.'

'There you are then, the lass isn't so bad after all,' Grace laughed. 'We moan about them but we wouldn't change them for the world.'

'No, that's very true.'

'Wonders will never cease you know. Jonathan is sprucing himself up and spends ages in the bathroom.'

'Jonathan is a nice-looking boy.'

'He is now that he has stopped slouching about.'

'Maybe he's got an eye for the girls.'

The cardboard boxes lay opened and Miss Ramsay and Jenny were checking the contents and admiring the hand-knitted children's Fair Isle jumpers.

'Aren't they lovely?' Moira said holding one up.

'Yes and beautifully knitted.'

'Funnily enough I don't like to see an adult in a Fair Isle jumper but on children they look delightful.'

'I'm inclined to agree with that. Mother used to knit me

Fair Isle jumpers when I was a child and the girls when they were younger. Nowadays she just knits Fair Isle gloves.'

'Cosy for the winter.'

'Yes.' Jenny was waiting for the right moment but Miss Ramsay got in first.

'Anything to report or is it too early?'

'No, I was about to tell you. Paul isn't likely to sell the house, Miss Ramsay, he did make that clear. He would, however, be interested to know what it would fetch.'

'Testing the market.'

'That was the expression he used.'

'A face-saver if there are no offers.'

Jenny shook her head. 'Paul will hold on, he sees property as the safest investment. Ours is a very average, small family house in a good district. When we bought it I remember Paul saying it is far better to buy a poor house in a good area than a good house in a poor area. One can improve a house but one cannot improve a district.'

'I can only agree with that.'

'We don't have a poor house but I have to say it is nothing special although, that said, it is special to us.'

'You might come to like another one even better.'

'I suppose that's possible,' she said but without conviction in her voice. Then she smiled. 'The girls were a bit upset at the thought of a move until I told them not to worry, that come another year the likelihood is that we would still be living in the same house. The difference, and all thanks to you, is that I won't have serious money worries. If Paul was to miss a payment the building society won't come down on us. I could pay without any great hardship.'

Moira was smiling as though she was genuinely amused by something Jenny had said although for the life of her she couldn't think what.

'What this boils down to is that the offer would have to be extremely good before Paul would be tempted to give up ownership.'

'Yes.'

'We'll just have to wait and see.'

Jenny nodded. 'Yes, we'll just have to wait and see.'

'When is the house going on the market or don't you know?'

'Paul said he would do it straight away.'

'His mistress might be pushing him, it could be in her interests, had you thought of that?'

Jenny hadn't. 'No,' she said, 'I hadn't thought of that.'

'By the way who is your solicitor?'

Jenny told her.

Chapter Twelve

There was an immediate response to the advertisement. Jenny wasn't long home when the solicitors' office phoned to say a Mrs Wiseman was interested in the house and would like to view it as soon as possible.

'Does that mean in the next day or two?' Jenny asked the girl.

'Before that, Mrs Richardson, she said this evening if you could manage that.'

Jenny was taken aback. She hadn't expected anyone so soon and she didn't feel ready. That was silly, of course, she was as ready as she would ever be.

'I suppose that could be arranged.'

'Good. What time shall I say? The lady left a number where I could contact her.'

'Give me time to get the house tidied and my two daughters fed.'

The girl laughed. 'Could we say seven thirty?'

'Yes, seven thirty would be fine. What was the woman's name? You did say but I didn't write it down.'

'Mrs Wiseman.'

'Oh, before you ring off. Surely this is very quick, is that unusual?'

'Not at all. A house comes on the market, it seems to meet someone's requirements and they want to be the first to view in case it is snapped up.'

'For something very desirable I imagine that could be the case.'

'Someone must think your home is just what they want.'

'Then they are going to be disappointed. Don't get me wrong, I do like my house but I am not blind to its shortcomings. We fully intended redecorating the whole house and making some improvements to the kitchen but we didn't get round to it.'

'That isn't necessarily a drawback, Mrs Richardson, most people would redecorate anyway. For instance I might like something that you would positively hate.'

'Very true. Only it would look fresher.'

'Yes to that.' She laughed and Jenny thought her a very friendly girl. 'There are those who rush around with a paint pot before putting the house on the market believing it will fetch a better price. That is seldom the case. It is the location of the house that is important. For a couple with a young family it could be its close proximity to a school.'

'Come to think of it we did give thought to that when we bought the house. The school isn't on the doorstep but it is within reasonable distance. Am I keeping you back?'

'No, you aren't and this is my job anyway. I'm here to answer questions.'

'About this Mrs Wiseman—'

'I can tell you a little, I have some notes here.' There was a pause. 'Apparently she and her husband and their two children have been living abroad and now that the children are of school age, just little more than a year between them, they want them educated here. The husband still has three years of his contract to go before he returns to the UK. Mrs Wiseman particularly wants a house in this district where she has family.'

'I see.'

'Yours is not too big and might well suit them until her husband returns and they look for something bigger.'

Jenny felt her heart plummet. She could see herself saying goodbye to her home. This woman would not be short of money, her husband would very likely be in a well-paid job. If she wanted the house she might be prepared to go well above the asking price, enough to tempt Paul.

'Thank you very much,' Jenny said, 'you have been very helpful.'

'All part of the job, Mrs Richardson. Goodbye.'

'Goodbye,' Jenny said faintly and put the phone down. She looked about her and wondered where she should begin. The house wasn't a mess, just a bit untidy with a thin film of dust on the furniture. With a coal fire that couldn't be avoided. What to do first – get the meal started or chase around with a duster and give a polish to the outside door brasses. First impressions were important. Jenny stopped herself. For heaven's sake, she didn't want the house to sell so why try to make it look nicer. She wanted to put the woman off so that she would go and see other houses and forget 16 Abbotsford Crescent. Her plan of action should be concentrated on the meal and leave the housework until the woman had gone.

Wilma and Katy arrived home at their usual time and chattered happily about their school day. Katy had got praise from her teacher for her essay on 'A Day in the Life of Katherine Richardson'.

'What on earth did you write?' Jenny smiled.

'I knew you would ask that.'

'I had to do that years ago. You only have to take one day, any day, and tell what you did from the time you got up until you went to bed.'

Katy frowned and looked a bit uncertain. 'Miss Paterson was pleased.'

'There you are then,' her mother said, 'you must have made your day interesting.'

'How could it be interesting when we don't do anything special, unless you cheated and made up something?' Wilma went on eating.

'I never cheat, not like some people.'

'Eat up, both of you, I want the table cleared. We have someone coming to view the house.'

'When?'

'Half past seven.'

'Do we have to keep out of the way?'

'No, Katy, you do just what you always do.'

'Mum, there are crumbs on the floor, shall I get the sweeper?'

'No, Wilma, leave them. We'll have a good tidy up once our visitor has gone.'

'Mum,' Wilma was giggling. 'That's awful and not like

you. Are you trying to put off whoever it is from buying our house?'

'Do we want to leave our home?'

'No,' they shouted together.

'Then we'll leave the crumbs where they are.'

'And the dirty dishes, we'll leave them in the sink,' Wilma said gleefully.

Jenny hated to see unwashed dishes. She liked to have the table cleared as soon as they had finished eating and the dishes washed and put away.

'All right, for this once only but don't let us overdo it. The woman who is coming has relatives in the district and I wouldn't want word to get around that Mrs Richardson doesn't keep a clean house.'

A minute or two before half past seven a car stopped at the gate and Katy dashed over to the window. It was grey dark and the street lights were on.

'Mum, a lady is just getting out of the car but whoever is driving is going to stay there I think.'

'Come away from the window, Katy,' her mother said sharply.

Katy did but not before the lady had seen her and given a smile. In a few moments the bell rang and Jenny went to answer it smoothing down her skirt as she walked. She wore her shop clothes as she called them. Usually she favoured a straight black skirt but today it was the turn of her navy blue box-pleated skirt and a very attractive navy and gold jumper. Wilma hoped the jumper would shrink in the wash and she would fall heir to it.

The woman looked to be in her early thirties, Jenny

thought. She wore a camel coat, expensive looking, with a big collar and a gold and brown silk scarf at the neck. No one could call her beautiful, not with those flat features, yet she was undoubtedly attractive. What saved her from being plain was the dead straight, thick, glossy blue-black hair worn in a fringe. Her face broke into a wide smile and Jenny responded to the friendliness.

'Good evening, I'm Mrs Wiseman and I do hope this isn't inconvenient.'

'Not at all. Please come in.'

'Thank you.' She stepped inside.

'Shall we start with the sitting-room?'

'Yes, that would be fine. The family room?'

'Yes.'

Jenny pushed open the door and could barely control her laughter. The girls were playing their part. The cushions had been thrown to the floor and Wilma was sprawled out on the sofa and attempting to read the newspaper spread open on the floor. Katy was sitting crosslegged on the chair with a book on her lap.

The woman was smiling. 'Your family, Mrs Richardson. Mine are younger. Sarah is six and Robert five. Absolute darlings one minute and little horrors the next.'

Little horrors or not Jenny heard the pride in her voice.

'This is perfect.'

'It can't be. I mean,' she said hurriedly, 'we never got around to redecorating. It all needs to be papered and painted.'

'Maybe it does but I could live with it. I mean if it is already finger-marked a few more isn't going to matter. My husband, poor darling, had a very strict upbringing and even as a small child he had to sit up properly.'

As though it were a signal, Katy brought out her legs from under her and both women laughed.

'Charles vowed that his children would have their freedom.'

'Quite right.'

'They are children for such a short time and it is so much better if one can look back on one's childhood as a happy time.'

Jenny smiled her agreement. She would go along with that.

'Are you and your husband looking for something bigger?'

Why not tell the truth, half truths only confused every-body.

'No, we are not looking for something bigger, smaller more like. My husband walked out on us.' Jenny purposely avoided looking at Wilma as she said it. She could feel the hostility. Wilma would be thinking she had no right to say that to a stranger. She wanted to protect her father which was commendable in its own way. Jenny saw no reason why she should.

'Oh, I'm sorry, so very sorry, how clumsy of me.'

'Don't apologise, how were you to know.'

'Even so I should not have just presumed.' She was clearly distressed.

'Don't feel badly,' Jenny said leading the woman into the kitchen. 'I'm over the worst.'

'And the girls?' she said very softly.

'The younger one got over the break very quickly. The older one as you may have noticed is clearly upset that I should say such a thing to a stranger. She idolised her father, still does. How do you find this?'

'Functional.'

Jenny burst out laughing. 'How very tactful. It's a mess.'

'Oh, the dirty dishes, that's excusable, I came before you were ready. I might, just might, make changes here, more wall cupboards for a start but nothing drastic. It would only be for three years.'

'Are you a good housewife?' Jenny asked.

'No, I am not. In India everything was done for us and we women just lounged about. Mind you, one couldn't do much in that heat.'

'The men would have to work in it.'

'Yes, but they avoided the worst of it.'

'This is going to be a rude awakening for you.'

'Not really. We are staying with relatives not far from here and my sister-in-law assures me that getting help in the house would be no problem.'

Jenny knew that was so. There were plenty of cards displayed in the newsagent's window offering services in the home. Not all were good but that was the chance one took.

'Three bedrooms?'

'Two bedrooms and a boxroom would be a more accurate description.'

'Forgive me saying this, Mrs Richardson, but you are very unusual. People wanting to sell their houses are desperate to hide the bad points and play up the good. This is so refreshing. I admire your honesty.'

Jenny went ahead and up the stairs. Both girls made their bed before leaving for school. How it was done depended upon the time available. Wilma knew how to make a bed and Katy was learning. The double bedroom was neat and tidy. Mrs Wiseman nodded and said it was a good size. Wilma's bed was made but the top cover was uneven. Katy had made a half-hearted attempt to pull up the bedclothes but had obviously given up. Jenny crossed over to rescue her nightdress which was half under the bed. She folded it and put it under the pillow.

'The bigger bedroom will be perfect for Sarah and your younger daughter's room will do for Robert. It is small, I agree, but he will only be sleeping there.'

'Cupboards, not too many I'm afraid. I often think they should let women design the houses.'

'Yes, we would make a much better job of it. After all it is the woman who has to work in the home. Don't bother showing me the cupboards, we'll make do with what is there.'

'The outside. Not easy to see in the semi-dark.'

'I saw all I needed to. There is a garage?'

'Yes. If you would like to come back for another look once you have given it some thought, you are welcome.'

'Thank you, that is kind of you but it won't be necessary. This would suit us and I do want to be settled as soon as possible. My husband's relations have been marvellous putting up with us but I don't want to prolong their agony. Poor things they must be longing for a bit of peace and quiet.'

'If you are sure, it wouldn't be any trouble.'

'No, as I say this will suit us beautifully. I just hope we get it. I'm the first am I?'

'Yes.'

'I'll be in touch with the solicitor first thing in the morning. Goodbye and many thanks.'

'Goodbye.' Jenny closed the door and for a moment shut her eyes. Mrs Wiseman was going to be the future owner of 16 Abbotsford Crescent. It was almost certain and Jenny felt depressed. Going into the sitting-room and finding Wilma scowling didn't help.

'That was a bit thick, Mum.'

'What was?'

'Saying that about Dad walking out on us.'

'How would you describe it?'

'That's not the point. At the start you didn't want people to know.'

'Perhaps, Wilma, because I thought your father's desertion would be short-lived. I was wrong.'

Wilma looked miserable. 'I used to love him so much.'

'You still do, dear, you always will. What happened between your father and me had nothing to do with you.'

'I don't think I love him as much as I used to and he doesn't love me like he did.'

'Of course he does but it isn't so easy for him to show it.'

'In case it makes Vera jealous?'

'That's possible.' Jenny wanted to change the subject. 'How about if we have a cup of tea and a chocolate biscuit before we tackle the washing up?'

'I didn't make my bed,' Katy said as though just re-membering.

'So I noticed.'

'Did the lady say anything?'

'No.'

'She was nice.'

'Yes, she was, very nice.'

Wilma went upstairs and Katy took the chance when she had her mother to herself.

'Mum,' she said worriedly.

'What is it, dear?'

'I told you about my essay, you know a day in—'

'Yes, you did tell me Miss Paterson was pleased with your effort.'

'I didn't do what Wilma said she did.'

'No, well, it wouldn't be the same, this was your story.'

Katy nodded. 'It was all true, not made up. I said a day in my life was different now because Daddy had left us and my mum had to go out to work. Then I said I got up in the morning a bit earlier and before leaving for school I helped you by making my bed and keeping my room tidy.'

'You told it as it was, Katy. You must have made it a very good essay or Miss Paterson wouldn't have given you praise.' She felt a lump in her throat and reached out to give Katy a hug. A mother shouldn't favour one child more than another, only, of course, it happened. What was important was never to show it. Jenny loved Wilma, she loved her very much but she didn't always like her. Paul had never hidden his preference for his elder daughter and that had been a mistake. Perhaps he thought Katy didn't notice but children were quick and noticed far more than they were given credit for.

193

Wilma came downstairs. 'Thought we were having tea and a chocolate biscuit.'

'So we are but the kettle doesn't fill itself. I'll see to the tea and you put out the cups.'

'I'll get the biscuits – I know which tin they are in.'

'More dishes to wash,' but Wilma was smiling.

'I'll wash and you two can dry. It won't take long.'

Jenny had four callers to see over 16 Abbotsford Crescent. A mother and daughter thought the house had possibilities though it would need a lot spent on it. The older woman seemed obsessed with cupboards.

'Poor for cupboards.'

'Fairly average, Mother.'

'My cupboards are far bigger.'

'Most old houses have large cupboards.' She gave Jenny an apologetic look.

Jenny thought if she had a mother like that she would have left her at home in her big house with its huge cupboards.

'Bigger rooms would set off your furniture better. Still I'm not the one who would be living here.'

'No, you are not.'

'Could do worse I suppose and it is the district you want.'

'If you've seen all you want downstairs shall we go upstairs?' Jenny asked.

'Mother you stay here and I'll pop up.'

The old lady was having none of it. She would manage the stairs she said. She was very stout and short of breath but after a lot of puffing and blowing and a rest halfway she was at the top to give her opinion. There weren't too many faults and she managed the going down easier than going up.

'Thank you, Mrs Richardson,' her daughter said when Jenny was showing them to the door. 'I do like your house and I believe it might suit us. My husband leaves all this to me. He says as long as I am pleased he and the boys will settle anywhere.'

'Nice obliging husband,' Jenny smiled.

'Bone lazy more like,' the old lady said with a sniff.

The daughter gave a slight shake of her head as though to say one had to make allowances. 'We have another two houses to view so I can't say whether or not we would be offering for yours, but many thanks for your trouble.'

Jenny disliked the couple who followed. She knew they were an awkward pair as soon as she set eyes on them. The husband had a florid complexion and wore a loud tweed suit. His wife was taller and heavily built with what Jenny could only describe as a bad-tempered face. Maybe living with that man had done that to her. They were hardly in the door before they started.

'That is a ridiculous price you are asking for a property so obviously in need of redecorating.'

Jenny said nothing.

'Don't you think so yourself?'

'I had nothing to do with it. That was left to the solicitor.'

'Surely you don't expect to get it?' the man said with a thin smile.

'We shall just have to wait and see.'

'Solicitors, can't trust them, crafty lot,' his wife said. 'They would suggest a ridiculous price. Maybe you don't know it, Mrs Richardson, but the more the property goes for the more they make. Call it their commission or something.'

'I was aware of that but one must remember solicitors have to make a living.'

'A killing more like,' the man said laughing heartily as though he had said something extremely funny.

'From that I gather you are not interested.'

The woman drew herself up and looked shocked. 'We didn't say that did we, Harold?'

'Indeed we did not. That is the downstairs and now, if you please, we would like to see the bedrooms.'

Jenny went upstairs, her lips pressed together and they followed. The double bedroom was declared reasonable and they had no complaints about Wilma's.

'This is a boxroom not a bedroom,' Harold said nastily when Jenny opened Katy's bedroom door.

She remembered describing it as a boxroom to Mrs Wiseman but she wasn't having Katy's room insulted by these two.

'This, I'll have you know, is a single bedroom. It is exactly as described in the house particulars which also gave the floor measurements. You should have read them and not wasted your time and mine.' When they left she all but slammed the door.

Two days went by and her next caller was a quiet, pleasant-mannered, middle-aged man in a business suit and carrying a briefcase. Jenny had no idea if he was a family man or not. She didn't ask and he offered nothing. Before he left the man thanked her very courteously for showing him around.

At the end of the week Paul came on the phone and sounded pleased.

'Hello, Jenny, everything fine?'

'I think so.'

'You've had a few callers?'

'Four to be exact.'

'Would you say they were interested?'

Yes, Paul, one is very interested and I'm worried sick that she is going to offer enough to tempt you, she said silently. Aloud she said, 'Hard to tell.'

'You must have some idea,' he said impatiently.

'Not really. One couple thought the asking price was ridiculous.'

'If you hadn't insisted on appointment only—'

'I did so because it suited me,' Jenny said shortly.

'I would call that selfish.'

'You can call it what you like. If you think back, Paul, you were only interested to know what the house was likely to fetch.'

'That still stands. Mr Jamieson wasn't in his office. I'll phone him tomorrow morning to get the latest.' He rang off and after a few moments Jenny put the phone down.

Chapter Thirteen

———❖———

'When you are ready, Jenny, come along to my office and we'll have our coffee together.'

Jenny gave a smile and nodded her head. 'Five minutes and I'll be with you.'

They were quiet at the moment with only two businessmen in the tea room. It was to be hoped that come the spring there would be a sharp upturn in trade. The cold, changeable weather didn't entice many out but, even so, there was the occasional bus load of hardy tourists with the Log Cabin on its list of places to visit. Toilet facilities of a high standard had been added on to the end of the building and the Log Cabin was now one of the regular 'comfort stops'. By popular demand the time spent there was increased so that tourists could enjoy a leisurely morning coffee, a midday snack of soup, roll and butter or afternoon tea. Following that would come a browse round the shop and a look at the paintings. A great many were tempted to buy from the attractive and unusual display.

Once Jenny was seated, Miss Ramsay poured the coffee and handed her a cup.

'Thank you.' She helped herself to sugar and milk and Miss Ramsay did the same.

'A biscuit?' She pushed the plate nearer.

'No, thank you, I won't. I'm being strong-willed, too many sweet things and the pounds go on.'

'I can't say it shows but I'll follow your example. Really I only take one because it is there. In future I'll tell Doris to bring coffee on its own unless I have a visitor.'

They sipped in silence for a few moments then Moira put her cup down.

'Jenny, satisfy my curiosity if you will and tell me what the position is with your house.'

'So far I have shown four parties over it,' Jenny said carefully.

'Any of them likely to put in an offer?'

'One lady appeared very interested and said she would be putting in an offer. She is home from India with her two children and wants our house because she has family living close by. The other three,' Jenny shook her head, 'possible I suppose but not very likely.'

'Had there been an offer you would have heard from your husband?' She looked at Jenny enquiringly.

'Paul phoned to ask how many folk had been to see it. He didn't mention an offer. When I told him I'd shown four parties around he said that was disappointing, he had expected more interest. He blamed me.'

'Why should he do that?'

'Because I insisted on appointment only. He said people were put off by that.'

'What nonsense. Would he have preferred you spending

your day showing the house to those who have no intention of buying?'

Jenny sighed. 'I just wish Paul would take the house off the market, the girls and I would hate to leave our home.' She hadn't meant to say that but it was out and it was the truth.

Moira Ramsay looked thoughtful. She took a sip of her coffee and put the cup down.

'Jenny, a blunt question and a straight answer if you please,' she said brusquely. 'How much do you trust your husband? Think about it.'

Jenny did, it was a question she was beginning to ask herself. 'Miss Ramsay, before Paul left us I had complete trust in him. I want to believe that I could still trust him but I have to say I am less sure. To give Paul his due I think he would always have the girls' best interests at heart. However, that said, if it was to be between them and Miss Cuthbertson I'm all but sure it would go her way.'

'Not a situation to give you any confidence?'

'No.'

'Bearing that in mind wouldn't it be in your own interests for the house to be sold?'

'I accept that but leaving my home and the friends I've made, especially my neighbour, is going to be such a wrench. And I know it will be the same for Wilma and Katy.'

'Jenny, I wish I could be more forthcoming but I can't, not at this moment. It is, as I said before, a case of trusting me. Things will work out.'

Jenny nodded but she was feeling far from happy. Her

future was being decided for her and it was an uncomfortable feeling. Deep down she felt resentment and had to be careful not to show it. She would just have to go along with what was being planned. She had no choice if she wanted to hold on to her new position and its rewards. It was as simple as that.

'More coffee?'

'No, thank you.'

'Oh, come on, these are small cups. We might as well finish what is in the coffee pot.'

'Thank you, I will then.'

'Can you drive?'

Jenny almost choked on the coffee. 'What?'

'I asked if you could drive.'

'A car you mean?'

'Of course a car, what else could I mean?' Moira sounded amused.

Jenny laughed suddenly. 'Stupid of me but the question was so unexpected. No, I don't drive.'

'Have you never wanted to learn?'

'I never seriously thought about it though I do remember once, and it must have been in jest, that I suggested to Paul that I would like to learn.'

'You got no encouragement?'

'None at all. Paul said I would be hopeless, that I was too timid ever to be at the wheel of a car.'

Moira bristled. 'Had that been said to me the person responsible would have got his answer and the words I fear would not have been very ladylike.'

Was that what making your own way in life did for you?

Did it give you the confidence to stick up for yourself? Jenny thought it must. Already she felt herself to be stronger and becoming a more forceful character. Maybe it wasn't before time.

'We can discount what your husband said. If he was to do the instructing then you were doomed from the start. That, I might say, does not just apply to your husband. It is a well-known fact that one should only take driving instructions from a stranger. I feel that at the present moment you have enough on your plate but one day, quite soon, you should take lessons from a professional instructor.'

'Keeping a car on the road would be expensive,' Jenny said timidly. She was wondering where the money was coming from.

'The car would be for business and belong to the Log Cabin.'

'Paul has a company car, something like that?'

'Yes, something like that. Now that you are to be my business partner there is a lot you will have to learn. The car would be necessary when you visit the warehouses. You will have to learn how to buy, bearing in mind what would sell in the Log Cabin. We are rather specialised and what we stock wouldn't be readily available in the town stores. Waiting about for buses would be a thing of the past and you could come and go as you please.'

Jenny felt excited at the thought of learning to drive. 'Do you honestly think I could master it?'

'Of course, why not? Other people learn, why not you?'

★   ★   ★

Jenny was in the house on her own when Paul phoned. He sounded jubilant.

'I've just had Mr Jamieson on the phone.' Mr Jamieson was the solicitor dealing with the sale of the house.

'No more callers, Paul.' Jenny thought she should get that in first.

'That doesn't matter. It would appear we have two parties fighting it out and Mr Jamieson is confident that the house will go well beyond the asking price.'

'Who are the parties?'

'I don't know and I didn't ask.'

'One would probably be a Mrs Wiseman. She and her children are home from abroad and looking for a house in our area. I can't think who the other interested party could be.'

'Jenny, I couldn't care less who gets the house. I am only interested in what it would fetch.'

'And now that you have some idea you will take it off the market.'

'Certainly not.'

'Paul, you did say you were only testing the market,' Jenny said desperately. 'The girls would hate to move away from their friends.'

'There was no mention of that before. Let me remind you, Jenny, that I have been kept completely in the dark,' he said angrily. 'You have refused to tell me where you would be living in the event of the house being sold. If things are not working out as you wished then too bad. Two can play at that game. From the beginning I said if the house failed to reach the asking price then there would be no question of selling. However, the way things look I would be a fool not to sell. I'm not likely to get another opportunity like this. I am going to do very well out of it and so are you with your insistence on a half share of the profit. It strikes me now that I was being far too generous.'

'I disagree. All I was doing was claiming my rights. How fortuitous that I did insist on everything being written into the agreement. Sadly I have to say, Paul, that I no longer trust you to keep your word.' She waited for the explosion of anger but it didn't come. There was silence for a few moments then his voice came over icily cold.

'You will be kept informed and let me suggest that you get started on the packing. It could be that whoever is buying the house may insist on early possession.' He rang off.

Jenny felt close to panic. What was to happen to them? She felt like weeping with frustration. What was Miss Ramsay playing at? Why all this secrecy? In the meantime she thought she must try and keep a grip on herself. There was no need to tell Wilma and Katy, not yet, and they wouldn't be visiting Paul for another three weeks. Let them go on thinking that all was well for as long as possible. She prayed for a miracle but didn't expect one.

The call she was dreading came two days later and was made by Paul's secretary, Betty Morgan. Betty sounded embarrassed when she came on the phone and Jenny felt sorry for the woman. She couldn't enjoy being the messenger between her boss and his estranged wife. She would keep the conversation short and businesslike.

'Hello, Betty, how are you?'

'Very well, thank you. Mrs Richardson, your husband is very busy at present and he asked me to inform you he has received official word that the house is sold.'

'I see. Was that all he said?'

'Yes, that was all.'

'Tell Mr Richardson message received and understood. Thank you, Betty.' Jenny put the phone down and began laughing, it was near hysterical laughter. She wondered if Betty would actually give Paul that message. Jenny thought it possible and wished she could see his face. She knew she was being silly and childish but at least it kept the worries away for a little longer.

By evening Jenny felt drained. The worst had happened and she had only herself to blame. Miss Ramsay, for reasons of her own, had interfered and no matter how well-meaning it was still interference. Paul wouldn't have considered selling if it hadn't been suggested to him. Sadly it was too late for regrets and tomorrow she would have to tell Wilma and Katy and telephone her mother. By then she would surely know what plans Miss Ramsay had for housing them.

That night her head ached and she tossed and turned in the bed she had once shared with Paul. Sleep claimed her for a short time and she awoke early in the morning. With her hands behind her head she lay against the pillow and wondered how many more mornings she would waken up in this room.

Jenny felt vaguely annoyed that Miss Ramsay should look so cheerful when she was feeling so miserable.

'Good morning, Jenny, that's a depressing day but I do think the mist will lift by midday. You look a bit down.'

'That's the way I feel.' She swallowed. 'Paul has sold the house.'

'Yes, I know.'

'You knew?' Jenny stared at her.

'Do you know who the new owner is?' She was smiling.

'No, I don't but I imagine it to be a Mrs Wiseman, she was very keen to get it.'

'So I understand. Jenny, take off your coat and stop looking so worried and bewildered.'

'Bewildered because I'm wondering how you come to know so much about it.' Jenny hung up her coat and at Miss Ramsay's invitation sat down.

'I owe you an explanation.'

Jenny thought that was the understatement of the year.

'Let me give you the good news right away. Jenny, you will not have to move out of 16 Abbotsford Crescent—'

'I have to. Paul more or less told me to get started to the packing. Not more or less, he did tell me.'

'That gentleman is in for a big surprise. Oh, dear, where do I begin? As I said, you do not have to move out of your home because it is now yours. No, please do not interrupt, I've been longing to tell you this but I couldn't be sure that if I put you in the picture, you wouldn't somehow give the show away. Jenny, my solicitor has been working on your behalf. I gave him instructions to get 16 Abbotsford Crescent and to top any bid. I have to confess that we didn't expect the house to go so far above the asking price.'

Jenny bit her lip. 'You must have offered far more than the house is worth.'

'I have to agree with that and my solicitor was becoming

concerned. We hadn't expected this Mrs Wiseman to be so anxious to obtain possession. In the end her solicitor must have advised her not to go any higher.'

'She particularly wanted it because she has family in the area. I—I don't know what to say.' Jenny was trembling.

'You can tell me how it feels to own your own home.'

'How do I feel? Where do I find the words? I feel so happy, so relieved and proud—yes proud. How can I ever repay you? Even yet I haven't taken it in. How did you manage it?'

'I didn't have a great deal to do, that was all left to my solicitor. He had his instructions to get the house and to top whatever offer came in.'

'I'm so sorry you had to pay so much and it makes me feel guilty.'

'Then don't. You knew nothing of this so why feel guilt? Having another party so interested was unfortunate but then one takes that chance and it ensured that Paul would sell. Remember too it is not as much as would appear at first. Whatever profit Paul makes from the transaction half of it comes to you.'

Jenny took a deep, shaky breath. 'That wouldn't have been the case if I hadn't taken your advice and got everything down in writing and signed. Had it just been verbal I don't think Paul would have kept his word. He more or less admitted it. I can't recall his exact words but they were to the effect that he regretted being so generous.'

'A lesson my dear Jenny for the future. We want to trust people but sadly one is sometimes disappointed. To avoid that and any unpleasantness always insist on a written agreement and a signature.'

The first shock was wearing off and Jenny's brain was beginning to work furiously. 'I think I am starting to understand, the building society doesn't come into this. I pay you instead.'

'Yes but unlike a building society I won't be charging you interest and that makes a very big difference. My accountant and I have worked it out and we suggest, with your agreement, that a small deduction be taken from your salary each month and you will receive only fifty per cent of your share of the profits until the debt is paid in full.'

'That is perfect and so good of you.' Jenny was looking flushed and happy.

'Am I forgiven for putting you through all that? You must have thought I had a terrible cheek taking so much on myself.'

'I'm glad you did. Had I known I might well have given the show away.'

'And alerted Paul. He is going to think you very devious.'

'He can think what he likes.' She chuckled. 'It's awful of me, I know, but I can't wait to see his face when he finds out I am the new owner.' Jenny's eyes were dancing.

'I felt you should have that satisfaction after your worrying time. My solicitor will not divulge the identity of his client or the new owner.' She smiled. 'The way is clear for you.'

Did she feel a little sorry for Paul? No, why should she? He only thought about himself and Vera. 'My husband is going to be absolutely furious,' Jenny said and her voice shook.

'You will be able for him?' There was a trace of anxiety in the look she gave Jenny.

'Yes, Miss Ramsay, I'll be able for him,' she said striving to control her voice. Paul didn't deserve her sympathy and wouldn't want it. She was nothing to him now. The love he had once held for her had gone – perhaps it had never gone very deep. Love between husband and wife is never equal. There is always the one more in love than the other. She had been that one giving her whole heart to Paul and now it would appear that he was in that position with Vera Cuthbertson. Thinking of her own heartbreak and suffering Jenny was filled with a whirlwind of rage. How dare he treat her the way he had. And how grateful she was to Miss Ramsay. Without her where would they be? Eking out a living and worrying about the future no doubt.

'Good.'

'I am no longer the timid woman he married. Paul isn't a bully or anything like that, but he would hate to be made to look a fool and particularly by me.'

'You can tell your husband in all honesty that you knew nothing about this.'

'I could, I might and then again I might not. Is it so awful that I should want my moment of glory?'

'Very understandable I would say.'

'I can't believe how much I have changed in these last months. Actually, when I think about it I have only contempt for myself for being such a spineless creature.'

'Jenny, there are many, many women like yourself with a good brain who have been conditioned to believe they are incapable of making an important decision. That said there are those who are unable to make a decision at all but thankfully not too many. Now you know what you can do.'

'Thanks to you.'

'No, Jenny, it started the day Paul walked out on you and the girls, that was when you took control.'

'I made it easier by convincing myself that Paul would come back to us, that what he was going through was a temporary madness. By the time I accepted that he wasn't coming back I had rearranged my life.' Jenny smiled. 'I don't think I believed in fate before, but now I do. Fate and my mother,' she laughed, 'brought me to the Log Cabin and changed my life.'

'For the better I hope.'

'No question about that.'

'Wilma and Katy are going to be greatly relieved to know they won't be moving out.'

'Neither the girls or my mother know anything about this. They believed and I encouraged them to go on believing that Paul was only testing the market and had no intention of selling the house. For a while I firmly believed that myself. When it looked as though he might sell I saw no reason to worry the girls or Mother. Time enough, I thought, when it happened.'

'You took all that worry on yourself. That was very brave and thoughtful but then you are that kind of person.'

Jenny shook her head. 'I am far from brave.'

'I think you are and I also think that the Log Cabin isn't going to get much work out of you today.'

'Oh, no, I'm ready to start—'

'You'll put on your coat and take the rest of the day off. This is a slack time and we'll manage very well.'

'I'd much rather work, honestly.'

'Do what you are told, Jenny, it is an order.'

Jenny bit her lip. 'You are very kind. I'll–I'll phone Mother to come over in the afternoon and that way I can give them the news over a meal.'

'A special meal?'

'Special for my two means a steak pie.'

Jenny phoned her mother as soon as she was inside the house. She could have phoned from the Log Cabin but decided against that. Her mother could be difficult to get off the phone. She liked to talk.

'Mum?'

'Jenny, it's you, where are you phoning from?'

'Home.'

'Why aren't you at work? Somebody ill?'

'No, we are fine. I was given the day off.'

'Why?'

'Miss Ramsay suggested it.' Jenny was glad of the chair beside the telephone even though it looked out of place. This could be a long call. Janet Scrimgeour enjoyed a chat on the phone and was annoyed if it was cut short.

'Why would she do a thing like that unless business is falling off?'

'Considering this is still winter, the Log Cabin is doing quite well. Enough to keep everything ticking away nicely as Miss Ramsay puts it,' Jenny said patiently.

'That's a big relief I must say. Jobs like that don't come easily. You have to hang on there.'

'I have every intention of doing so.'

'Is this just a chat or is there another reason for the call?'

'There is a reason. I want you to come over in the afternoon.'

'Very short notice I have to say.'

'Why, have you another engagement?'

'As it happens, no. I wouldn't describe my social life as hectic but it could have been the afternoon I was going out.'

'Then you would have declined the invitation and that would have been that.'

'With me left wondering what this is all about. Can't you tell me?'

'I suppose I could but I am not going to.'

'Jenny, you can be very exasperating at times.'

'Like mother, like daughter. Mum, will you stop blethering, you have all day but I don't. When I come off the phone I'm going to the butcher's to get steak.'

'We're having steak pie then?'

'Yes, followed by jelly and fruit salad.'

'That'll suit the pair of them and me too. Is this Sunday best or everyday clothes?'

'Everyday clothes. Cheerio, Mother, see you when you come.'

Jenny had kept on her coat since she knew she was going out again and it took only a couple of minutes to collect a shopping bag and check she had enough money in her purse. The day hadn't improved much. It was cold and damp and a thin mist lay all around.

Jenny felt herself bursting with energy as she tackled the housework and brought in coal and logs from the cellar. She prepared the meat, browning it slightly, Jenny had a light hand with pastry and after rolling it out and covering the dish she trimmed and fluted the edges and brushed the top with egg yolk. The pie was ready for the oven.

'Mum, what a marvellous smell, what have you made?' Katy asked as she came in the back door and left it open for Wilma.

'Shut the door, Katy, you're letting in the cold.'

'I thought Wilma was coming.' She went to have a look outside. 'Wonders will never cease, she's talking to Jonathan, standing talking.'

'Close the door when you are told and why shouldn't Wilma talk to Jonathan?'

'She never does that's why, I do, I like Jonathan.' Katy had been about to say more when her grandmother came in.

'Hello, Gran, what are you doing here?'

'And what kind of a welcome is that?' Janet smiled as the two hugged each other.

'We weren't told, we didn't know, that's why. Mum, I asked you what was in the oven and you didn't answer me.'

'Steak pie.'

'Goody, goody, I'm absolutely starving.'

'You'll have to keep on starving until five o'clock. No biscuits so keep your eyes away from the tin.'

The door opened and Wilma came in. 'Hello, Gran, what are you doing here?'

Janet opened her eyes wide. 'The same welcome as your sister gave me. I think I should put on my hat and coat and go away.'

'Not your usual day, that's why.'

'What were you saying to Jonathan?' Katy asked.

'As if I would tell you.'

'I tell you lots of things.'

'Nothing of any importance. For your information Jonathan spoke to me first.'

'We're having steak pie.'

'Really,' she drawled. 'I'm going up to change. The person who introduced school uniform should be shot.'

'Very smart I would say.'

'You would, Gran, because you are old-fashioned.'

Janet shook her head and Jenny smiled. Wilma liked her school uniform but it wasn't the thing to say so. Individual choice was what they wanted or so some of them said and the others followed.

'Katy give yourself a wash and change out of your school clothes.'

'Must I?'

'Yes, you must.'

'What a bother.'

'It was a bigger bother for me to dash to the butcher's for steak to make your favourite meal.'

'That's different. You like cooking and I expect I'll like it too when I'm older.'

'Katy!'

'Yes, on my way.'

Janet was laughing. 'Never a dull moment with those two.'

'Try the patience of a saint,' but she was smiling.

Jenny postponed the telling until the pie had been eaten and enjoyed and they had a plate of jelly and fruit salad in front of them. From the looks she was getting her mother was becoming impatient.

She took a little of the jelly and put the spoon down. 'I have something to tell you,' Jenny began and three pairs of eyes turned to her. 'I thought it better to have Gran over so you could hear it together.' It wasn't only the jelly that was wobbling, her voice was doing it too.

'Hear what?'

She took a deep breath, surprised to find herself so nervous. 'You knew that 16 Abbotsford Crescent was to go on the market?'

'Yes, of course we knew that,' Wilma said impatiently, 'Dad wanted to know the present-day value of the house.'

'Jenny, what has happened?' her mother said quietly. 'Surely Paul hasn't changed his mind—'

'Changed his mind about what?' Wilma said looking from one to the other.

'Yes, Mother, I'm afraid Paul has changed his mind. The house reached substantially more than the asking price and he has decided to sell. In fact the house is sold.'

There was a stunned silence. The jelly and fruit salad remained untouched.

'Where does that leave you?' Janet said looking strained.

'There is nothing to worry about.'

'That is you all over, Mum, nothing to worry about.

Dad wouldn't think about selling our house, that was what you said. You were so sure, so very sure.'

'Stop it,' her grandmother said sharply.

'I didn't want to worry you, any of you.'

Wilma wasn't going to stop. 'Meaning you weren't as convinced as you pretended to be?'

'At the beginning I was almost sure we were safe and then when Mrs Wiseman showed such an interest I was less sure.'

'She's bought our house,' Katy said on the verge of tears. 'I liked her, she was nice, but I don't want her or anybody else to live here.'

'Don't get upset, just give me a chance to explain.'

'Explain what? Explain how you let us go on believing the house wouldn't be sold. We should have been told the truth.'

'Wilma,' her grandmother said severely, 'do you think of no one but yourself? You can't even begin to know what your mother has come through these last months and everything she has done has been for you and Katy.'

'I do wish you would all be quiet and listen. What I am trying to tell you, if you would give me the chance is that we will not be leaving here.'

'The house isn't sold after all.'

'The house is sold, Wilma. Your father no longer owns it.'

'I'm lost.' She raised her arms.

'I'm lost, too, Jenny. If not Paul, who does own it?'

'I do,' Jenny said quietly.

There was silence then a babble of voices.

'I can't answer everybody so will the three of you be quiet. Try to understand that I am still suffering from shock myself because I only learned this morning that I am the owner of our house, the owner of 16 Abbotsford Crescent to make it absolutely clear. No, no interruptions, I tell this in my own way or I don't tell it at all.'

Three people fell silent.

'Yesterday, when your father's secretary phoned to tell me the house had been sold I was in complete despair. I knew it was always possible but I made myself believe it wouldn't happen.'

'Mum, I have to interrupt. Did Dad really do that, get his secretary to phone?' Wilma said quietly.

'Yes, Wilma, apparently he was too busy to phone himself.'

Wilma looked shattered. 'That was awful of him, I didn't think Dad would do that.'

Jenny was sorry for Wilma. She was finding out her adored father was not so perfect after all.

'Eat up your jelly.'

'Never mind the jelly, get on with the story,' Janet said pushing the plate aside.

'Very well. I can't remember just when, but it was some time ago that Miss Ramsay asked me how I was placed regarding the house.'

'Now why would she do that?'

'Because, Mother, she thought I looked worried and I was. It was something you said, Wilma, about Miss Cuthbertson having expensive tastes and your father's wish always to please her.'

'You weren't meant to take that seriously.'

'I did take it seriously, I took it very seriously. Had there been a real problem with money I felt I would be the first to suffer. Your father couldn't reduce what he allows me since it is so small which only left the house.'

'You thought Paul might sell?'

'I just wasn't sure, Mother, it was a niggling worry that wouldn't go away.'

'You confided in Miss Ramsay?'

'No, I tried to keep my personal affairs to myself, but she can be very persistent and I found I was telling her about my concern over the house.'

'If the worst came to the worst I would have put you up, surely you knew that?'

'I knew that, Mum, and we both know you don't have the accommodation.'

'We would have managed until you made other arrangements.'

'A cheap rented house was the only answer.'

'Dad would never have done that to us, I mean expect us to live in a cheap rented house,' Wilma said sounding scandalised.

'Probably not, Wilma, but the possibility was there. Anyway, to get back to the story, Miss Ramsay must have given the matter a lot of thought and when I admitted that I couldn't be certain that Paul wouldn't sell she suggested to me that I tackle him and find out if he would ever consider putting the house on the market.'

'What did Dad say?'

'That he would have to think about it. You see he wasn't

just dismissing it. Then he got back to me – there I am using your father's office jargon,' Jenny laughed.

'That means office language, Gran.'

'I had gathered that much, Wilma.'

'Mum, do you want your jelly?'

'No, Katy, I don't. You have it.'

'Have mine too,' her gran said handing over her plate.

'Where was I?' Jenny asked.

'Dad was getting back to you.'

'Thank you, Wilma. Paul said there was little likelihood of him selling though he wasn't ruling it out. What he would be interested in was finding out what the house would fetch in today's market.'

'Mum, you sound just like a businesswoman.'

Jenny smiled. 'Do I, Katy? Your father put our house on the market and there was some interest shown in it. Had the offer not been so good I do not believe Paul would have sold the house because he has always believed in property being a good investment.'

'Too good an offer to refuse?'

'Yes, Wilma, when he came on the phone he sounded jubilant. Two prospective buyers were fighting it out. What he didn't know and remember I didn't know it either, was that Miss Ramsay had instructed her solicitor to top any offer to get the house.'

'For herself?'

'No, Wilma, on my behalf. When a solicitor is acting for his client he is not required to divulge that person's identity.'

Janet was shaking her head as though she didn't understand the half of it. Wilma was puzzled too.

'Mum, wait I need to get this straight. Miss Ramsay was buying the house for you and going to charge you rent?'

'No, the house is legally mine. I own 16 Abbotsford Crescent.'

'Which means you have to pay Miss Ramsay back and how are you going to do that?'

Janet was wondering the same.

'A building society would charge interest, a great deal of interest, that is how they make their money. Miss Ramsay won't be charging me interest and I'm not quite finished, I have something else to tell you.'

'Something good?'

'Very good, Katy. I am no longer a shop assistant.'

'I knew it,' Janet said showing her worry, 'I knew there was something wrong when you weren't in at work.'

'What a worrier you are, Mum. I have gone up in the world. Miss Ramsay has appointed me to be her business partner.'

'In plain language what does that mean?'

'A great deal financially. I now have a salary not a wage and in due course I'll be in line for a share of the profits. That is confidential maybe I should have waited before telling you.'

'Why not, that is wonderful news.' Janet was crying and, getting up from the table, she went round to give Jenny a hug. 'Many, many congratulations you clever girl. You should both be very proud of your mother.'

'I am, I've got the best mother in the whole world.'

Jenny waited for Wilma to speak.

'It's great about your promotion and I'm glad about the house, I mean that we won't have to move but—'

'But what?' Jenny said quietly.

'Dad is going to feel such a fool.'

'Why, because I've bettered him?'

'No, because you've made him look foolish. It was a bit underhand.'

'I did nothing underhand, how could I when I knew nothing of what was going on.'

'Dad won't believe that.'

'That is up to him. He knows I am not guilty of telling untruths.'

'Will you tell him how it happened?' she was almost pleading. 'Or are you going to leave him to find out?'

'I don't know and with all the excitement I almost forgot to tell you that I've agreed to a divorce.'

'You weren't going to.'

'I'm allowed to change my mind.'

'You are going to let Dad divorce you?'

'No, Wilma, he can't do that, he has no grounds. I am the innocent party.'

'You have to agree to it before the divorce can go ahead?'

'That's right. The way will be clear for your father to marry his fancy piece and make an honest woman of her.'

'That is a horrid way to speak of Vera,' Wilma said flushing angrily.

'Maybe it is but the truth can be horrid.'

'You and Gran are the same – you have a down on Vera and she can't do anything right,' Wilma shouted.

222

'Is that so surprising that we should have a down on her as you call it?' Jenny was becoming more than a little angry with her daughter. She shouldn't have said fancy piece but it was out before she could stop herself. 'I had thought you were becoming a little less enamoured of late but it appears I was mistaken.'

'I'm not blind to Vera's faults.'

'You were until recently.'

'She's selfish. I accept that just as Dad does. What you don't understand is that women who look marvellous like she does usually are.'

'I'll need that explained,' her grandmother said.

'Waste of time – you would never understand, you are too old.'

'Don't use that tone of voice to your grandmother.'

'I'm not too old to understand that you are a very silly child. I say child because that is what you are. You need to grow up and learn some sense.'

'I understand a lot more than you think,' she pushed back the dessert plate spilling some of the jelly on to the tablecloth.

'Now look what you've done. Go and get a cloth to wipe it up.'

With a face like thunder Wilma did as she was told.

'You might as well clear the table when you are at it.'

'Why me?'

Jenny didn't answer. The three of them got up. Jenny signalled to her mother to sit down in the easy chair and she began helping Wilma. Katy was finishing off the fruit salad before the plates disappeared. The activity had helped to restore peace and once Jenny had steeped the tablecloth in cold water to remove the stain, they were seated round the fire.

'Mum, once you pay Miss Ramsay back the house will be ours.'

'It already is mine just as it was your father's before. Most people have repayments to make on their home.' She smiled to Katy.

'When it's all paid we'll be rich?'

'I don't see us ever being rich but we'll be comfortable and I would never look for more. Money doesn't bring happiness but security does.'

'We should all be grateful to Miss Ramsay.'

'I shall be grateful to her for the rest of my life,' Jenny said quietly. 'There is no way I can properly repay Miss Ramsay except through my work and she won't find me wanting there.'

'Jenny, a cup of tea would go down very well.'

'Just what I was thinking myself.'

'I'll make it,' Wilma said jumping up from her chair.

'Thank you, dear, that would be nice.'

'I'll help.'

'You can put some custard creams on a plate, Katy.'

Chapter Fourteen

Moira Ramsay was looking thoughtful as she locked up the premises and walked round to where her car was parked on the gravel at the side of the Log Cabin and well away from the area where the customers left theirs. She didn't mind staying behind when the others had gone if there was something she wanted to finish. Being alone in the grey dark with only the bleak hills for company held no terrors for Miss Moira Ramsay. She wasn't the nervous type. Single women couldn't afford to be. They had to know how to look after themselves.

Her brow puckered as she wondered uneasily if, perhaps, she had taken too much upon herself. A helping hand was one thing while organising another person's life was quite another. Moira recognised the bossy streak in herself and was surprised that more often than not she got away with it. Her justification was that being assertive had got her where she was today.

It was little wonder that Jenny had been so over-whelmed. First by her new status and then finding the house that had been in Paul's name was now in hers. Moira had thought she looked alarmed and a little frightened. In spite of her disclaimers to the contrary, was Jenny afraid of her husband? Many women were afraid of their partners. Was she worried about what he would say when he found out? No man likes to be made to look a fool and Paul would not be easily convinced that Jenny had known nothing of what was going on. Would she be able to stand up to her husband after all the years of docile acceptance? Whether it was the case or not it made little difference.

What was done was done.

The balance of power had shifted or was beginning to if only Jenny could see it that way. It was unlikely she would refuse her husband entry into what was now her house but the choice was hers. Moira thought about the house keys. Paul would have his set and might not be prepared to surrender them. He could always say he had mislaid them. Far better if Jenny changed the locks, that would solve the problem. She would suggest it but not right away.

Moira was trying to put herself in Jenny's position and wonder how she would feel. Grateful on the one hand and deeply resentful on the other. Resentful because her life was being arranged for her without her having any say in the matter. Moira didn't dwell too long on that. If Jenny was upset she would get over it and see that it was all in her own interests. From now on her life would be a lot easier. There would be security for her and the girls. And as for herself she had got what she wanted. Jenny was intelligent, quietly efficient and with an eye for display. She was also blessed with patience. Together with those qualities she was well liked and there was no danger of her new status going to her head. Moira already thought of her as a friend.

Forty minutes later Moira drove into a quiet cul-de-sac of Victorian houses that provided an oasis of peace and tranquillity yet were no more than a few miles from the busy and picturesque city of Perth. On the death of her parents and her sister, everything including the house where she had been born had come to Moira. Well-meaning friends advised her at the time of her mother's death to sell the house and look for something smaller and easier to manage. It had seemed like good advice and Moira had gone to see several houses in the same area since she didn't want to move too far away, only to return to her own house with a sigh of relief. This was home and always would be, she couldn't see herself settling anywhere else. How could she bear to part with the heavy handsome furniture in High Oak House. It belonged there just as she did. In a modern house such furniture would be over-powering and completely out of place. The rooms were too small and the ceilings too low.

Moira Ramsay had always been interested in antiques and had seriously considered studying the subject and perhaps one day opening her own business. It had not happened but one of her great pleasures was visiting antique shops and searching for the unusual.

Over the years she had made some changes to her home. It was possible to add modern comforts and marry those with the old, she found. It was a question of care and attention to detail. The downstairs floor coverings were worn and had been replaced with Wilton carpet. The heavy brocade curtains in the drawing-room came down and in their place went deep blue velvet ones, floor-length and rich-looking. For the dining-room Moira had chosen dull red velvet. The cluttered look that had been there in her mother's time disappeared when Moira removed the small tables and footstools from the drawing-room. They sold quickly and for a good price.

All the rooms were beautifully proportioned and the drawing-room had particularly lovely cornices. Large though it was Moira still used it when she was on her own. Regency bookcases filled with leather-bound books graced one complete wall. Against another was a display cabinet holding exquisite china and sparkling crystal. Valuable figurines had a glass case to themselves. The wide sofa, softly cushioned, faced the fire with matching armchairs on either side. There had always been a live-in housekeeper at High Oak House but once Mrs McDonald retired and left to make her home with a relative, Moira Ramsay decided she would prefer someone to come in daily. She advertised and a Mrs Stephen applied and was given the post. She proved to be entirely satisfactory since she was quiet, methodical, hard-working and honest. Moira paid her well but she was worth every penny since it allowed her to go about her own business knowing her house was in good hands.

The weather was bitterly cold but both girls were wearing warm coats, scarves and gloves. On their feet were shiny black wellington boots and inside those was a pair of old woollen socks. Evelyn Bannerman, Wilma's school friend, was eating a caramel and chewing it as though her life depended on it.

'Want one?' She held out the bag.

'Thanks.' Wilma took one, put down her bulging satchel and began to unwrap the paper. 'Toffee is bad for your teeth,' she said after popping it into her mouth.

'Who says?'

'My gran for one. Anything you enjoy and you can be sure it will be bad for you.'

'Mine is a bit like that, always looking on the gloomy side. Born pessimist. She hasn't got any teeth, just false ones.' Evelyn grinned. 'Know what she says?'

'How could I?'

'She says the benefit of having false teeth is you never suffer from toothache, all you have to do is take them out.'

That struck them both as being hilariously funny and they went into gales of laughter.

'Jonathan Turnbull lives near you, doesn't he?' Evelyn said when the laughter ceased.

'Next door. Why?'

'Nothing.'

'Must be something or you wouldn't have asked.'

'Not really. I just think he's nice, don't you?'

'He's all right I suppose.'

'A lot more than all right.' Evelyn rolled her eyes.

Wilma looked aghast. 'Don't tell me you've got a crush on Jonathan Turnbull,' she all but screeched.

'What if I have,' Evelyn said and began to poke about in her mouth. 'Hate it when I get a piece of toffee stuck between my teeth.' She poked some more until she had dislodged it. 'That's better.' Evelyn licked her finger then took out her woollen gloves from her coat pocket and put them on. 'You've got to admit that Jonathan Turnbull is nice-looking and I'm not the only who thinks so.' She paused. 'Don't you like him?' she added curiously.

'I neither like nor dislike Jonathan Turnbull, I never thought about it, you don't when someone lives next door to you.'

'I would.'

'Oh, you would, I know that, you're boy daft.'

'I am not.'

'Yes, you are, any boy we talk to and you simper. It's sickening.'

'I do not and if I did it's better than acting all hoity-toity.'

'I do not,' she said outraged.

They walked a bit apart and in a huffy silence.

Wilma was finding it disturbing hearing Evelyn talking about Jonathan. She thought she must have a good look at Jonathan when next she saw him. If the others thought he was special then maybe he was and she hadn't noticed. Or had she noticed without it actually registering? Her mother had thought Jonathan was smartening up and that could be because he was suddenly taking an interest in girls her mother had said and she had thought that a stupid thing to say and typical of her mother.

'Are we speaking again?'

'Expect so,' Wilma mumbled.

'I'm bored if you want to know and I think I'll be glad when the summer holidays are here and I can leave school.'

'I'm staying on,' Wilma said shaking one gloved hand to get some warmth.

'Since when? It isn't long since you told me you were definitely leaving.'

'I've changed my mind, I can do that can't I?'

'Why do you want to stay on?'

'I can sit my Highers and if I get good grades it will help me to get a better job.'

'Doing what?'

'Don't you ever listen, I told you ages ago I want to be a journalist.'

'I know you told me that. A reporter was what you actually said and let me remind you that you said you could be it without staying on at school. So there.'

'I did say it, you didn't require to remind me and it is possible but not very probable. As a matter of fact my mum's boss advised me to stay on.'

'She doesn't count, what does your mum say?'

'She says I can be anything I want to be.'

'Is that what your dad says as well?'

'No, he thinks I should go in for teaching. He's always saying I'd be silly not to. I think he's got teaching on the brain.'

'I wouldn't like to be a teacher. Think of all the names we call ours.'

'They don't know and what you don't know can't harm you. Another pearl of wisdom from my gran, she's full of them.' Evelyn sighed. 'I'm not staying on just because you are.'

'I didn't expect you to.'

'My parents think staying on would be a waste. They want me to do a year at business college, then I should get a good job in an office.'

'Is that what you want?'

Evelyn shrugged. 'As long as there is a pay packet at the end of the week I'm not bothered. Dad says it will only be for a few years then I'll get married and be off their hands. My dad is all for me finding a rich husband.'

'You wouldn't marry someone old and ugly just because he was rich?'

'Not old and ugly but maybe one or the other wouldn't be too bad if he was a millionaire that is to say.' She looked at Wilma's face. 'My dad was only kidding you know.'

'Think I'm daft, I know that, you dope. I'm not supposed to tell anyone this.'

'Whatever it is I won't utter a word.'

'After a while it won't matter but Mum is really, really excited.'

'About what and hurry up, my bus will be along any time. Why is she excited? There's always something happening in your family.' She sounded disgruntled.

'Like what?'

'Like your dad going off with another woman.'

'That wasn't exciting, if you want to know it was just awful.'

'I thought Vera was supposed to be very nice.'

'So she is but it was better when Dad was at home and we were a real family.'

'If he got tired of Vera or she of him would your mother have him back?'

Wilma took her time before answering. 'She would say no to begin with, well what would you expect? She has some pride.'

'After a while she would?'

'I think so but not, of course, if they got divorced.'

Evelyn was kept up-to-date with events. 'Your mum refused.'

'Yes, she did refuse but she's changed her mind and says Dad can have a divorce and guess what?'

Evelyn shook her head.

'Dad and Vera don't seem too keen to go ahead. They like things as they are. That's your bus coming. Are you going to take it or wait for the next?'

'If you do the same or will Katy be waiting?'

'She'll go home by herself and tell Mum I've missed the bus.'

'Better walk about my feet are getting cold.'

'Come on we've time to go round the block.' They began walking.

'I was telling you about the promotion but I think I've got the wrong word. Miss Ramsay, she's the boss, has made my mum her business partner and before you ask I'll tell you what that means. It means doing some of the buying and making important decisions.'

'That's good. Does that mean a rise – you know more money?'

'Of course. You can't expect someone to do something important like buying and not pay them more.'

'Suppose not.' They walked on. 'That's great about your mum, she can call herself a buyer now.' Evelyn was impressed. 'I forgot to tell you my mum and my Aunt Violet spent an afternoon at the Log Cabin and they said it was much better than they expected.'

'What did they expect?'

'Well, of course, they expected it to be nice but it was better than that. My mum was going to introduce herself to your mum but she didn't like and anyway the place was busy.'

'This isn't a busy time, must have been a coach tour or something like that,' she said off-handedly.

'Could be I suppose.'

'She should have spoken, my mum would have been pleased.'

Evelyn nodded. 'That's what I said. She'll do it if they ever go back. All the same that's great news about your mum and my Aunt Violet, my dad says she's a right know-all, says she can see the Log Cabin becoming a wee gold mine.'

'I don't know so much about that,' Wilma said but she was smiling and looking pleased.

'All right for some,' Evelyn said gloomily.

'Comfortably off will do for my mum, she wouldn't want to be rich.'

'She's only saying that,' Evelyn said scornfully, 'everybody wants to be rich.' She swopped her satchel to the other hand. 'Bet your dad wouldn't like it if your mum started to earn more than he does. Stands to reason, men don't like it you know.'

'Maybe my dad wouldn't but that isn't likely to happen. My dad has a very good salary.'

'Why do you call it salary and not wages? My dad always speaks about his wages.'

'I'm not absolutely certain but I think wages are paid weekly and salaries once a month. If you are salaried I think you get more.'

'That's not fair,' Evelyn said indignantly, 'your dad is an accountant and that might be important but not as important as my dad's job. If he didn't stoke the fires the engine wouldn't move and the railway would come to a standstill.'

'You told me a lie, Evelyn Bannerman, you said your dad was going to be an engine driver.'

'I did not. You should clean out your ears. What I did say was that he was hoping to train as a driver – that's funny what I said. Did you get it?'

'I got it before you – train and driver. Ha! Ha!' Wilma was wishing she hadn't suggested waiting for a later bus, the conversation wasn't going her way. A fireman or stoker working on the railway didn't sound all that marvellous but an engine driver did, especially a driver of a passenger train. Fancy being in charge of a whole train! If it was to happen and Mr Bannerman got to be an engine driver Evelyn would be impossible. The whole school might get to know. By that time though Evelyn could be in business school and they would both be looking for a new best friend. That was a bit sad. Evelyn could be a real pain sometimes but they were used to each other.

Jenny stood in the middle of the sitting-room floor and looked about her feeling the pride of ownership. I can do exactly as I please, she thought and that has to be a first for me. The gilt mirror above the fireplace would come down and go in the hall. Wilma could titivate there without putting herself in danger. In fact she would take it down this very day and give herself peace of mind. Wilma had been warned time and time again about the danger of using the mirror but she still went on doing so. Jenny had seen her elder daughter checking her appearance and her skirt all but brushing the fire. Paul hadn't seen the danger and said she was fussing over nothing.

She looked at the furniture. Would Paul want any of it? Jenny thought not. Miss Cuthbertson wouldn't give it house room and Jenny would hardly blame her for that. When it came down to dividing the wedding gifts, most had come from her side of the family but she wouldn't be greedy, Paul could have his pick. She was already looking forward to a time when she could redecorate and furnish to her own taste. The money she had in the bank for a rainy day could be spent. She would allow herself that. Jenny liked to visualise the new-look sitting-room. Nothing too striking, she would aim for a room of quiet good taste. Something one could go on living with and never grow tired. The walls would be plain with a good quality wallpaper. That would show off the paintings she would buy. Jenny had promised herself when she could afford it, to buy two paintings from the Gallery. She liked and got on well with the young artists and did her best to encourage them. When they made a sale her pleasure was almost as great as their own.

Wilma and Katy would get a free hand to choose the

paper and paint for their own bedrooms. No matter how awful that might be she would make no comment. They would have to live with it and it could be a lesson for the future.

Paul had said he would come over today but would phone her before leaving. Jenny was nervously excited about breaking the news and needing something to occupy her time, she set about packing the rest of Paul's belongings. She had two strong cardboard boxes to hand which should take care of everything. There were books, some from Paul's schooldays and those she put at the bottom of one of the boxes. A pair of brown shoes, still good but requiring to be heeled and a pair of worn leather slippers joined the books. Paul had taken only the best of his clothes and hadn't bothered to return for the rest. Jenny folded up what was there which included underwear and socks, the socks she put one in to the other to avoid getting them mixed up. Paul could never differentiate between black and navy. Using a strong piece of cord she tied up the boxes, carried them into the hall and left them beside the telephone for him to uplift.

Although she had been expecting it, the sudden shrill ringing of the telephone startled her into spilling the coffee she had just poured. With a shaking hand she put the cup down on the saucer and took a deep breath. Her throat had gone dry the way it did when faced with an ordeal. This should not be an ordeal but it was. Anger at her own stupidity helped to calm her and she went into the hall to lift the phone.

'Hello.'

'Paul here, Jenny, would this be a good time to call? It shouldn't take long, just a few loose ends to be tied up.'

She wondered what those could be. 'Yes, quite convenient,' she said.

'Good. Have you got a cold?'

'No,'

'Thought you sounded hoarse. By the way, are you on your own?'

'Yes.' Had he thought her mother might be there?

'Fine. This is better between the two of us, no use involving anyone else.'

'I wouldn't dream of it, as you say this is between the two of us.'

'Expect me in about twenty minutes.' He rang off.

She stood there motionless then replaced the receiver. The moment of truth was close, the time to confess if that was the right word. It wasn't, she had done no wrong. Then why did she feel guilty? Because it made her appear underhand and in spite of everything Jenny didn't want her husband to think badly of her. His good opinion did matter. She wasn't prepared for the wave of desolation that washed over her and the lump in her throat was getting bigger.

In a short while every sign that Paul had once lived here would be gone. Belongings were easy to remove but what did one do about memories? How could you forget, just blot out, someone you had loved so much. A little of that love was left, would always remain. It was difficult to know what she felt when it was a mixture of so many emotions. The past kept intruding. Jenny was remembering that first meeting, the moment their eyes had met and the instant attraction. Then that first kiss, clumsy but so sweet and she had known then it was love and Paul had said it was the same for him. How could it have gone so wrong?

Would the day come when Paul would regret what he had done, the pain he had caused his wife and family and try to make amends? Jenny gave a small shake of her head. She didn't see that happening, it was just wishful thinking. They had both changed and there was no going back. There was no future for them just a past full of memories and those in time would fade.

Jenny wept for what had been then rushed upstairs to repair the damage to her face. When she came down she was composed.

Twenty minutes or thereabout after his phone call and Paul was ringing the bell of what had been his front door. He still had a set of keys though he had never made use of them. Unhurriedly, Jenny crossed the hall and opened the door. How well he looked, she thought. Her husband was one of the lucky ones who wouldn't age quickly and when in the fullness of time the years did begin to show it would only be a touch of grey at the temples and if he didn't exercise, a slight thickening of the figure.

'Come in,' she said putting a smile on her face, then turning away she left him to close the door and follow her.

'Ah, I see you've made a start on the packing.' He pointed to the boxes looking both pleased and relieved.

Jenny turned her head. 'No, I haven't. What is there belongs to you. I collected all your stuff together and that is the lot, I think.'

'Heavens! I don't want them. Vera hasn't room for anything else.'

'Then she'll have to find room.'

He frowned. 'Why this now? What is the immediate hurry?'

'I want rid of them, in other words I want them out of my way.'

'All in good time. I came to tell you that no date as yet has been set for vacating the house. Even so I strongly advise you to get a move on or you may be caught out and have to do things in a rush. Do we have to stand here?'

She didn't answer but went ahead into the sitting-room. The fire was quite low and she added a log. Then she sat down and Paul took his usual chair as though it was his by right. Jenny caught him looking around the room and thought he must be comparing the shabbiness of 16 Abbotsford Crescent with the elegance of the house where he now lived.

'Will you be taking all the furniture to wherever you are going?'

'Why, do you want some of it?'

'God! No! You're welcome to the lot.'

She thought he seemed a little ill-at-ease and his next words proved he was.

'Look Jenny, I don't like to see you getting yourself into a mess. In case you hadn't realised it, packing can take up a lot of time.'

'I imagine it would but it won't bother me since I'm not moving. I'm staying put.'

Paul looked at her with mounting concern. Had Jenny

taken leave of her senses? 'Don't be stupid and childish, Jenny, that attitude won't get you very far. And don't try to blame anyone, you brought this on yourself.' He crossed his long legs and sat forward. 'Tell you what,' his voice softened, 'I'll come over one evening and give you a hand.'

She looked at him in surprise. 'That was a kind offer.'

He smiled. 'I'm not all bad you know.'

'I never thought you were. As I said, it was kind and I am touched by the offer, Paul, but you won't have to put yourself about, it isn't necessary.' She thought it was time to tell him. 'Paul, brace yourself for a shock.'

'What kind of damned nonsense is this? I wish you would stop playing games.'

'This is no game, this is fact. There will be no packing done because I am not going anywhere. This is where I live and I shall continue to do so. No, don't interrupt. You see, Paul, the house is mine, I am the new owner.'

'How can – you're in a bad way.'

She laughed. 'Thanks very much and most certainly I am not in a bad way. Quite the opposite. You didn't know it but you or your solicitor sold the house to me. When I say me, of course, I mean someone acting on my behalf.'

His mouth fell open as slowly the truth began to sink in. She saw his look of incredulity, then his face turned an ugly red with anger.

'You – you would do that to me?' he spluttered.

'Why not, you did worse to me.'

His eyes bored into hers and for a moment Jenny felt threatened and instinctively moved back in her chair. She could see he was striving for control and when next he spoke his voice was dangerously quiet and she shivered. It would be unwise to let him know she was alarmed at his behaviour and it was her turn to fight for control. She was winning, Jenny felt almost calm.

'You owe me an explanation, I think,' he was saying.

'Wrong, Paul, I don't owe you anything but I am prepared to answer any questions you care to put to me.'

'How very kind,' he sneered.

'Why, I ask myself, are you so distressed? It doesn't make sense. No one forced you, you wanted to sell the house and you did. Everything was working out for you. I even recall you saying that you couldn't care less who got it just as long as you made a good profit from the deal.'

'Nevertheless you won't deny the suggestion to sell the house came from you in the first place?'

'No, why should I? The suggestion came from me and it was no more than that, a suggestion. Whether you took it further or not was entirely up to you. There was no pressure, none at all. To be perfectly honest I was very surprised when you did decide to test the market, as you called it, and even more surprised when you made the decision to sell.'

Paul's lips tightened, he had no answer to that. 'I wouldn't have believed you could be so devious.'

'It is not in my nature to be devious and you should know that as well as anyone.'

'That was then, this is now. You've changed.'

'Of course I have, how could I not change? Circumstances saw to that. You can believe it or not just as you please but I had no idea what was going on. My surprise, when I was told, was every bit as great as yours.'

His eyebrows shot up. 'You expect me to swallow that?'

'Why should I lie? And why have you got yourself into this state? You got what you wanted which was a very good offer for the house and one, you said, you couldn't refuse. Money is very important to you these days and not having to pay the mortgage was going to make life easier.'

'My financial affairs are no longer your business.'

'I can't recall a time when they were my business,' she said tartly. 'What possible difference does it make who bought the house?'

'A hell of a lot of difference.'

'How sad. It shows you in a very bad light. You should be happy to know that Wilma and Katy can stay where they are and not have their life turned upside down.' Her eyes met his. 'Is it possible that you would rather a stranger was taking possession. Yes, I believe you would. You would prefer that to seeing your wife and daughters—'

'Don't be ridiculous.'

'Sadly I don't think I am being ridiculous.' Jenny paused and moistened her lips. 'Incidentally you should know that Wilma was shocked and surprised to learn that you hadn't the decency to tell me yourself that the house was sold but left it to your secretary.'

'You are trying to blacken me in Wilma's eyes.'

'I don't need to, you are making a good job of that yourself,' she said swiftly.

Paul looked at his watch. 'Before I go I'd like to hear how you are going to keep up the payments. Don't expect me to help you out.'

'I wouldn't accept a penny of yours for myself. Your only responsibility is to Wilma and Katy.'

'Vera thought there was a man behind all this and it looks as though she is right.'

'That is the kind of remark I might have expected from your mistress.'

He winced. 'You don't have to call her that.'

'No, I don't, I could call her a lot worse but I won't.' Jenny smiled pleased with her performance so far. 'Your mistress is wrong as it happens. One day there might be someone and then again maybe not. Giving up my new-found freedom, my independence, could be too big a price.'

'The money is coming from somewhere and it isn't out of a waitress's wages.'

'I was never a waitress, Paul, though I am always willing to help during busy spells. Until very recently I was a shop assistant.'

'Not exactly a well-paid job.'

'I got a fair wage for what I was doing but my status has risen.' Jenny couldn't keep the edge of excitement from her voice.

'Your status has risen. Spare me that,' he said sarcastically. 'How many of a staff is there? Two, perhaps, and now you are senior assistant.'

'Sorry to spoil your bit of fun and this might take the smile off your face. Miss Ramsay has made me her business partner. She has sufficient faith in me to offer me the position which I was delighted to accept.'

'I don't believe you.' He did, Paul just didn't want to

believe it. 'Let me get this straight. One day you are a humble shop assistant and the next you are a partner in a growing concern. Pull the other one.'

'It is a growing concern as you say yourself. I have every right to be insulted by your remarks but I must try and remember that you only knew me as a wife, the mother of your children and a housekeeper. Miss Ramsay is a business woman to the tips of her fingers and not given to reckless decisions. She must have seen I had some potential. Whatever it was I am over the moon.'

Paul was shaking his head as though in total disbelief.

'The sale of the house would probably never have happened if Miss Ramsay hadn't thought I looked worried.'

'Worried about what?'

'What was to happen to us. Wilma, you see, mentioned that you were becoming concerned about Miss Cuthbertson's extravagance.'

'What nonsense.'

'I couldn't be sure that it was nonsense. My eyes have been opened, Paul, and I was fairly sure that if money became a problem I would be the first to know about it. Then I began to wonder about the house, the roof over our head. I couldn't see you selling it but then again I couldn't be sure that you wouldn't. In the event I was proved right.'

Paul had another look at his watch. 'I'm late, I expected to be away from here long before this.' He got up.

'Rather more to talk about than you expected. Don't go without the boxes.'

'I haven't time to be bothered with those,' he said irritably.

245

'I took the time and trouble to get them ready and don't worry they are securely tied.'

'I don't want them,' he said his voice rising.

'Neither do I. Kindly take them out of my way.'

'Let me repeat myself, I don't want that rubbish.'

'Then carry that rubbish out to the dustbin. You should remember where it is. If you don't remove them I'll put them there myself.'

His lips tightened as he lifted one box and went down with it to the car. Then he came back for the other.

'Paul?'

'What?'

'The keys of the house, you have a set and I would like to have them.'

'I don't have them with me, in fact I don't know where they are.'

'It doesn't matter, I'll get new locks put on the doors.'

They looked at each other, a long look and he was the first to look away.

'Goodbye, Paul,' she said gently.

He didn't answer or perhaps he mumbled something she didn't catch. Then he was gone.

Chapter Fifteen

———◆———

Paul was desperate to share the news with Vera and after
dropping the car keys on the hall table he quickly opened
the door to find her sitting well forward in one of the deep-
cushioned chairs that Wilma so loved. An open bottle of
crimson nail polish was on the glass-topped table brought
up close to the chair. For a split second, Paul compared the
room with the one he had just left and surprised himself by
thinking how much more comfortable 16 Abbotsford
Crescent was than the high style that now surrounded
him. He never felt completely at ease in the cottage and
had frequently to remind himself that it was Vera's and the
setting was right for her. There was always a price to pay for
happiness but surely this was a small one. At the sound of
the door opening, Vera glanced up then carried on with
painting her fingernails.

'You've taken your time, darling,' she drawled, 'I
thought you said you weren't going to be long.' There
was no censure in her voice, Vera wasn't complaining, it
was a pleasant change having the cottage to herself. Paul
was becoming tiresome of late and she was becoming
restless. Perhaps she had been long enough in this job

and should be considering a move. When it came to money Paul was too careful, bordering on the mean, and he had taken to lecturing her on the need to save. Not that it did any good, Vera had her own philosophy which was to spend today and let tomorrow take care of itself. Why save for a time, she argued, when they would be too old to enjoy themselves. It was the present that was important.

'So did I,' he said answering her question. 'God! I still can't believe it.'

Vera lifted her eyes and gave him a long, cool look. 'I can see something has happened. Poor darling, you look as though you've had a bad shock.'

'Believe me I have, I'm still reeling from it.'

Paul didn't sit down but instead began to pace the floor to Vera's annoyance.

'Must you?'

'What?'

'Do that. How can I keep this brush steady with you pacing the floor like a caged animal. If I make a mess of this I'll have to start again.' Her head went down and the tip of her tongue protruded as she concentrated.

'Sorry.' Paul sat down as though defeated. He smoked only the occasional cigarette which was just as well since Vera strongly objected to the smell of cigarettes. She had never taken up the habit herself and couldn't understand the craving others had for the weed. Right now he could have done with one.

'I'll just be a few more minutes, dearest, let me finish then you'll have my undivided attention.'

Paul felt irritated that something as important as the news

he had to impart should take second place to her wretched nails. He didn't like bright, crimson nails and in particular long, crimson nails. They made him think of claws dripping with blood. The paler shades were more to his liking. Some time later she held out both hands, the fingers splayed, to admire the result. Satisfied, the tiny brush was replaced and the cap on the bottle secured. That done she sat back in the chair and stretched her stockinged feet towards the electric fire.

Jenny, he was remembering, had never gone about the house without wearing shoes or slippers. Vera did. Once in the cottage the first thing she did was to kick off her shoes. She said it was relaxing and that chiropodists, who should know, recommended it. Toes needed freedom after hours of being squashed into narrow, high-heeled shoes.

Vera was taking great care not to touch anything in case her nails got damaged. For the moment she seemed to have forgotten that Paul had something important to say. He became increasingly annoyed and, feeling he couldn't sit a moment longer, jumped to his feet.

'I need a drink. How about you, darling, can I get you your usual?'

'No, thanks.'

'Quite sure?'

'Quite sure, but do have one yourself, you obviously need it.'

'I do.' Paul crossed the room and opened the cupboard of the sideboard where the glasses were kept. Then glass in hand he went to the kitchen to find the whisky bottle and poured himself a generous measure. He took his first mouthful where he was standing and found the fiery, amber liquid begin to do its work and calm him down. With the glass held between finger and thumb, Paul went to join Vera. He had already removed his jacket but even in shirt sleeves the room was too warm for him. Vera was very proud of her electric fire with its flame effect and the lovely surround of polished wood. Paul agreed that it looked very attractive and that it did send out immediate heat. It also saved work which was important but for Paul it could never take the place of a brightly burning coal fire. Jenny had never complained about the work involved but he must remember his wife, when he was there, had been home all day and had the time. Vera didn't. She worked full time as she wasn't slow to remind him when it came to allocating the chores.

In his mixed up state of mind, Paul was no longer sure that selling 16 Abbotsford Crescent had been such a good idea after all and in fact he found himself regretting it. The advantages were not as great as he had at first thought. Not having to pay the mortgage on the house wouldn't make such a huge difference and the profit made on the transaction would not for long remain in the bank. Vera didn't plan for the future, she lived for the present. Sometimes he made a half-hearted attempt to get her to curb her passion for spending but even as he spoke the words he knew it was hopeless.

Was it just the sale of the house that depressed him? Would he have had the same regrets, he wondered, if his home had gone to a stranger? The answer was no. It was shameful of him to be so small-minded but he couldn't help it. Paul hated the idea of Jenny owning the house they had once shared. It had seemed to him like theft. He was being stupid and knew it. Jenny should still need him, still want him, but that no longer was the case. His wife, thank you very much, was doing very well for herself, too well, he thought sourly. Would she really have thrown away his belongings, those two cardboard boxes? Too true she would. There had been that look, a new one for Jenny, that showed she wasn't to be messed about with. Take them with you or they go in the bin, the rubbish bin, was what she had said. The cheek of her.

'Darling, I'm ready and waiting, you can tell me now.' Aware that he was annoyed, Vera gave him a particularly loving smile.

'Who do you think has bought the house?'

'Silly question, how could I possibly answer that.'

'Have a guess then.'

'I'm not in the mood for guessing games.' She was beginning to show impatience. 'Just tell me who has bought your house.'

'Jenny has.'

'You have to be joking.'

'Only wish I were but I'm not.'

'Paul, there has to be some mistake. How could Jenny afford to buy the house?'

'Good question, I asked that too.'

Vera frowned. 'You had no idea what was going on?'

'Absolutely not.'

'How on earth did your wife manage to fool you?' She smiled grimly. 'I've been proved right. Haven't I said all along that there was a cunning streak but you wouldn't have it?'

Paul found himself defending Jenny. He had accused his wife to her face that she had been devious but in his heart of hearts he knew that not to be true.

'Jenny is not devious.'

'You can't know that.'

'People don't change that much, Vera.'

'Wrong, Paul, people do change, they change all the time.'

'Not Jenny.'

'Yes, Jenny. When you walked out on your wife she became a different person. It stands to reason, Paul. The woman had to if she was going to survive. Remember you were the one who made the decisions and she the one who carried them out.' Vera paused and went on in a quiet voice. 'For the first time, Paul, she was making the decisions and that for her must have been terrifying. Then as time went on it got easier until she thought nothing of it.'

'I had walked out, yes, but I hadn't deserted her. I was a phone call away that is all and Jenny knew that.'

'I would have said you deserted her completely and I believe Jenny would have thought that too. You will recall at the start that you were pushing for a divorce and that has to be final.'

'That no longer applies.'

'The difference between then and now is that we wanted a divorce at the beginning and she refused. Now she is the one who wants to make the separation permanent.'

'So where does that leave us?' He smiled ruefully.

'I have no idea. What I am fairly sure about, however, is that Jenny has someone, a man, who is looking after her interests.'

'No, Vera, not a man.'

'You know something I don't?' Her eyebrows shot up.

'Jenny said her surprise was as great as mine when she heard that the house was hers.'

'Don't tell me you believed her?'

'I took a bit of persuading but in the end I accepted what she said.'

Vera was looking puzzled. 'Presumably this has to do with the solicitor not divulging the identity of the new owner. You did say that secrecy has surrounded it from the start.'

'Not unusual for that to happen, darling, and that I assure you didn't give me a thought.'

'Let me try and make sense of this. Jenny has no money. Jenny was as surprised as anyone to learn she was the owner of the house. The house went well beyond the asking price which would indicate that there was keen competition to get the property. Someone was determined to get it for Jenny and topped every offer made. Which makes it very clear that whoever was behind this is not short of money.'

'She isn't short of money.'

'Who isn't?'

'Jenny's employer, Miss Ramsay.'

'Really!' Vera drew out the word slowly and widened her eyes. 'This is becoming very interesting. Paul, tell me this – why would a successful businesswoman like Miss

Moira Ramsay, do that for a humble employee? A mere waitress in the tea room.'

'Jenny was engaged as a shop assistant not a waitress.'

'No matter, the wages wouldn't be all that different.'

'You underestimate Jenny, darling, she has a good brain when she takes the trouble to use it. I had expected her to take an office job but Jenny felt she had been away too long.'

'Are you telling me everything?'

'I'm trying to but I haven't as yet got it all sorted out in my own mind.'

'Think aloud. I'll only interrupt if I can't stop myself.'

'I imagine Wilma was the unwitting cause of all this with you playing your part though you didn't know it.'

'I certainly did not and I need that explained.'

'It just shows that a joke, a casual remark, can have unfortunate consequences.' He paused, aware that he would have to go carefully. 'Dearest, do you remember when we came back from that Paris shopping spree?' Paul was smiling in an attempt to make light of it.

'Heavens! That was ages ago and I would hardly describe it as a shopping spree.' She was frowning. 'A few dresses that was all. It was a chance to get something different when we were there. What on earth has that to do with Jenny and the house?'

'Nothing one would think. A jocular remark I apparently made about your extravagant tastes bankrupting me—'

'Joke or not that was a bit thick. My salary takes care of quite a lot you know.'

He could have said that most of it went on clothes, make-up and expensive hairdos. And she would have been ready with her reply that it was for his benefit. She dressed to please him as well as herself.

'Of course it does, I'm not complaining, darling, I'm only trying to explain how all this came about,' he said soothingly.

'Maybe I'm beginning to see the light.'

'I'm relieved one of us is.'

'Women grasp these things quickly whilst men are notoriously slow. Poor dears they need everything spelt out.' Vera drew in her long, shapely legs and tucked them under her in the wide chair. 'Of course, Jenny was worried, in her place I would have been too. She takes what Wilma said as gospel truth and immediately worries about her financial position. If money was to be tight then she and the girls would get less—'

'Jenny knows I wouldn't do that to Wilma and Katy.'

'Perhaps she did but she would see her own allowance disappearing and in the worst scenario, the house as well. It could be sold and Jenny and the girls would have had to find other accommodation.'

Paul showed his annoyance. 'What nonsense.'

'Is it, Paul? Isn't it exactly what has happened? You did put the house on the market.'

'You forget the suggestion about selling the house came from her. The idea had never crossed my mind.'

'And who put it there? I was wrong about a man being behind this. We now know it was this Miss Ramsay.' Vera puckered her brow. 'Why I keep asking myself, is a woman like Miss Moira Ramsay, going to all this bother and expense for an employee? What is so special about your wife?'

'Jenny would be a conscientious worker and completely trustworthy. She has a pleasant manner and put those together—'

'You mean not so many have those qualities in this day and age,' she said sarcastically.

'I might mean just that. Maybe the woman wanted to hang on to Jenny and saw this as a way to do it.'

'Possible I suppose but highly unlikely. This, my dear Paul, was a lot more than a helping hand to a valued employee.'

'Fair enough but it might be that Miss Ramsay wants to shed some of the responsibility for the Log Cabin—'

'And has no one close or at least no one suitable?'

'Just a suggestion. As well as being dependable Jenny can work on Saturdays now that the girls spend the day there. Wilma says Miss Ramsay is very generous to both of them.'

'We are getting nearer.'

'Pieces are still missing.' He was frowning. 'Jenny was adamant that she knew nothing of what was going on and I believe her, Vera, because my wife is no actress. If she told a lie her face would betray her.'

'Could be that Miss Ramsay knew that, hence the secrecy. For her own reasons she wants Jenny free from worry. Maybe she confided her fears to her boss. Whatever, Jenny's only part in this was to suggest to you that it might be a good idea to put the house on the market.'

'And I fell for it?'

'If you say so. Certainly you were sufficiently interested to want to know what the house would fetch. Jenny wasn't showing any particular interest herself.'

'No, she wasn't, she said it was entirely up to me.'

'Clever. Then she threw in a carrot, sell the house and she would agree to a divorce.' Vera paused. 'How is she going to find the money to meet the payments? Where is it coming from?'

'You haven't heard everything,' Paul said slowly.

'Oh, for goodness sake, Paul, you can be the absolute limit. Here am I wasting my brain power.'

'I'd forgotten about it myself until you mentioned money. Jenny told me she is no longer engaged as a shop assistant in the Log Cabin.'

'Then where is she working?'

'She hasn't moved. Wait for it – Miss Ramsay has made her a partner in the business.'

Vera was momentarily struck dumb, then she got to her feet, her face was flushed and she was looking agitated. 'I do not believe that, not for a single moment.'

'Happens to be true,' Paul said looking at her curiously. He hadn't expected such a reaction.

'How could something like that slip your memory?'

He shrugged.

'That drink you offered me I'll have it now.'

Paul was glad to have something to do to give her a chance to calm down. He got a glass from the sideboard and went to prepare her drink in the kitchen. This had been one hell of a day, he thought and he wished with all his heart that he had held on to his house. Why hadn't he thought it through? At the back of his mind he had always known he could return to 16 Abbotsford Crescent since it was in his name. He couldn't do that now. The uncomfortable truth was facing him, he would no longer be welcome. He felt deeply hurt that Jenny would go as far as have the locks changed. Paul went through to put the drink in front of his mistress.

'Thanks.' She was more composed though there were patches of red on the usually pale cheeks. Vera had experienced a blinding rage and a fierce jealousy that someone as ordinary and inexperienced in the business world as Jenny could have landed such a prize. No doubt Paul's wife would be on a good salary and in time entitled to a share of the profits. Vera's quick mind was leaping ahead. Repaying the money for the house would not be a problem. No doubt they had worked something out that made it easy. Paul, for all his intelligence, could be slow in the uptake. He didn't seem to realise what this new position of Jenny's meant. She did or had a good idea. Like Wilma's friend, Evelyn's Aunt Violet, she saw the Log Cabin as having a wonderful future. She didn't use the expression, little gold mine, but it was what she thought.

'No wonder you looked sick when you came in. Heavens! I wouldn't mind a share in that business, your wife has landed on her feet.'

'Don't get carried away. No business is secure and especially one that depends on tourists.'

'I totally disagree. Scotland attracts tourists and the Log Cabin pulls them in.'

'Maybe.' He felt dead tired.

'*You* have changed, Paul.'

'In what way?'

'Not so long ago you were congratulating yourself on having sold the house and making a substantial profit.'

'Not all that substantial when it had to be halved.'

'You knew that.'

'I wasn't going to sell at all,' he said grumpily.

'That is not true. The possibility was always there. From the very start, Paul, you said if the house didn't reach the asking price you wouldn't sell and that it would take a very good offer before you gave it serious consideration. Well, you got a very good offer and you took it which was very sensible.'

'Was it?'

'Yes, it was,' she snapped, 'such an offer wasn't likely to come again. That is not what is bugging you but I can tell you what is.'

'Go ahead.'

'You can't stomach the fact that Jenny is the new owner. Anyone else and it wouldn't have mattered. You liked to think of little Jenny in the background grateful for the crumbs offered.'

She'd got him on the raw and Paul felt his temper rise. 'To hear you, Vera, one would believe you cared about Jenny.'

'I don't, I scarcely ever give her a thought but whatever my faults, Paul, I am honest with myself. I feel positively sick that she's done so well for herself but I have to admire her too. Try to be generous and accept what you can't change and then we can get on with our lives.'

'You amaze me,' he said getting up from the chair to sit on the sofa. He patted the place beside him. 'Come on, darling, come and sit beside me.'

Vera smiled and with a slow, languid movement got up to join him.

'I've just had another thought,' she said as his arm drew her close.

'Don't you think it is time we gave the subject a rest?'

'Hear this first.' She paused to make herself more comfortable. 'Remember that time when Jenny came to serve us in the tea room? Now that to me was brave. Not many would have put themselves through what had to be an ordeal when all it needed was a quick word to someone and she could have disappeared behind the scenes until we'd gone. She didn't, Paul, she chose to face up to the situation.'

'She was prepared, we weren't.'

'Even so, there is more to her than I would have believed.'

He shook his head.

'Clearly Miss Ramsay must have been impressed.'

'Mmmm,' he said closing his eyes.

'On a sobering note, sleepyhead,' she gave him a poke, 'in a year or two your wife could be earning more than our two salaries put together.'

He groaned and pulled her close. Suddenly she was remembering the two boxes in her hall and moved out of his embrace.

'Those two boxes in the hall—'

'Can't they stay there for the time being?'

'No, they cannot, I won't have it. Please remember,' she said haughtily, 'that the cottage belongs to me and I do not like to see it cluttered.'

'Perhaps I should remind you that I pay for most of the household expenses.'

Paul held his breath. He was amazed that he had actually said that and Vera looked taken aback. It was a dangerous moment, their first ever near quarrel.

'Darling, I can't help it, things lying about upsets me.'

'I know. I'll open the boxes shortly and see what is there. No doubt some of it can be thrown out but there will be other things that mean something to me.'

'That was mean of Jenny to choose to do it now. She must be in a hurry to remove all traces of you.'

The words weren't meant to hurt but they did. He wanted Vera but Jenny should be there as well.

Vera began to laugh. 'Maybe Jenny is thanking her lucky stars that you walked out on her when you did.'

'Not funny.'

Chapter Sixteen

———◆———

Jenny put up the collar of her coat as the first few drops of rain began to fall and just wished the bus would come. The girls were going to a concert in the evening and Grace was coming round. Jenny and her next-door neighbour hadn't had a proper chat for what seemed like ages and there was a lot of catching up to do. It hadn't looked like rain when she left the Log Cabin and, of course, she had no umbrella. Her evening was carefully planned but it hadn't allowed for the late arrival of the bus. She hoped this wasn't going to be a long wait. No wonder there were complaints, she thought. This was a particularly unreliable route and those waiting at the stop had the long-suffering look of folk well used to delays. One or two kept moving out to peer into the distance to see if there was any sign of the bus coming. Jenny didn't bother, it wouldn't bring it any quicker. She was aware of the car slowing down and stopping but paid it little attention. Someone was going to be lucky enough to get a lift and only when she heard her name did she jerk to attention. The man had the passenger door open and was leaning out.

'It is Mrs Richardson?'

'Yes,' Jenny said going forward quickly.

'I'm going your way if you'd like a lift.'

'Yes, I would, thank you very much.' She got in, shut the door and the car moved off smoothly.

'The bus is late,' she said.

'Out-of-town buses very often are.'

Jenny didn't know the man's name which put her at a disadvantage. She thought she ought to put that right.

'You must forgive me, I know you have come to live in our area but I'm afraid I don't know your name.'

'Stewart Taylor and if you want to know how I happen to know yours, I overheard it in the newsagent's.'

'And you remembered?'

'Oh, yes, Mrs Richardson, I remembered,' he smiled.

Jenny found that she was remembering too. She had just paid her papers and was looking at the display of birthday cards for one suitable for her mother. Wilma and Katy would choose their own for their grandmother and pay for it out of their own money. Strangers stood out in Blackford and since the man was arranging to have the daily paper delivered he was obviously a newcomer. After paying for the card and before leaving the shop, Jenny made some remark to the assistant behind the counter and her smile included the stranger. She recalled him being quite tall, maybe five ten – Paul was six feet and she judged from his height – and of slim build. Now she could add to that a thin, clever face and with what looked like worry lines round the mouth. He had a good head of iron grey hair and if asked for his age she would have said middle or late forties.

'Are you and your wife quite settled in to your new home?'

'More or less. The boxes are all unpacked but as yet we haven't found a place for everything. Our old home was in Perth so we haven't come very far.'

'It takes time to get settled.'

'Yes.' He fell silent and Jenny thought that maybe he didn't want any more conversation. Paul had never been one for talking and driving.

'Mrs Richardson, I am aware that we are considered an odd couple, my wife and I. Although I don't as a rule broadcast our problems I would like to explain.'

'You don't need to,' Jenny said hurriedly.

'I know but I find I want to tell you.' He paused for a moment. 'Phyllis, my wife, had a nervous breakdown some years ago. It happened after our child, a boy, was stillborn.'

'That must have been very upsetting for you both,' Jenny said sympathetically.

'It was. We were heartbroken but life has to go on. Everybody, including the doctors, said to give it time. That and rest and she would be all right. They were wrong.'

'How very sad,' Jenny murmured and wondered how she would have coped if she had had to come through that.

'She does have spells when she is almost her old self and during those times she manages to cook the meals and look after the house. My sister-in-law, who is a widow has been marvellous and comes over as often as she can. Phyllis will go out with Beatrice after some persuasion but she won't venture out on her own.'

'Is that just lack of confidence?'

'That and the fear that she may wander off and get lost. The worry is that there is little or no warning. Something comes over her and she sinks into a depression and when my wife is like that she takes no interest in anyone or anything.'

Jenny felt there was nothing for her to say and waited for him to continue if he so wished.

After a few moments he continued. 'When that happens Phyllis has to go back into hospital.'

'Having to go into hospital, does that distress your wife?'

'No, not at all. She makes no fuss and it is as though she knows herself that she needs professional help and in hospital she gets that.'

'Can't be easy for you and then there is your work.'

'I'm lucky, I work for Harris the pharmaceutical company and provided I produce results—' He broke off to overtake a slow-moving vehicle and she finished the sentence for him.

'No one bothers about the hours you work?'

'Exactly. There you are, my life in a nutshell, Mrs Richardson, and I apologise if I've bored you. No one enjoys hearing about someone else's problems.'

'Wrong, we all need to unburden at times. You haven't bored me, far from it, what you have done is make me feel ashamed. I have a lot less to complain about than you yet from time to time I get a fit of the doldrums.'

He turned briefly to give her a smile. 'It doesn't show. What I see is a happy, contented person.'

'That might have applied before—'

'Before what?'

'Before my husband walked out on me and our two young daughters.'

His eyes were on the road but he was shaking his head.

'I couldn't imagine anyone wanting to leave you, Mrs Richardson.'

'Kind of you to say so but then you haven't seen my replacement. She's tall, blonde, slim and beautiful and as if that wasn't enough she is also highly intelligent.'

She was making light of it but even so she hadn't expected him to laugh and certainly not so heartily.

'Mrs Richardson, may I ask your first name?'

'Jenny.'

'May I use it?'

'Yes and you can tell me what is so funny. I tell you I've been deserted by my husband—'

'I do apologise but honestly I couldn't help myself, it was your description of your replacement as you called her.'

'I'm not exaggerating. My older daughter, Wilma, is quite bowled over by her.'

'That isn't so funny,' he said quietly, 'and deeply hurtful I imagine. I was laughing because you described the kind of woman I would run a mile from. I bet she is cold and unfeeling.' His voice softened. 'It won't last, Jenny, he'll tire of her and look back with longing to what he had and threw away.'

Jenny was shaking her head. 'No, Mr Taylor—'

'Stewart.'

'Stewart, Paul is besotted. You are probably right about the relationship not lasting but she will be the one to call it off. He'll know that, too, Paul is no fool.'

'He's all kinds of a fool but we'll leave it at that.'

Jenny was glad to get off the subject and surprised at herself for having spoken so freely to a stranger.

'Have you paid a visit to the Log Cabin?'

'Not as yet but I hear good reports.'

'That is where I am working.'

'In that case I will pay it a visit.'

Jenny gave a start, the time had gone so quickly and she was home.

'Slow down, Stewart, I wasn't paying attention.'

'Neither was I. Which road is yours?'

'The one you've just passed, Abbotsford Crescent. No, don't reverse, I'll get out here. Two minutes will take me to my door.' She had her hand on the handle.

'Are you sure? It would be no trouble.'

'This is fine and I'm very grateful for the lift.'

'My pleasure, thank you for your company.' He smiled, a warm smile that made her think he really had enjoyed her company. 'I hope we meet again very soon.'

Jenny didn't answer but maybe her smile answered for her. She liked him, she liked him very much. Stewart Taylor was easy to talk to and in that short space of time they had learnt a lot about each other.

'Goodbye and thanks again.' She walked away smartly. Her plans for the evening should go smoothly thanks to Stewart Taylor giving her a lift.

Once inside the house, Jenny hung up her coat and went through to see to the fire. She pushed the poker in. Once the red showed through the coal and dross she would remove it. In no time it would be a good going fire. Humming to herself she went into the kitchen to prepare the meal. Amazing how one's mood could change and all because a very pleasant man had taken the trouble to stop and offer her a lift home.

Grace arrived shortly after the girls had left for their concert. She came clutching a bottle.

'What on earth have you got there?' Jenny asked once the door was shut.

'Sherry,' she said showing the Bristol Cream label. 'I thought we should be good to ourselves.' Grace put the three-quarters filled bottle on the oval table which was one of the few pieces of furniture to have been bought new. 'The only time when we have a selection of drink in our house is at the New Year. And all that remains from the festive season is a half bottle of Johnnie Walker and this. Arthur doesn't touch the stuff, spirits I mean, but his brother makes up for him. His better half finished off the port. Port and lemon is her tipple.'

'I didn't know Arthur was teetotal.'

'Not completely, he likes the occasional glass of beer. The only time he takes whisky is when he feels a cold coming on and then it is bed, a hot water bottle and a strong toddy.'

Jenny looked at the sherry. 'Are we celebrating something?'

'I am if you're not.' She took off her coat and handed it to Jenny. Under it she wore a woollen dress in a pale rose pink that Jenny had admired before.

She sat down in the chair close to the fire and after hanging up the coat on the hallstand, Jenny returned to claim the other chair beside the fire.

'Of course we have something to celebrate. Honestly, Jenny, I'm just so relieved and happy to know you are not to be moving away from Abbotsford Crescent and I think it is marvellous about this job you have landed. If anyone deserved their luck it is you.'

'Grace, I've just been incredibly lucky. I know I am nothing special I just happened to be in the right place at the right time.'

'Maybe so, maybe you were in the right place at the right time but don't put yourself down. Someone saw that you had what was wanted.'

'Thank you.' Jenny thought this had been a good day for compliments.

'I have to say it about these houses, they are not difficult to heat. In the winter when the curtains are drawn like now they are really cosy.'

'My mother always says that. She finds it warmer here than in her own home. Mind you, Grace, she has only herself to blame. Half the heat goes out of those badly fitting windows. She needs new window frames but will she do anything about it, not her. Do me all my days is what she always says.'

'Maybe she can't be bothered.'

'I've offered to see to it but she won't allow me and I can't just go ahead without her permission.'

'No, perhaps not, old folk can be very stubborn. Maybe one day we'll be the same.'

'You know, I'm just remembering there is sherry in the house though I wouldn't like to say how long it has been there. Paul took the whisky.'

'Probably improves with age which is more than can be said for me. These days, Jenny, I'm scared to look too closely in the mirror in case I see yet another wrinkle. I do so hate the thought of growing old,' she said morosely.

'No one looks forward to it but if it will cheer you up let me say that I fail to see any signs of advancing age. You have nothing to fear, Grace, you are one of the lucky ones who will always look younger than their age.'

'That, my kind friend, is a load of rubbish. Good, you've brought the glasses.'

'Yes, and you can do the pouring.'

Grace poured the sherry until it reached the brim and handed a glass to Jenny.

'A bit full, you need a steady hand for this.' She took a small sip.

'Not so fast, this is a toast we are drinking. First, on you, Jenny, becoming the owner of this very desirable residence and second, on your promotion.'

Jenny giggled. Grace had risen and looked as though she were addressing a company.

'Thank you for your kind words.'

'To your continued success let us drink to that.' They touched glasses. Grace drank some of hers then put down her glass and sat down. 'Joking apart, Jenny, when you told me the house had been sold I felt positively sick and I could have wept. Then what joy, what relief, when you came round to tell me that you and the girls would not be moving after all. Arthur and Jonathan were all smiles when they heard. They didn't want new neighbours.'

'Bless them,' Jenny said softly. 'I did go through a worrying time myself not knowing what to expect. It was easy enough for Miss Ramsay to say not to worry but how could I not worry? I did trust her in so far as us not being without a roof over our head but it was the not knowing what to expect, what was ahead of us.'

'In your place I would have felt the same.'

'Later, once I was in the picture, I could understand the need for secrecy. Miss Ramsay was afraid I would give the show away and alert Paul to what was going on.'

'Which, let us face it, you might easily have done.'

'No question about it. Paul would have known something was up, he knows me too well. I would have tripped myself up.' She paused to sip her sherry. 'Grace, everything Miss Ramsay did was for my benefit yet I couldn't help feeling—'

'Used.'

'No, not used, more as though I was being manipulated like a puppet with my employer pulling the strings.'

'For all you know she was probably feeling very un-comfortable but decided the end justified the means.'

'Grace, you are right that was how she did feel.' Jenny smiled. 'Miss Ramsay apologised for putting me through all that but said it was in both our interests. In mine I could see that, but how could it have been in hers?'

'No matter how kind your boss might be she would still be looking after number one. Business people always do, if they didn't they wouldn't survive.'

'I'll go along with that but until a short time ago I was only a housewife. Miss Ramsay would have had no difficulty in getting someone with qualifications.'

'Possibly not but maybe she didn't want someone like that. A very efficient person might be inclined to throw her weight around whereas you won't.'

'True.'

'She will have thought it over very carefully and decided that you fitted the bill.'

'In what way?'

'I don't know but this is what I think. You, Jenny, are intelligent, you have a pleasant manner, you will give an opinion when it is wanted. In other words you will do as you are told and not cause trouble. Take that frown off your face I'm not finished. That said you won't be a push-over.'

'Not a weak character?'

'Most certainly not. Jenny, she wants you most of all because she can trust you.'

'I'll do my very best.'

'No one can do more,' she said draining her glass.

'I'll get the kettle on.'

'No hurry for that. We'll have another glass of sherry.'

'Not me, I never take more than one glass, Grace.'

'Neither do I come to think about it. This is a special occasion, we have an excuse.'

Grace was already refilling the glasses.

'I'll be light-headed.'

'Nonsense. No one ever got drunk on two sherries.'

'I'm not so sure.'

'You're happy and Miss Ramsay is happy but Paul must be feeling positively sick.'

'He was. He was really angry and that made me sad.'

'You thought he should be pleased?'

'I wouldn't go that far but I never imagined he would be so upset. He should have been happy that the three of us wouldn't have to move out of our home.'

'Maybe you are seeing the real Paul now.' She paused

and looked across at Jenny. 'Forgive me asking and it is none of my business but are you still in love with your husband?'

Jenny played with her glass before answering. 'I still love Paul but I am not in love with him. Does that make sense?'

'Frankly it does not.'

'I'll try and explain. You can't stop loving someone at will. Paul is a part of me, Grace, and although he would want to deny it, I must be a part of him. We had so much together and for a lot of the time we were happy. Maybe I was the more contented but I don't accept that he was unhappy. I'm talking too much.'

'No, you aren't. It is only to me and we know we can trust each other.'

Jenny nodded. 'I know that. Paul does love his daughters, we have that in common.'

'If Paul wanted to come back to you, would you have him?'

'No.'

'As sure as all that?' Grace sounded surprised.

'As sure as all that. The love I have left for Paul isn't enough.' She smiled sadly. 'Grace, I can't think of anything worse than living with someone you don't trust.'

'No second chances?'

'No. Do I sound very hard?'

'You sound very sensible.'

'Why did you look surprised?'

'I had a feeling you might weaken.'

'Would you if you were in my position?'

'If it was Arthur you mean?'

'Yes.'

'I'd murder him. Seriously, I'm not sure, Jenny. Maybe I would but it would never be the same again.'

'No fear of Arthur straying, he adores you and now I am going to see about the tea and I am light-headed.'

'Need any help?'

'No, thank you, I'll manage. Everything is ready. The sandwiches are mine and so are the scones but the cakes are by courtesy of the Log Cabin.'

In a short time Jenny came through with the teapot and placed it beside the fire on the pottery tile left there for that purpose.

'This is nice we must do it more often,' Grace said as she helped herself to the dainty sandwiches. 'That is if you have the time.'

'I'll make time. Wilma thinks the woman is marvellous,' Jenny said abruptly. She finished her sandwich before continuing. 'A very serious Wilma informed me that she is not blind to Vera's faults – heavens, I had a job getting that name out but I managed – she accepts that the woman is selfish—'

'Good.'

'No, not so good. She is excused her faults because they are to be expected from someone with film star looks.'

'She has got it bad, Young girls can be so silly.'

'Don't I know it. On one occasion, I didn't tell you this, I got so mad hearing how wonderful that creature was that *I* told Wilma to pack her bag and go and live with her father and his mistress.'

'You didn't?' Grace said admiringly.

'I did. Mind you, after I said it I felt horribly guilty but I wasn't going to take it back.'

'I should think not. Good for you, Jenny, I'm glad you didn't apologise, there was nothing to apologise for. Wilma would have got a fright, she wouldn't have expected that.'

'She was shocked.'

'It wouldn't do the young lady any harm. Next time Jonathan tries my patience I'll tell him if he isn't satisfied he can go and find other accommodation.'

'Two hard-hearted Hannahs,' Jenny grinned.

'While on the subject of our youngsters, have you noticed the growing friendship between your Wilma and my Jonathan. Not so long ago they practically ignored one another.'

'I hadn't until Katy brought it to my attention. The poor wee lass isn't at all happy about it. She always considered Jonathan to be her property. I was told in confidence that when she was old enough she was going to marry Jonathan.'

Grace laughed. 'Let us hope it will be a long time before my son considers marriage. He would do well to keep his mind on his studies if he wants to qualify as an architect.' She smiled. 'Katy would be a lovely daughter-in-law and one never knows. Jonathan has always had a soft spot for her. I sometimes think she takes the place of the little sister we failed to give him. Arthur, too, is fond of Katy and I've heard him say that if we had been blessed with a daughter he would have wanted her to be like your Katy.'

Jenny was touched. 'Thank you, that was nice of Arthur to say that.' Jenny did feel enormously pleased. 'We all like to receive compliments but those for one's family most of all.'

'Enough about the family, you are entitled to a reward. Why don't you treat yourself?'

'To what?'

'Oh, I don't know, replenish your wardrobe perhaps. It's what I would do.'

'I will buy a few things but at the moment I am more interested in the house and before you say not before time—'

'I was going to say nothing of the kind.'

'There won't be money to burn, the house has to be paid for but isn't going to be the drain on my purse that it might have been. The difference being that I don't owe money to the building society, I owe it to Miss Ramsay and she isn't charging interest.'

Grace's eyebrows rose. 'Now that is what I would call generous.'

'Yes, I know, it is absolutely wonderful. It means the money I've saved can be spent on doing up the house, starting on this room. It's a mess.'

Grace looked about her. 'I don't see anything wrong with it.'

'Right with it, you mean, nothing matches.'

'Maybe things don't match but that isn't necessarily bad. This, I would say, has a charm all its own.'

Jenny threw her a look. 'My sitting-room is a disaster. Yours as you very well know is lovely. Everything matches or at least tones in.'

'Agreed, everything I have matches or tones in and I'm

bored with it. My sitting-room lacks character. I was careful where I should have been adventurous.'

'Don't tell me you are contemplating—'

'No, much as I would like to I wouldn't dare. Arthur would have a fit if I suggested refurnishing.'

'Quite right too, you've hardly had it any time. I'm determined so don't try to make me change my mind.'

'Wasted effort,' she smiled.

'Yes.' Jenny paused to add a log to the fire. 'Paul and I furnished this whole house from salerooms and second-hand shops. I might, just might, hang on to the display cabinet. I always thought it was a genuine bargain. What I will do is remove the clutter in it and display a few choice pieces.'

'Don't be impulsive and throw what you have away. One man's rubbish is another man's treasure, isn't that what they say?'

'Something like that. The unwanted today is the sought after tomorrow. Grace, I can't imagine anything of value lurking there but just to be on the safe side I'll pack them away in a box and shove it in the attic with the rest of the junk.'

'That would be sensible.'

'Maybe I've shown sense there but I have a horrible feeling I've done something I'm going to regret.'

'What have you done?'

'Given Wilma and Katy free rein to choose their wall-paper and paint for their bedrooms.'

Grace let her mouth fall open. 'Heavens, that was rash.'

'A moment of madness.'

'What if they choose colours that will make you violently ill? Like red and purple striped wallpaper.' She took a fit of the giggles.

Jenny shuddered. 'Don't, I can't go back on my word.'

'Maybe they will surprise you by having quiet good taste.'

'Not a chance. Wilma will see this as her way to shock and she may have some influence over Katy's choice.'

'You asked for it.'

'Don't remind me. If it turns out to be just awful I can avoid going into their rooms. They can't, they will have to live with their mistakes for at least two years.'

'An expensive one, too,' Jenny sighed. 'On a lighter note I got a lift home today. Glad of it as well since it saved me getting soaked waiting for the bus.'

'Anyone I know?'

'Stewart Taylor.'

'Who is Stewart Taylor when he is at home?'

'The new people, they bought that house—'

'Got you,' she said snapping her fingers. 'Heavens, Jenny, he's the other part of the mystery couple.'

'He's very nice.'

'Apparently the man is quite pleasant, I mean he always passes the time of day but his wife, if anyone approaches her, scuttles off like a scared rabbit.' Grace continued before Jenny could get a word in. 'Mrs Sievwright, you know the old woman in the next house, spoke over the wall. She was going to invite her new neighbour in for a cup of tea but she didn't get a chance. From what I gather the old lady was quite upset. Her new neighbour ignored her and went into her own house and shut the door.'

'Maybe it looked like rudeness, Grace, but it wouldn't be and probably Mr Taylor has explained to Mrs Sievwright by now. Stewart Taylor told me his wife had suffered a nervous breakdown. It happened after they had a stillborn son and she has never recovered. If anything she is getting worse.'

Grace looked annoyed. 'Why couldn't your good Samaritan have explained at the start. People, most people, are not unkind but they need to be told something like that.'

'Grace, be fair, men don't find it all that easy.'

'Maybe not,' she said reluctantly.

'Stewart said that there are times when she copes quite well and manages to cook a meal and keep the house tidy. What she won't do is venture out alone.'

'What about his job? How does he manage to hold one down? It can't be easy.'

'I wondered that too. He works with Harris the pharmaceutical company and I imagine his hours to be flexible.'

'Surely he has someone in to help?'

'His sister-in-law is there quite a lot. She is nearer to them now than she was when they lived in Perth.'

'I've seen him about the village. Quite nice-looking I thought.'

Jenny thought so too but didn't want to say. They had said enough about Stewart Taylor.

'Come on, don't stop there, I'm interested in our newcomer. After all this is a village and in time we all get to know each other.'

'I don't know everybody.'

'Neither do I but near enough,' she laughed. 'Don't you want to talk about him?' she said slyly.

'Not much more I can tell you.'

'You liked him and not just because he stopped to give you a lift.'

Jenny laughed. 'Grace, you don't give up do you?'

'Not if I think I'm being short-changed.'

'You aren't. There isn't much more to say. The man was aware that he and his wife were considered an odd couple. He wasn't looking for sympathy, he just wanted to put me in the picture.'

'So that you would tell the rest of us.'

'Possibly. Phyllis, that is her name, is in and out of hospital quite a lot. It doesn't upset her, or appear to, she has come to accept that she needs treatment and for that she has to go into hospital.'

'Not much of a life for either of them.'

'No, it can't be but I suppose he just accepts it and resigns himself. In sickness and in health isn't that what we promise?'

'True but not everyone remembers the vows they took.'

Jenny smiled sadly.

'Oh, heavens that was clumsy. Sorry, Jenny, I wasn't thinking.'

'Don't apologise for speaking the truth. Paul forgot his when it suited him.'

'Jenny, you are attracted to this Stewart Taylor.'

'No, I liked him that's all. Don't try and make something more of it.'

'I'm not. I think you are two people drawn together by a common need.'

'What rot. All this drawn together nonsense in the time it took for the car to travel from the Log Cabin to Abbotsford Crescent.'

'Haven't you heard of instant attraction?'

'For teenagers yes but not mature people like me. Stop it, Grace, I've had quite enough.'

'OK. Sorry if I'm embarrassing you.'

'You haven't, I'm just being silly. So much has happened to me in such a short time and I'm still coming to terms with it.'

'All the more reason why you have to be careful. Don't get involved. Does he know that you and Paul are separated?'

'Yes, it came out in the conversation.'

'Two lonely people.'

'I'm not.'

'You are when it comes to male company.'

'I'll get by without that.'

'If you have to, yes, but if a presentable man comes along and invites you out what then?'

'A refusal, what do you think?'

Grace's eyes went to the clock. 'I had no idea it was that time. The girls will soon be home and my two as well. No matter how substantial a meal they get before going off to a football match they are always starving when they arrive home. That was lovely – I enjoyed our evening and a chance to talk. And now if you wouldn't mind getting my coat.'

Chapter Seventeen

———◆———

Paul and Vera got up at seven o'clock on a weekday and breakfasted on fresh orange juice and a bowl of cereal followed by weak tea and lightly toasted bread. Although Paul found it insufficient to satisfy his needs he was reluctant to say so since in the early days he had assured Vera that a healthy, rather than a filling breakfast, was fine by him. What he had insisted and insisted on firmly, was a cooked breakfast at the weekend irrespective of how bad it might be for him. Paul was proud of his recently acquired skills with the frying pan which he had had to buy. He was able to produce a hugely satisfying breakfast consisting of rashers of crispy bacon, sausages cooked to perfection and two eggs, sunny side up with their yolks unbroken.

While Paul upped his intake at the weekends, Vera reduced hers. He sat in the kitchen and Vera, who couldn't stand the sight of a cooked breakfast, set a corner of the dining table and sat down to a glass of orange juice and fingers of toast with a scraping of butter. There was no cereal on a Saturday or Sunday.

Paul always cleared the breakfast table and cleaned the kitchen. He did the washing-up and left the dishes to dry on the rack. Vera said it was more hygienic. She didn't approve of dish towels and had given a shudder as she explained to him that dish towels were a harbour for germs and the cause of a great many illnesses, chiefly among them being stomach upsets. Paul accepted all she said but it didn't stop him from wondering how he and those close to him had survived all those years. They had been remarkably healthy. In his mother's time and later with Jenny, he recalled that dishes were washed in hot water with some kind of liquid squeezed in it to make it soapy. A fresh dish towel did the drying. Jenny's ways were a bit like his late mother's and, of course, Jenny's own mother. As soon as the family had finished eating and sometimes before they had, Paul recalled occasions when he had had to hang on to his cup to save it being whipped away in the hurry to get the table cleared. No matter how pushed for time everything had to be cleared away, washed, dried and put out of sight. Vera didn't hold with any of that. She was a modern woman with modern ideas. One had to accept change, one should welcome it and move with the times. It was a favourite saying of Vera's.

While Paul attended to his chores in the kitchen, Vera made the bed and gave a quick flick round with the duster. The cottage got a proper clean at the weekend. For those not very onerous tasks Vera wore an attractive housecoat and Paul wore his second best dressing-gown. His other had been a gift from Vera when they were in Paris and was kept for lounging about in the evenings while they had a drink and listened to the wireless or more often to Vera's collection of records.

Paul used the long mirror on the wardrobe door to adjust the knot of his tie and to check his appearance. Vera's dressing-table held a neat row of jars and pots of various creams that promised, if used regularly, to give a wrinkle-free future. Vera was blessed with a lovely skin that needed very little make-up, she knew it wouldn't always be that way and to keep her skin young looking for as long as possible she was prepared to buy expensive creams and lotions.

For the office, Vera preferred to look businesslike as well as elegant and the well-tailored grey pinstripe costume with its neat jacket and straight skirt with a small inverted pleat at the back was perfect. She took a last critical look at herself then picked up her black patent handbag.

'Ready, dearest?' Paul said dangling his car keys from his finger.

'I think so.'

Neither of them spoke until they were inside the car.

'Darling, you are remembering the girls are coming this Sunday?' Paul said as he switched on and set the car in motion.

'I hadn't forgotten, but you will have to count me out.'

'Count you out? Why?' he said turning his head to show his surprise.

She frowned. 'Because it just so happens, Paul, that I have another engagement which I mean to keep.'

'Fair enough but if you had only said the girls could easily have changed to another day. Still, no problem, a phone call will take care of that.'

'No, Paul,' she said very firmly, 'keep the arrangements as they are.'

'May I ask where you are going?'

'If you must know, Mavis Ingram has invited me to lunch at the Queen's Hotel and after that she is taking me to see her new home. Her husband, as I think I told you, is in the navy and for a lot of the time Mavis is on her own.'

Maybe she had mentioned it but he couldn't recall. 'I see,' he said in a clipped voice.

'I don't think you do. This is not just any old lunch, Paul, this is special. One of the top stores is showing the new season's fashions.'

His lips tightened. It was beginning to irritate him how much importance she put into studying the next fashion craze.

'On a Sunday?' He sounded incredulous and that put her back up.

'Yes, Paul, on a Sunday. No one is doing anything outrageous you know.'

'I wasn't suggesting anything of the sort. Sunday seemed to me a strange day for a fashion show, that's all.'

'Not at all, you are well behind the times. It is the one day when women have more time. This is the new approach to showing clothes and it is completely different from the catwalk. Lunch is served and while it is being eaten models walk around the tables displaying the fashions or rather showing them. That way one gets a much closer look.'

'Wilma and Katy are going to be very disappointed.' Paul didn't add that he would be disappointed too. The fear that she was drifting away from him was growing stronger.

Vera was growing increasingly annoyed and was not too successful at hiding it. Paul was expecting too much. She after all was the one, not him, who had to entertain his two daughters. To begin with Vera had enjoyed Wilma's open admiration and the way she hung on to her every word. Now it had become tedious. The younger one didn't have a lot to say for herself. Probably she was bored and Vera suspected she was relieved when the visit came to an end.

'Your daughters will just have to be disappointed then.'

'Poor kids, they don't get a lot from us. A few hours once a month is all it amounts to.'

'I don't recall you making any objections when that was arranged.' The windscreen was misting over and finding the cloth she gave it a clean.

'That was because I felt it was what you wanted and what you want is important to me.'

'You do accept that I have done very well—'

'Of course you have, you have been wonderful with the girls. That is why you not being there will be such a disappointment to them.'

'I doubt it, they will enjoy having you to themselves.'

'No, that is where you are wrong. Once I've checked on their progress at school that's about it. I've nothing more to say.'

'A sad confession,' she laughed and he was relieved that her good humour appeared to be restored. Earlier in their relationship he hadn't needed to watch what he was saying. Now he had and the constant fear of doing or saying the wrong thing was like walking a tightrope.

'As you say, darling, a sad confession but it happens to be the truth.'

'The truth, Paul, if you would face it, is that you have become lazy and left it all to me. I didn't find it easy having to entertain two schoolgirls. Not exactly my idea of fun I have to say. I did it for you.'

'I know you did and I'm grateful, but I didn't realise it had been such an effort.'

'Now you do.'

'Damn! What is that fool doing?'

'Taking evasive action I would have said,' Vera said coldly.

'My fault I suppose,' he said through clenched teeth.

'Yes, Paul, it was entirely your fault. If we are to arrive safely I suggest you give more attention to your driving.'

Paul swallowed whatever it was he wanted to say. He had been in the wrong. Better to slow down, he wasn't normally an aggressive driver. Paul adjusted his speed and gave himself time to cool down before he spoke.

'What you are telling me is that you don't care for Wilma and Katy?'

'Don't be so silly and childish,' she said witheringly, 'of course I don't dislike them. As a matter of fact I think I have been very generous with my time. There were a great many things I would rather have been doing.'

'Am I right in thinking that this is the end as far as you and the girls are concerned?' he said rather pompously.

'Yes, Paul. Finish it now rather than have it drag out.'

'What do I tell the girls? That you have better things to do with your time?'

'What you tell them is entirely up to you. Wilma will soon get over her disappointment and as for Katy I rather think she will be relieved. The poor child was bored for most of the time but did her best not to show it.'

The remainder of the journey passed in silence and in a short time they had arrived at the premises of Easton & Hutcheson. Paul parked in his usual place and before he had time to switch off, Vera had the passenger door open and with one graceful movement was stepping on to the gravel.

'I do wish the powers-that-be would get a firm to tarmac the parking area,' she said irritably, 'it wouldn't cost the earth. As it is, this stuff ruins shoes, particularly the heels. Why don't you suggest it?'

'Wouldn't do any good. A waste of money they would say. After all darling, I think you are the only one who complains.'

'That lot are so stupid they would put up with anything.'

'That lot as you call them don't have cars so they have no need to come round here.'

She smiled. 'Point taken.'

'And we men don't find it a hardship,' he said and wished he hadn't.

'All right no need to go on about it.'

They walked round to the front of the building and up the three steps to the main entrance. The reception desk was occupied and a few members of staff were lingering to talk. There was the sound of laughter. Vera knew she could expect only the coolest of good-mornings but it bothered her not a whit. The smiles were for Paul. Rightly or wrongly, the staff of Easton & Hutcheson blamed Vera for the break-up of Paul's marriage. Apart from that they didn't like Vera's arrogant manner and jealousy could have played its part. It was unfair they thought that someone should have it all. Beauty and brains. Women like that could get away with murder and men were putty in their hands. Paul, being the most presentable male, became the chosen victim. The fact that he was a married man with a family had been no great hindrance. Vera had little interest in the young, unattached male still finding his way and having to watch the pennies.

They all liked Jenny and agreed she hadn't stood a chance. Not once Vera Cuthbertson got her clutches into Paul. His wife, poor thing, was a pleasant-faced woman with a warm friendliness. Sadly heads didn't turn for Jenny the way they did for Vera.

Paul and Vera smiled to each other as they parted company in the corridor. She to go upstairs to her office and he to continue along the corridor to his. His secretary, Betty Morgan, looked up when the door opened and gave him a smile. She had been upset about Jenny but was careful not to show it. Paul was her boss and it was wise to remember that. He was considerate and that was important. All bosses weren't, some were impossible and, after all, his private life was his own affair. What Betty was noticing just of late was a look of strain on the handsome face. They were all agreed, the female staff, that Vera Cuthbertson would not be easy to live with. Perhaps there were times when he wished himself back with Jenny and the two girls. Maybe at the back of his mind had been the comforting thought that if this relationship fell through, Jenny would welcome him back. A secretary got to know rather a lot about her boss's private life. There was complete trust between Paul and Betty Morgan and Paul had no fear that anything of a confidential nature would go beyond the four walls of the office. Divorce, she knew, had been mentioned at the start but never since. At that time Jenny had refused to consider one and only when Paul was no longer interested, or had that been Vera — whatever it was or whoever had lost interest, Jenny had shown her hand and offered Paul a divorce when it suited her. Betty Morgan had smiled to herself. Jenny had surprised everyone. She hadn't wept and lamented or stormed into the office causing a scene. She had been dignified throughout. Jenny had faced up to life without Paul and was, by all accounts, doing very well for herself. Her employer at the Log Cabin where Jenny had been given some responsibility, had been marvellously supportive. The house was now in Jenny's name which gave her security which should have pleased Paul only it didn't. She couldn't remember ever seeing him so upset. Men were strange creatures, she had always thought so, not pleased unless they were top dog. She knew her boss well enough to know that he would never have abandoned his wife and family but he would want to be the one in charge. If Jenny had to be grateful to anyone it should be to him and not that Miss Ramsay. Jenny no longer needed her estranged husband and that for him was a bitter pill to swallow.

The pavements were dry and there was a pale sun showing when Paul drew up at 16 Abbotsford Crescent. He had no need to announce his arrival since the girls would have been watching for the car. Paul looked at the house that was no longer his and felt an overwhelming sense of sadness. That looked like new curtains at the window and the garden looked neat and tidy. Much nicer than it had ever been. Could it be that Jenny had someone coming in to do it? It looked that way. Was she paying for it or did she have an admirer who offered his services? He would get round to asking the girls, keeping it casual. The outside door opened and he caught a glimpse of Jenny before the girls spilled out and then the door was shut. To him it was like a slap in the face, although that was ridiculous. He hadn't bothered getting out of the car so what did he expect? That she would wave to him, a cheerful, friendly wave. Yes he had and been ready to return the wave. She had done it before only not recently.

There was a difference in Wilma and Katy. In the last few months they had both grown. Katy had lost a lot of her puppy fat and there was the promise of beauty. Not the head-turning kind of beauty that was so rare but rather a soft loveliness. She was going to be like her mother. Wilma was much too thin but once she filled out in the right places she would be a very attractive young woman. Meantime she was delightfully gauche and both girls were wearing new coats. Paul felt very proud of them.

'Hello, you two,' he smiled as they got into the back seat of the car. 'And, Katy, may I say how very smart you look.'

Katy beamed. Her dad had noticed her new coat before Wilma's.

'This is new,' she said proudly, 'usually I have to wear

Wilma's cast-offs but Mum said she wanted me to have a new trench coat. She said she could afford it because she didn't have to pay the full price.'

'Why not?' he asked as he eased away from the pavement.

'Because, Dad, Mum can go to the warehouse for anything she wants,' Wilma said. 'Miss Ramsay gives her a line to say that she is entitled to get goods at cost price.' She paused and fingered the rich softness of her long jacket. 'You haven't said I look nice in this and you haven't seen it before.'

'Neither I have but give me a chance, I did notice. You suit that shade of blue—'

'Hyacinth blue, Dad,' she said to help him out.

'Very, very nice but I wouldn't have thought warm enough for this time of the year. The odd blink of sun doesn't mean that spring has arrived.'

'Of course it's warm enough, this is mohair and mohair is particularly warm.' She put her hands in the large pockets and brought the warmth around her.

He smiled. 'Presumably that came at cost too?'

'No, it didn't. There is a tiny little mark on it but you wouldn't notice unless you had it pointed out.'

'She got it for nothing, Dad.'

Wilma rounded on her sister furiously. 'I was talking, why do you have to finish what I was going to say?'

'Because you do it to me all the time.'

'No, I don't,' she snapped. 'What I do is help you out when you get stuck.'

'What a cheek.'

'Calm down at the back there.'

'Dad, I hadn't finished what I was saying,' Wilma said haughtily.

'Go on then, I'm listening.'

'Miss Ramsay said her reputation would suffer if she sold something that was below standard. She is very, very particular.'

'And you came by it?'

'Miss Ramsay said if it fitted me I could have it.'

'And you just prayed it would fit,' he laughed.

'I knew it would, I had tried it on before.'

'Lucky you.'

'Dad, this isn't the way to the cottage,' Wilma said suddenly noticing the direction they were taking.

'I'm aware of that, Wilma.'

'Where are we meeting Vera?'

'We aren't, she isn't coming.'

'Why not?'

'Because, Wilma, Vera has another appointment.'

'But she can't have, this is our day. Didn't you remind her?'

'She didn't require reminding.'

'You mean,' Wilma said incredulously, 'she knew but she is going with someone else or – or to some other place?'

'That would appear to be the case.'

'She shouldn't have done that to us – we only see you once a month and that isn't very often.'

'I know,' Paul said gently, 'but you have to remember, Wilma, that it was good of Vera to come in the first place.'

'Yes, I suppose so,' she said miserably. 'I'm disappointed that's all.'

'Never mind we'll do something different, we'll go further afield for our meal. There's a place, Shenval is its name, that is gaining a reputation for its food, I thought we might go there.'

'That would be nice, Dad,' Katy said cheerfully.

'It won't seem right, just the three of us, it should be four,' Wilma said nursing her disappointment. She had so wanted Vera to see her new hyacinth-blue mohair jacket.

'It didn't have to be just the three of us, you should have said about Vera before we set off, Dad. Mum wasn't doing anything special and she might have come instead of having to eat her meal on her own.'

Wilma clapped her hand to her brow. 'I don't believe what I have just heard. Is it possible for anyone to be so stupid?'

'I'm not stupid,' Katy said close to tears. 'I know Mum can't come when Vera is there but Vera isn't coming. That should have made it all right.'

Paul was seldom angry with Wilma but at this moment he was. There had been no need to have Katy reduced almost to tears. No doubt about it, she was the kindly one. Wilma could do with being brought down a peg or two.

'Wilma, if you are hoping to be a lady one day I suggest you adopt a nicer manner and especially to your sister. No one likes a sharp-tongued young woman and that is what you will become if you are not careful.'

Wilma gaped, she was completely taken aback and it was she who now looked on the verge of tears. Her father never spoke to her like that.

She had to get back into his good books and that meant an apology although she didn't think what she had said was so terrible. Katy was silly at times.

'I'm sorry, very sorry,' she mumbled and kept her face down.

Paul had been surprised at the strength of his anger and his need to comfort Katy. He had never bothered much about his younger daughter, but that was because she had always run to Jenny with her troubles whereas it had been to him that Wilma had come.

'Katy, you are not stupid, far from it but what you suggest isn't possible.' He paused and slowed down to give a wide berth to a wobbly cyclist. 'Your mother and I are estranged which means, my dear, that we have decided to go our separate ways.'

'Will it always be like that?' Katy didn't believe her mother had had any part in the separation but maybe her father was forgetting what really had happened.

'Will it always be like that?' he repeated. 'That's difficult to say, Katy, none of us knows what the future holds.'

'You might not always live with Vera,' Katy persisted.

'There is that possibility.' A few short months ago he wouldn't have been able to accept that possibility. He could now and if it happened he would survive.

Wilma wished she could see her dad's face and see what was written there. Was he falling out of love with Vera or was Vera tiring of her dad? She couldn't ask anyone, she could only wait and watch.

'Dad, I'm hungry, how much further is this place?'

'Nearly there, Katy.'

'What does nearly mean?'

'Ten minutes should see us there. Incidentally I meant to ask, which of you is the gardener?'

'What do you mean?' Wilma said puzzled.

'The front garden, I thought, was looking especially nice.'

'Oh, that,' Wilma said dismissively, 'no, we had nothing to do with it. Mrs Turnbull managed to get someone to do her garden and since he was making such a good job, Mum asked him to do ours as well.'

'On a regular basis?'

'Yes, Mum is much too busy to do it herself and the gardener is going to do the back as well.'

'My! My! Things are looking up at 16 Abbotsford Crescent.'

Wilma didn't like that remark, she felt annoyed. Her mother was doing wonders, she was always cheerful now and life was good. She gave them surprise little treats and that had been great about allowing them to decorate their bedrooms the way they wanted. She said she wouldn't interfere and she hadn't. And because of that Wilma had taken her eyes away from a particular garish wallpaper and chosen one she thought would meet with her mother's approval. Thinking about their life Wilma realised they were happy. She was too loyal to say her dad wasn't missed, but he wasn't missed the way he used to be. She supposed it would be the same when Evelyn left school. For the beginning of the new term it would be awful then it would get better until she was hardly missed at all.

There was a scattering of gravel as Paul drove towards

the front of the long, low building and parked the car. They got out and for a few moments stood together looking at the front of the restaurant.

'It's not very big, Dad,' Katy said.

'No, but quaintly attractive wouldn't you say?'

'Yes, Dad, that's exactly what it is,' Wilma agreed as they moved towards the entrance.

Shenval was two cottages knocked into one with extensive kitchen premises built on to the back. Voices and laughter could be heard and a dog barked, probably to warn of their arrival. A buxom woman in a snowy white apron came to greet them.

'A chill in the air, we haven't got rid of winter yet.' She smiled. 'Do you have a reservation?'

'Yes, Richardson.'

'This way, Mr Richardson and the two young ladies.' The dining area was a long, narrow, low-ceilinged room with tables down either side and in one corner was a trolley laden with a wonderful selection of sweet dishes. Katy felt her mouth watering. 'Shall I take your coats?' the woman said when they arrived at their table.

Katy was willing to part with hers and handed it over. Wilma said she would keep hers on.

'It gets very hot in here, my dear.'

'I don't mind that,' Wilma said. She knew she couldn't bear to see her precious jacket being borne away to some place behind the scenes where she couldn't keep her eye on it.

The woman smiled and seemed to understand. They were each given a menu, leather-bound with gold lettering and a tassel. Katy was intrigued.

'Are we allowed to take it home, Dad?' she whispered.

'Afraid not, pet, those would cost a lot of money to produce.'

Katy nodded, she had expected as much. Three heads bent over the menus.

'Dad, I don't know what some of these dishes are.'

A waiter in a short white coat had overheard. 'May I be of assistance?'

'Thank you,' Paul smiled. 'When it comes to food my daughter likes to have everything explained to her.'

He bowed. 'A very sensible young lady and one after my own heart. Food should be appreciated and not just eaten to satisfy hunger.'

Katy went pink with pleasure. Normally she didn't like to be the centre of attention but this was different, she was enjoying every moment. She listened very carefully, nodding her head when she thought she should as the waiter, who turned out to be the proprietor and the husband of the woman who had shown them to their table, explained the different dishes and how they were cooked. Paul was amused and greatly relieved. How lucky that he had heard about this place and made the decision to come. The girls were loving it.

The meal had been a great success, there was a friendly atmosphere and not once had Vera's name been mentioned. Only when they were leaving did Wilma say that next time they must bring Vera instead of going to their usual restaurant. Paul had smiled and said nothing. Why spoil the day which was turning out to be unexpectedly enjoyable, by telling Wilma that there would be no next time.

Katy wiped her mouth with the napkin then put it down beside her plate. She felt comfortably full.

'Dad, I'm glad you found this place, that was great. I think it is the best meal I have ever had and as for that orange soufflé,' she closed her eyes as though in ecstasy, 'it was a dream.'

Paul was nodding. 'I must say I enjoyed it too.' He had paid a lot more many a time when what was served hadn't been half as good.

'I know what I'm going to do when I leave school.'

'You want to be a nurse, you've told us often enough.'

'Not now I don't,' Katy said to her sister then looked over to her father. 'Instead of training to be a nurse I'll go to classes and learn to be a good cook. And later,' she said hardly pausing for breath, 'when I'm old enough to get married, we can open a restaurant like the Shenval.' Wilma and Paul were sharing a smile. She knew they were smiling about what she was saying but she didn't mind. 'If you ever get to be a reporter, Wilma, you can give me a—' she stopped.

'Write-up,' Paul suggested with a grin. Why had he ever thought that entertaining his daughters would be difficult? They were doing the entertaining. Possibly it was because they were natural with him whereas with Vera they were always on their best behaviour. Wilma trying too hard to impress and Katy feeling left out of it and not knowing what to say.

'That was what I meant, thanks Dad. Would you, Wilma?'

Wilma adopted her most haughty expression but it was in fun, she wasn't trying to put Katy down.

300

'Yes, I would, provided the standard of food and service was sufficiently high,' she drawled. 'It wouldn't do my reputation any good if people went to your restaurant and were disappointed.'

'They wouldn't be,' Katy said earnestly.

To put off time Paul took the long way home to 16 Abbotsford Crescent. He supposed they could have gone to the cottage for an hour or so but he knew they wouldn't be comfortable. It was Vera's home and he was merely living there. To go might take the shine off the day and that would be a pity.

'Here we are, girls,' Paul said when he drew up opposite the gate. In the grey dark the lighted window looked very inviting.

'Thanks, Dad,' they said as they scrambled out.

'About next time,' Wilma said anxiously.

'I'll be in touch before then.'

She saw his eyes stray to the lighted sitting-room window. Her mother had closed the curtains but hadn't pulled down the blind. With just the curtain to move she could always take a peep out to see if they were coming. Wilma couldn't be sure but she thought that was a wistful look. Would he want to come in and talk for a while? Should she ask him? Better not. If her dad was desperately keen he wouldn't need her to suggest it. Then there was her mother. Although she made everyone welcome that might not include her estranged husband. It didn't matter now it was too late, the car was moving away with Paul giving a final wave.

He couldn't understand his feelings. For a moment he

had wished himself in that lighted room with the curtains closed and his long legs stretched out in front of a cheerful coal fire. He at one side of it and Jenny at the other. The girls would be occupied doing something or other. Why, he wondered, should he want that now when he had been happy to give it up? It wasn't as though he had fallen out of love with Vera, he didn't see that ever happening. The end would come when she tired of him. Strangely the thought of that no longer filled him with dread. He could almost see it as a relief when it was all over.

Which brought his thoughts back to the house. That had been a monumental mistake selling 16 Abbotsford Crescent, he must have been out of his mind to agree to it. That error of judgement had left him with no place of his own. The cottage belonged to Vera and 16 Abbotsford Crescent was owned by Jenny. Both the women in his life were comfortably settled. He, on the other hand, had nothing. Just his job and dwindling savings. Paul began to feel sorry for himself. He had no house, not even a stick of furniture. Once the day came when Vera asked him to leave he would be back to the life of a bachelor. Then he would be reduced to furnished accommodation or buying a small house or flat and furnishing it himself. Years ago that would have had a certain appeal but not now.

Paul imagined the scene, with Wilma and Katy telling Jenny about their day and the absence of Vera. Would his beloved be home when he got there or would he be returning to an empty house?

Jenny had moved the curtains a fraction to confirm that it was Paul's car that had stopped. She hadn't expected

Wilma and Katy for another half hour. Quickly going to the front door she unlocked it so that they only had to turn the knob and come in.

'You're home early,' she smiled and folded the Sunday paper she had been reading.

'That was because Vera didn't come and we weren't at the cottage,' Katy said dismissively. 'Dad liked my new coat, he said I looked very smart.'

'So you do. Take it off and remember to hang it on a coat hanger.'

'He liked Wilma's too,' Katy said generously as she undid the buttons.

Jenny looked at her elder daughter curiously. It was usually she who did most of the talking when they returned from a visit but not this time. Katy was flushed and happy and stumbling over the words in her eagerness to get them out. Wilma didn't even interrupt. She was standing in front of the fire with her hand constantly smoothing her jacket. Jenny thought she must remember to tell Miss Ramsay that Wilma was so in love with her mohair jacket that she could hardly bring herself to take it off.

After these visits, Jenny made a point of not asking questions, leaving it to them to tell her what they wanted her to know. By bedtime it would all come out, she just had to be patient.

It was typical of Katy to have had all weekend to do her homework and then to remember just before bedtime on Sunday that there was more to do.

Jenny shook her head in exasperation. 'Go upstairs and do it now.'

'Do I have to? Tomorrow would do, it isn't much.'

'You'll do it now, Katy, and no arguments if you please.'

Paul hadn't agreed with homework being done at the kitchen table. Wilma had a desk in her bedroom with a shelf for books. Katy had to make do with a folding table in her bedroom since there was so little space.

With Katy gone upstairs, Jenny looked at her elder daughter who hadn't moved. 'Wilma, would you kindly take off that jacket unless you intend to sleep in it.'

'I wanted Vera to see it,' Wilma said slowly taking it off and putting it carefully over the back of the sofa.

'She'll see it next time.'

'If there is a next time,' Wilma said gloomily.

Jenny looked at her sharply. 'What makes you say that?'

'Just a feeling. She didn't bother to come today after all.'

'Maybe she had a previous engagement.'

'How could she arrange something when she knows this is our day? Every fourth Sunday shouldn't be difficult to remember. She puts everything down in a diary.'

'You don't know, it could have been very important.'

Wilma threw herself on the sofa. 'Why are you taking her side?'

'I'm not, I'm merely putting forward suggestions. Didn't your father offer some explanation?'

'No, he hardly mentioned her.'

Jenny smiled. 'Maybe they had a tiff.'

'Or more likely Vera has got tired of us.'

'I'm sure it's not that,' Jenny said kindly although she thought it could well be true.

Wilma decided it was time to change the subject.

'Dad said the garden was looking very nice.'

'He noticed?' she said raising her eyebrows.

Wilma laughed. 'He asked if Katy and I had taken up gardening.'

'That was a joke. I doubt if you two could tell a flower from a weed.'

'Mum, we're not as bad as that and it has been known for us to help.'

'You told him we had a gardener?'

'Yes.'

It was like drawing teeth. 'What did he have to say to that?'

'Nothing much. I told him you were far too busy to do the garden and that you'd asked Mrs Turnbull's gardener to do ours, the back as well. Mum,' she said uncertainly and stopped.

'What?'

'I think Dad would have come in if he had been invited.'

'What makes you think that?'

'He sort – of had – a wistful expression, the kind of look you have when you wish something.'

Jenny smiled and waited.

'If Dad came to the door would you ask him in?' she said in a rush.

'I don't see me keeping him standing at the door.'

'I could have asked him to come in and you wouldn't have been angry?'

'Not angry, Wilma, but I would rather you didn't. Your father and I have nothing to say to each other and if we had there is always the telephone.'

'What it boils down to is you don't want him back.'

'That's right, I don't and that is the last word on the subject.' Jenny got up. 'I'll put the kettle on and we'll have a cup of tea when Katy comes down.'

Chapter Eighteen

---◆◆◆---

Paul kept hoping that Vera would be home before him but he wasn't at all surprised to find the cottage in darkness. There was a shed at the back with an accumulation of rubbish dating from when Vera's great-aunt had occupied the house. Thinking he should, Paul had half-heartedly offered to clean it out and get someone to take away the broken furniture and other useless items. Vera had agreed it was a good idea but not urgent. They had no plans to use it. There was no garage though space for one and he parked as he usually did opposite the front gate. Paul didn't always remember to lock the car door but this time he did. The house key was on the same ring as the office keys and after selecting it, he let himself in. Darkness enveloped him and as he fumbled for the switch and flicked on the hall light, the thought struck him that there was something very depressing about entering an unoccupied house. During the years of his marriage he'd had very little experience of it. Jenny had always, or nearly always, been there to welcome him. In the colder days there would be a good going fire with the flames leaping up the chimney. Not aware he was sighing, Paul went along to the sitting-room and switched on the centre light quite forgetting that Vera never used it. Much too harsh she would say. The softer light from the table lamps was all that was required.

Paul put them all on flooding the room with light, then had second thoughts and turned off the lamps. The main light would let him read the Sunday papers without strain. Paul required a stronger light for reading than the lamps gave but made no mention of this. Vera had excellent eyesight and he wasn't going to admit to any weakness with his own. Sadly the day wasn't far off when he would have to pay a visit to the optician's. Someone who had come through it himself had told Paul that the first sign of failing eyesight was difficulty in reading the telephone directory. Paul had been telling himself that the printing was getting smaller.

The meal at Shenval had satisfied him. It had been well cooked and appetising. In the hotel where Vera was dining he knew she would have asked for a small portion of her chosen dish. If that was refused and very often it was, she would leave most of the food on her plate. Then someone would come over looking concerned and ask if the dish had not been to madam's liking. Nothing wrong with the food, she would have said clearly, just too much of it. I have a very small appetite. There would be an understanding smile and relief that the food was not at fault. The plate would be quickly removed to the kitchen before others could see it and wonder the reason for its return.

A drink would go down well but Paul decided he wouldn't have one just yet. Vera might join him later on in the evening. He knew that he was drinking more than he used to but not enough for it to be a problem. He would never let it get out of hand. Reaching for the Sunday papers he sat down to read. The cottage was never completely cold. There was a small heater that Vera kept on when they were out.

In little more than half an hour he heard the key in the door.

'Hello, darling, I wondered who would be first in.'

Paul dropped the newspaper and was preparing to get up when she gently pushed him down.

'Stay where you are, dear,' she said bending over to give him a kiss and a whiff of her perfume. Then she was frowning. 'What on earth are you doing with that centre light on and no fire glow. Honestly, Paul, will you never learn,' she said teasingly but with some exasperation too.

'Forgot about the fire glow and I don't agree about the centre light being harsh. I don't find anything wrong with it.'

'I do,' she said going over to switch on the lamps before turning off the centre light. 'How you can sit without the fire glow I do not know, it makes such a difference.' She attended to the glow and switched on a bar of the fire.

'I haven't had a drink, thought I would wait for you.'

'That was sweet of you. Yes, please, you can pour me one.'

Paul got to his feet. 'How was your day?'

'That'll keep for the moment.' She picked up the court shoes she had removed when she came in and stood looking uncertain. 'I'm wondering if it is worth changing?'

'No, it isn't, just stay the way you are.' He went off to

the kitchen to prepare the drinks and Vera went along to the bedroom. She took good care of her clothes and Paul knew she would be putting shoe trees into her shoes and hanging up her costume jacket.

The drinks were on the table, the Sunday papers folded and put into the magazine rack. The room would soon be cosily warm helped by the pinkish glow from the lamps. Paul had moved from the chair to the sofa and they sat close together. His arm was around her and she had her head on his shoulder. For Paul time stood still, this was what he liked. These moments were paradise and the little irritations and annoyances, which were more frequent these days, no longer mattered.

'How did things go?' she asked.

'You first,' Paul said dreamily as he stroked her hair.

'I wanted you there and you should have been.'

'Not quite my scene.'

'Nonsense, you wouldn't have been the only one, I counted half a dozen.'

'Probably dragged along against their wishes.'

She lifted her head to look at him. 'It didn't look that way, I would have said they were taking a keen interest.'

'Would that be in the fashions or the models?' he joked.

She knew it was a joke but didn't like it because it was very close to the truth. A few of the women were visibly annoyed at their menfolk openly flirting and it was unlikely the husbands would be asked to accompany them on a future occasion. The models were playing up to the balding, overweight men. Maybe it helped sales and it didn't bother them. Paul, on the other hand was a very attractive man, the kind that women liked to flirt with and the models knew how to use their charms.

'How would I know? What I do know and you don't is that a lovely figure doesn't always mean a lovely face. Not one of those modelling the clothes today would have had a look in far less taken a prize at a beauty contest.'

'Aren't you being rather hard?' Paul said enjoying himself. She didn't often do it but he liked it when she showed her claws. If Vera could still be jealous then he had nothing to worry about. There would be no need for jealousy if she was tiring of him.

'No, I don't think I am being hard, just truthful. You, poor lamb, are like a lot of other men who think models are—'

'Gorgeous,' he finished for her and she had to laugh.

'Seriously, Paul, some models are extremely plain. On the catwalk it isn't noticed because they are some distance away. It is a different story coming up to the tables like today, one can see the blemishes that make-up cannot hide.'

'They can't all be plain.'

'No, but there wasn't a real beauty among them.'

'Then I am truly blessed to have you. What a wonderful model you would have made, perfect in every way.'

'Thank you, darling,' she said looking pleased. 'You aren't growing tired of me?'

'Never that, how could you even think such a thing?' Had he done something to make her say that? He must have though he couldn't imagine what. Unless – unless his hints that she should be less extravagant made him appear that way. Yet what else could he do? She wanted to have it all now and he preferred to save for the future. A compromise, of course, that's what it would have to be, although he hadn't a clue how that would work. Hadn't it already been tried. Whatever it took he had to keep her happy for as long as possible. He drew her closer.

'Did you buy anything?' Stupid question, why else was she there?

'No, I did not. One does not usually decide there and then. The whole purpose of the fashion show is to get you to visit the store and once there to try on the clothes you admired. Relax, my dearest, I wasn't terribly taken with anything apart from a black dress.'

'Black?'

'You like me in black?'

'I like you in anything.'

'This you would have to see me in before I decided.'

'Why?' In the past she had just gone ahead and bought what she wanted and expected him to like it and foot the bill.

'You might not approve, after all it is a very plain dress and figure-hugging. Very figure-hugging,' she repeated.

Paul liked heads to turn for Vera. It gave him a nice feeling, but he wasn't so sure he would be happy about something sensational which she was hinting at. He liked admiring glances not raised eyebrows.

'Wear it for me,' he suggested.

'What a waste.'

'Thank you very much.'

She gave him a dig in the ribs. 'Trust you to take it the

wrong way. All I meant was it is a bit pricey for wearing about the house. On second thoughts I don't think I'll trouble.'

Paul sighed with relief. 'What about your friend, did she go mad?'

'Mavis couldn't afford to go mad. She says her husband is becoming horribly mean and if she goes over her dress allowance it comes off the next.'

'Sounds reasonable.'

'It would to a man. Does that mean you would do the same?'

'All depends, Vera, I would hate to appear mean but if it was that or going bankrupt I know what it would have to be.'

'There is no question of going bankrupt.'

'Don't be too sure, it can happen.' He wondered how such an intelligent person could be so careless with money. 'Haven't they just bought a new house?'

'Yes.'

'Then, poor man, he's probably up to his eyeballs in debt.'

'Mavis thinks he might have some hidden expense.'

'Such as?'

'Another woman. He is away for long periods you know.'

Paul was about to say how awful or something like that when he remembered he was in the same position. Or not quite. His affair with Vera was out in the open.

'We are better off as we are, Paul. Mavis thinks so.'

'Why are we better off?'

'Because we are free to do as we wish.'

'All I wish is to stay with you for ever.'

'At times, Paul, you can be very slow in the uptake. The fact that we are free to end our relationship whenever we want keeps us together.'

Paul didn't want an argument he was bound to lose so he nodded in agreement.

'What did you think of the new house?'

'I wasn't greatly impressed. It was nice enough but Mavis's taste in furnishings and mine differ.'

Paul gathered that the outing had not been a great success. She would have been better with them.

'Was your day with the girls too awful or did you manage to carry on some kind of conversation?'

That angered Paul. He had suggested nothing of the sort. Or if he had then he hadn't meant it.

'As it happened the day turned out to be very enjoyable.'

She turned to look at him in surprise. 'What did you do?'

'I decided to take Wilma and Katy further afield to that new place just opened called Shenval.'

'Heavens! Was that where you went. Those two old cottages knocked into one?'

'That's the one and an excellent job they made of it. Quaint and quite charming was our opinion of the outside.'

'And the food?'

'Couldn't have been better. A good choice of menu and the food when it came was well cooked and appetising.' He smiled as he remembered. 'Katy was overheard to say that she didn't know what some of the dishes were and someone who turned out to be the owner, explained what they were and how they were cooked.'

'How boring.'

'Anything but. Katy was absolutely delighted, in fact she was so impressed that she now wants to learn to cook when she leaves school and one day open her own restaurant.'

'I take it I wasn't missed?' Vera was miffed. She didn't want the bother of entertaining the girls but she had expected Wilma at least to make a fuss about her non-appearance.

'Of course you were missed. Wilma had on a new jacket she was dying to show you. Why not come next time and see what you think of Shenval?' he said hopefully.

'No, darling, that doesn't sound like my sort of place at all.' She yawned. 'This is a good time for me to bow out as I said before.'

He wasn't going to plead. 'If that is your decision, so be it. My daughters are good company. They did most of the entertaining and as I said the day was a success.'

Jenny was rearranging the glassware in one of the cabinets when Doris Roberts hurried over. Doris was always rushing whether it was necessary or not.

'Someone in the tea room wants to see you, Jenny, if you can spare the time.'

'Thank you, Doris, I'll come now.' Before she could ask if the visitor was male or female, Doris had gone.

Jenny closed the glass doors of the cabinet and went along to the tea room thinking as always how attractive it looked with the freshly laundered red and white patterned tablecloths and the small flower arrangement in the centre. She wondered who it could be who wanted to see her. As she looked at the only two tables occupied, a man in a slightly crumpled suit got to his feet. Jenny saw to her surprise that it was Stewart Taylor and remembered him saying that he would call in to the Log Cabin when he was in the district. With so much happening in her life she had all but forgotten the man who had been kind enough to stop and give her a lift home.

'Mr Taylor – Stewart, I mean, how nice to see you.' She smiled as they shook hands.

'I do hope I'm not taking you away from something important.'

'You aren't, at least nothing that can't wait.'

'Would you join me?'

'Of course, I'd be delighted to. I'll make this my coffee break.' She saw that his coffee was untouched. 'Do sit down and have yours, Doris will bring me one.'

Doris heard and popped her head up above the counter. She stopped what she was doing to pour a cup of coffee and put it down in front of Jenny.

'Thank you, Doris,' Jenny smiled.

Stewart picked up the spoon to stir his. 'You are looking very well, Jenny.'

'Thank you, I never felt better. The busy life seems to suit me.'

Their eyes met across the table. 'I've thought of you often, Jenny,' he said softly.

Jenny felt her colour rising and not knowing what to say she dropped her eyes to the table.

'I'm sorry, I didn't mean to embarrass you.'

Jenny was annoyed with herself. How stupid of her to be embarrassed by a compliment. 'It's all right,' she said. It must show how few compliments came her way.

He was looking at the changing expressions. 'I only spoke the truth.'

'How – how is your wife?' Jenny said quickly, then wished she had waited before asking that. It must look as though she was reminding him that he had no right to make such a remark.

If it did he gave no sign and went on to answer her question.

'Phyllis is back in hospital. I'm afraid the times when she is at home are getting shorter and shorter. Phyllis is no longer the girl I married, Jenny; she has become more child than woman, a difficult child,' he added.

'That must be dreadful for you,' she said, her voice full of concern. 'Is visiting a strain? I suppose it must be.'

'It has become a strain. Awkward is the word that springs to mind. We sit and look at each other and I make an attempt at conversation then I dry up. There is so little to talk about. Phyllis has no interest in what is happening at home. I thought I must be at fault but her sister is finding it just as difficult. When visiting time is over I think we are all equally relieved. Sounds dreadful but that is the way it is.'

Jenny nodded. She could imagine the scene.

'My wife is happier with the nurses. They are good with her and I am grateful for that but I didn't come here to talk about my problems. I came because I wanted so much to see you.'

They were back on dangerous ground. She would have to be careful. Life was complicated enough without adding to it.

'Have dinner with me, Jenny? Please say you will?'

She saw the pleading in his face but hardened herself. Had it been possible, which it wasn't, she would have enjoyed an evening out. It would have certainly made a change. She shook her head.

'Stewart,' she said gently, 'that was kind of you to ask but I couldn't possibly accept.'

'Why not?'

'You know why not. Neither of us is free. I might be separated from my husband but I am still a married woman.'

'And I am a married man,' he said heavily.

'Yes.'

'You can say that, even though I have told you how it is, that I have no marriage in the true sense of the word?'

She heard the anger in his voice. 'Life can be very cruel, Stewart.'

'Just my bad luck,' he said bitterly.

'Stewart, if I had only myself to consider it might be different but there are three very good reasons why I cannot accept your invitation to dinner.'

'May I hear them?'

'My two daughters and my mother. Wilma, my elder daughter, would be quite horrified. Strangely enough she can excuse her father for what he did though at the time she was terribly upset.'

'But not you?'

'No, not me.'

'You must be beyond reproach.'

'That's it. Katy wouldn't be very happy about it either but wouldn't be so upset as her sister.'

'Which leaves your mother.'

Jenny smiled. 'Ah, yes, my mother. I love her dearly but I could wish she wasn't so old-fashioned and set in her ways. She is of the old school, Stewart. For better, for worse in her book means just that. She believes that marriage, be it happy or otherwise, is for ever.'

'A life sentence.'

'That is one way of putting it.'

'How can she say that, when your husband walked out on you and his family?'

His voice had risen slightly and she gave him a warning look.

'Sorry, I got carried away,' he apologised.

She leaned forward. 'Mother believes that Paul will come back, that if I am patient, all will be well.'

'She honestly believes that you could take up again where you left off?'

'No, she isn't as naïve as all that. She would say it will take time.'

'I'm amazed she wants her son-in-law back after the way he treated you. I would have expected her to say he was good riddance.'

'No, she has always liked Paul,'

'She would forgive him?'

'Yes, I'm sure she would and I'm equally sure that he would get a piece of her mind,' she laughed.

'You can laugh?'

'I hope so, it would be rather awful if I couldn't.'

'Could you forgive him?'

'In time, I imagine so.'

'That is very noble of you?' Did she detect a faint note of sarcasm.

'I don't think so.'

'You would forgive all and have him back?'

'Stewart, don't put words in my mouth, I did not say that. Forgiveness is one thing and why, I ask myself, should I withhold that, what good would it do? Taking Paul back, now that is something totally different. When he is free of Vera Cuthbertson he will be filled with remorse and fully expect me to take him back. Knowing Paul he will use his very considerable charm to win me over but he won't succeed.'

'I'm glad to hear it.'

'The truth is I don't need Paul, I can support myself and the girls.' As Jenny said it a wonderful feeling of independence came over her. 'My husband does give something towards Wilma and Katy's keep and I don't see him stopping that. If he did it wouldn't bother me.' She laughed at his expression. 'No Stewart, some long lost relative hasn't departed this earth and left me a fortune. Miss Ramsay, the owner of the Log Cabin has – how shall I put it – given me a share in the business.'

'That's absolutely wonderful, I couldn't be more pleased for you. A partner is what you mean?'

'I suppose I do but I feel embarrassed calling myself that.'

'Don't be embarrassed, be proud of yourself.' He paused.

'Be strong, Jenny, don't go back to him, no matter the pressures on you.'

'I was never a forceful person, quite the opposite in fact but I am learning. Once my mind is made up on important issues that is final. Paul belongs to the past and that is where he will remain.'

'You'll divorce him?'

'When I'm good and ready,' she said a trifle sharply.

'Am I asking too many questions?'

'You are getting dangerously close. No,' she said when she saw his face, 'if I hadn't wanted you to know I wouldn't have said a word. You have been open with me about your life and now you know something about mine.'

'Thank you.' He smiled winningly. 'After all that, dare I ask if you have had a change of mind about dinner?'

She shook her head. 'I'm afraid not.'

'Dinner is out I have to accept that, but surely that doesn't include lunch? No babysitter required—'

'My two wouldn't need to hear you say that.'

'No, I wouldn't be very popular. You, I take it, wouldn't be happy leaving them alone?'

'Not at night, no. I would worry all the time.'

'Mothers!'

'I know we can't help it,' Jenny smiled.

'Is lunch on or is it that you don't want to see me.'

'It isn't that at all.'

'Then say yes and prove it.' He paused. 'I very much want to see you again.'

Why shouldn't she, where was the harm? Be honest with

yourself, you want to have lunch with this man. You like him and you trust him. And face it, to be found attractive is just what you need. She'd talked herself into it.

'Lunch would be lovely.'

'Thank you. Jenny, you are a delightful person, so refreshingly honest and straightforward. You say what you mean and mean what you say.' He was laughing.

'Paul wouldn't agree with that, he called me devious.'

'You couldn't be that if you tried. Jenny, I don't know your husband but I heartily dislike him.'

'Paul isn't all bad, he has a lot of good qualities and calling me devious when he did was understandable. I might as well tell you this since you already know quite a lot about me, but before I do I think we should have another coffee. Doris?' she called.

'More coffee is it?'

'Yes, please.'

'There you are,' Doris said putting down the coffee cups and removing the others.

'Lovely. Doris, this is Mr Taylor, a friend of mine who was in the district on business and decided to pay the Log Cabin a visit.'

Doris smiled. 'I hope it has come up to expectations.'

'That and beyond as far as the tea room is concerned. Another time I may be lucky enough to get a conducted tour of its other attractions.'

'You won't be disappointed.' The woman smiled again and walked away.

'Thought I should do that,' Jenny whispered, 'since we are taking rather a long time over our coffee.'

He nodded. 'I want to hear why your husband had the nerve to call you devious.'

'Oh, yes, I was about to tell you. Miss Ramsay was to blame, she was the culprit and at the same time she was and is my saviour. The house as you would guess was in Paul's name and although I never believed it would happen there was always a niggling doubt at the back of my mind. The vague worry that one day I might be asked to leave it.'

'Surely not. The man couldn't put you and the girls out of your home.'

'As I said it was highly improbable. It's a long story and I'll spare you most of it.' Jenny took a sip of her coffee and thought she should have spared him all of it. She hardly knew Stewart and already he knew too much about her.

'You are having second thoughts?'

'No, not really,' she lied. 'I don't want to bore you.'

'You couldn't do that.'

'Unknown to me, Stewart, Miss Ramsay and her solicitor were working on my behalf. To let you understand she persuaded me to ask Paul if he would consider selling the house. After some thought he said no but that he would be interested in what it might fetch. The only way he would even consider selling was if the house went well beyond the asking price.'

'Jenny, I think I am ahead of you. Let me take a guess. Your Miss Ramsay through her solicitor made sure that a tempting offer was there and your husband was unable to resist.'

'Exactly how it was. That is how the house came to be mine.'

'Good for you.'

'Paul was congratulating himself, he was as pleased as Punch until he discovered that I am the new owner. That has really upset him.'

'Very small-minded I must say.'

'His pride was hurt. I know him so well. Paul didn't want me to be independent. In his own way he liked to see himself in the role of the provider.'

'He was hardly that.'

'Paul thought he was. He suggested I get myself a job to help out.'

'You did that.'

'I have been incredibly lucky and that is enough about me,' she said firmly.

'I agree, we'll talk about us,' he smiled.

'About lunch you mean?'

'Yes. When shall we say?'

His thin, clever face had lit up. Why did she think of it as a clever face – it must be the eyes, the intelligence behind them. When his hand moved to cover hers she let it remain there. She liked its comforting warmth and from where they were sitting no one could see.

'This is Monday, shall we say Wednesday or is that too soon for you?' Jenny suggested since he was leaving it to her.

'Wednesday is perfect. I take it you would rather we didn't go too far afield?'

'No, I don't want to be away too long. I am a working woman.'

'The Parkview is within reasonable distance and I can recommend it.'

She nodded.

'I'll book a table though at this time of the year I don't imagine they will be full up. Twelve thirty and I'll pick you up just after twelve. How does that sound?'

'That would suit me fine. I'll be ready.' She made a move and he got up quickly.

'Let me see to the bill then I'll get on my way and let you get back to your work.'

'No bill, Stewart, this is by courtesy of the management,' she smiled.

'Thank you, that was very enjoyable.'

They walked together to the door and Jenny went down the steps and outside to get a breath of fresh air. There was a chill in the air but the signs of spring were all around.

'This is a lovely spot.'

'Yes, it is and I know it well. When I was small my parents used to bring me here for a picnic. Dad would look for a sheltered piece of ground near to a clump of trees so that he could lean against one. Mum would spread the cloth for the food and I would be despatched to find four flat stones of similar size to put on the corners and keep the cloth in position.'

'Happy times.'

'They were, although looking back I think we make them out to be happier than they actually were. Am I making sense?'

'Yes, I think most of us do a bit of that. Remember the good and forget the not so good.'

'My father was a difficult man. He was honest and hard working and determined to get his own way and I have to say he was usually successful. I used to think my mother was weak always giving in to him but I was wrong. She had the good sense to know she couldn't change him.'

'So why bother,' he smiled.

'Exactly. Instead she would suggest something to him and much later make out that it had been his idea in the first place.'

'Crafty woman your mother.'

'It usually worked, she said. If it had been father's suggestion then there was no question about its merit.'

Stewart was in no hurry to depart and began to look around him. 'No wonder the tourists flock to the Log Cabin, it looks so inviting.' He pointed to the glazed pottery tubs filled with spring flowers and stretching the length of the building.

'I love it here and feel very privileged,' Jenny said looking up and squinting in the sunshine.

'I really must go,' he said, but reluctantly. He kissed her on the cheek. 'Until Wednesday, Jenny.'

'I'm looking forward to it.'

Jenny went indoors and Stewart walked smartly over to his car. As he did two cars drew in. The bonny day was bringing the people out.

Jenny was smiling when she went inside to complete the job she had left half done. Miss Ramsay stopped to talk.

Jenny thought she should explain her absence from the shop. 'I spent rather a long time in the tea room,' she said sounding apologetic.

'And why not? You can take as long as you wish over your coffee break. You don't have to ask permission, I thought I had made that clear.'

'Yes, you did, Miss Ramsay.'

The woman sighed. 'Jenny, will you please stop calling me Miss Ramsay. What is wrong with Moira?'

'Nothing,' she laughed. 'All right I'll address you as Moira when we are on our own but in front of the others it will be Miss Ramsay. I would be more comfortable.'

'Just as you please and now may I be terribly inquisitive and ask you about your gentleman friend?'

'You saw him?'

'Of course I saw him. Not much misses me and certainly not a presentable looking man. There aren't too many of them around.' She paused. 'This is silly but may I make a guess at his occupation?'

'No harm in that.'

'Someone who spends a great deal of time in a car – perhaps a travelling salesman?'

Jenny laughed. 'Why should you think that?'

'Crumpled suit and—'

'No, that will do. I noticed too but his wife is in hospital and I don't think Stewart would be greatly bothered about his appearance.'

'More on his mind, poor man.'

'Yes. Stewart does travel about. He is employed by Harris the pharmaceutical company.'

'Hand me the yellow duster and I'll give these silver dishes a rub before you place them. This can be described as talking while you work whereas standing and talking is more like gossiping.

'I can't recall seeing him in the Log Cabin before and I know most of the commercials,' she continued.

'This was his first visit and he was very impressed with what he saw.'

'When I glanced your way I would have said he had eyes only for you.'

Jenny blushed.

'I'm sorry I'm a tease.'

'Moira, Stewart Taylor is his name and he has only recently come to live in our village. He happened to see me standing at the bus stop and he offered me a lift home. I was very grateful with the rain beginning to fall, no umbrella and no bus in sight. Apart from then this is the first time I have spoken to him.'

'A wife in hospital you said.'

Jenny was surprised at the interest Moira was showing but there was no harm in answering her questions. Moira was inquisitive and didn't try to deny it but she was not a gossip.

'Yes, she had a nervous breakdown and never got over it. Stewart says she is getting worse and is almost permanently in hospital.'

'That is tragic. Some people do have it hard.'

'Moira?'

'What?'

'I think I might be in danger of making a fool of myself.'

'Not you, Jenny, you are too level-headed.'

'I don't think I am. Stewart asked me to have dinner with him.'

'Before you say any more let me check this. Do you like this Stewart or are you just sorry for him?'

'I'm sorry for him, who wouldn't be, but I do like him. To be honest I like him very much.'

'Then I do hope you accepted his invitation. No, Jenny, that isn't quite in the middle. Move the sweet dish a fraction to the left.'

Jenny did. 'That it?'

'Almost. Yes, that's it now. He asked you to have dinner with him and I hope you said yes.'

'Of course I didn't. How could I?'

'Very easily I would have thought.'

'Then you aren't thinking. How do I go about asking my mother to come over and be with the girls while I have dinner with a man I met recently.'

Moira frowned. 'You don't think she would approve?'

'You know my mother so you shouldn't have to ask. She would be scandalised and wonder where she had gone wrong with my upbringing. Wilma and Katy would take a poor view of it as well.'

'Seems such a shame. I'm sure you would enjoy a night out.'

'When he suggested lunch I accepted that.'

'Good.'

Jenny frowned.

'Having second thoughts?'

'Yes, but too late to do anything about it. Stewart is collecting me here just after twelve on Wednesday. He said he would book a table at the Parkview.'

'You'll get a good meal there. The service is slow or it used to be. Still, that needn't be a bad thing,' she smiled, 'more time for you two to talk and, Jenny, take a tip from me and don't dare look at your watch. Men just hate women to do that, it can be very off-putting. Relax and take all the time you need or want. We have no large bookings for Wednesday so none of us is going to be rushed off our feet.'

'You are very good to me, Moira.'

'Nonsense.'

'I hope I don't see anyone I know.'

'Don't let that bother you. Give whoever it might be a wave and a smile. Good heavens, woman, you are only having lunch.'

'That is enough for the village gossips.'

'Jenny, I've raised a few eyebrows in my day, perhaps I still do, I hope so – it makes life so much more interesting. You are laughing but it is true, one begins to see the funny side.'

Jenny didn't see herself ever doing that. She would hate to be talked about behind her back.

'Remember too that if they are talking about you some other poor soul is getting a rest.'

'That won't help me,' Jenny laughed.

'Seriously, Jenny, as my mother used to say we only come this way once so we should make the most of it. Take what happiness is offered, you deserve some.'

'Moira, I won't accept another invitation if he asks.'

'Scared he might be serious?'

'He *is* married.'

'I'm not completely sure about this but I believe in certain circumstances a marriage can be ended.'

Jenny looked shocked.

'Better to know these things.'

'Do you believe there is such a thing as platonic friendship between a man and a woman?' Jenny asked.

'Some would say so.'

'Would you?'

'Now you've got me in a corner.'

'Sorry.'

'Don't be, I started this after all.' She paused for thought. 'I am a single woman which puts me in a different position from you. I make no apology when I say I enjoy male company and I can do that without wanting to spend the night with them if I can put it crudely. So for me there is such a thing as a platonic friendship, I have one as it happens.'

'You didn't have to tell me all that. I'm sorry.'

'Don't be. From the little I saw of your friend I would say he isn't looking for a platonic friendship but if that is the only way to keep you then he will settle for it. You are a very attractive woman, Jenny, and the fact that you won't believe it makes you all the more desirable.'

Jenny closed the cabinet door.

'Time to change the subject. Tell me about the driving lessons, how are they going?'

'Very well. I'm amazed at my progress and all thanks to Mr Mason. He couldn't be more helpful and he most certainly has the patience of Job.'

'I thought you and he would get on well. Have you told the family yet?'

'No, I haven't. With me taking the lessons during working hours there was no hurry to tell them.'

'Prefer to wait until it is a *fait accompli*?'

'Yes. If I wasn't going to be any good then I could keep that knowledge to myself.'

'Learning to drive is not difficult.'

'No, it is much easier than I expected.'

'The fault of that wretched husband of yours daring to suggest that you were too nervous to learn. I wouldn't say you are nervous, no more than the average person. And as your instructor would tell you, nervous folk, once they overcome their nerves, very often turn out to be good drivers. It is the over-confident who are more likely to come to grief.'

'I enjoy the lessons.'

'Good. Tommy is pleased with your progress. He'll know when you are ready to take your test.'

'That does make me panicky I have to confess.'

'Most people are. Give yourself a few minutes then you will forget it is a test and drive as though you had Tommy beside you.' She smiled. 'Have no fear, I won't rush you. Once you are declared fit to drive a four wheeled vehicle, Tommy will sit beside you in the new car. I am shortly to be taking delivery of a Morris Minor, a very similar model to the one you are learning on.'

Jenny felt butterflies in her stomach. 'You would have passed first time?'

'I never passed at all. When I was learning to drive there was no such thing as a test. My father taught me so any bad habits he had would have been passed on to me. I can't be too bad though. In all the years I have been driving I have never been the cause of an accident.'

Chapter Nineteen

———◆———

Jenny was still in her dressing-gown when the girls left for school although underneath she was fully dressed apart from her blouse. This she occasionally did, leaving it off until the breakfast table was cleared and the dishes washed and put away. It saved rolling up the sleeves and crushing them. This morning the dressing-gown was to save questions that Jenny didn't want to answer. The pinafore she usually wore would not have hidden everything and nothing much missed the pair of them.

Upstairs, in her bedroom, on a padded coat-hanger and secured by its hook to the top of the wardrobe, hung the pale gold, fine-knit jersey suit. It had been an impulse buy that had made Jenny feel guilty for days. Money wasn't tight but even so that had been an unnecessary extravagance. When, she asked herself, would there be an occasion to wear it? She never went anywhere all that special. Not that a jersey suit was particularly dressy, it was the colour. Gorgeous but impractical.

The assistant kept telling her how well she suited the colour and she could see that for herself in the full-length mirror. The fit was perfect too which was quite wonderful since she was not what could be considered stock size. Not to snap it up would be foolish and the minute Jenny was outside the building and on the pavement she knew she would regret it. Price was usually the deciding factor but this was the warehouse and the discount Jenny was allowed made it affordable. There was a question mark about the Dry Clean label. She usually avoided those.

The girl was waiting, not pushing for a sale, just hoping. She was thin, pale-faced and tired looking but with a ready smile and lovely small, white teeth. Poor thing, Jenny thought, she had probably been on her feet all day waiting for customers to make up their mind. Folk like her who were swithering.

'Dry Clean Only — I suppose it does mean what it says?' Jenny said.

'Sometimes I think it is just a safeguard for the manufacturer in case something goes wrong in the wash.'

'You could be right.' Jenny smiled. 'I am careful and it won't be the first label I've ignored. On the other hand . . .'

'A risk?'

'It has to be that.'

'Would you keep this for special occasions?'

'Yes, I expect I would.'

'Then, barring accidents, you wouldn't have to send it to the dry cleaners for ages and when you did it would come back looking like new.'

'You've talked me into it,' Jenny said, making up her mind. 'I'll take it.'

She was upstairs in the bedroom and nibbling at her lower lip. Did lunch or maybe it was called luncheon at the

Parkview Hotel, really call for her jersey suit? Wouldn't her everyday clothes be all right? She was always neat. The answer to that was probably yes but it would be a lost opportunity. When would she get another? If Stewart wanted to see her again she thought she would refuse and if this was to be a one off then she had better make it a day to remember.

Should she wear her working clothes and change into her jersey suit just before lunchtime? No she wouldn't do that – it was making too much of the occasion. Come to think about it there was a smock belonging to her in the Log Cabin. She would wear it to protect her clothes. With that settled in her mind, Jenny quickly dressed, then almost changed her mind again when she looked at herself. Heavens! the colour seemed lighter than ever. She turned away and reached for her loose-fitting oatmeal coat and slipped it on. The weather seemed slow to make up its mind. The dull start might mean a bright day or there again it might remain dull. At least there were no rain clouds.

Jenny went through the usual routine of checking that the windows were closed and the gas on the cooker turned off. Satisfied, she locked the back door and let herself out the front, double locking it. Jenny had thought there was no need for all this locking up, the village didn't have a problem with burglars although there had been one or two break-ins in the distant past. Jenny's mother had been very firm about it. She was much more concerned about security than her daughter.

'Maybe it was reasonably safe, Jenny, when you were going out at different times but not now you are getting the same bus in the mornings and remember you are away for most of the day. Someone up to no good could notice when the house would be empty. A back window left slightly open would be enough for them to gain admittance. That type are clever, Jenny, don't underestimate them.'

'No, Mother, I won't.'

'Surely worth the small effort, that is all it takes.'

'Yes, Mother.' There was no use arguing and she was talking a lot of sense.

It was a last minute rush to catch the bus and Jenny was out of breath when she got on.

'Sleep in this morning?' the conductor said cheerfully as he punched her a ticket.

'No, I didn't sleep in, I just didn't realise the time.'

Two of the passengers were known to Jenny but since they were sitting together she could go further back and take a seat on her own. She smiled to the two ladies, made some remark about the weather and walked on. The journey was a time when she liked to be alone to gather her thoughts. In two weeks' time she would be sitting her driving test and if she passed first time there would be no more running for buses. She would have the use of a car. Jenny still couldn't imagine it happening. She, Jenny Richardson, learning to drive, it was like a dream. The dream could become reality if she didn't get too excited. Her instructor was quietly confident, he told her, otherwise he wouldn't be putting her forward for the test. No one, he said, could foretell how a pupil would perform on the day but he thought Mrs Richardson would be fine. Reversing round a corner had given her most trouble but she had mastered the technique as she had with a hill start. Her horror had been the car rolling back down the hill. She had overcome that too.

No one knew she was learning to drive, she had told no one. What would the family say? The thought of her secret sent shivers of excitement down her spine. Would Wilma and Katy be proud to have a mother who could drive? When Paul had left them the girls had missed the family car just as she had but little had been said about it. In the midst of all the trauma it hadn't seemed so very important. Jenny allowed herself the luxury of imagining Paul's reaction when he heard that his wife had her own transport. Not too pleased would be an understatement, shocked incredulity more like. It hadn't happened yet and there was always the chance that she would require two or more attempts before the examiner was satisfied.

Jenny came out of her daydream with a start. Goodness, this was where she got off. Hurriedly she got to her feet and was further embarrassed when the conductor shook his head and grinned.

'Too much on your mind, lass.'

'I know.' She could have gone beyond her stop and had the walk back.

The morning went in quickly. Merchandise had arrived earlier than expected and had to be checked then priced before going into stock. There was a blink of sun slanting in the windows which was promising.

'Jenny, watch your time,' Moira said as she held up one of the mohair jackets for Jenny to admire.

'Lovely and as for time I'm early yet.'

'Since Wilma was so delighted with her jacket I thought we should get in a few more. We must cater for the young as well as the young in heart,' she smiled. 'Wilma will keep us right in that department.'

'I'm not so sure. She and her friend drool over fashion magazines and seem to like the most extreme styles.'

'To drool over, Jenny, but not to buy. Off you go, I'll finish here.'

'I'd rather—'

'And I would rather you went away and got yourself spruced up. If I need any help, which is unlikely, then Doris will give me a hand.'

Jenny was glad of the chance to freshen up. She took extra care with her make-up and her hair, which was professionally cut every four weeks and required only a comb through it to fall into place. She changed her shop footwear for a pair of cream-coloured court shoes with a higher heel than she usually wore. A last look in the mirror and she was ready. Picking up her handbag, Jenny went in search of Moira. She had been talking to a customer and left her to make up her mind what she should buy for her grandchild's birthday.

'Over here, Jenny, where I can have a good look at you. Perfect and just right for you.'

'Far too light, I should never have bought it.'

'An excellent buy. You look very elegant.'

'Me? Elegant?' Jenny shook her head. 'That is something I could never be.'

'How wrong you are. Elegance has nothing to do with

338

beauty, it is something quite different. I could say you look smart and you would be satisfied.'

'Yes. I could accept that, you see. In other words, Moira, I know my limitations.'

'Away with you. Other people see what you don't. Enjoy your lunch and stretch it out for as long as you want.' She gave a wave of her hand.

Jenny waited until it was almost twelve fifteen, then she went out of the door and down the steps. She began to walk slowly towards the area used for parking. She thought Stewart must have been sitting in the car for some time because she had heard no car arriving and she had been listening for ten minutes or so.

The car door opened and closed and Stewart was striding quickly towards her. How smart he looked, there was nothing crumpled about his appearance today. His dark suit was well-pressed, the shirt snowy white and his shoes shone with polish. It couldn't be easy for a man on his own yet he had made the effort for her. How very glad she was to be wearing her new outfit. She was paying him the same compliment. As they neared she saw his face wreathed in smiles and Jenny felt her own smile stretching.

'Jenny,' he said, taking her hand in both of his. 'I've been looking forward to this so much.'

'So have I,' she found herself saying.

'How lovely you look,' he said softly, 'that is a wonderful shade. Daffodils in springtime is what you remind me of. My favourite flower as it happens and very soon now they will be out in all their golden splendour.'

'That sounds poetic,' she laughed.

'I have my moments,' he said laughing with her.

'Let me say how smart you look,' and was glad she had said so when she saw how pleased he was.

Together they walked the few yards to the car. Stewart saw her settled in the passenger seat then went round to the driver's side. He started up the engine and manoeuvred out of the parking area and over the bumpy ground until it evened out and they were joining the traffic on the main road. Jenny hadn't been aware she was doing so until he remarked about it.

'Are you interested in driving, Jenny?'

'What made you ask that?'

'You were giving a great deal of attention to me changing gear.'

'Was I? How we give ourselves away.'

'If you are keen I would be only too happy to give you lessons.'

'An offer you might live to regret. That was kind of you, Stewart, and brave.'

'Why brave?'

'You can't know what I would be like behind the wheel.'

'At a guess I think you would pick it up very quickly and become a good, careful driver.'

How different to Paul, Jenny was thinking. He would never have offered to teach her which was probably just as well. A husband wouldn't have the patience whereas an instructor is trained for the job, and a stranger or even a friend might want to shout and hurl insults but would hold back. They would make excuses not to have to go through another hair-raising experience.

'Thank you. As it happens, Stewart, I have been taking instruction in driving from a qualified instructor and I am due to sit my test in two weeks' time.'

He turned his head to look at her admiringly. 'Well done, Jenny.'

'I haven't passed yet,' she protested.

'I think you will but don't be disheartened if you fail first time. Many do and the extra lessons are money well spent.'

'Give you more confidence you mean?'

'This doesn't apply to you but there are some who become over-confident because they passed first time.'

She nodded. Jenny could imagine that being the case but he was right. Over-confidence would never be one of her faults.

'I'm full of admiration for you, Jenny.'

'Why? Because I am learning to drive? Many women do, you know.'

'The admiration was in general. You didn't sit about feeling sorry for yourself and many in your position would. You faced a very different future with courage. And speaking of the future you won't have to hang about waiting for buses.'

'That's true, but the car will belong to the Log Cabin, I will have the use of it that's all. Miss Ramsay, my employer, wants me to take on some of the buying which means going to the warehouses and that wouldn't be easy without a car.'

'There are many advantages in having a company car, for one thing you don't have the upkeep.'

'I know. Paul's is a company car. Is yours?'

'No, the car belongs to me and I get expenses. There isn't much to choose between a company car and claiming expenses. I'm speaking about the financial side but I have to say I prefer to—'

'Own your own,' she finished for him. 'Let me tell you this, Stewart Taylor, apart from Miss Ramsay who suggested I learn to drive, you are the only one who knows I am taking lessons.'

'Then I am honoured, but are you saying you have kept this from your two daughters and your mother?'

'Yes.'

'Any particular reason or shouldn't I ask?'

'If I wasn't going to make anything of it they didn't have to know.'

He was smiling. 'And then you discovered it wasn't anything like as difficult as you thought?'

'That's about it. Before starting the lessons I was apprehensive but now I am enjoying them. Mind you, I feel very confident when my instructor is sitting beside me. He happens to be excellent and at the stage I am he gives only road directions. Once I have an examiner sitting beside me it might be a different story.'

'A lot of learners go through agonies before their test then after about five minutes settle down. You will, don't you worry.'

'Thanks, you've made me feel better already.'

'Good. Incidentally, do you know the Parkview Hotel?'

'By name only.'

'Occasionally I do business over lunch and I find the

Parkview is quiet which is welcome when one is trying to get an order.'

'Is that difficult, getting an order I mean?'

'No, not too difficult at all, not in my line. You see, Jenny, I visit hospitals in the main and doctors' surgeries. After the usual patter I leave samples and orders follow. Perhaps I should qualify that, orders more often than not follow.'

'I'm sure it isn't as easy as you are trying to make out.'

'Very few of my problems are associated with work.'

'No,' she said quietly. They were both silent until he said, 'This is where we turn off.'

Parkview Hotel was approached by a winding, tree-lined road that was badly potted in places. Paul reduced his speed to a crawl.

'You would think the management would keep this road in reasonable repair. It wouldn't cost much to fill up the pot holes and the saving on car springs would be enormous. You avoid one hole and go into another.'

'Annoying but never mind, this is a lovely setting. Look at the way the branches almost meet,' Jenny said admiringly. 'Would you happen to know what the Parkview was before it became an hotel?'

'A mansion house with rather an interesting history. I've heard bits and pieces but I'm not up on it. We'll pick up a brochure from the desk and you can read all about it.' He went on a few yards and pointed though he didn't need to. Through the trees Jenny saw it, a magnificent structure she was to learn that had been built in Victorian times for a wealthy family who through greed and misfortune had to sell.

'Fancy being able to call a house that size your home,' Jenny laughed.

'Personally I give the hotel full marks for keeping the frontage much as it was and having the sense to build bedrooms to the back as well as kitchens. Mind you, Jenny, perhaps they had no choice, it could have been written into the agreement.'

'Very sensible if it was.'

'The parking area is to the back but there are a few places just to the side and we could be lucky. Yes, we are,' he said, driving into a space between two cars. 'I'm probably out of order and taking a private space but if called to task I can always plead ignorance.'

'It should be marked private if they want to keep people away.' Jenny was out of the car before Stewart got round.

'You should have allowed me to open the door.'

'No need,' she smiled as together they crunched their way up the gravel drive to the impressive entrance. The heavy glass door was opened for them by a young man in hotel uniform. It wasn't part of his duties to open the door, it just so happened that he was on his way out when they were about to enter. The very large entrance hall was also a sitting area. It was beautifully carpeted and a log fire burned brightly and gave out a welcome heat. On either side of the fireplace were two sofas and between them a long low, heavy-looking table. An elderly couple were occupying one of the sofas drinking coffee and reading a newspaper. The woman looked up briefly, gave a half smile and returned to her reading.

Stewart went over to speak to the young lady in

reception and Jenny heard him say that it was all right, he knew the way to the dining-room. He came back with a hotel brochure.

'Put that in your bag, Jenny, to read at your leisure.'

'Thank you.' She was looking about her and allowing her imagination to wander. Without the reception desk this could still be a stately home. There was an old-fashioned feel to the place and maybe a lot of the furniture had been sold with the house. The tapestry chairs set around appeared to be completely at home as though they had always been there.

'We can do a tour later on, Jenny, but I think we should head for the dining-room now.'

Once inside the door of the dining-room, a woman smart in her dark dress with touches of white, smiled a welcome. There was a lot of talking and then a burst of laughter and the woman winced.

'This way, please, and I'll show you to your table.'

Jenny followed with Stewart behind. A few of the small tables were taken but the noise and hilarity was coming from a long table with a party of women sitting round it. Whatever the other guests thought the ladies were thoroughly enjoying themselves. Stewart and Jenny were given a table some distance away from the long table and once settled were each given a menu.

'The waitress will come to take your order,' they were told before the woman made her departure.

Stewart looked upset. 'Sorry about this, Jenny and after me saying how quiet it would be.'

'I don't mind, I like to see folk enjoying themselves.'

'So do I but I could have wished they had chosen another hotel.'

'Just to cheer you up I notice they are now at the sweet course or as my younger daughter would say, the pudding stage.'

'Katy is quite right and long ago it was always pudding. Why it suddenly became a sweet I'll never know.' There was another burst of laughter and someone was choking with merriment. 'Maybe the ladies will take their coffee elsewhere, we can but hope.'

'Stewart, don't think you have to apologise. Laughter is infectious and I want to laugh with them even though I wouldn't know what I was laughing at.'

'Not me. I enjoy a good laugh if I am part of that company but not unless.' He tapped the menu. 'Let us see what they have to offer.'

The waitress came over to the table. 'Would you like something to drink?'

'Jenny, what would you like?'

'Nothing for me, thank you.'

'Are you sure?'

'Quite sure but don't let that stop you.'

'No, I won't either. Perhaps we could see the wine list?'

'Certainly, sir.' She went away and returned with a rather shabby leather-bound wine list which she handed to Stewart.

'Better to decide what we are going to eat before choosing the wine. What appeals to you?'

'Everything,' she laughed, 'but for starters I'm going to have orange and grapefruit segments.'

346

'The soup for me I think.'

It was a good and varied choice for the main dish and they both took a while to decide.

'Whole lemon sole, that would be a treat – yes, I'll have that.'

'That was getting my consideration.' He nodded. 'I'll have the fish which will mean a bottle of white wine.'

'Stewart, this is lunch time and we both have work to go to.'

'True, though I wanted this to be special.'

'It is special,' Jenny said softly. He was trying so hard.

'Shall I order two glasses?'

'That would be very nice.'

Stewart gave the order and with the menus removed, Jenny leaned over the table and whispered.

'Your wish is about to be granted, the ladies are going somewhere else for their coffee.'

'Praise be,' he grinned.

The ladies were being taken to a small sitting-room usually reserved for overnight guests and to get there they had to pass Stewart and Jenny's table. None of the ladies was known to her and she breathed more easily.

The starters arrived. A glass dish well filled with segments of orange and grapefruit was placed before Jenny and a few moments later the vegetable soup arrived piping hot. Warmed rolls arrived in a basket lined with a white napkin and was left on the table with a dish of butter. The rolls were light and delicious and Jenny ate two. She could have eaten more but as she told Stewart she had to keep a space for what was to follow which was just as well when she saw the size of the sole. It occupied most of the large plate and tasted as delicious as it looked.

'Everything to your satisfaction?' the waitress came back to ask.

'Lovely, thank you.'

To follow, Jenny had Bakewell tart with custard and Stewart had apple pie and cream. Stewart told the waitress they would have coffee in the lounge.

'I'll bring it to you there when you are ready.'

They went through to the main lounge and got comfortable seats opposite each other. No one else was there. The waitress brought the coffee on a silver tray, poured out two cups and left the pot on the table. A tiny plate held four small squares of fudge.

Stewart smiled across to Jenny then leaned far forward.

'This is lovely, my idea of happiness, don't you agree?'

'It was a very enjoyable meal, Stewart,' Jenny said moving further back in her chair. She took a piece of fudge and put it in her mouth. The other diners must be having their coffee at their table in the dining-room and Jenny wished Stewart hadn't suggested the lounge for theirs.

'Jenny, we must do it again and soon,' he said urgently. 'In fact we must arrange to see each other as often as possible. Surely you can plan your home affairs—'

'No!' Jenny was startled. She hadn't expected this. Lunch once in a while was all she had had in mind though it looked as if Stewart had other ideas. She took a deep breath. 'Stewart, if I am in any way at fault I apologise but I really did think that I had made it clear that lunch very occasionally was all it would be.'

'Maybe I did agree to that at the time but we both know it isn't enough. We want to be together and why should we deny ourselves? We are tied in one way and free in another.'

She frowned. 'I think I would need that explained.' Jenny was becoming more uncomfortable by the minute.

'Obvious I would have thought. Your divorce will no doubt be straightforward but even so these things take time. Mine would be more complicated and though there is no guarantee of success I have reason to believe that eventually I will gain my freedom. Phyllis won't be hurt, she will not be harmed in any way and I do have a right to some happiness.'

'You have every right to happiness but whether you gain your freedom or not it has nothing to do with me.'

'It has everything to do with you.'

Jenny sipped some coffee and put the cup down with a hand that trembled.

'You must listen to me, Stewart, and please try not to interrupt.'

'You look very serious.'

'I am serious.'

'All right you have my full attention.' He drank some of his coffee, looked at the two remaining pieces of fudge and handed the plate to Jenny.

'No, thank you. Why don't you have both?'

'Might as well since you don't want yours.' He popped both squares into his mouth.

Jenny swallowed and began. 'For the first time in my life,

Stewart, I am in charge. I have my independence and it is a wonderful feeling.'

'That needn't—'

'No interruptions, you promised.'

'Sorry.'

'From the time we were married Paul made all the decisions and I went along with whatever he said. He was the breadwinner and it was no more than I expected. My role, as I saw it then, was to keep Paul happy, look after our two daughters and manage the house without being extravagant. In other words my life was like that of hundreds of other women and I was perfectly content. Which made the shock of suddenly having to manage on my own all the more terrifying. My mother was very supportive and I came through it bruised but wiser. Luck played its part but my determination helped.'

'I'm sure it did.'

'I hold down a good job and if Paul for some reason were to stop maintenance for the girls, it would be no great hardship. Being able to say that makes me feel very proud. This is my life and the way I want it. No one, you included, is going to change that.' She paused and looked at him but it was difficult to read his expression. 'My girls and I are happy, genuinely happy. Paul was once essential to their happiness but no longer. They do see him from time to time and are satisfied with that. As for me Paul belongs to my past and there is no way back for him.'

'Jenny, I wouldn't want to spoil anything for you but when you come down from the clouds the novelty of having your independence will have worn off. Nothing surer. Your Miss Ramsay might be a hard-boiled business-woman but you could never be that. You are made for loving, Jenny, and that I might say is the greatest compliment one can make to a woman.'

She smiled. He was rather sweet but totally wrong.

'Thank you for the compliment. Maybe the old Jenny was made for loving but the new Jenny sees a whole new world opening up for her. She won't give that up.'

'An occasional lunch or nothing at all. Is that what you are saying?'

'We should say goodbye now. Don't waste your time on me, Stewart. Someone much more suitable might walk into your life.'

'Until such time we can have the occasional lunch. Surely you wouldn't refuse me that?'

'No, I won't do that,' Jenny said quietly, 'just so long as you understand the situation.' She looked at her watch and smiled to herself when she remembered Miss Ramsay's words – whatever you do don't look at your watch, men just hate it. 'Stewart, this has been a very long lunch break but I must get back to the Log Cabin.'

'Of course and I must put in a couple of calls before I head for home.'

Jenny gave a sigh of relief. It was going to be all right.

Chapter Twenty

'Wilma, wait for me,' Evelyn shouted as she hurried to catch up with her friend.

Wilma turned round then slowed down. 'I thought you'd missed it when you didn't get off your usual bus.'

'Got a lift. A new neighbour of ours said he was going past the school and to hop in if I wanted a lift.'

'And you hopped in?'

'Too true I did. Saved my bus fare if nothing else. Wait until I tell my mum, she thought they were a bit standof-fish. I wouldn't know about his wife but he's nice, old of course, but nice. Hang on that's my shoe lace undone.' She bent down to fasten it in a double knot. 'This, I can tell you, is to be the last pair of lacing shoes I get. From now on it will be something decent. You know what – I fancy those with a single strap across. Very smart.'

'I have a pair like that.'

'You would. I can never get anything without you having it first.'

'Can't help that can I? I'm only allowed to wear them at the weekends.'

'Before I forget my mum said she saw your mum.'

'When was this?'

'Wednesday I think, yes it was Wednesday.'

'Where?'

'The dining-room in the Parkview Hotel.'

'Not my mum, she didn't see her there. She works all day in the Log Cabin.'

'My mum was very sure.'

'How could she be sure? Your mum saw my mum only the once so how could she be sure?'

Evelyn was thinking hard. 'It was a Guild outing, they have one about this time every year. They book up at a different hotel, you know try them all. I remember now how she was so sure. She wasn't absolutely certain until then. The man your mum was with called her Jenny. She heard him when they were passing the table. Jenny is your mother's name isn't it?'

'Yes.'

'You see my mum's got a good memory,' Evelyn said proudly. 'That time she was in the Log Cabin she must have heard somebody call your mother Jenny.'

Wilma shook her head. 'It still wasn't my mum she saw.'

'Well, she was awful sure.'

'You ever heard of coincidences?'

'Of course I have but that would be quite a big one, wouldn't it?'

'No, it would not. I keep telling you it wasn't my mum your mother saw. It could be her double though, everybody has one.'

'Not called Jenny, that would be a bit much,' Evelyn said stubbornly.

'That is where the coincidence comes in.'

'You could ask your mother, no harm in that.'

'I will if I remember. She'll have a good laugh.'

Janet Scrimgeour came over once a week to have her meal with Jenny and the girls. Jenny did most of the preparation before leaving for work. She set the alarm and got up half an hour earlier than usual and marvelled at how much could be done in that extra thirty minutes.

Janet never came empty-handed. She arrived with a sponge she had baked that morning.

'Mum, you shouldn't have but thanks,' Jenny said taking the sponge from her mother. It was in a biscuit tin that was almost a perfect fit to take it. The box travelled frequently between the two houses.

'Keeps me occupied and you've so little time.'

Jenny smiled. 'We'll have a quick cup before the girls get in.'

Katy arrived first and gave her gran a beaming smile.

'Hello, dear, how was school?'

'Like always. Awful.'

'You don't mean that.'

Wilma had come in and shut the door noisily. 'Why should she not mean it? School is awful.'

'If it is as bad as all that why are you staying on?'

'Just because – that's why,' she said annoyingly.

'That is no answer.'

Jenny was laughing as she checked the oven. 'Mum, you won't get them to say they like school. It is just not done.'

'I don't understand the young of today. Why can't they say what they mean?'

'I don't know but be like me and just accept. It took me a while but I now know not to ask anything. If they have something to tell me I'll get it when they are ready and not before.'

'Times I wonder who is boss. You were never like that.'

'I was a different generation. Hurry up you two, get your hands washed and be down in five minutes.'

There was no move.

'You heard your mother?'

'Yes, Gran, we heard.' Wilma was sprawled on a chair and got up slowly. She winked to Jenny who shot her a warning look. Katy glanced from one to the other then shrugged and went upstairs.

'You do have a lot to put up with.'

'No, I don't, Mother, this is just a stage they are going through. I wouldn't change them for the world. That doesn't mean I don't find them exasperating at times but they know not to go too far.'

'I think you are too soft.'

'No, I don't think I am. And you, Mother dear, should be glad they are not on their best behaviour when you are here. If they were it would mean they weren't comfortable with you.'

'They are always comfortable with me and frankly I don't know what I would do without them.'

'Live in peace and quiet.'

'Bored out of my mind more like. Here they are. Sounds like a regiment coming down those stairs and not two young ladies.'

'Are we young ladies, Gran?'

'Not yet but I have hopes.'

They were eating rice pudding with raisins when Wilma remembered what Evelyn had said.

'Mum, where were you last Wednesday at lunch time?'

Jenny looked up startled and felt a cold band of dread grip her. With difficulty she swallowed the mouthful of rice. It gave her a moment to think.

'I can tell you where your mother was last Wednesday and every Wednesday. She was in the Log Cabin.'

'I know that is where she was supposed to be.'

'Why do you ask?' Jenny managed to get out.

'Only because Evelyn's mother saw you.'

'I don't know Evelyn's mother.'

'I know you don't but she knows you by sight. Remember I told you that Mrs Bannerman and Evelyn's aunt visited the Log Cabin. Evelyn's mother was going to introduce herself but I think you were busy or something.'

Jenny nodded. 'I seem to recall you saying that.'

Janet Scrimgeour finished her rice pudding and put the spoon on the plate. She had taken a very small portion saying it was all she had room for.

'Tell me this,' she said smiling to Jenny. 'Where was your mother supposed to be or didn't Evelyn say?'

'She did say. It was in the Parkview Hotel, Gran. Evelyn's mum was on some kind of outing and she was with a lot of other women.'

Jenny felt herself go clammy. Evelyn's mother had been one of the ladies at that top table. She was caught, there was no way out of this. She wouldn't tell lies. Once you started that you were on the slippery slope.

She had felt her colour changing and knew her mother's eyes were on her. She might have tried a little lie. Lunch with a friend which was true, no need to say it was a male friend. Not unless it couldn't be avoided.

'The really, really strange thing about it, Mum, was that the woman who was supposed to be you was called Jenny. Evelyn's mum heard the man she was with call her that.'

Jenny closed her eyes. This was as bad as it could be.

'What man?' Katy said absently. She hadn't been taking much interest in the conversation. 'Any rice pudding left, Mum?'

'Yes, I'll get you some.'

Katy handed over her plate and kept hold of her spoon. Jenny got away from the table and had a moment or two to compose herself. They would have to be told the truth, difficult though that would be. Why, oh, why, had she agreed to have lunch with Stewart? Not that it was too terrible, what was shaming was the deception. She had kept it a secret as though she had something to hide. She had done nothing wrong but would others be convinced of that? Jenny spooned the rest of the rice pudding on to Katy's plate and carried it through to the table.

'Thanks, Mum.'

'You eat like a horse Katy Richardson.'

'Mum?' Katy protested.

'Never mind, dear, it shows you enjoy your food and better that than picking away like your sister.'

'I do not pick at my food,' Wilma said haughtily. 'I do

what Gran says everyone should do and that is leave the table still feeling a little bit hungry.'

'Did I say that?'

'Yes, you did.' Wilma turned to her mother. 'Mum, I'll tell Evelyn it wasn't you her mum saw.'

'No, don't do that.' Jenny sat down and pushed the half-empty plate to the side. She couldn't have swallowed another mouthful to save her life. 'I have a confession to make,' she said quietly. 'Not a confession, rather an explanation.'

Three pairs of eyes fixed on her.

'I wouldn't have recognised Evelyn's mother but she was quite right, I did have lunch in the Parkview Hotel last Wednesday. There was a party of ladies in the dining-room when we arrived.'

'We? Then you were with a man?' Wilma looked puzzled and uncertain.

'Yes. The man's name is Stewart Taylor. We have become friendly and he asked me to have lunch with him. I accepted.' Jenny could see that her mother's lips were pursed in disapproval. She would say very little in front of Wilma and Katy. It would be saved until they were on their own.

'Fair enough having lunch with a friend but why all the secrecy?'

'There was no secrecy intended, Wilma.'

'You didn't tell us.'

'No.'

'Why not?'

'Because I didn't choose to.'

'Why was that?'

'How often have I asked you where you were going and got the answer – out?'

'That is different, you had a good idea where I would be.'

'Maybe so but you weren't prepared to say.'

'Gran?' Wilma looked to Janet for support.

'I am saying nothing, Wilma, nothing at all.'

'Was it a good lunch at the Parkview, Mum?'

Jenny laughed. Dear, darling Katy, she always came in at the right moment.

'Yes, dear, it was a lovely lunch.'

'For any favour it doesn't matter what they had to eat,' Wilma almost shouted. 'Food on the brain that's you.'

'I only asked and Mum can do what she wants, she's an adult.'

'Last Wednesday,' Wilma said slowly, 'I remember now, your bedroom door was open and that yellow jersey suit you bought not long ago was hanging on the wardrobe door. I wondered why it was there and I meant to ask only I forgot. You must have been going to wear it, that is why you were in your dressing-gown,' she said accusingly.

Jenny gave a forced laugh. 'Really! Is this an interrogation?'

'No, Mum, it is not. I just cannot understand why you couldn't have said. Did you think we wouldn't approve?'

'I'm your mother, I don't need your approval and this is becoming ridiculous.'

'You weren't hungry that night,' Katy grinned. 'You hardly ate anything and no wonder if you had a big tuck-in at lunch time.'

No one laughed.

'Mum, I need to know one thing and it is important.'

'What do you need to know, Wilma?'

'Was it because you thought I might say something nasty if you told us?'

Jenny stared at her daughter. 'What nasty thing could you have said?'

'I might have said you were as bad as Dad.'

'Is that what you think?' Jenny said faintly.

'No, of course I don't. I wasn't fair to you before. I knew I was wrong but I had to blame someone and I didn't want all the blame to go on Dad.' She gulped. 'I used to think he was perfect and Vera marvellous but I was wrong. Vera got fed up and dumped us and Dad is so – so stupid about her that he'll forgive her for anything.'

That had been quite a speech, Jenny thought and brave – yes brave.

'Darling, everything is just fine. With hindsight I should have told you but then we don't always do what is sensible.'

'Where did you meet Mr Stewart, Mum?'

'Mr Taylor, Katy. Stewart is his Christian name. He has only recently come to live in Blackford and when I was waiting for the bus home he very kindly offered me a lift. In the conversation I told him I worked in the Log Cabin and he said when he was passing that way he would come in for a coffee.'

'And he did?'

'Yes. His wife—'

'The man is married then?'

'Yes, Mother, Stewart's wife is a poor soul.'

'All the more reason why she should be getting his attention and not you.'

That infuriated Jenny and she spoke angrily. 'You know nothing of the circumstances?'

'I know when something is right or wrong.'

'Black or white, Mum. No shades of grey for you.'

Katy looked puzzled. 'What does that mean?'

'I'll explain it some other time, dear,' Jenny said wearily. She looked at the clock. 'Katy, if you are going to Brenda's it is time you were on your way. What about your homework, when do you propose doing that?'

'I'm taking my school books to Brenda's and I'll do it there.'

'See that you do.'

'I'll have to. Brenda's mother is strict, nearly as bad as you,' she said cheekily before galloping upstairs.

'I'll have to watch my time.'

'Nothing to hinder you staying overnight.'

'No, I won't, I'll be better in my own house tonight.'

'Want a hand with the dishes, Mum?'

'No, I'll manage. You said you had a lot of work to do.'

'So I have. I get more to do because I'm staying on.'

'Off you go. Gran and I will have a cup of tea and then you can take her to the bus.'

'Sure, shout when it is time.'

'Thank you, Wilma, I'll be glad of your company.'

Jenny sent her mother into the sitting-room and followed a few minutes later with a fresh pot of tea.

'You've made a lovely job of this room.'

'So you said before. Come on, get it off your chest. We need to clear the air.'

'To say I am disappointed in you is to put it mildly. I would never have believed that you would take up with a married man. After the agonies you suffered when Paul left you I would have thought you would have considered that man's poor wife.'

'I am not having an affair if that is what you are thinking.'

Janet looked shocked. 'Not for a moment did I think that.'

'Yes, you did. You didn't want to think it but you did.'

'It was all this secrecy. You must admit—'

'I admit that was a mistake. My reason for not shouting it from the roof tops—'

'No need for that, Jenny,' Janet said holding herself stiffly.

'Sorry, but I have every right to be angry. Had I said that Stewart Taylor had invited me to lunch I can just imagine what you would have said. As a matter of fact, Mother, the invitation was for dinner which I declined.'

'I should hope so.'

Jenny's lips tightened. 'I told Stewart that there were three reasons why I couldn't accept his invitation. You, Wilma and Katy were the reasons.'

Janet attempted a smile. 'Rather than disappoint him you agreed to have lunch?'

'Yes.'

'What is wrong with his wife?'

'She had a nervous breakdown a number of years ago after a stillbirth.'

'Poor soul. It takes time to get over that.'

'She hasn't got over it. Stewart says she is getting worse and just living in a world of her own.'

'Terrible when the mind goes. A tragedy, Jenny, no one would deny that but you should stay out of it. You have enough problems of your own.'

'Have I? I thought I had overcome them.'

'You've done wonders but at the end of the day Paul is still your husband. Be patient as I have said all along. It will all come right in time. Look at Wilma – she's had her eyes opened. She sees that Vera woman for what she is, a scheming, ruthless besom. Paul will too.'

'Perhaps he will but it won't make the slightest difference to me.'

'Don't become hard and bitter. Can't you find it in your heart to forgive him? Paul has a lot of good qualities.' Janet was almost pleading.

'I forgave him long ago. Once the affair with Vera Cuthbertson is over I genuinely hope he will find happiness but it won't be with me.'

'You seem so certain.'

'I am. You can believe it or not but I am very happy as I am.'

'You would go through life alone?'

'Many do and I don't have to be alone. When the divorce—'

'What divorce?' she said sharply.

'My divorce from Paul. I have set everything in motion and Paul should have heard from the solicitor by now.'

Janet was shaking her head. 'Divorce is so final and this could be a terrible mistake.'

'Divorce is final, that is the whole purpose of it.'

'You've changed and I find that so sad.'

'I'm sorry, Mother, but that is the way it is. And I am not rushing you out but if you want that bus you had better get ready and I'll give Wilma a shout.'

She got up hastily. 'I'll get home, Jenny, and you think carefully before you do anything stupid.'

Wilma came back from seeing her gran to the bus stop.

'She caught it?'

'Just. The conductor saw us hurrying and waited.'

'Your gran could have stayed overnight there was nothing to stop her.'

'I said that too but she said when she was upset it was better to be upset in her own house.'

'Oh dear, I seem to have caused a lot of trouble.'

'It'll blow over. Any tea in that pot?'

'Yes, but it will be cold.'

'I'll make fresh.'

'I'm full of tea.'

'Bet you won't refuse though.'

'No, I don't suppose I will. You take a cup up to your room and that will let you get on.'

'We'll have it together, I want to talk.'

Jenny sighed inwardly. How much more of this did she have to take?

'Couldn't it wait, this talk?'

'No, this is a good chance when Katy is out.'

'I'm not sure if I can take any more.'

'You don't know what I'm going to say.'

'That's true.'

'You shouldn't have let me get away with the things I said to you. I thought you were such a soft mark, that you would let anybody walk over you but you are not like that at all.'

'What am I like?'

'Honest and straightforward.'

'I thought I was secretive and worse.'

'You could have denied everything and nobody would have been any the wiser. You didn't because you are you. That was brave confessing all.'

'I didn't feel brave.'

'You shouldn't bother too much what Gran says, I mean she is old-fashioned and what was right in her day doesn't have to be right now. You are entitled to a life of your own and we have no business to find fault.'

'A man friend is acceptable,' Jenny smiled.

'Men friends are acceptable,' she grinned.

'Now! Now!' Jenny laughed. 'Seriously, dear, if I were to have lunch with Stewart again would you find that upsetting?'

'No, I wouldn't and don't feel you have to tell us. That isn't to say I wouldn't like you to, but the decision is yours. As for Evelyn who caused all this bother I'll just say I forgot to ask you and she'll let it drop. Maybe she's forgotten already.'

Jenny was shaking her head and looking on the verge of tears.

'Wilma, you sound so mature, so grown-up and I'm not sure I want that, not yet' she said unsteadily.

'If I'm not grown-up I very soon will be. Mothers and daughters should be friends, that's what I want to be, your daughter and your friend. Katy is going to be the baby for a while yet.'

'Better not let her hear you say that.' Jenny got up still fighting the tears. 'Come here and let me give you a hug.' For a few moments they clung together.

'Is it true? Gran said you were filing for divorce.'

'I'm surprised she told you.'

'She wouldn't have only she wanted my opinion.'

'And what is your opinion, Wilma?'

'Go ahead and get your freedom. The way you are placed at the moment you are in – are in—'

'Limbo?'

'Yes, that's it, in limbo. You are neither married nor single.'

'That's what it amounts to. Wilma, are you happy or do you think you have lost out? Think carefully before you answer.'

'I do have to think about it. If—'

'Life is full of ifs.'

'I know. If Vera hadn't come on the scene I suppose the four of us would have been happy together. Don't worry about us. Katy and I haven't missed out. At first we thought we had, or I did anyway, but that was because suddenly life was different and a bit scary. We've all changed, well maybe Gran hasn't but you have changed most of all. You've been terrific.'

'Luck had a lot to do with my changed circumstances.'

'Maybe it did but you took those first steps and showed

everyone what you could do. I honestly believe that you would succeed in anything you put your mind to.'

'Thank you, darling and I'm afraid I have another confession to make—'

'You're joking?'

'No, I'm not. Your mother has been taking driving lessons.'

Wilma's eyes opened wide. 'Driving lessons on the quiet. Gosh!'

'I sit my test next week.'

'Why keep it to yourself? Why didn't you say something?'

'This is between us?'

'Sure.'

'I was afraid that driving a car would be beyond me—'

'And if it was and it most certainly isn't?'

'If it was beyond me then no one need know. Silly pride.'

'Dad would have been dead against you taking lessons.'

'He thought I was too nervous. Maybe I was then.'

'If you are taking your test next week then that means you can drive.'

'Only with a qualified driver beside me.'

'Can we afford a car?'

'No. In the years to come probably yes, but not yet. The car will belong to the Log Cabin but I will have the use of it. Miss Ramsay wants me to visit the warehouses and buses would be hopeless for that.'

'Miss Ramsay has been wonderful to the three of us.'

'Yes, she has and we must never forget it.'

'Isn't it sad that she didn't marry and have children? She would have made a good mother.'

'I must tell her that.'

'No, don't do that, she might not like it.'

'I won't then.' Jenny looked at the clock. 'What about all that work waiting for you?'

'I'll get down to it presently. We've had a good talk haven't we?'

'A very good talk, Wilma. We understand each other. Maybe I should finish by saying that when the divorce comes through you mustn't let it make any difference to you. Your father has his problems—'

'Meaning Vera?'

'Yes. She isn't important and you no longer see her through rose-coloured glasses but Paul does. When it ends it will be awful for him and he will need you and Katy. He loves you both. Remember that.'

'I won't forget. He is still Dad after all and the three of us have a lot of fun. Vera isn't missed and we hardly ever mention her name.'

Jenny nodded.

'Could be Dad is getting tired of her.'

Jenny wasn't particularly interested.

'Wait until Dad and Vera hear that you have—'

'My own transport,' Jenny finished for her. 'Say nothing, I haven't passed yet.'

'If you fail will you get another chance?'

'As many as it takes.'

'What kind of car?'

'A Morris Minor.'

'A brand new one or a second hand?'

'Brand new. Nothing but the best for the Log Cabin,' Jenny laughed.

'Forgot. What colour?'

'Dark blue.'

'Life is good, Mum, isn't it?'

'What you make of it, Wilma.'

'It will be nice having a car again.'

'Very nice. We'll be able to collect your gran and save her all those bus journeys.'

'Until you get a lot of experience we won't talk to you when you are driving.'

'That is sensible. I have to concentrate on the road.'

'Mum, it isn't worth going upstairs.'

'What about the work you have to do for tomorrow?'

'Not tomorrow, just when I get it done. Senior girls are not treated like children you know.'

They were all crowded at the window. Miss Ramsay, Lily Anderson, Doris Roberts and the odd-job man who was taking a break from collecting the wrappings and cardboard boxes for removal. The best of them would go into the cupboard for future use and the remainder would be for the rubbish pile.

The car had just drawn up. Jenny wasn't at the wheel and believing this to be a bad sign Lily gave a sympathetic clucking noise.

'Poor lass, she'll be that disappointed.'

'Don't jump to conclusions,' Miss Ramsay said, straining

to see the expression on Jenny's face when she got out of the car.

Jenny got out and turned her back to say a few words to her instructor who smiled, shook her hand and then drove away. She began walking and then became aware of the faces at the window. With a broad smile she held up both thumbs.

'The clever girl, she's passed,' Doris said.

'Of course she has,' Moira smiled as she went to the door to meet Jenny.

'Many congratulations. I take it the thumbs-up mean you have passed.'

'Yes. I can't believe it. I made mistakes, I know I did.'

'Not serious ones or you wouldn't have passed.'

'I wasn't as nervous as I expected to be but when he, the examiner I mean, told me I'd passed, I began to shake. That's why Tommy took the wheel coming back. I don't think he trusted me.'

'That is quite normal. It is an ordeal for most people. You'll be fine by tomorrow which is when the new car should arrive. I'll get on to the garage right away and as I said before, Tommy will sit with you until you get the feel of it. A sherry is called for, we'll have that in my office.'

Chapter Twenty-One

―――――❦―――――

The dry-spell of weather was over and the rain was falling steadily, hitting the pavements and running in rivulets down the kitchen window. The tubs outside the Log Cabin were at their flowering best and the surrounding countryside was ablaze with golden daffodils which, in the far distance, looked like a huge yellow carpet. A gentle fall of rain would have been welcome, the earth was crying out for moisture, but not a damaging deluge. The tall, proud daffodils would be broken and flattened unable to survive such a battering. Jenny could only hope that the area around the Log Cabin was escaping the worst.

She had driven home, arriving before the rain had properly started but with the clouds dark and threatening. Wilma and Katy hadn't been so lucky. They ran when they came off the bus and came into the house wet but not soaked. Jenny served the meal at the usual time and when they had finished the three of them did the clearing up. Jenny checked that no dirty dish was left before emptying the basin and almost jumped when the front doorbell rang. Not a short ring but one that went on rather too long as though whoever was there was making sure it would be heard in every part of the house.

'Who on earth can that be? Whoever it is is determined to be heard.' Jenny dried her hands and went to answer it. Opening the door she found Paul standing there under cover of an umbrella.

'Paul?' she said sounding her surprise. There was just the tiniest hesitation before she moved aside to let him in.

He stepped quickly into the vestibule, gave the umbrella a shake before shutting the door then closed the umbrella and handed it to Jenny.

'I'll let you deal with that,' he smiled.

She put it in the umbrella stand where it would drip.

'Lucky I had it in the car, I didn't expect the weather to turn like this,' Paul said, wiping his feet on the recently purchased doormat that said WELCOME.

Jenny hoped he wouldn't notice and if he did that he wouldn't take it personally.

The girls recognising the voice came into the hall.

'Hello, Dad.' They were smiling but looking and sounding unsure.

Paul was the only one who appeared completely at ease. He could have been still living at 16 Abbotsford Crescent and it occurred to Jenny that an onlooker could have mistaken this man to be the owner and the bread-winner. A husband being welcomed home by his wife and family.

In the sitting-room the fire was burning brightly. The lamp was turned on and the curtains drawn. It was early to be closed up but it did keep out the depressing night. Jenny had been about to suggest that they go through when Paul turned to address Wilma and Katy.

'How about you two making yourselves scarce for say fifteen to twenty minutes? Your mum and I need to have a private talk.'

Jenny looked at him sharply and drew in her breath. The nerve of him. If she wasn't careful Paul was going to walk right over her. Wilma and Katy were looking at their mother to see what they should do.

'Paul, you may go into the sitting-room,' Jenny said coldly. 'I give you permission to do that.' She paused. 'You will not, however, order any of us about. This is my house in case you have forgotten.'

He raised his eyebrows and Jenny could see that he was taken aback. 'Sorry! Sorry! I seem to have put my foot in it. My humble apologies, Jenny. All the same, what we have to talk about is private and I'm sure Wilma and Katy won't find it a hardship to go upstairs. A chance to get on with their homework I would have thought.' He made it sound so reasonable and the girls must have thought that.

'Come on, Katy. All right, Mum?'

Jenny nodded. Paul had gone ahead of her into the sitting-room and was standing in the middle of the floor looking about him.

'Wilma said you had been making some changes to the house.'

'Yes.'

'Quite a transformation I have to say and very tastefully done. I am impressed.' He was impressed and wondered how much Jenny had spent. Quite a bit he was sure. That was quality furniture and over and above that was the redecoration. Very obviously professionally done.

'Thank you.'

He gave his lopsided smile. 'Mind you and with due respect I rather liked the way it was.'

'I didn't. It was a mess.'

'Not a mess, Jenny, you don't mean that. Just a rather nice mishmash. Remember the fun we had getting it together, searching second-hand shops and salerooms and finding wonderful bargains. Those were happy days.'

She didn't bother to answer. 'You can tell me why you are here and what is so private that it cannot be said in front of Wilma and Katy?'

'I'll come to that in a minute,' he said moving over to examine the two paintings. 'These are rather good. Did you buy them?'

'Yes.'

'Local artists are they?'

He wasn't going to give up. 'Two unknown artists, Paul, who might well be famous one day.'

'You hope,' he smiled, 'then you could cash in.'

'No, I would hold on to them. I bought them because I enjoy looking at the paintings.'

'Where did you get them as a matter of interest?'

'In the Log Cabin. They came from the display in our Gallery.'

'Might be worth a visit or again maybe not,' he said seeing her expression.

'With your curiosity satisfied perhaps you will answer

the question I put to you,' Jenny said sitting down in the nearest chair. 'What brings you here?'

'You don't sound very welcoming,' he said sitting down in the armchair beside the fire.

'I'm glad you noticed,' she said sarcastically. 'You are not welcome.'

'Bitterness doesn't become you, Jenny.'

'I am far from bitter. My life has never been better.'

'Fallen on your feet.'

She looked at him with contempt. 'Whatever you came to say get on with it or I am calling the girls down.'

His face hardened. 'This is what I came about.' His hand went to his jacket pocket and he brought out a long white envelope which he placed on the arm of the chair.

'Is this a guessing game or am I supposed to know what is contained in the envelope?'

She saw by the set of his mouth that she had angered him and smiled to herself. She felt rather pleased to have managed that.

'You know damn well what it is.'

'I imagine it has to do with our divorce.'

'I don't want a divorce and neither do you if you were honest with yourself.'

'I'm staggered by your arrogance but then you always have been arrogant. You are very wrong if you think I do not want a divorce. I do want one.'

'If you go ahead you will regret it.'

'Why should I?'

'Because my dear Jenny—'

'I am not your dear Jenny.'

'Slip of the tongue,' he grinned and she could have hit him. 'Be sensible, Jenny, it isn't necessary. Different if you were in love with someone and contemplating marriage but there is no one in your life.'

'How can you be sure about that?'

'It would have got to me.'

She supposed he meant Wilma or Katy. Jenny smiled, a secret smile that she thought had him worried.

'You were keen enough on a divorce at one point, what a pity I stood in your way then. I do genuinely regret that.'

He gave a shake of his head. 'All talk, I wouldn't have gone through with it.' He paused to stretch his long legs and enjoy the heat of the fire. Paul looked very much at home and she resented it.

'And why wouldn't you have gone through with it?'

'Whatever you might think I didn't want you out of my life.'

'No, you wanted to hang on to me in case your new relationship failed. Very sensible of you.'

'Jenny, one doesn't forget and what we had together was very precious.'

'So precious that you threw it away.'

'That is how it must have appeared to you.'

'Am I stupid or something? How could it appear otherwise?'

He looked at her for a long time then sighed. 'You would never understand, Jenny, never in a million years.'

'Try me, you never know.'

'Maybe if you had been more like you are now then it

wouldn't have happened. No, that isn't true it would still have happened.'

'Satisfy my curiosity if you will. Have I changed all that much?'

'I would say so. For a start you take more interest in your appearance.'

'I was letting myself go?'

'Yes.'

'Thanks. My housekeeping allowance wasn't over generous.'

'You never complained.'

'That was where I went wrong. I never complained. I managed on what I got and we lived comfortably but there was very little left for extras. By extras I mean a decent hairdo and some new clothes.'

'You are suggesting I kept you short.'

'Yes, I suppose I am but since I didn't complain I accept that I was partly to blame.'

'Why are we talking about money?'

Why are we talking at all she could have said. 'I have no idea.'

He laughed. 'We'll get back on track. Let me be completely honest with you, Jenny, and say that there are times when I wish I had never met Vera. Before she came on the scene life was uncomplicated.'

'Or that could be boring.'

'You said it. Life was dull, the same dreary routine day after day. One accepts the sameness in the working day but one looks for a bit of variety at home.'

'You did have variety at home as you put it. What you had was family life with all its ups and downs. When you wanted peace and quiet I kept the girls out of your way and as for me I waited on you hand and foot and that was my greatest mistake. If I had done a bit less you might have appreciated me more.'

He shrugged. Jenny remembered he had done a lot of it before the break-up of their marriage. She had found it annoying. Did it irritate Vera Cuthbertson? Or there again maybe he didn't shrug when she was around.

'Paul, this is getting us nowhere.'

'I want you to understand how it happened. The plain truth is that our marriage had gone stale and Vera offered excitement.'

'A last fling before you were too old.'

'Maybe it was. I know I was surprised and thrilled to bits when Vera began flirting with me. Contrary to what you might think I didn't make the first move.'

'I do believe you. There are women like your mistress who would do just that. She saw you, thought you were the most presentable and made her move. The fact that you were a married man with a family was no obstacle.'

'You've got it all worked out.'

'Long ago.'

'Vera is very beautiful and I fell in love. I couldn't help myself.'

'Doesn't she want marriage?'

'At first yes, but not now. She sees no need for it and neither do I.'

'What does she do when her looks go?'

'I don't see that happening for a very long time. Her kind of beauty will last.'

'Not for ever and it could be that she is making plans for her future, a future that doesn't include you. Aiming higher in other words,' she said cruelly.

'You could be right,' he said heavily and for a moment she felt sorry for him. 'The new Jenny doesn't mince her words.'

'The old Jenny was too trusting or too stupid.'

'Not stupid you were never that. Don't change too much, I wouldn't want that.'

'What do you want, Paul? Are you leaving your mistress?'

'I only wish I could but I can't.'

'She will when she is good and ready.'

'Could we stop talking about Vera and talk about us?'

'No, I don't think they can be separated. She dropped your daughters when it suited her and Wilma, for a little while, was devastated.'

'A little while, it is over now.'

'Not completely. Wilma honestly believed that Miss Cuthbertson was her friend and that cut deep.'

'Vera wouldn't mean to be unkind and you have to remember, Jenny, she works a full day and that doesn't give her much time to herself.'

Jenny didn't bother to answer, what was there to say.

'Something you said—'

'What?'

'You said she would leave me.'

'That much is obvious. She doesn't want marriage to you and, as I said before, she is probably aiming higher. Until that person comes along I imagine you are safe.'

He looked wretched. 'If I truly thought that . . .'

'You do but you won't face it.'

He sat up. 'Jenny, if you will just forget about the divorce I promise I'll leave Vera.' The wretched look had gone and in its place was the old winning smile. 'It can be like it once was, no not like that, it would be better.'

'Better for whom?'

'For the four of us.'

'You believe that?'

'I do. What has happened will strengthen the marriage.'

She began to smile and the smile grew wider.

'What is so funny?'

'You, Paul. What an idiot you must think me. As always you are thinking of yourself. If you leave your mistress or she gives you your marching orders you will have no place to go. Your wife owns her own house and so does your mistress. What would you do? Where would you go? It would have to be furnished accommodation or buy a house and furnish it. I'm not weeping for you. Not with your salary, and Wilma and Katy tell me you are now quite domesticated.'

'Have your moment of glory, I suppose you've earned it. I have always regretted selling the house.'

'Correction. Not selling the house but selling it to me. There is no going back, Paul, so you had better understand that. I don't need you and what is more I don't want you. My life has never been better. I have a job I love which pays well and gives us a comfortable living, and Wilma and Katy are not missing out in any way. The three of us are very happy as we are.'

She thought he looked defeated. Maybe she had been hard but he had to know the position.

'How is Ma Scrimgeour?'

That had been Paul's way of addressing his mother-in-law.

'My mother is well, thank you.'

'Always got on well with the old girl. Be sure to give her my best regards.'

'I'll do that.' She wondered if she would.

'Bet she would like to see us together again and that goes for Wilma and Katy.'

She had to hand it to him. Paul wasn't giving in without a fight.

'Mother is old-fashioned about marriage. She believes that couples should stay together no matter what, so you could be right in what you say. However, she isn't married to you and I am. And don't be so sure about the girls.'

'I am very sure about them. They know how much they mean to me and that I am always there for them.'

'So you are, once a month isn't it?'

'I do the best possible,' he said angrily.

'I'm sure you do in the circumstances. I remember you saying before you walked out that children accept and adapt to change and you have been proved right. They haven't been harmed in any way.'

'We all make mistakes, Jenny, but everyone should be given a second chance.'

'It wouldn't work because I am no longer in love with you.'

'There is someone else?'

'I am not answering that and now I think you should go.'

He got up. 'May I say cheerio to my daughters?'

'Of course. I'll tell them they can come down now.'

Paul was in the hall when they came downstairs.

'What a long time,' Katy grumbled. 'It was a lot longer than twenty minutes.'

'Sorry, Katy, I have been trying to persuade your mother to take me back. I have apologised again and again for the unhappiness my departure caused but your mother is not in a forgiving mood.'

'Are you leaving Vera or has it already happened?'

'No, we are still together but I am prepared to leave her. I have told your mother that.'

They were talking as though she wasn't present, Jenny thought. She was about to say, am I invisible, but stopped herself.

'Mum has to make up her own mind, Dad. If she wants a divorce from you she will just go ahead and get one. That won't pose problems.'

Jenny's eyes almost popped, she hadn't expected that.

'If your parents divorced would that not upset you and Katy?'

Wilma didn't hurry with her answer, she was obviously giving a lot of thought to it. 'We were very upset when you left us,' she said slowly, 'but we got over it. If it comes to a divorce we'll get over that too.'

Katy thought she should get a word in. 'If you are not to be living with Vera and Mum won't let you live here where will you go?'

'Good question, Katy. Your poor dad would be home-less.'

'Don't start and feel sorry for him, Katy. Your father has enough money to see to his comforts. Once I had the real worry of becoming homeless with very little money but it worked out. As your gran would say we just have to have faith.'

'I'll go,' Paul said abruptly.

'I'll show you out.'

'Incidentally, I had to park further along the crescent, there was a car right outside the gate.'

'It belongs to me,' Jenny smiled.

'What good is a car to you when you can't drive?'

'Mum can drive, she passed her test first time,' Katy said gleefully.

'Well! Well! Wonders will never cease. Quite an achie-ver, your mother.'

'We are very proud of her, aren't we, Katy?'

'Very.'

For the first time Paul felt what it was like to be shut out. Jenny had the door open, then remembered the um-brella.

'Katy, get your dad's umbrella, will you?'

She took it out of the stand and handed it over then went ahead outside.

'It isn't raining, you won't have to put it up.'

'See you soon, you two. Cheerio.'

'Cheerio, Dad.'

He hurried away and Jenny closed the door. That had been an ordeal and she had come through it rather well.

Even so her head ached and in a few minutes she would go upstairs and take an aspirin.

'Katy, you've been out in the wet with your slippers,' she scolded.

'Only a little bit wet, Mum. You know something—'

'What?'

'You didn't offer Dad a cup of tea.'

'Neither I did.'

'You forgot?'

'I must have.'

Paul started up the car feeling utterly depressed. His whole life seemed to be falling apart. He had been so sure she would forgive and forget but she had made it clear that she wouldn't. There was no future for him at 16 Abbotsford Crescent. Funny that he should want Jenny and want her quite badly. Thinking about Vera now, after that talk with his wife, made him wonder if he was falling out of love with Vera. Maybe it had been just infatuation all along. Before he couldn't have listed her faults because he didn't believe she had any. Now he could. She was shallow and selfish and a lot more besides.

The rain started again and he set the wipers going. Vera was out somewhere, he couldn't remember where. She hadn't asked where he was going and he wouldn't tell her. He hadn't expected an easy victory with Jenny but that had been total failure.

The cottage looked bleak and uninviting. He had never been greatly taken by it. It should have had a comfortable cottage feel with furniture to suit. Modern stuff had no place. Jenny hadn't made that mistake. She hadn't gone for the ultra-modern and must have given careful thought to both comfort and appearance and managed both. Best of all she had kept the coal fire.

Paul let himself in, switched on the lights and went to the kitchen to fill the kettle. His wife hadn't offered him a cup of tea and it left him feeling outraged. She wouldn't have done that to anyone else. No one left 16 Abbotsford Crescent without being offered a refreshment. No one but him.

Maybe he should start looking for another job and make a new life for himself. His qualifications should get him a position without much difficulty. The thought began to excite him. Why not? What was to stop him? In a way he would be playing Vera at her own game. She was stringing him along until someone with more to offer came on the scene. How satisfying if he got there first and walked out on her. She wouldn't need to get hint of it. He would begin looking for another job and be very discreet. The replies would go to the office and not to the cottage. Where would he go? It wouldn't much matter. Where the best jobs awaited and that could be London or any other major city.

Having no home of his own was an advantage. No house to dispose of. On the downside he would miss Wilma and Katy but not all that much. They would be all right with Jenny and he would keep in touch by letter.

The tea he had poured out was cold and he went and threw it down the sink. This called for a drink. All wasn't lost, he had a future after all.

Chapter Twenty-Two

Having her own car was a new and exciting experience for Jenny and it was making life very much easier. Waiting about for buses had been such a waste of time. Jenny couldn't help feeling guilty about her short working day and when she mentioned this to Moira it was dismissed with a wave of her hand. The hours they had settled on were to suit Jenny's home life and that would continue. Moira had smiled and reminded Jenny that she was no longer a member of staff with fixed hours but part of management. As long as the work got done she was free to come and go as she pleased. She had every confidence that Jenny would not take advantage.

In return for her many privileges, Jenny had insisted on taking some of the office work to do at home. She could do the books in the evening and any typing that was required. Moira, as Jenny knew, thought nothing about staying on at night after the others had gone home but Jenny worried. The Log Cabin was so cut off and what chance would a lone woman have against intruders? Security could never be one hundred per cent.

Business was expanding but there wasn't enough office

work to engage a clerkess. Moira and Jenny could deal with that between them. Now that the holiday season was approaching and coach tours becoming ever more popular, the greater need was for extra staff for the shop and the tea room. They must advertise soon and show a preference for employing the mature woman with time on her hands and a willingness to work part-time in pleasant surroundings.

Saturday morning was when Jenny did the shopping then around midday she would drive the three of them to the Log Cabin. Wilma continued to work in the tea room and was now a confident and experienced waitress. Katy had outgrown her clumsiness and could be trusted to clear the tables and carry the trays of dirty dishes to the kitchen. They earned their wages which pleased their mother and tips, as Wilma said, were always gratefully received.

Jenny set off on this bright and cold Saturday with a list of shopping and a basket over her arm. She preferred it to a shopping bag and since there was a rainproof cover for it, there was no danger of the food coming to grief should the heavens open. There were smiles from those women also doing their shopping. Some had stopped to chat but Jenny didn't linger since there was little enough time to do all she wanted. She made the fruit and vegetable shop her first call. Displaying the fruit the way they did was nothing short of a piece of art and it seemed a shame to disturb it. The window would remain that way until the boxes outside on the pavement were depleted. The good folk of Blackford ate healthily of the home-grown products and the shop did a roaring trade. Jenny went inside and was examining the turnips.

'Can I help you Mrs Richardson?'

'Yes, Nan, if you would. These are all so big, haven't you anything smaller?'

'No, I am afraid not. How about if I halve one?'

'That would do.'

'Choose the one you want and I'll go and get the knife.'

'Massive, aren't they?'

Jenny turned round and smiled. 'Ruby, it's you? I should have paid you a visit before now, it isn't that I haven't thought of you,' Jenny said apologetically.

'I know, Jenny, I do understand. You have such a busy life.'

'Even so I should have made time. I was so very sorry to hear about your mother.'

The woman nodded. 'She got a quick call in the end.' Ruby's mother had been an invalid and a difficult one for years.

The assistant came back to show Jenny the halved turnip, leaving the choice to her.

'That bit and I'll take a pound of carrots.' Jenny got her fruit and vegetables packed into her basket and paid for them. 'I'll wait,' she said to Ruby feeling she could do no other.

'I won't take long. A body on her own doesn't need much.' She smiled to the assistant. 'Two bananas, not hard, they give me indigestion and two, no make that three apples, and I like them crisp.'

'Pick your own, Miss Cruickshank, then you'll have nobody to blame but yourself.'

It wasn't said in a nasty way and everybody was smiling.

The shop was filling up and Jenny went outside to wait for Ruby. In a few minutes she came out carrying two brown paper bags.

'Ruby, I wish there was more time to stand and talk but I have my work to go to.'

'I knew you had a job, Jenny. I do hear about you from time to time.'

'Gossip?'

The smile was apologetic. 'You know how it is in a village, nothing remains a secret for long.'

'I know.'

'Let me just say you came in for a lot of sympathy. Most folk were shocked. Paul and you always seemed such a happy couple. As for me I was sorry to hear that you were separated.'

'Paul found someone else, Ruby.'

'That must have been a difficult time for you but I would say you were over the worst judging by how well you look.'

'I am over it. To begin with I was shocked and devastated but I'm fine now,' Jenny said as they began to walk along the Main Street towards Archibald the butcher. Ruby Cruickshank was a tall, thin, maiden lady with bobbed grey hair, a high forehead and a pale complexion. She was in her early forties but looked older. The fact that she was all in black didn't help.

'I'm glad to hear it. Someone said you were coping magnificently.'

'That was kind of whoever it was. I have been very lucky, you wouldn't believe just how lucky. I have a good job and I love it and best of all I can say in all honesty that the girls haven't suffered. They do see Paul from time to time and have just accepted the changed situation. And that is enough about me. I want to hear how you are coping. Your whole life was devoted to your mother and you must miss her dreadfully.'

'I do miss Mother but I am glad she didn't suffer in the end. She just slept away and is now at peace. Mother wasn't easy and my patience was often sorely tried but being an invalid couldn't have been easy for her either. I should have made more allowances but it is too late for regrets.'

'Don't you dare have regrets. No one could have done more than you did. You were a devoted daughter and as for occasionally losing patience, who wouldn't?'

'Thank you and maybe you are right. I have to admit that for a while I did enjoy my new-found freedom. No more demands, no more disturbed nights and that was such a welcome change. Now I find the days too long for me and life seems so empty. If I were the outgoing type it would be easier, but I'm not and that won't change.'

'You have no wish to become involved—'

She shuddered. 'In village life – absolutely not. I'm not sure that I know what I want.' She smiled. 'What a confession.'

'Why not try and get a little job? It would help to fill in the time and take you out of the house.'

'A job? I hadn't thought of that. Mother was always very careful with money and if I am equally careful there will be enough to keep me.'

'You wouldn't say no to a little extra?'

'No, I wouldn't. A little extra would come in very useful. The problem is that I am not qualified to do anything except look after an invalid and I've had my fill of that.'

'What about housework?'

'A small cleaning job, you mean? Maybe I would consider that, I don't mind housework.'

Jenny was doing some quick thinking. She could do with some help in the house.

'Ruby, would you come to me? Say for four hours a week. My house isn't getting the attention it should. I do try to organise myself but there aren't enough hours in the day. Wilma and Katy help but I don't want to ask more of them.' Jenny was hoping quite desperately that Ruby would agree to come to 16 Abbotsford Crescent. It would be perfect, the answer to a prayer. The woman was honest, dependable and a good worker. The house would get a proper clean, corners and all. There would be no instructions unless those were requested. Ruby would have a free hand. Four hours should do, one could get through a fair amount of housework in that time.

Ruby was showing her surprise. 'Are you sure? I wouldn't want you to be giving me a job because you are feeling sorry for me.'

'Nothing could be further from the truth. This is me praying inwardly that you will accept. Advertising for help is such a risk whereas I can leave you with an easy mind.'

'I'm flattered,' she laughed.

'Then you will consider my offer?'

'Very seriously.'

'Ruby, I must dash, I've masses of shopping still to do. How about coming round to me – say Monday evening? We'll have a cup of tea and a chat and discuss it all then.'

Her face lit up. 'Thank you, I'll come just after seven o'clock.'

'That would be splendid.'

'Jenny?' she called.

Jenny stopped in mid flight.

'I'll help you out, don't worry.'

'Bless you.'

'Mum, we thought you were never coming home. The milkman has been and I paid him and Katy paid the papers.'

'That's fine. Take the shopping would you, Wilma, and put it away. I'm breathless from hurrying.'

'Shops busy?'

'No more than usual for a Saturday morning,' Jenny was saying when Katy came running downstairs.

'I've tidied my room.'

'Good girl.' Jenny took off her jacket and hung it over the back of a chair. She would need it when they went out. 'I was talking to Miss Cruickshank, you remember I told you that Ruby had lost her mother.'

'That's a daft thing to say when somebody dies,' Katy said.

'Not really, dear, maybe it seems silly to you but death is losing someone. I'm hoping Ruby will agree to come here for a few hours each week – we got talking about it and that is why I'm so late.'

'A few hours doing what?'

'Housework.'

Wilma looked pleased. 'That's great.'

'Is it like a real job, will you have to pay her?'

'Of course Mum will have to pay her, she'll need more than thank you,' Wilma said scornfully to her sister. 'Who would do a rotten job like housework for the love of it?'

'Not you, that's for sure, but there are some women who genuinely enjoy housework. And, no, before you ask, your duties will remain as they are. Ruby will do the corners and all the neglected bits. I've asked her to come round on Monday evening and we'll talk about it then.'

Jenny had no idea what the going rate was for housework and she didn't imagine that Ruby would either. Moira Ramsay would know or make it her business to find out. Jenny's mind was busy, there was so much to think about. There was a spare key and Ruby could have that. That would be better then leaving one next door with Grace. Jenny didn't want to bother anyone if she could avoid it.

Moira came up with the information. 'How perfectly splendid, Jenny, and so much more satisfactory than getting someone through an advertisement. Even with a recommendation it is a risk. This is someone you know and trust.'

'If I have one worry it is that she will work herself too hard.'

'If you feel that is at all likely then give her strict instructions that she is to stop for a rest, a proper rest with feet up, a cup of coffee, a plate of biscuits and the morning newspaper.'

They were both laughing when Moira gave a gasp of surprise. Jenny saw her face break into a delighted smile.

'Do excuse me, Jenny, a very dear friend of mine has just come in.' She sounded slightly breathless and hurried forward. Jenny thought this must be one of Moira's gentlemen friends she had once mentioned.

The price tickets had to be done and Jenny busied herself with them. At the same time she managed to study the man who had kissed Moira on both cheeks and was looking equally delighted at the meeting. It was very obvious they were good friends or maybe more than friends. The man was tall and thin but with good shoulders and thick dark hair peppered with grey. Jenny liked the careless elegance about him. His tweed suit was shabby, Jenny's mother would have described it as having seen better days, but it looked well on him. A country gentleman was what she put him down as.

'Why didn't you phone to tell me you were home?' Moira was saying with a reprimand in her voice.

'I was going to then I thought it would be nice to surprise you.'

'It is a lovely surprise.'

'Having missed the opening of the Log Cabin and I apologise again for that, I had to come and see it at the first opportunity.'

'I'm so glad.' She took his arm. 'We'll have a cup of coffee and exchange news then I'll show you around.'

'What I have seen is very impressive but no less than I would have expected from a perfectionist like yourself.'

They moved out of earshot. The outside door opened and two couples who looked like tourists, came in. Jenny stopped what she was doing and went over to offer assistance.

Doris served coffee to Moira and her friend and put down a plate of biscuits. Moira had chosen a window table with a lovely view of the Perthshire hills.

'How was the trip, Andrew?' she asked and handed him the sugar bowl.

'Thank you.' He took two heaped spoonfuls and stirred briskly. 'The trip was both enjoyable and worthwhile. Mixing business and pleasure can be very successful. I saw quite a bit of Europe.'

'Lucky you. What treasures did you find?'

'Quite a few interesting pieces. When it came to antique furniture I would have appreciated your opinion.'

'Andrew, you are the expert, I am but an amateur.'

'An amateur with a good eye. Marguerite always said that about you. We agreed that you should have studied the subject.'

They were silent for a few moments.

'Five years seems like a long time only it isn't. You must still miss her dreadfully. I know I do.'

He nodded. 'Marguerite was very special. A short but happy life she would have called it. She would want to be remembered but not mourned.'

'That's true.'

'Tell me about business,' he smiled.

'Can't complain. The winter months were slow as one would expect but, that said, there was enough to keep us going. Advertising is having an effect and we are becoming quite well known.'

'I'm intrigued about this Gallery. Only you would think of something like that. Our young artists must love you.'

'I'm guaranteed a few hugs when they make a sale and we do make a few sales, Andrew.'

'I thought it a wonderful idea and an added attraction for the Log Cabin.'

'Much as I like to help our young artists I saw the benefits to myself.'

'Naturally,' he laughed. 'A businesswoman to the fingertips.'

'And one who wondered if she had maybe made a mistake when she saw the way they dressed. Positively weird some of them, but it is their way of expressing themselves and after a time one hardly notices.'

'Adds a bit of colour and if one is to dress outrageously let it be when one is young. Youth can get away with anything.'

'I have to agree with that. They pop in and out but are never a nuisance. A few are very talented but you can judge that for yourself.'

'Staff, any problems there?'

'One mistake at the start but I very quickly got rid of her. In this kind of business we depend a lot on part-time assistants for the summer months. My small permanent staff are excellent. We work as a team and help out where and when it is needed.'

'You took a chance. Even with your business experience this is very different to what you were used to.'

'I did have a few sleepless nights wondering if I had made an expensive mistake. Worst of all was having no one to share my worries but happily that is no longer the case.'

'You've taken a partner?'

'I have but not maybe in the way you mean. You must meet Jenny, Mrs Richardson, she is a lovely person. Fate sent her to me and she says the same, that she was guided here.'

'Someone with the right experience.'

'Someone with no experience at all. I think I was first drawn to her by her honesty. It was cards on the table for both of us I should say. Jenny told me she had worked in an office before her marriage but hadn't a hope of getting back. That at thirty-eight she was too old and who was going to employ her when they could get a young woman with all the skills.'

'She spoke the truth I have no doubt.'

'More coffee?' She held up the pot.

'Yes, please, but don't fill it.'

She stopped when his hand went up and then she filled up her own.

'I explained to Jenny what was wanted and she said though she had no experience she thought she could do the work and would certainly do her best.'

'So you engaged her?'

'No, I did not. You forget I am a businesswoman. A month's trial was what I agreed to. If at the end of the month I wasn't satisfied or she didn't like the work then I would look for someone else.'

'Happily she fitted the bill.'

'More than that, she was exactly what I wanted. Jenny has a lot of character. Her husband is an accountant and she had no need to work. Then all that changed—'

'The husband died or lost his job?'

'Neither, he walked out on her and their two young daughters and went off with another woman. From being comfortably off or near enough to it she was reduced to what he allowed her. It was he who made the suggestion that she should find herself a job.'

'A thoroughly nice chap by the sound of him.'

'I won't say what I think of him. That apart and to cut a long story short we hit it off right away. My worry was that she would look for a job nearer to her home so the offer was made earlier than intended. Jenny is now my business partner with a share in the Log Cabin. After hearing all this you must be dying to meet Jenny.'

'Can't wait,' he laughed.

'Have you quite finished?'

'I have, that was very nice.'

They got up and walked back to the shop. Jenny had just seen a customer to the door and was about to clear up the goods spread over the counter.

'Leave it, Jenny, and come and meet a friend of mine.'

Jenny wasn't in her usual skirt and blouse. She wore a navy blue dress with a large white lace collar and a slim navy belt.

Moira made the introductions. 'This lucky man has just returned from a trip around Europe and managing to mix business with pleasure.'

'Very nice,' Jenny smiled.

Andrew Harrison took her hand and held it gently. 'I'm delighted to meet you Mrs Richardson,' he said in a quiet, well-modulated voice. Their eyes met and Jenny found herself confused and breathless. She must have answered, made some comment and then, thankfully, Moira was talking and Jenny's heart settled to a regular beat. She hoped and prayed that her confusion hadn't shown. It was humiliating and she couldn't understand herself.

'Was it a worthwhile trip from the business point of view?' Moira was asking and smiling into his face.

'I would say so and once the shipment arrives you must come and judge for yourself.'

Jenny thought she should go and waited for a break in the conversation.

'Will you both excuse me. I must tidy up the counter before another customer arrives.'

He nodded. 'Of course, Mrs Richardson.'

'Andrew, I'm sure we could dispense with formality. Mrs Richardson prefers to be addressed as Jenny—'

'And Andrew will suit me.'

'I'm about to show Andrew the Gallery and to find out what he thinks of our young artists.'

'You won't be disappointed.'

'I have a feeling I won't.'

They watched Jenny hurry away. 'Well?' Moira looked at her friend and raised her eyebrows.

'My opinion of your business partner? A very delightful and charming lady and I am sure you have made a wise choice.'

The day was well on before Jenny and Moira had a chance to talk.

'What did you think of my friend Andrew?'

'I thought him charming.'

'That was the word he used to describe you.'

'Oh.' She found herself blushing.

'You do know who he is?'

'No. Should I?'

'His is a very well-known and respected name in the antique business.'

'I should have made the connection. John Harrison, Antiques.'

'A family business going back to Andrew's grandfather. It is quite near to Simpson's, one of the warehouses we use and some day when you are in Perth you must pay the shop a visit and get Andrew to show you around.'

'Moira, I wouldn't expect your friend to go to all that trouble for me. If I did go I would just look around on my own.'

'Hopeless, a waste of time. It needs an expert. Andrew has fascinating little stories about how such and such an object got into his hands. And he enjoys showing folk around even though he is well aware there will be no sale at the end.'

'Didn't you tell me that you once thought of studying the subject?'

'Did I? I'm not sure how serious I was. Certainly it is a fascinating hobby collecting antiques in a small way. I was going to tell you a little about Andrew. He is a widower, Jenny, and has been for about five years. Marguerite and I were at school together and our friendship continued after that. She was a very pretty girl but Marguerite was always delicate. At school she could never take part in any of the energetic sports and had to sit and watch from the sidelines. For me that would have been utterly frustrating but

Marguerite never complained or hardly ever. She was fun to be with.' Moira closed her eyes for a moment. 'Life can be so unfair. She and Andrew were so happy and he was always so protective. When she died Andrew and I tried to console each other. We had always been close, the three of us, but I believe her death brought us closer. If you are wondering why I am telling you all this – you are wondering?' she smiled.

'I'm not.'

'Whether that be true or not I want no misunderstandings. Andrew and I are the best of friends but it is no more than that. If there was more than friendship we wouldn't be so comfortable with each other.'

Jenny smiled and nodded. She wasn't at all convinced. Moira's face had lit up with sheer joy when Andrew Harrison had appeared but if that is what she was supposed to believe then so be it.

Chapter Twenty-Three

———◆———

'That must be the third or is it the fourth time recently that my friend, Andrew, has paid a visit to the Log Cabin, Jenny, and delighted though I am to see him, I know I am not the attraction.'

They were sitting in the office with the sunshine streaming through the window. There was no need for a heater, the warmth from the sun through the glass was enough. A representative had called and left several books of samples and these were lying at Moira's feet. She had one open on her knees and was studying it. Jenny was busy checking the order books and referring to the invoices. She was frowning.

'Something not quite right here, Moira—'

'Never mind that just now, we'll go into it later,' Moira said a little impatiently. 'In case you didn't hear what I said, I'll repeat myself. I was talking about Andrew and I wondered if you found him attractive.'

'I suppose I do,' Jenny said carefully. The conversation was making her uncomfortable. She did find Andrew Harrison attractive and that was what troubled her. So far she hadn't had much luck with the men in her life, she thought, then smiled to herself. That sounded as though she had had a few when, in fact, it was two. The husband who had left her and Stewart Taylor who had turned out to be such a disappointment. She wasn't blind. Jenny knew perfectly well that Andrew Harrison was seeking her out and that it was becoming increasingly difficult to avoid him without appearing rude.

That lovely slow smile and the way his eyes crinkled at the corners would be her undoing. She had only to see Andrew coming in the door to feel her breath catch in her throat. Some, perhaps most, would call him handsome though she would prefer to describe Andrew as tall and distinguished looking. What, she wondered, would she do if an invitation did come her way. She could be sensible and turn it down and be firm about it so that there would be little likelihood of the invitation being repeated. Jenny didn't see herself being sensible and that was why she was trying to keep her distance.

Moira might only be teasing but Jenny wished she wouldn't. Not so bad if she knew how to handle it but she didn't. It was embarrassing and made her feel foolish. Another thought crept in. This could be Moira's way of letting Jenny know that she was noticing.

That first time Andrew Harrison walked into the Log Cabin was etched on Jenny's memory. He had turned up unexpectedly and Moira had positively sparkled, there was no other word for it. To show elation when a close friend appears unexpectedly after a lengthy absence is perfectly normal but Moira's delight had been nothing short of ecstatic. And that had made Jenny wonder if the woman's feelings went beyond those of friendship and were not reciprocated. Should that be the case how hurtful it must be for Moira to see him show an interest in someone else and even more hurtful should that someone else be her new business partner.

'Is that all you can say?' Moira said incredulously.

'What do you expect me to say?'

'I don't know but you could show a little more interest, a bit more enthusiasm.'

Jenny was becoming irritated. 'With due respect, Moira,' she said with a hint of sharpness in her voice, 'I think you are being rather ridiculous asking me such a question. I hardly know your friend.'

'And whose fault is that, may I ask? The minute the poor man goes anywhere near you and you are making some flimsy excuse to get away.'

'That is simply not true.' It was true but she hadn't realised it was so noticeable.

'I am afraid it is true.' She paused. 'Jenny, will you please look at me.'

Jenny lifted her gaze from the floor and a pattern book lying open.

'I hope this has nothing to do with me. Has it?'

Jenny looked blank.

'Oh, come on, stop acting the innocent and answer the question.'

'Moira, I honestly have no idea what you are talking about.'

'I am talking about this reluctance of yours to be in Andrew's company and whether it has anything to do with me.'

Jenny shook her head.

'I sincerely hope it hasn't because you are so wrong if you are thinking that Andrew and I are more than very dear friends. There is no romance, never has been and never will be.'

'You don't have to tell me all this, there is no need.'

'I am aware of that and my only reason for telling you is because I do not want any misunderstanding.'

Jenny remained silent.

'Oh, dear, I know, Jenny, you are thinking there she goes again interfering in your affairs.' She gave a little tinkle of a laugh. 'An unfortunate choice of word, let me try again. I am interfering with what is none of my business.'

It was exactly what Jenny was thinking.

'Your silence is answer enough but I am going to have my say and then we'll let the matter drop. I like and admire Andrew and it was his late wife who brought us together. Marguerite was my best friend and someone I had known all my life. We started infant school together and over the years we never lost touch. After five years I still miss her.'

Jenny heard the sadness in her voice.

'I appreciate all you are trying to do but truly my life is fine as it is. Without you and the Log Cabin my circumstances would have been very different. Believe me the three of us are very happy.'

'Can't you spare a kind look for Andrew?'

Jenny laughed. 'I could manage that.'

'I know you are happy but even so you should have a bit of social life.'

Jenny shook her head.

'If friendship is all you want then make that clear at the beginning. It could be that the other party will be satisfied with that.'

'Maybe yes, maybe no. I tried that with Stewart Taylor and it didn't work. He actually had the nerve to accuse me of leading him on when nothing could have been further from the truth.'

'So that is what happened. It didn't last long and I wondered.'

'Two lunches, that was how long it lasted.'

'An unfortunate experience, you were unlucky.'

'A lesson I won't forget in a hurry.' Jenny was looking thoughtful.

'Why the thoughtful look?'

'Life is full of surprises, don't you find that?'

'I've had my share.'

'I was led to believe that going through a divorce is a very stressful experience.'

'Are you finding that?'

'No, I'm not and that is what is so surprising. Actually, Moira, I feel no emotion whatsoever, just a longing to have it over and done with.'

'To be free of your husband?'

'Yes, I do want Paul out of my life but that doesn't mean I want to forget him. I don't. That, I believe, would be wrong. We had happy times and those are worth remembering.'

'No bitterness?'

'Not now. At the beginning there was but I am over that. I feel sorry for Paul but not for myself. She, the

Cuthbertson woman, will drop him and until he finds someone else he will be lost.'

'Don't dare tell me you are going to worry about him?'

'No, but I do hope there is happiness ahead for Paul.'

'A generous soul, that is you. Not many would be so forgiving.'

'I can afford to, I've fallen on my feet.'

Moira laughed. 'Is that what you call it?'

'Actually it was what Paul said when the house became mine.'

The phone rang and Moira reached for it. After a moment or two she made a face and signalled to Jenny that this could be a long call. Jenny nodded, got up quickly and left the office. The order book could be dealt with another time. There were other jobs more pressing and Jenny wanted to get ahead with them when she had the chance. Much of the next day would be taken up with interviewing.

From now until the end of October the Log Cabin could expect to be busy with coach parties as well as passing motorists. The need was for part-time staff. Two assistants to help in the shop and another who would be prepared to work between the shop and the tea room.

'Jenny, I would like you in at the interviews.'

'Thank you.'

'We can discuss the applicants and decide which if any will be suitable.'

'Knowing me I am going to feel sorry for the unsuccessful who are probably most in need of the job.'

'Jenny, business and a kind heart do not go together.'

'They did when I was interviewed.'

'You were different and remember you were on a month's trial.'

'So I was.'

There had been a good response to the advertisement which had appeared in the morning and the evening papers. The replies varied from a page torn out of a jotter to one written on good quality notepaper. It was easy to do but wrong to attach too much importance to the written application. One could get the wrong picture.

The ages of the applicants ranged from thirty-six to fifty-one. Two were almost begging to be considered for the vacancy and both of these women could only work in the mornings. The final two made no mention of preference and Moira assumed, rightly as it turned out, that they would work whatever hours were required. One letter was badly typed and another was full of spelling errors.

The replies, minus the envelopes, were on Moira's desk under a paperweight.

'We should see them all, I think, that is if they bother to turn up.'

'Surely they will otherwise what was the point of going to the trouble of applying?'

'Second thoughts or a husband who had just been informed and who objected.'

Jenny typed the letters requesting that the women attend for an interview on Thursday afternoon or Friday morning. No time was stipulated.

A lot of Jenny's thinking was done at the end of the day when she was in bed. Katy was usually asleep by half past nine and Jenny, on her way to bed, would look in to check that she was covered since the quilt was as often as not on the floor. Katy was a restless sleeper. Wilma liked to read in bed and Jenny had no objection to that. Unfortunately her elder daughter had a bad habit of falling asleep with the book fallen to the floor and the light left on. Unless sleep claimed her early and for her own peace of mind, Jenny would get up and slip along. She didn't have to open the bedroom door, if there was no light showing under it then all was well and Wilma had remembered to switch off.

Tonight they were both sound asleep and their mother wide awake. Jenny lay on her back, her hands behind her head and smiled into the darkness. It seemed unbelievable and rather amusing that she should suddenly find herself in demand. Paul wanted to get his foot back in the door of 16 Abbotsford Crescent and to more or less take up where he had left off. The errant husband returning.

Jenny had found to her cost that she wasn't such a good judge of character as she'd thought. Stewart Taylor had been a big disappointment and the experience had certainly opened her eyes. Men, she was finding, could be unpredictable creatures and a nuisance into the bargain. The occasional lunch together was all it was to be. She had made it very clear, she knew she had, yet it hadn't been clear enough for him. Jenny had enjoyed his company then he had to go and spoil it. They must meet in the evenings, he'd said and spend more time together. Wilma and Katy were old enough to be left in the house, younger children were and came to no harm. He had even gone as far as suggest they spend a weekend together.

Rather shocked at the way things were developing, Jenny had tried to be gentle but his temper had flared. Stewart had rounded on her, accusing Jenny of leading him on and that had been too much for her. Her temper had matched his. They were finished, she told him and when he had calmed down he had been full of apologies but all his pleadings were in vain. When losing control one does say things one doesn't mean, Jenny accepted that, but they had been said and that was enough. She had learnt her lesson. Or had she? Was she about to go through the same with Andrew Harrison? Her heart told her no, that this was different, but could she trust it?

One only had to look at Andrew Harrison to know he was a perfect gentleman, someone who could be depended upon to keep his word. She had thought the same about Stewart Taylor and she would do well to remember that. All this soul searching was probably for nothing. The man in question hadn't asked her out and maybe had no intention of doing so. Nevertheless the possibility was there and surely it was better to be prepared.

In due course she would become a divorcée. Jenny didn't like that word but she would have to get used to it. Her divorce would go through with the minimum of fuss but Stewart Taylor could have a battle on his hands. Tying the knot was easy enough, untying it was not so simple.

Andrew had been a widower for five years and surely that said something. Someone so presentable and respected as Andrew would be much sought after by the unattached ladies of Perth. Men who had lost their wives and wished to remarry usually did so within the first two years. Others having survived those two years might be content to live alone with their memories. Andrew could be perfectly happy with his life just as she was with hers.

Three weeks went by without Andrew putting in an appearance at the Log Cabin. Jenny was disappointed when she should have been relieved, and when he did arrive a few days later she could barely hide her joy. He saw her and came straight over.

'You aren't going to run away, Jenny, are you?' he asked softly.

'Run away? Why should I do that?' she said breathlessly.

'I don't know, but that is what you have been doing and I was worried that I had offended you in some way.'

Jenny was shaking her head when Moira breezed over.

'Andrew, dearest, you are a stranger, I was beginning to think you had deserted us.'

'Never. Good morning, Moira.' He smiled. 'To be honest I thought I was making a nuisance of myself coming so often so I purposely stayed away.'

'That was very silly of you, Andrew, you should know better than that. You are always welcome, isn't that so, Jenny?'

'Of course.'

'I'm afraid you will both have to excuse me, I have work to do which can't be put off any longer.' She gave a long-suffering look. 'I am going to have my coffee in the office. Jenny, you haven't had yours so why not join Andrew in the tea room and keep him company?'

'Excellent suggestion, Moira. How about it, Jenny?'

'Thank you, I'd love to.'

No one was in the tea room though a number of tables were laid ready for the arrival of a touring bus which was due to arrive in about half an hour.

'A window table, Andrew?'

'Anywhere will suit me.' He was looking at the set tables. 'Is this the calm before the storm?'

'Yes. We are prepared for a small invasion but not for at least half an hour. Touring buses are usually behind time rather than before it.'

'Not easy judging.'

Hetty, the new assistant and the only one who had been able to start on the Monday after the interview, came over to the table. She had been the oldest applicant but was as smart on her feet as a much younger woman.

'What can I get you and the gentleman, Mrs Richardson?'

'Andrew?'

'Coffee, please and am I too early for the scones?'

The woman beamed. 'No, sir, you aren't and they will still be warm.'

'A plate of scones, Hetty, and perhaps you should bring some plain biscuits as well.'

The woman hurried away and Jenny and Andrew spoke pleasantries until they were served.

'Do you take sugar, Andrew?'

'Do you know a man who doesn't?' he smiled taking the sugar bowl and helping himself to two heaped teaspoonfuls of brown sugar.

'Now that you mention it I don't think I do.'

'Jenny, I am going to ask you now before someone snatches you away and I don't get the chance.'

'Before I have my coffee, no one would dare,' Jenny laughed.

'In that case I shall wait.' He took a bite of the scone. 'Excellent.'

'They always are, our Mrs Wallace is a wonderful baker.'

'Why, then, aren't you having one?'

'Because I have to be strict with myself and you have to remember that I am faced with temptation every day.'

'A little of what you fancy—'

'Is fine but too much and I'm going to have a weight problem.'

'That I do not believe.'

'Spoken like a gentleman but alas it is true.'

'You look delightfully trim if I may say so.'

'Thank you. A compliment like that makes it almost worthwhile depriving myself.'

'Almost you said. Go on, spoil yourself, one scone isn't going to make much difference.'

Jenny reached for a scone and put it on her plate. 'See how easy it is to talk me into it.' She split the scone and buttered both sides.

Andrew leaned forward and spoke very softly. 'Jenny, will you have dinner with me?'

This was it and she was supposed to be prepared. Jenny took a deep breath.

'It is lovely of you to ask me but I can't.' She saw his disappointment.

'Why not? Is it because you don't want to accept or that you can't?'

'I can't. Andrew, try to understand, I have two young daughters—'

'I know. Moira told me they are two delightful girls.'

Jenny smiled, that had been nice of Moira. She took a sip of her coffee then put the cup down. 'Let me try and explain the difficulty. Wilma is sixteen and considers herself old enough and responsible enough to be left in charge of the house and her young sister.'

'You don't?'

'I do as a matter of fact. Wilma is a sensible girl and we have a very good next-door neighbour who could be called on in an emergency but even so I would be poor company. I would try not to but I would be worrying the entire evening. Stupid, I know, but I am a mother and I couldn't go out and leave them alone in the house.'

'You don't have to apologise. Sixteen is young and as they are still at school it is only right and proper that there should be an adult in the house. My late wife and I were not blessed with children but had we been, Marguerite would have been like you.'

'Thank you.'

He took another scone. 'What we need then is a responsible adult.'

'My mother would have been the obvious choice but I would rather not ask her.'

'I see.'

'I'm not sure you do. My mother is a very obliging person but she does have very decided views on what is acceptable and what is not. Until my divorce comes through I am a married woman.'

'And a married woman does not accept an invitation to dinner from a man.'

'That is about it.'

'Mother is ruled out. Is there someone else you could ask?'

Jenny nodded slowly. 'There is but I can't be sure that the person I have in mind would be prepared to oblige.'

'You could ask?'

'I could and I will.' All her good intentions were forgotten.

'To find out the answer shall I phone you here or at home?' He saw her hesitation. 'You phone me, that might be easier.' Andrew reached into his pocket and brought out a business card, another pocket yielded a pen. 'That is my business number and should I not be available leave a message with my assistant. I'll write my home telephone number on the back and the same applies. Mrs Brown, my housekeeper, is not deaf as she keeps telling everybody, just a little hard of hearing so you may have to repeat yourself.'

'I'll remember to speak loud and clear. When would be the best time to phone?'

'Difficult to say – I am sometimes called away during the day but if you were to phone in the evening there is a good chance you would get me. I don't go out a great deal and after a long day just give me a comfortable chair and a good book and I am content.' He closed his eyes. 'I've just remembered that I have agreed to give a talk on Wednes-day evening but other than that you choose the evening.'

'The talk will be on antiques,' she smiled.

'Yes, it is about all I can talk about with any specialist knowledge.'

'When it comes to questions what do people want to know?'

'Some of the questions would surprise you but most want to know how to recognise the genuine article and what they should avoid. Mistakes can be very costly.'

'I'm afraid I am completely ignorant about antiques.'

'Then it will be my pleasure to introduce you to a fascinating subject.'

There was a commotion outside. From their window they couldn't see the carpark but the sounds were un-mistakable. The chattering and laughter of folk enjoying themselves and hungry for a refreshment.

'This is where I leave you,' Andrew said getting up. Jenny got up too. 'I'll look forward to your phone call and hope the answer is yes.'

Chapter Twenty-Four

Jenny kept telling everybody that Ruby Cruickshank was a godsend. The house had never looked better, everything shone, even the saucepans in the kitchen gleamed. Before Ruby arrived on the scene, a tin of furniture polish would have lasted for months. Now that it was being used regularly the woman had suggested they buy the larger size since it was better value for money. Jenny agreed and marvelled at the amount of work Ruby could get through in four hours. She was very methodical. Downstairs got a thorough clean one week and upstairs the next.

Perhaps it all went so smoothly because they had a perfect understanding. There were no little notes left on the table or propped up on the mantelpiece, to do this or that. There were no instructions, none were necessary. Jenny went off to her work leaving Ruby to get on with hers. The woman had her own key and only occasionally did she and Jenny meet in the morning. This particular morning Jenny had lingered purposely. She was dressed and ready to leave with the car keys in her hand. When the gate clanged as it always did Jenny went over to the window to have a quick look. It could have been the postman but it was Ruby. Jenny went to open the door.

'Good morning, Jenny,' Ruby sounded surprised. 'Am I early or is this you late?'

'Neither,' Jenny smiled as Ruby stepped in and the door was shut. 'I wanted a word with you before I left.'

For a moment the woman looked startled. 'There's nothing wrong, is there?'

'With the house, you mean? Of course not, I couldn't be more pleased. No, Ruby, this is me wanting to ask a favour of you that's all.'

Ruby relaxed and began to unbutton her coat. She still wore black.

'I hope I can oblige,' she said carefully, 'but first I would need to hear what it is.'

'And so you shall. You cannot promise and I wouldn't expect it of you until you know what is being asked.' Jenny paused. 'Sit down, Ruby.' Ruby did and Jenny perched herself on the arm of the settee. 'I have had an invitation to dinner and I wondered if you would be prepared to keep Wilma and Katy company. I wouldn't be late and I'll drive you home.'

'That shouldn't be any problem. Which evening is this to be?'

'It hasn't been decided but it would be one evening next week other than Wednesday. I am left to choose and I thought Thursday.'

'Thursday is fine for me.'

'You must be wondering why I haven't asked my mother?'

'I suppose I am. Won't she be offended? I mean, Jenny, you are choosing the evening—'

Jenny nodded. 'I don't intend telling her.'

'Oh!'

Jenny sighed. 'Let me try and explain.'

'You don't have to. Your private life is your own affair,' Ruby said a little stiffly.

'Yes, it is my own affair or it should be. Believe me, Ruby, I am not proposing to do anything outrageous—'

'Such a thought never entered my head.'

'Ruby, this is a gentleman friend, a widower, who has invited me to have dinner with him. He knows the position, the position being that I will only accept his invitation if I can get a reliable adult to stay with the girls. On no account would I leave Wilma and Katy alone in the house. If I have to refuse the invitation I'll be disappointed, I admit that.' She smiled. 'That is nothing new. I have had disappointments before and got over them.'

'Jenny, I didn't say I wouldn't do it.'

'No, you haven't but before you decide one way or the other you should know why I am not asking my mother. You might feel the same way about it as she does.'

It was Ruby's turn to smile. 'And what way is that?'

'Mother thinks that I have no right to spend an evening with a man until my divorce is through and I am once again a single woman or should that be a divorcée?'

'The divorce is definitely going ahead?'

'Yes.'

'Then I see no reason whatsoever why you should turn down an invitation which, clearly, you would like to accept. Paul deserted you, it wasn't the other way round. Your mother, with due respect, is of another generation.'

'To be fair to my mother, Ruby, although she would be cold and disapproving, she would probably agree to stay with the girls. I would rather she didn't, that's all.'

Ruby looked wise and nodded slowly. 'All that cold disapproval would spoil your evening.'

'Too true.' Jenny's face cleared. 'Dare I believe that you wouldn't mind?'

'Mind? It would be a pleasure. Being in young company would be a pleasant change for me.'

'Thank you, Ruby. Thank you very much.'

'So that I don't put my foot in it what will you tell Wilma and Katy?'

'The truth. Early on we discovered that it was better to be honest and straightforward. My two have been quite marvellous and surprisingly understanding. I am very proud of them.'

'You are a good mother, Jenny, and you work very hard. A bit of social life is no more than you deserve.'

'Ruby, this is so good of you, it really is.'

'Don't sound so surprised, I am not as old-fashioned and strait-laced as I appear.'

'Wrong, I never thought you strait-laced and as for old-fashioned—' Jenny stopped, thinking she shouldn't say what was in her mind.

'Say it. Say what you were going to say.'

'All right I will. When are you going to stop wearing black? Black can be very chic but—'

'Not on me.'

'Don't keep picking me up before I fall down. What you are wearing does nothing for you. The summer is just ahead and you should be thinking of—'

'Print dresses and sun hats,' Ruby laughed. A good hearty laugh that showed she wasn't in the least offended.

'Why not on you? I can see you in a lovely pale green and cream summer dress or any soft colour.'

'Do you really think so?' Ruby said doubtfully. 'Mother always said I should wear dark colours.'

'Then your mother was wrong.'

'Jenny, my mother was never wrong. She always knew what was best for me.'

'What she thought was best for you.'

Ruby smiled. 'Same thing.'

Jenny knew that Ruby's father had died suddenly when she was about school-leaving age.

'When your father was alive did he ever take your side?'

She shook her head. 'I adored my father; he was a very nice man but he was all for a quiet life. He took the easy way out and just agreed with what mother said. Maybe if he had lived longer things would have been different. I would have been able to take a job on leaving school like my peers. But that wasn't to be, I had to stay at home, look after the house and mother too since she was beginning to think of herself as an invalid even then. That sounds uncharitable but the doctor said as much. Once you think of yourself as an invalid you become one.'

'You had your hands full,' Jenny said sympathetically.

'A full-time occupation.'

'Everyone knew that.' Jenny was being careful but it was

too good an opportunity to miss. The woman had never spoken so freely before and perhaps never would again. 'What about your life? Didn't you feel resentful?'

'Many a time, but looking back I have to feel sorry for my mother – she didn't have many friends and she didn't encourage neighbours to come about the house. Poor soul, Jenny, she was afraid of growing old and being alone and forgotten. She made me understand that my first duty was to her and said it often enough for me to believe it. How would she manage if I were to leave home?'

'The same as anyone else,' Jenny said drily. She could have added that Mrs Cruickshank had enough to live on and a bit over. How many were alone and had to watch every penny?

'Yes, I suppose so. What started me, why am I telling you all this?'

'Because we are friends, I hope.'

'Maybe I needed this outpouring and you are a sympathetic ear, Jenny. Since I've started I'll finish what I was going to say rather than leave a story half told.' She paused. 'There was someone I cared for but I sent him packing when he called my mother a selfish so-and-so. She was a selfish so-and-so but it wasn't his place to say it.' Ruby laughed. 'Any hope I had of having mother to live with us after that went out the window. It could have been that he wasn't right for me and mother spared me heartache but I'll never know.'

'You should have been given the chance to find out.'

'Don't waste too much sympathy I am not blameless. Perhaps there is quite a lot of my father in me. We both accepted what we felt we couldn't change and, Jenny Richardson, would you look at the time. You are going to be very late and I should have had my sleeves up and started the housework.'

'Don't worry about me. No one is going to take me to task for being late and as for you, Ruby, stop feeling guilty. You do a power of work, more than you should and I don't want you to slave.'

'This isn't slaving. I'm enjoying the wee job and it takes me out of the house.'

Jenny wanted to do something for Ruby if only she would agree.

'Ruby, how about the two of us going shopping. Shopping for clothes for you, I mean. Don't worry, I promise you this won't burst the bank. Miss Ramsay always looks marvellous and she was quick to inform me that the best dressed women don't spend a fortune on clothes. They mix and match, choose carefully and try to avoid mistakes. The addition of a scarf or a colourful blouse can transform an outfit, give it a lift.'

'Are you hinting that I should throw everything out and start again?' she laughed.

Jenny would have gone along with that but she had to be tactful. 'Nothing as drastic as that but you could make a start by putting that black coat to the back of your wardrobe. Your dark skirts are fine or will be when we take a couple of inches off the hem. Wear them with light-coloured blouses and they will take you through most of the year. Cotton dresses cost very little and always look fresh and cool. Buy yourself a few.'

'Which shops had you in mind?'

'We won't go to the shops, we'll visit the warehouse since I have the advantage of discount.'

'I didn't mean that,' Ruby said hastily, 'I can afford to buy myself new clothes.'

'I know you can, but why pay more? The warehouses have a wonderful selection so no argument if you please.'

'I'm not going to argue because I would like that very much. Having you to keep me right is what I need.'

'Too true, I am going to keep you right. Knowing you, Ruby, I bet you bought the first thing you were shown.'

'Not quite. I did check that it fitted.'

'What we will buy will not only fit you, it will suit you. And this time I am going.'

'Tell your gentleman friend that you have a baby-sitter.'

Jenny put her finger to her lips. 'Don't use that word in Wilma's hearing. She would be mortified. My daughter likes to think of herself as grown-up but secretly I know she will be glad to have you there.'

Jenny was smiling as she drove to the Log Cabin. She might be very late but a lot had been achieved.

She rang Andrew at the shop and was greatly relieved when he answered the phone himself.

'Andrew Harrison speaking.'

'Hello, Andrew, it's Jenny,' she said trying hard not to sound breathless.

'Nice timing, Jenny, you just caught me on my way out.'

'I won't keep you—'

'Now that would be a pity.' She heard the laughter in his voice. 'I don't want you rushing off.'

'It was just to let you know that Ruby, a friend of mine, has kindly agreed to stay with Wilma and Katy.'

'Splendid.'

'I made it Thursday, is that all right?'

'Of course. I did say any evening other than Wednesday. Thursday it is. Jenny, is there anywhere special you would like to go or will you leave that to me?'

'I'll leave it to you.'

'Thank you. I don't have your home address so don't be ringing off before I take a note of it and instructions on how to get there.'

'I won't.'

'We need to arrange a time. If I call for you at half past seven, would that suit you?'

'Yes, Andrew, half past seven will suit me.' Then she added quickly, 'A few customers have just come in so let me give you my home address.'

'Pen and paper at the ready, go ahead.'

Jenny was spending a lot of time over her appearance. She didn't know where Andrew was taking her but wherever it was she wanted to look her best. Moira knew about the invitation for Thursday evening and thought Andrew might choose the very fashionable Pinegrove Hotel or the exclusive Miranda Restaurant on the outskirts of Perth. It was small and it was necessary to book well in advance although as always in these places a special guest could always be accommodated.

Jenny had come downstairs ready for the comments. Wilma was looking at her mother admiringly.

'Mum, you look great, doesn't she Miss Cruickshank?'

'Indeed she does, Wilma. That shade of pink, is it dull rose, is a favourite of mine. You suit the colour.'

'Mum, I think it makes you look thin.' That was Katy.

'Does it, dear?'

'Yes, I think so. Is it true that some clothes make you look thin?'

'Dark colours are supposed to do that.'

'You had better start wearing black, Katy,' Wilma teased.

Katy put out her tongue. 'Skinny malinkie long legs and big banana feet, that's you, Wilma Richardson.'

Jenny was trying to keep her face straight. 'That is enough both of you, what will Miss Cruickshank think?'

Ruby was quietly enjoying this glimpse into family life. 'Katy, don't ever wish yourself thin, I was one of those gangling girls with legs and arms like matchsticks and I longed to put on a bit of flesh.'

'Dad used to say I was all arms and legs,' Wilma said.

Ruby wondered what she should say now. 'The difference is, Wilma, that you are slim not thin and one of the lucky ones. I wasn't slim, I was just plain skinny.'

Jenny thought it was time to bring this conversation to an end. 'We are all different and that is how it should be. Think how dull and uninteresting life would be if we could choose how we looked and we all ended up looking alike.'

Wilma was about to argue that point but Katy got in first.

'When is he coming, Mum?'

'The gentleman has a name,' Jenny said with raised eyebrows.

'I know that, everyone has but I just forget what it is.'

'Mr Harrison.'

'What is his first name?'

'You don't require to know that but I'll tell you. His Christian name is Andrew.'

'Andrew. Does he get called Andy?'

'No, he does not and you will kindly remember to address him as Mr Harrison.'

Katy nodded and went back to her jigsaw puzzle. A few moments later the doorbell rang.

'That's the doorbell, Mum,' Wilma said unnecessarily, 'are you going to answer it or do you want me to do it?'

'I'll go, Wilma.'

Jenny hoped she looked calm and relaxed which was what she was not. She was nervously excited. She went to open the door and for a split second the man standing there was a stranger, a handsome stranger. Any time she had seen Andrew he had been wearing tweeds and looking the country gentleman. In his dark, perfectly tailored suit, he was more like a successful businessman. Jenny supposed he was both.

'Come in, Andrew,' she smiled. 'No problems getting here?'

'None at all.' He stepped in and she shut the door then led him through to the sitting-room. The talking had stopped and Jenny made the introductions. 'My daughters Wilma and Katy.'

Andrew shook hands with both girls.

'And this is my very good friend Miss Cruickshank. I can't tell you how helpful she has been.'

'It goes both ways, Mr Harrison,' Ruby said as they shook hands.

'I daresay it does.'

There was no awkwardness, Jenny thought as Andrew went over to the coffee table where Katy had her jigsaw set out. For a few moments he stood looking down at it then lifted a piece and slotted it into place.

'Good! I was looking for that bit,' Katy said.

He smiled. 'Never could resist a jigsaw, there was always that other piece I wanted to put in place.'

'You wouldn't be able to finish this one.'

'Too difficult you mean?'

'No. Two of the pieces are missing, that was what I meant.'

'You can't find them?'

Katy shook her head. 'Mum must have thrown them out when she was cleaning up.'

'I'm glad it wasn't me,' Ruby said.

'No, it wouldn't be, this was ages ago.'

'I'm not so sure that I am guilty but it might teach you to tidy up instead of leaving it to me.'

They were all laughing. Jenny had draped a lovely gossamer-thin shawl round her shoulders thinking it would be warm enough on this early summer evening.

To save Andrew having to make the first move Jenny thought she should.

'That's me ready,' she said.

Andrew turned, admiration in his eyes. 'Then we should be on our way I think. Good night,' he said addressing the three of them. 'It was a pleasure meeting you.'

They left to goodbyes.

'I hope that wasn't too much of an ordeal,' Jenny said lightly as they walked down the drive.

'How could it be an ordeal? They are delightful. I think Moira is particularly fond of Katy and I can see why. She is just so natural.'

'Katy never thinks before she speaks and we never know what to expect.'

Andrew wondered what kind of man Jenny's husband could be to leave such a charming wife and two delightful daughters. Maybe he would discover his mistake but by then it might be too late. Andrew hoped she wouldn't be persuaded to go back to her husband. That was selfish but if the man could leave her once he could do it again. Jenny would never be able to trust him completely.

Andrew held the passenger door open for Jenny to get in then when she was settled, he went round to the driver's seat.

'Let me say how very lovely you look,' he said giving her a smile before setting the car in motion.

'Thank you.' Jenny wasn't very good with compliments on her appearance. They still embarrassed her but, thanks to Moira, she now knew how to make the most of herself. Play up the good points and play down the bad. She must have succeeded when someone as distinguished and charming as Andrew wanted her company. She had left behind her that discarded feeling which for a short time had engulfed her. Life was different, life was good and she was looking forward to the evening ahead.

'Jenny, I've booked a table at the Miranda Restaurant, do you know it?'

'I have heard it is very exclusive.'

He laughed. 'I don't know so much about that but I can recommend the food and very important, to me anyway, there is no overcrowding. The tables are far enough apart not to have one's conversation overheard at the next table.'

'Saves whispering.'

'It does. For some people, thankfully not too many, scraps of conversation can be fascinating. A friend of mine has this deplorable habit of listening and trying to make sense of what she hears. She says it is harmless and just a bit of fun.'

The lights of the restaurant were welcoming and Jenny imagined how much more effective they would be in the dark winter nights. Andrew parked the car and they walked across the cobblestone courtyard to the door. Immediately they were inside a pleasant looking woman came forward. She wore a black dress with a broad white collar and a narrow white band at the cuffs.

'Good evening.'

Andrew smiled. 'I have a booking. Harrison.'

'This way, please, Mr Harrison.' The lamps on each table had a red shade which gave a welcoming glow without making it too dim. Jenny remembered being in one restaurant where the lighting was so subdued that they had difficulty reading the menu.

Once they were seated the woman departed and a waiter came over to give them each a menu. He left the wine list on the table.

'The secret of a good restaurant is the chef and doesn't he know it,' Andrew laughed. 'A really good one can state his terms and expect to get what he asks. If not he won't be greatly troubled, there will always be someone anxious to employ a first-class chef.'

'I must tell Katy. She was going to be a nurse when she left school and then that was shelved in favour of opening her own restaurant. Paul had taken them both to some new place where the owner and his wife went out of their way to be obliging. Apparently Katy – this is Wilma's version – had complained in a too loud voice that she didn't know what to choose because she didn't know what anything was. Come to think about it that didn't say a lot for her mother. The one in charge, who turned out to be the owner, spent time explaining the dishes, what was in them and how they were cooked.' Jenny smiled. 'Wilma would have been terribly embarrassed, she is at that stage.'

'I can see there is never a dull moment in your house.' They began to study the menu.

Chapter Twenty-Five

———◆———

The two people sitting at one of the tables seemed to have very little to say to each other. Married couples could dine out without the need to talk but theirs was usually a comfortable silence. This wasn't. The woman was beautiful and elegant and admiring glances were coming her way. If she noticed she gave no sign. She was more interested in looking to see if she recognised anyone. About to give up, her startled eyes rested on Jenny. An animated Jenny who was deep in conversation with her male companion. Unable to believe what she was seeing Vera Cuthbertson blinked and looked again.

'Paul,' she said urgently and making him look up, 'you are not going to believe this.'

'What am I not going to believe?'

'Behind you and sitting at a table beside the window, I am almost certain it is Jenny dining with a man.'

'No law against that, is there?'

She frowned. 'You could look.'

'How do I manage that with my back to whoever it is? It won't be Jenny, what would she be doing here?' Paul said carelessly.

'I don't know but I am almost positive it is your wife. For goodness sake, Paul,' she said exasperatedly, 'it is easy enough to turn round without making it too obvious.'

Paul sighed. He wasn't going to get peace until he could say categorically that the woman Vera was talking about wasn't Jenny. He moved his chair slightly and then turned round. It took Paul a moment or two to locate the table.

'It is Jenny.' He turned back quickly not wanting to be recognised.

'I knew it,' she said triumphantly. Vera was craning her neck for a better look then her eyes narrowed. 'Good heavens!'

'Stop it, Vera, you will have everyone looking at you,' Paul hissed.

'Not all that unusual, darling, I thought you liked it that way?' she smiled.

'Maybe I did at one time but this is different. The way you are carrying on will make folk curious to know what you are looking at.'

'Very well, since it is getting you in a state I'll tear my eyes away. What I was about to tell you when you interrupted so rudely, was that I know the man Jenny is with. Well, to be honest, I don't exactly know him but I do know who he is.'

Paul couldn't care less whom Jenny was with and he was only half listening. He had no wish to come face-to-face with his wife and he was already planning their escape. The Miranda had two doors. To leave by the main door would mean having to pass Jenny's table. The other, which was nearer to where they were sitting, led directly to the carpark.

They were dining earlier than usual and had reached the coffee stage. Paul had made up his mind that when the waiter arrived to offer them more coffee he would ask for the bill. He was anxious to be out of the Miranda.

'He gave a talk—'

'Who gave a talk?'

'I am about to tell you if you would take the trouble to listen. The gentleman Jenny is with gave a talk at something I attended. Does the name, Harrison Antiques, mean anything to you?'

'Don't be stupid, Vera, of course I know of Harrison Antiques.'

'Your wife happens to be dining with Andrew Harrison who is Harrison Antiques. What is it about Jenny – how does she manage it?'

It was said nastily and Paul's mouth tightened. Vera could be a real bitch when she wanted, he thought. He was no longer making excuses for her. Of late he was becoming increasingly irritated and what hadn't bothered him before now made him angry.

'Maybe Jenny manages it because she doesn't try. Unlike you, Vera, she doesn't push herself forward. Your approach would put some men off.'

Her eyes opened wide. 'It didn't put you off. You should have realised by now, my dear Paul, that men come to me – I don't have to do anything.'

'Wrong. With me it was you who made the first move.'

'So it was. That was because you were so pathetically

slow. You needed a little push, a very small one and I landed you hook, line and sinker.' She smiled a hard smile that didn't reach her eyes.

'You did, I don't deny that. I was dazzled for a time but these days I am not so gullible.'

Vera looked at him sharply. Maybe she should go carefully. She was tired of Paul but she hadn't thought he was tiring of her. She couldn't afford to lose him, not yet, not until she had someone else in her life. Her own salary wasn't anywhere near enough for her needs and there was the car. She would miss it. Catching a bus to and from the office would be humbling. Jenny could drive and had her own car. Damn Jenny Richardson.

Her temper was rising. 'Maybe you should have stayed with your sweet little wife,' she said viciously then wished the words unsaid. 'I'm sorry, darling, forget I said that.'

'More coffee, madam?'

Vera moved back in her chair. 'Yes, please.'

'And you, sir?'

'Yes, please and bring the bill, will you?'

The waiter gave a small bow. 'I'll see to that right away.'

'To return to Andrew Harrison,' Vera was saying, 'the man is a widower and has been for a number of years.'

Paul nodded. Where did she get all her information he wondered. That figured though, him being a widower. Jenny would never be the one to break up a marriage. He remembered how she had tried to save theirs and when she failed there was no fuss. She had been dignified through-out. Instead of lamenting she had set about making a new life for herself and by heavens hadn't she succeeded. He still hadn't got over it.

They drank the rest of their coffee in silence, both of them in deep thought. Vera kept glancing over to that other table and each time the couple smiled to each other with that special togetherness, Vera felt a stab of envy. It was humiliating to be envious of someone like Jenny Richardson and difficult to believe that a sophisticated man of the world like Andrew Harrison could be attracted to her. She, Vera Cuthbertson, was much more his type of woman.

The coffee cups were empty, the bill had been settled and Paul was suggesting they leave by the side door.

'Certainly not,' Vera said indignantly. 'We are not going out that way. Why should we sneak out?'

'I wouldn't call it sneaking out. The side door is nearer to us and it would save a walk to the car.'

'No. A short walk in the cool of the evening is very pleasant.'

'Vera,' Paul said between clenched teeth, 'I am trying to avoid an awkward situation.'

'It needn't be awkward.'

The waiter was there with her cape. Paul took it and placed it round Vera's shoulders.

'Thank you,' she said coldly and began to move forward.

Paul's lips tightened but he could do no other than follow. A few steps further on Vera fell back forcing Paul to take the lead. He had already made up his mind to say good evening to Jenny and then move quickly to the door. Vera had other ideas.

Blissfully unaware that their tête-à-tête was about to be interrupted, Andrew was leaning forward to ask Jenny if her poached salmon, decorated with twists of lemon, was to her satisfaction.

'Andrew, this is absolutely delicious,' she said, then froze when she heard her name. For a moment she was too shocked to speak but recovery was swift. The old Jenny would have been covered with confusion and embarrassment, and probably rendered speechless.

'Good evening, Paul.' Jenny managed the introductions in a perfectly normal voice. 'Andrew, this is my husband,' then she deliberately paused before adding, 'and Miss Cuthbertson.'

Andrew had risen to his feet then sat down again. The two men nodded curtly to each other.

'Jenny, I couldn't believe it was you at first and I had to get Paul to confirm that it was indeed you.' Vera was deliberately studying Jenny's outfit. 'Pretty shade. You do look nice.' It was said in a voice rich with surprise and condescension.

Inwardly Jenny was seething. There had been no need to mention what she was wearing, in fact it was extremely bad manners. 'You look nice' said by a friend would have been welcomed, but this was no friend. Jenny gathered it was to draw attention to herself and emphasise the difference between them.

Paul felt sickened as well as ashamed. He thought Jenny looked uncomfortable. His wife was no match when it came to bitchiness. It wasn't in her nature. Vera was in a class of her own.

'You are looking very well, Jenny,' Paul said quietly.

Jenny knew he was being sincere and husband and wife exchanged a smile. A smile that wasn't lost on Andrew.

Vera ignored Paul and Jenny, her whole attention was on Andrew Harrison.

'You must forgive me, Mr Harrison,' she gushed, 'for a moment or two I couldn't remember where I had seen you but now I do. You gave a very interesting talk on antiques, I can't remember where it was held but I do recall being fascinated.'

Andrew looked amused. 'I'm glad to hear that all my talks don't fall on deaf ears,' he laughed.

'No danger of that I assure you. You made quite an impression on us all and I remember wishing that I wasn't so ignorant on the subject.' She turned briefly to Jenny. 'Don't tell me this is another achievement. Are you knowledgeable about antiques?'

'No, I am not,' Jenny said shortly. She looked down at her plate and wondered if she should take a mouthful of salmon. It might chase them away but she didn't want to appear rude to Andrew. What was he making of all this?

Vera smiled her brightest. 'One day quite soon, Mr Harrison, I intend paying a visit to your premises.'

'We make everyone welcome.'

'I know. You said so after your talk but did you really mean it?' she said coyly.

'I would hope to mean what I say. You can be sure that my very able assistant, Miss Grey, would be only too happy to show you and your friends what we stock.'

Vera made a face. 'I would be coming on my own, Mr

443

Harrison, and hope that you would be available to show me around. I promise not to be greedy and take up too much of your valuable time.' It was blatant and shameless yet she managed to carry it off.

'I make no promises,' Andrew smiled.

Paul had had enough and he only just stopped himself from walking out of the restaurant and leaving her. What he did do was take a firm grip of Vera's arm.

'I do apologise,' he said with a strained smile, 'we are keeping you from your meal. Come along, Vera.'

Vera hid her fury. Paul was hurting her, his fingers digging into her arm but she managed a warm smile for Andrew.

'Yes, we must go. How lovely to have met you, Mr Harrison and don't forget I will be paying you a visit.'

'I shan't forget.'

'Good night, Jenny,' she said as though it had been an afterthought.

Andrew and Jenny watched their departure.

'I really am sorry about that,' Jenny said wretchedly.

'Why should you be? You couldn't have foreseen it and to be honest I found the whole thing rather amusing.'

'I didn't.'

'No, you couldn't have and let me say you handled the situation very well.'

'Did I?' Jenny looked pleased. She had thought so herself but it was nice to hear Andrew say so.

'Your husband was anxious to be gone.'

'I know. Poor Paul. Left to him he would have said good evening and walked on.'

'That is one very strong-willed woman who is used to getting her own way.'

'I couldn't disagree with that.'

'Goes after what she wants and lets no one stand in her way.' Andrew frowned and looked annoyed at himself. 'Oh, dear, that was tactless of me.'

'Never mind tact. She did go after Paul. I like to think he didn't make the first move and I am fairly certain he didn't. That said he wouldn't have required much persuasion.'

'To leave you? I don't believe that was easy for him.'

'You are being very kind,' she smiled. 'Paul told me our marriage had gone stale. Maybe it had for Paul but not for me. I was quite happy. Half of Paul's trouble or maybe the whole of it is that he hates the thought of growing old and to have someone like Vera Cuthbertson, with her marvellous looks, take a fancy to him was too much. He couldn't resist.'

'If it is any consolation I would say that your husband is not a happy man and unless I am very much mistaken he is bitterly regretting leaving you and his daughters.' Andrew looked over at her plate, he had finished his. 'Are you going to finish that salmon or shall I have the waiter take it away?'

Jenny looked shocked. 'Certainly not. If you think for one moment that I am going to allow my husband and his mistress to put me off my food you are very much mistaken.'

'Glad to hear it.'

Jenny ate the last few mouthfuls then placed the cutlery together on the plate and sat back. A waiter who had been hovering nearby came to remove the dishes. Another

445

waiter, slim-hipped and silent, topped up their glasses. For some diners the wait between courses was too long while for others it was an opportunity to spin out the evening and enjoy the wine. At the Miranda eating was a serious business.

The chicken served with wine sauce arrived and as if by mutual consent Paul and Vera Cuthbertson were not mentioned. Andrew kept Jenny entertained with his stories, some of them hilariously funny and all to do with the antiques trade. Jenny thought Andrew would use one or two during his talks to bring a lighter touch to the serious business of collecting antiques.

Over coffee they became thoughtful.

'Are you as content as you appear to be, Jenny?'

'Yes, I am and with good reason. Independence is something I have come to value.'

He was smiling and she frowned at him.

'That may seem strange to you, Andrew, but you must remember that men have always enjoyed a degree of independence denied to women.'

'Are you trying to tell me that women would like greater independence?'

'Not all women, not by any means,' Jenny said hastily. 'Some only feel safe when there is someone there to look after them, bring in the money and make the important decisions. Until not long ago I was one of them.'

'Then you found that you had to make the decisions?'

She nodded. 'It was terrifying to begin with and I was luckier than many. Paul, to his credit, hadn't deserted us completely – he never would, I was nearly sure of that – but money was going to be very tight. And I had Mother, she was there to give her support. No doubt the girls and I would have muddled through somehow but thanks to Moira our fortunes changed. Andrew, your friend opened up a whole new world for me. My confidence, I never had too much of it, was at a low ebb but Moira let me see that I was capable of more than cooking and looking after the house.'

'Moira has a heart of gold but she is also a very astute businesswoman. You must have measured up or she wouldn't have taken you on.'

'We got on well from the beginning and she had this way of making me feel good about myself. In short, Andrew, she was my saviour and I will always be grateful. Thanks to her I have a job which is also a challenge and I love it. Financial worries are a thing of the past.' Jenny laughed. 'Do you know this, Andrew, I used to put money aside in different tins. One for this and one for that but before the week was out I would be dipping into the coal money to pay the milkman.'

'My poor Jenny.'

'Not so much of the poor Jenny. I am doing very well thank you very much. We, the girls and I, have a comfortable living, the house is in my name and best of all, Andrew, Wilma and Katy haven't been harmed by the upheaval in their lives.'

'What you have now, is that all you want from life?'

Jenny looked puzzled. 'I'm not sure I follow you.'

'Let me put it another way. Would such an independent woman as you have become give any serious consideration to a second marriage?'

This was dangerous ground and she would have to be careful. There was no denying she was greatly attracted to Andrew Harrison. Love was too strong a word and she didn't want to use it.

The mention of a second marriage. Was he being flippant or serious? It was hard to know. What would be her answer if this was to be a proposal? Could she give up all she had now? That is what it would mean. She would be mistress of Andrew's house rather than a housewife. Not as fulfilling as the life she was enjoying. The Log Cabin was a challenge and would continue to be that. Its success depended to a large extent on she and Moira working together. They were a good team. To leave would be to destroy that and was no way to repay her debt. Moira wouldn't see it that way. She would say to do what is best for you.

'Have I posed such a difficult question? You are certainly taking your time to answer.'

'I'm not sure that I do have an answer,' Jenny said slowly.

'You could try.'

'I will and I'll try to be completely honest. If I ever thought about marrying again and it is a very big if, it would not be for a very long time. The girls – no I am not going to blame them. If Wilma and Katy liked the person and believed I would be happy then they would tell me to go ahead and marry him. That isn't the same thing as saying they would welcome me marrying again.'

'Go on.'

'It would never come to that because I would never ask it of them.'

'Ever?'

He was being very persistent. 'Ever is a long time,' she said lightly. 'When Wilma and Katy are old enough to look after themselves then who knows?' She laughed. 'By then, Andrew, no one will bother to give me a second look.'

'Don't be too sure.'

Jenny thought enough had been said. 'Your turn now.'

'My life is an open book, you know all there is to know.'

'I doubt that very much.' She paused. 'Freedom to ask anything?'

'Of course.'

'I do know that you were happily married, Moira told me.'

'Yes, Marguerite and I had a good marriage. There were no children and that was a disappointment but we didn't let it cloud our happiness. If anything I believe it drew us closer together.'

'You still miss her,' Jenny said softly.

'I always will, Jenny, but the mourning was over a long time ago. Memories remain but life must go on.'

'You could have married again.'

'I could.'

'Why didn't you?'

'The right person didn't come along.'

'Five years is a long time for a man to be on his own. Isn't there a saying that if there is to be a wedding it will be within two years of losing one's partner?'

Andrew laughed. 'I don't set much store by those old sayings.'

'Not taking another wife could be because you are very content as you are.'

'That is possible.'

'Possible for me too, I mean not taking another husband.'

'We'll leave it there for the present. And now tell me this, when can I expect a visit from you or is that low on your priorities?' he teased.

'On the contray it is very high but finding the time is not easy. Still I'll work it some way.'

'Is that a promise?'

'Yes, it is a promise.'

Chapter Twenty-Six

The opportunity to visit Perth came sooner than Jenny expected. Moira had developed a summer cold which she was having difficulty in throwing off. Jenny thought she looked pale and tired and scolded her for coming in.

'A day or two in the house and resting would let you get rid of that cold.'

'Dreadful thought. The cure would be worse than the disease. No, Jenny, sitting about feeling sorry for myself is not for me. I need to keep busy.'

'A good book, your feet up and your housekeeper providing light, tasty meals, what is wrong with that?'

'Nothing I suppose, not the way you describe it.'

'Can't stay away from the Log Cabin, that's your trouble.'

'That is so, I can't and here I am. To keep you happy I'll go home early.'

'That's something I suppose, only see that you do.'

'I am not being completely thoughtless. If I believed I was spreading germs I would have stayed away but I feel that I am beyond that stage. Nevertheless I will keep out of everyone's way and work in the office. You keep your distance, Jenny.'

'I'm safe enough, we've all had the sniffles, Mother included.'

'Jenny, visiting the warehouses is out for me, I'm afraid, but you could go.'

'Of course I'll go,' Jenny said quickly, 'but remember I've never gone alone before.'

'Time that was changed and this is the perfect opportunity.' She looked at Jenny. 'And the answer is yes to your silent question. I could very easily phone for a repeat order but I prefer not to. New stock is always coming in and we pride ourselves on being one step ahead.'

'I know.'

'You know too what is likely to appeal to the customer and in particular to the tourist. If something takes your fancy don't hesitate, just order a small quantity. Many a time I have been surprised by goods I thought would go quickly only to find they remained stubbornly on the shelves while others that had been bought on the spur of the moment disappeared quickly.

'Do you want me to go now?'

'Yes, as soon as you are ready. Don't hurry back, take time to do some of your own shopping.'

'Thank you.' Jenny saw her chance. 'Andrew is always asking me to visit his shop. Would you mind if I popped in?'

'Of course I don't mind but, my dear Jenny, no one pops in to an antique shop, one takes time to look. Andrew will want to show you his treasures. Special pieces that he will never sell no matter what he is offered. Each article has a history and only those with a genuine interest in antiques get to hear it. You will be fascinated just as I was. Are you going to phone Andrew?'

'No, I won't. He might feel obliged to cancel an appointment and I wouldn't want him to do that. I'll take a chance.'

'If Andrew isn't around you will meet Miss Grey, his assistant. Andrew calls her his treasure and she is a darling. She was there in Andrew's father's day and he inherited her with the business. What she doesn't know about antiques is not worth knowing. Andrew frequently asks her opinion.'

The sun was slow to break out though it would later. Jenny enjoyed driving and was equally confident in town and country. As she clocked up the few miles she was beginning to regret not having phoned Andrew. Not everyone enjoyed a surprise visit.

Jenny had no problems in the warehouse and when she told the staff that Miss Ramsay was unwell and couldn't come they gave her every assistance. In the end she was well satisfied and thought Moira would approve. The dozen Chinese lacquered boxes were lovely and even if they did not sell they would look very pretty on the glass shelf.

Once outside where there was a pleasant breeze blowing, Jenny thought about having a light lunch before visiting Andrew then changed her mind. That might not be a good idea and Andrew could be annoyed if he hadn't eaten. He would say they could have dined together.

Jenny didn't need to ask directions, she knew exactly

where she was going. Marshall Street was directly off the High Street and was one of the few remaining cobbled thoroughfares. Harrison Antiques was about halfway down and over from it was a restaurant. Jenny felt smart and summery. Her linen dress in pale lemon was buttoned down the front and had a matching blazer type jacket. Jenny always kept an old pair of shoes in the car and had remembered to change out of them into a pair of slim-heeled court shoes in a mushroom colour that toned with her outfit.

A thrill of excitement went through her at the thought of meeting Andrew and she quickened her step. When she came to an abrupt halt the person behind bumped into her and Jenny was almost knocked off her feet.

'Of all the stupid things to do, what were you thinking of?' The stout, perspiring, red-faced woman sounded alarmingly breathless and very angry.

Jenny was shocked at her own stupidity. 'I *am* sorry,' she said knowing it wasn't enough but what more could she say?

'Sorry! I would just think you should be. Hurrying along like that then without any warning coming to a stop. You could have had us both on the pavement and me in my state of health.'

'I do apologise, it was my fault entirely.'

'It most certainly wasn't mine,' the woman said indignantly as though somehow Jenny had suggested it was. 'Some folk! Honestly!' After a final glare and clutching her shopping bag, the woman waddled on her way leaving Jenny shaken and upset. Jenny had been looking out for the two bevelled windows of Harrison Antiques and was about to cross over the road when she saw them coming out of the Victoria Restaurant which was almost directly opposite. They made a handsome couple standing below the red and gold canopy. Vera Cuthbertson was looking into Andrew's face and laughing at something he had said.

Desperate not to be seen, Jenny quickly turned round and half ran down the first opening which was a lane that brought her back to the High Street and not far from where her car was parked. She could go and sit in the car but she didn't want to do that and she knew she was in no fit state to drive. The café didn't look inviting but it offered a seat and just then all Jenny wanted was a pot of tea and the chance to pull herself together.

The tea did help, her brain was beginning to function normally and now she was asking herself if she hadn't overreacted. Vera Cuthbertson had made it very clear in the Miranda Restaurant that she was going to pay a visit to Andrew and expected him to show her around. Jenny could accept that, what she couldn't accept was them having lunch together. They must have, there was no other reason for them being there. That Cuthbertson woman was brazen enough to invite herself but, Andrew, had he wished, could have made some excuse.

On the other hand, she reasoned, why should he make an excuse? He was a free agent and he had every right to have lunch with an attractive woman if that was what he wanted. He and Jenny were no more than friends. She frowned. If only the woman hadn't been Vera Cuthbertson. Anyone but her.

He had called her a strong-willed woman who went after what she wanted. Whether he suspected it or not he was being singled out as the next victim. Victim was the wrong word. Paul hadn't needed much persuasion and Andrew could be the same. Her beauty and cool confidence would be hard to resist.

It did look as though Paul would get his marching orders unless he got in first. Perhaps he was seeing the writing on the wall. Jenny felt her eyes fill with tears and impatiently brushed them away with the back of her hand. Where was her pride? She didn't need Andrew Harrison or Paul or for that matter any man. Life was what you made it and hers was just fine or it had been until Andrew came on the scene and upset the rhythm. She didn't want to remarry and she didn't believe that Andrew wanted that either. For Jenny there was a small void and Andrew had filled it and for him maybe she had done the same. An evening together enjoying each other's company was all she was seeking. That and to know there was someone she could turn to if the need arose. Wishful thinking was all it had been.

After paying the bill she went outside and walked about looking at the shop windows to put in the time. To be back early would cause comment and Jenny wanted to avoid that. No one need know, she would keep it to herself. Her excuse if she needed one would be that there hadn't been time to visit Andrew. Moira might not be taken in but there would be no further explanation.

Paul had once said that Jenny was no actress and it was true. She couldn't hide the hurt in her eyes. Everyone knew that something was wrong and those who ventured to ask wished they hadn't. Andrew phoned in the middle of the week but she pretended to be too busy to come to the phone. When this happened again Andrew drove to the Log Cabin determined to discover what had gone wrong. Something most certainly had. Moira was no help and said she didn't want to get involved. They could sort our their differences and the sooner the better.

Andrew looked baffled. 'Moira, tell me what am I supposed to have done?'

'Don't ask me, I know nothing about it.' Then seeing his face she relented. 'If you think it will help you may use my office and I'll slip along to the tea room. Get yourself behind my desk and I'll send Jenny in on some pretext. Then, my dear Andrew, it is up to you.'

'Thanks, Moira, sorry to put you through all this but I can't for the life of me imagine what I am supposed to have done.'

'Being a man you wouldn't,' she laughed.

He shook his head in perplexity and raked his fingers through his hair. This was out of character for him. Andrew Harrison was a proud man and there would be no begging. If Jenny, for reasons of her own, wanted nothing more to do with him then he would accept that and never bother her again. What he wanted and insisted on was an explanation for her sudden change of heart.

'Oh!' Jenny said, taken aback to see him sitting there behind Moira's desk. 'Excuse me, I came in for something—'

'No, you didn't.'

'I beg—'

'Sit down, Jenny,' he said sternly and when she did he got to his feet to close the door.

'We won't be disturbed for at least the next few minutes so you can begin by telling me what this is all about.'

'Telling you what what is all about?'

'You know perfectly well.' His hand went up when she made to speak. 'Let me say this first. You need have no fear that I will pester you. All I want is a reason for—' He shook his head. 'I am at a loss.'

Jenny felt trapped, she was trapped. She worried her lip then looked directly at him. 'I had no intention of giving you an explanation, I didn't think you were due one.'

'Then we must disagree there. I thought we were good friends.'

'So did I.'

'I did something to change that?'

'Yes, but let me add that you had a perfect right to do so.'

'If I was lost before I am totally lost now.'

'Perhaps it would help if I were to say that I was in Perth last Monday and decided to pay you a surprise visit.'

For a moment he looked blank then he closed his eyes. 'You came to the shop last Monday—'

'No, I was on my way to the shop when I saw you and my husband's mistress coming out of the restaurant opposite. You are not going to deny it, are you?'

'Not much point in doing that since you did see us coming out of the restaurant and yes, we had shared a table for lunch.'

'Which you had every right to do,' Jenny repeated stiffly.

'If only I had seen you, but I take it you turned tail and ran.'

'Nothing quite so dramatic. I turned and walked away.'

'Why didn't you phone to say you were coming?'

'To warn you,' she said sarcastically.

'Sarcasm does not suit you, Jenny. Had I known you were coming I would not have been forced to have lunch with Miss Cuthbertson.'

'Why don't you call her Vera, I'm sure she asked you to? I am the only one who has difficulty with her Christian name.'

'Jenny, would you please be quiet for the next few minutes and let me have my say without interruption.'

'I have work to do even if you haven't.'

'I have,' he said showing anger, 'coming here caused me quite a lot of inconvenience.'

'You shouldn't have bothered,' she snapped.

'No, perhaps I shouldn't but since I am here you can listen to what I have to say.' He paused and leaned forward over the desk. 'Vera Cuthbertson arrived at the shop much to my surprise—'

'It shouldn't have been a surprise since she prepared you.'

'So she did, but I didn't expect her to turn up. People make promises they don't keep. However, there she was and I could do no other than show her around the shop. She pretended an interest in antiques but I can always tell when someone is pretending. Miss Grey, my assistant, I shouldn't be telling you this, but we have a special sign known only to us and when used it is a call for help.'

Jenny couldn't stop a smile and Andrew smiled too. 'As it was lunch time or thereabout, Miss Grey was reminding me to have lunch now or there wouldn't be time before my appointment.'

'I think I am ahead of you, Andrew.'

'Maybe you are but since you brought it on yourself you are going to hear it all. Vera, as I was asked to call her,' he said with a twinkle in his eye, 'said she, too, was thinking about lunch and could I suggest somewhere close by. My brain wasn't working fast enough or I might have been able to get out of it—'

'Not you, you are too much of a gentleman.'

'Miss Grey wasn't so charitable, I'll spare you what she called me.'

'A big softy?' Jenny suggested.

'Something of the sort. I had said there was a restaurant opposite where I usually had lunch. As to whether I invited her or she asked herself I wouldn't care to say. What I can say is that we had a light meal in record time and we shook hands outside the door of the restaurant.' He leaned back and put his hands together. 'There I rest my case.'

'You didn't need to tell me all that.'

'Yes, I did, I had to set the record straight. Am I forgiven?'

'I should be asking your forgiveness. I'm sorry, I had no right to feel the way I did and I wouldn't have bothered if it hadn't been Miss Cuthbertson.'

'I'm glad it bothered you.' He looked at his watch and got up. 'I have to dash, all your fault, you've played havoc with my appointments for today.'

'I am sorry, I really am.'

'To show that you are truly sorry we will have dinner together and you can phone me to arrange an evening.' He kissed her on the cheek before opening the door. 'Tell Moira I had to dash and thank her for the use of her office.'

The open suitcase was on the bed and a pile of folded shirts beside it. Shoes wrapped in paper covered the bottom of the case and socks and handkerchiefs filled the spaces. He remembered Jenny doing that. When the door opened he didn't raise his head.

'Paul, what on earth are you doing?'

'What does it look like?'

She saw the suits, still on their coat hangers, over the back of one chair and an overcoat over the other.

Vera sat down abruptly. 'I don't understand.'

He looked up. 'What don't you understand?'

'Why are you doing this?'

'You don't know?' His eyebrows shot up.

'Would I be asking if I did?'

'Possibly not. For your information I have been considering leaving you for some time and I have been looking in the *Accountants' Journal* for vacancies that might suit me.'

She looked startled. 'Those two days you had off, that wasn't a conference?'

'It was and I attended but my main reason was to present myself for an interview—'

'In London?'

'That's right, in London.'

'You've got the job,' Vera said heavily.

'Yes, I was offered the job but I was reluctant to accept. Leaving you with all your faults was going to be difficult, then suddenly you made it very easy – shall I go on?'

She nodded and slipped off her shoes.

'Your behaviour at the Miranda finished me. I don't know which was worse the embarrassment or shame. Much as you flaunt your good looks, you are jealous of Jenny and all she has achieved.'

'How ridiculous can you get?' Vera spluttered. 'Me jealous of your nondescript wife – why that is laughable.'

'The way you threw yourself at that fellow Harrison sickened me. And as for all that nonsense about being fascinated with antiques you had nobody fooled. Your only fascination was for the man and his bankbook.'

'I am not going to listen to this.'

'Please yourself but I'll say it. That day you took time off to shop in Perth, a Monday I recall, I came looking for you. It didn't take me long to put two and two together. That was you paying your promised visit to Jenny's friend. I hope Harrison sent you packing and I rather think he must have.' Paul carried on with what he had been doing. The coat and suits would go on the back seat of the car.

Vera was very worried, she hadn't expected this. Now when it was too late she was regretting going near Andrew Harrison. They should have gone out the side door as Paul suggested and none of this would have happened. She couldn't accuse Andrew Harrison of being rude but he had left her in no doubt that he had no interest in her. Perhaps there was still time to work on Paul.

She walked over and put her arms around him waiting for the response that didn't come.

'I'm sorry, Paul,' she said gently, 'my only excuse for my behaviour is that work has been getting me down recently. So much so that I, too, was thinking about looking for another situation but I felt I couldn't do that to you.'

'You should have gone ahead.'

'I see that now.' She paused. This wasn't going very well and her brain was working feverishly. She couldn't afford to let Paul go. 'Darling, do stop what you are doing. We'll go through, have a drink and talk things over quietly.'

'There is nothing to talk over.'

'Of course there is. Paul, we have lost that special closeness we once shared and I take the blame for that. It will all come back and we'll be as we were before. I do love you.'

'Vera, the only person you have ever loved is yourself.'

'You are being horrid and I deserve it. Paul, we all make mistakes and, listen, I have just had an idea.' Her face broke into a smile. 'Good secretarial jobs are easy to get in London and I should have no difficulty. It could be a new beginning for us.'

The expression on his face made her think twice about throwing her arms around him, instead she sat down on the edge of the bed.

'You never cease to amaze me, Vera. You would stop at nothing to get what you want. This is one time you fail and let me be absolutely blunt. I am leaving you because, apart from not loving you, I don't even like you. Until I work my notice I shall be staying in a guest house. Financially, until you get someone to fill my place, you will have to be careful. You aren't stupid, you must know that.'

'I can't believe you would be so mean. You know I have no savings.'

'I do. I warned you often enough but you paid no heed. Now, if you will excuse me I'll continue with my packing.'

Chapter Twenty-Seven

Jenny was alone in the house when the doorbell rang and dropping the newspaper she went to answer it.

'Paul?'

'May I come in?'

She moved back and once he was inside closed the door.

'I've come to say goodbye, Jenny.'

'Goodbye?' She looked at him quickly. 'You mean you are going away?'

'Yes, Jenny, I'm going to London, I've got a job there.'

'This is all very sudden surely?' They were standing in the hall looking at one another. Jenny moved. 'We'll go into the sitting-room and you can tell me about it.'

Paul followed her and for a moment or two gazed about him. 'This will probably be the last time I'll see 16 Abbotsford Crescent,' he said sadly.

Jenny said nothing, just watched him sit down.

'I've left Vera.'

'You hinted before that all was not well.'

'I remember. That was when I asked you to take me back though I knew the answer. What a mess I have made of things.' He shook his head.

Jenny felt there was no need to say anything, what could she say? He had made a mess of things and now he was paying the price.

'I want to apologise for Vera's behaviour at the Miranda. It was unforgivable.'

'Not your fault.'

'No, I did try to avoid it. I was all for going out the other door but Vera would have none of it. I'm sorry she put your friend in such an awkward position.'

Jenny smiled. 'Your—'

'Ex-mistress,' he grinned, 'you can call her that.'

'Thank you, I will. Your ex-mistress did pay Andrew a visit—'

'But got nowhere with him, I gathered that, Jenny. Vera is worried but I am losing no sleep over that. There will always be another sucker like me. One day I might be able to laugh about it and wonder how I could have been such a fool.'

'Tell me about the job.'

'A good move in every way. Reasonable starting salary with excellent prospects.'

'Have you fixed accommodation?'

'The firm are seeing to that and once I'm there I'll look around for what I want.'

'You will see Wilma and Katy before you go?' Jenny said anxiously.

'Of course. I'm going to miss them.'

'They will miss you too.'

'I hope so.'

'You'll keep in touch, write to them?'

'Yes. Later on when I'm settled they can both come and spend a holiday with me. I'll be able to show them around.'

'That will make the parting easier, they will have that to look forward to.'

'In case you are wondering where I am living at the moment—'

'The girls will want to know.' She was curious herself.

'The Fairfield Guest House in Queens Avenue.'

'You should be comfortable there.'

He smiled. 'It came recommended.'

'How much notice do you have to give?'

'A minimum of two months. They wanted three but couldn't insist on it.'

There didn't seem much else to say and Jenny got up. Paul rose too and they faced each other. Neither seemed to know what to do. Did they shake hands? No, that was too cold, too distant. Jenny reached up to kiss his cheek and Paul quickly put his arms around her and for a few moments they clung together. Very gently Jenny moved away. The tears were close.

'Take care, Paul. I wish you every success and every happiness.'

'Thank you. We are parting as good friends, aren't we?'

'Of course.'

'I liked him, that Harrison chap and if he is your future I wish you both well.'

'I don't know what my future will hold but thank you.' Jenny saw Paul out then, her lips quivering, she burst into tears. It wasn't that she wanted Paul back in her life, it was because he looked so lost. He was hopeless on his own or perhaps that was no longer true. The girls said their dad could cook and do a lot of things he had never had to do before. If Vera Cuthbertson had given Paul nothing else she had given him a measure of self-reliance. He would manage and Jenny found herself hoping that he would find someone who would look after him and bring him happiness.

Jenny had recovered by the time the girls came home from the first house of the cinema. They came in arguing about the film.

'Did you both see the same film?' It was hard to believe.

'Mum, Katy gets it all wrong as usual.'

'I did not get it wrong. I just think she shouldn't have married him.'

'Don't be stupid. Of course she should have married him. Maybe he was awful to her at the start but that was all forgotten and she happened to love him.'

'All right, argue about that later. I've just had a visit from your father.'

She had their attention. 'What did Dad want?' Wilma asked.

'He came to tell me he is going away.'

'Going away?' Wilma said incredulously. 'When is he going?'

'Not for a few weeks and you will see him.'

'Wish we hadn't gone to the pictures.'

'Katy, the cinema not the pictures. Gran says pictures but it's old-fashioned.'

Jenny was sitting at the kitchen table and they joined her as though they were about to share a meal.

Wilma put her elbows on the table and stared across at her mother.

'Better tell us everything.'

'Not much to tell, but you will hear it all. Your father is going to London, he applied for and got a job.'

'A better job?'

'I'm not sure, Katy. The reason he applied for another position is because he and Miss Cuthbertson have parted company.'

'You mean they have had a quarrel and fallen out?'

'That would appear to be the case.'

'Did Vera put him out? It is her house.'

'No, he left of his own accord, Wilma.'

'I'm not terribly surprised, are you?'

'No. Paul hinted that things were not too happy.'

Katy was nodding her head. 'He wanted you to take him back but you didn't want that, did you?'

'No, I didn't want that.' Jenny paused. 'From now and until he leaves for London your father is to be living at the Fairfield Guest House.'

'Where is that?'

'About halfway along Queens Avenue, Katy.'

Wilma was biting her lip. 'That was a big step to take. What if he doesn't like his new job?'

'Then he will look for something else. With his qualifications your father will have no difficulty in the jobs market. That said, Wilma, he will probably be perfectly content where he is going.'

'I'll miss Dad, I'll miss him a lot but I think he is doing the right thing. If he stayed here Vera might try to get him back and—'

Jenny smiled. 'Paul might weaken?'

'Possible, don't you think?'

'I don't know.'

Katy was preparing to have her say. 'I'm going to miss Dad as well but not as much as the time when he left us. After all, we have only been seeing him once a month.'

'There is something to look forward to for you both. Once your father is settled he wants you to go down during the holidays and spend a week or two. He'll arrange time off to show you London.'

Katy brightened. 'Buckingham Palace, the Changing of the Guard and everything?'

'Those and many more. Paul will make a good guide.'

'Isn't it awful that when everything looks good something spoils it?'

'What is going to spoil it, Katy?'

'You won't be going, that is what spoils it.'

'Darling, I'll hear all about it from you and that will be second best.'

'Won't you be lonely without us?'

Jenny smiled. 'Don't worry about me, dear, I'll keep myself busy.'

'Mr Harrison will come and take you out, won't he?' Katy didn't want it to be all work and no play.

'Perhaps.'

The child moistened her lips, a sign that she wasn't too

sure how her next question would be received. A sign, too, that she was going to risk it.

'Mum, if Mr Harrison asked you to marry him would you say yes?'

Wilma gasped. 'Don't answer that, Mum, what a cheek she has asking you a thing like that.' She shot her sister a dark look but she was interested to know the answer to that question herself.

'I was only asking and where is the harm in that and anyway nobody else is going to hear. So there!' Katy sat straight up in the kitchen chair and glared.

Jenny had been taken aback but recovered quickly. In the circumstances, she supposed, it was a perfectly reasonable question since she and Andrew had been seeing each other regularly.

'I don't know, Katy, what my answer would be. All this is very personal and anything said in this room is not to go beyond these four walls,' she said severely.

'I wasn't going to say anything, not even to Gran,' Katy said sounding offended.

'All right, dear, I just had to be sure.' She paused. 'Mr Harrison and I are very good friends. I enjoy his company and he appears to enjoy mine, and that is all I am going to say.' Jenny thought this might be a good opportunity to find out how her two daughters would feel if, once the divorce was out of the way, she did decide to remarry. 'However, since you brought this matter up, how would the pair of you feel if I were to get married again?'

Neither of her daughters rushed to answer. It was obvious they were going to give the matter some serious thought.

'He's nice, I like Mr Harrison,' Katy said cautiously.

Wilma nodded her head. 'That goes for me too.'

'Be funny though, wouldn't it?'

'What would be funny, Katy?' Jenny asked her.

'Not funny, I mean strange, that's what it would be if Mr Harrison was living here instead of Dad—'

'Katy, do you know this, you are a proper numbskull,' Wilma said witheringly. 'If Mum married Mr Harrison she would have to go and live with him in his house.'

'Would you, Mum?'

'Yes, I expect so.'

'What about us?'

'I'm not likely to leave you, am I? Don't be silly, Katy, you and your sister would have to come with me wherever that was.'

'What about our house?'

'It would go on the market, wouldn't it, Mum?'

'Yes.'

Katy's lips were quivering. 'I don't want to live in another house, I like living here.'

'You started this, remember, and we were supposed to be playing pretend.'

Katy brightened. 'I forgot. Does Mr Harrison live all by himself?'

'No, he has a live-in housekeeper and now I really think that is enough on the subject.'

'Let me say something, Mum, and I know it is just pretend or make believe, but it could happen. You might want to marry again once Dad and you are divorced.'

'And if so?' Jenny smiled.

'I was going to say that Dad made a mess of things, but only after he did what he wanted to do. You have as much right to happiness as anybody else and if that means marriage to Mr Harrison,' she gulped, 'what I mean is don't refuse him because of us, Katy and me. We'll fit in, you don't have to worry,' Wilma said trying to sound very mature.

Jenny was touched. They didn't want change and who could blame them. One big upheaval was enough but they were prepared for more if it meant her happiness.

'Nothing is going to change for a long time but this has been a good talk hasn't it?'

Two heads nodded.

'You are old enough, both of you, to know that nothing in this life is certain so all I can say is that I am as nearly sure as I can be that 16 Abbotsford Crescent will continue to be our home for the foreseeable future. Does that satisfy you?'

They nodded and looked relieved. All was well in their little world and they could relax.

'I don't know about you two but I'm very thirsty.'

Wilma shot to her feet. 'I'll make the tea.'

'I'll help.'

Jenny left them to it and climbed the stairs to her bedroom. Crossing to the window she looked out to the back garden. Like the front it was always neat and tidy. The gardener came weekly and did what was necessary. All Jenny had to do was pay him and that posed no problem. The days of watching the pennies were over. They lived comfortably. In fact life had never been better. Jenny smiled to herself thinking that not so many months ago she would have done anything to have Paul back and to resume life as it had been before Vera Cuthbertson came on the scene. Yet if that were offered to her now she wouldn't want it. She had had a taste of independence and liked it. Liked it too much to give it up. With Paul to be living in London she had the full responsibility for Wilma and Katy but she no longer found that scary. Jenny had never imagined herself juggling with children and a career yet that is what she was doing and enjoying the challenge.

As for Andrew, Jenny was glad she had met him. She thought that what they both cherished from each other was their friendship. They had a good relationship and if there was a hint of romance it was no more than that. Marriage wasn't ruled out, it could happen one day but neither of them was in any hurry to change what they had now.

'Mum, that's the tea made,' Wilma shouted from the foot of the stairs.

'Lovely, I'm just coming.'

Jenny moved away from the window and she was smiling and giving up a small prayer. She had so much. She had two wonderful daughters, a job she loved and her new-found independence.

She would enjoy each day as it came and tomorrow – tomorrow is another day.